TO THE GRAVE

G. S. Hollaway

To Millie, a great inspiration and even better friend.

CHAPTER 1.

It was too late; they had passed the point of no return and now it was time. There was no avoiding what was coming. The tiny lantern in the corner above their heads gave the only light in the cellar, it might give them away, but they could not afford to fight in the darkness and that small, flickering light would keep them alive.

The sepulchral tones of the village bells rang deep, emanating from the deserted town square and penetrated the boarded-up windows and doors down to the cellar floor as they sat and waited. Each strike of the bell brought more dread into their hearts.

Their hands clenched around their swords with the subtlest of sounds above; she had forged that sword with his help mere hours ago. Long and sharp, swift and balanced; just as she was. Riddled with imperfections just like her, she had forged the sword with her own two hands; forged in heart and soul. If their plans failed, it was her only defence. The sword, and each other. They must not waver now.

It was time for her to use it.

It had found them.

They jumped to their feet at the shattering wood upstairs; it was inside the workshop. Glancing at each other one final time, they steadied their stance and watched the door: waiting, listening. Furniture clashed against the floor; thrown across the room, a roar in pain as several hanging swords clattered together and fell to the stone floor beneath, then a nose at the door. She saw the shadow in the crack under the door, huffing and snorting. A bead of sweat trickled down her forehead, her hands clammy and trembling. She only hoped the door was thick enough to mask their scent.

It was not.

The cellar door exploded, raining splintered wood, and

1

bathing the room in light. She cut the rope held taut above their heads and the heavy bookcase fell on its side with a crash behind the beast, blocking its exit. At the same moment, he had cut the second rope and the chain reaction pulled the cloth, releasing the steel mace heads down on the beast beneath.

Without hesitation they sprinted from their corner of the cellar to the thin window on the back wall. They were prepared and quickly unbolted it, prying off the plank and climbed on the crates below to reach and escape. The beast had recovered quicker than they had anticipated; still with maces embedded in its fur, it came for them. She was already halfway out the window, but he was still inside. She crawled out, spun around, and watched him leap, kicking over a wine-rack that landed on the beast. Wine bottles shattered, flooding the floor, but the extra momentum got him to the window. She grabbed his arms and pulled him through. Boy and beast roared together as a clawed paw ripped flesh and cloth from his back. She felt the shuddering of pain and tearing flesh as she pulled him out.

With his legs through the window, she dragged him to his feet and picked up their swords from the grass, they looked back as they ran; the beast could not fit through the window. Their plan had worked; it would have to break through the bookcase, exit the workshop and circle the building before reaching them, giving them a good head start. She threw him his sword and he caught it mid-run, but she stopped in her tracks.

"What are you doing?"

"Over here!" She screamed, waving her hands above her head. The knights were galloping down the street on horseback, noticing her display. She pointed toward the blacksmith's, "in the forge, go!" Without faltering, the knights changed their direction and the two of them kept running.

She reached the Manor gates before he did; his injury slowing him down, pain with every step but her stamina and adrenaline drove her forward. She could hear the knights in battle, all the way down the hill. "Raise the gates!" She called, shouting as loud as she could through the panting. "This is Evangeline Ravenhill, raise the gates!" The gates did not rise.

"Open the gates! *Please!*" He echoed just behind her.

Evangeline looked up as she ran, arrows were flying over her head down towards the hill. She shouted again and finally the gate began to rise but abruptly stopped. As soon as they both crawled under, it closed behind them.

"Why are they not opening the other one?" He asked, trying to pull up the second portcullis.

"No idea," she answered. She was not focused on the gate but watching the dip of the hill and the rain of arrows above, waiting for the beast to appear. They both jumped at the sound above as a fire ball was launched from the trebuchet behind them. Flying, lighting up the night sky and disappearing down the hill where they heard it hit something.

Silence fell, and they waited.

Panting, bleeding and terrified; they waited.

Finally, the Manor doors burst open and three figures made their way across the grounds toward them. The Manor Chamberlain: Cadmael strode toward them, scrolls stuffed in every pocket of his thick, dark robes. He walked in long strides, swinging his knees out giving him a bounce with every step.

To his right was Lord Horus Ravenhill; her father and Lord of the Manor, his once lofty proud gait now overshadowed by sickness and grief that weighed heavily on his shoulders. He still carried most of his brawn and at first glance, he was a strong and formidable man, but his eyes betrayed him; sunken and sombre, they were stranger's eyes to Evangeline.

The third figure was tall and thin; ambling along next to the two men beside her, managing to keep up with their fast strides with no effort. Zorya, set to marry Lord Horus the following day used to be Evangeline's mother's own handmaiden. Her jet-black dress was thin against her body and flowed out with lace at the knee. Her clasped hands at her breast were hidden underneath the floor length lace sleeves and her eyes were on *him* not Evangeline.

Taren, at her side, bowed to the three of them, battling against the excruciating pain of the scratch down the length of his back. Evangeline, however, remained upright and stoic as she stared at each of them, one by one, through the bars of the portcullis, lingering on Zorya.

"What do you think you are doing?" Lord Horus began.

"What if you were killed?" Why do you insist on putting yourself in danger?"

"If you were trying to kill yourself there are far easier ways," Cadmael smirked, leering.

"Do not joke about that," Evangeline spat. "You have no right."

"Why are you doing this, Evangeline?" Horus interjected, "on the eve of my wedding you go out there despite the danger to prove, what? That you are invincible? Just to rebel against my wishes to keep you safe? Are you trying to get my attention?"

"I am *not* doing this for attention! This is not about you or me. Our people are out there in the danger every night and we are safe behind our high stone walls sleeping soundly. I wanted to be out there with them to see things like they do, to experience what they do every full moon. They are forced to board up their homes, cowering in corners, hoping the beast will not pick their house that night. They must craft traps in their homes to slow it down just so they can get a head start and hope it runs into someone else. They are *smothering* their children, terrified their cries in the night will attract the beast. I will *not* sit back and do nothing."

"We are doing everything we can," Cadmael interrupted, "our knights are patrolling the village every night and every full moon we go to war with that thing. We are trying but we cannot stop it."

"What do you think you will accomplish by being on the front line with them? How can you help when you are dead? What can you do that our soldiers cannot?" Zorya finally spoke up and Evangeline found herself not being able to answer. She had done this a few times, evading the patrol on the Manor, stealing off into town and spending the night with Taren in his workshop; setting traps and waiting. She realised that perhaps she was not helping them, she fled to the safety of the Manor every time, the people did not have that privilege.

"I want to help." It was all she could say, and she hated it.

"Come on, we'll tend to your injuries." Lord Horus stepped forward and finally addressed Taren. He nodded to the Gatekeeper above and the portcullis rose. "Come on, my son, you may rest here."

Lord Horus led a limping Taren from the grounds and Evangeline saw the disapproving look spark between Zorya and Cadmael. When their gaze broke, Cadmael followed his Lord but Zorya remained at the gate watching Evangeline as she, too, went inside.

"Let the doctor do his thing," Horus said, blocking Evangeline from entering the infirmary. He placed a hand on her cheek and turned her to look at him. "I know you want to help, and I admire your effort but be honest with yourself, what can you truly do to help them?"

"At least I am trying. What are you doing?"

"Enough now!" His hand dropped from her face. "I am leading. Those are *my* knights out there fighting. *I* hand pick the best to protect us. It is *my* Manor workers out there rebuilding and healing in the aftermath. I am doing what I can. There is nothing more we can do. We have been living with this for several years now and that is all we can do; *live* with it."

"People are dying, father," She pointed to the infirmary door, "People are getting hurt every night, but you are safe here."

"I lost my brother to that monster, your uncle, have you forgotten? We have all lost people. Death comes for all, please do not make me bury another loved one and remain here, safe."

"I cannot sit by and watch."

He grabbed her shoulder with a vice grip and stepped forward, a hair's width apart. Then his voice fell quiet and deep.

"Enough with this stubborn child act. You are an *adult,* act like it. I am getting married tomorrow and I do not need you ruining everything just for a little bit of attention. If you are starved for it, go find your sister, you have three now or if they aren't enough drama for you, I will move up your wedding and move you far away from here then the drama will finally stop."

"Oh, father, don't you know? Attention seekers will always find drama wherever they go." She was being sarcastic and boldly grinned at him, but he looked at her as if deeply thinking over her words. Being so close to her father's face she could see the dark circles around his eye sockets and the cloudiness fogging his pupils. The sallow skin and terrible coarse complexion had aged him horribly before her. No one could tell her what was wrong with him only that it was getting worse.

"Do not disobey me again. You will not leave this Manor after dark and you will *not* be out in the danger on the next full moon. Do you understand me? I will assign Sir Thedamaine to keep a closer watch on you. You need babysitting."

"Do whatever you want." She pushed passed him and entered the infirmary, crossing the room to Taren in his bed; bandaged and smiling. "What are you so happy about?" She asked him, her father did not follow her into the room.

"This is great. I was *invited* to stay here; I did not even have to sneak in or anything."

"Well, you are not allowed to leave; he debriefed me before I came in. Your punishment for endangering a Lady is remaining in this room until you are healed, then you can go."

"That's it? Do they know that this is paradise compared to the village infirmary?" He put his hands behind his head and lounged back. "I could get used to this." He had obviously been given a high amount of pain relief. He barely flinched and his pupils were large and black.

"Perhaps you'll be my date to the wedding?" She grinned and busied her hands by picking up the medicinal jars on the table, pretending to read them.

"I do not think your husband will approve of that; he'll be there tomorrow." She sniffed a jar of laudanum twice and took a swig as Taren watched her.

"He is not my husband, *yet-*" she added the last word under her breath, "-it is just a political marriage. I can do what I want. Bring any date I want."

"And you wonder why your father calls you spoilt?" He was joking but it hurt Evangeline, touching a nerve.

"Stop that. You know that bothers me." Taren was tapping his fingers against his head, still lounging with his hands on his neck. It did bother her, but she wanted to change the subject before she lost her temper.

"I didn't even realise." He stopped and laid his hands on his lap, fidgeting from the pain. Evangeline passed him the laudanum jar and he drank the rest of it.

"He's really angry with me this time. I've done it before

but today, I really felt it."

"You haven't really been caught before, have you?"

"No, I have. They know what I do and how often I do it but today it seems like I stepped over the line and I don't know why."

"His wedding *is* tomorrow. That is a lot of stress, I just do not think he would like to wake up the morning of his wedding to the news his daughter is dead. He will be thinking of your mother a lot tomorrow, despite feeling guilty for thinking of her. He does not want to be reminded that he lost her and has moved on so quickly. Plus, inviting noble guests to a village branded dangerous, if any of his high-end guests were killed, your family would be bumped off the hierarchy quicker than you could say wedding. Like I said, it's a lot of stress. It adds up."

"Wow, you really thought this through."

"Well, I thought it was quite obvious." Taren smirked at her, smugly and she rolled her eyes at him, her temper flaring up again.

"I'm going to bed," she announced against a large yawn. He yawned also, smiling as she took his hand and squeezed it twice before silently leaving the room. He watched her leave and waited a moment, hoping she would return and stay with him, but the hallway candlelight left with her.

Rolling over onto his stomach to sleep, the growing throbbing pain now the only thing he could think about. With all distractions gone, he ended up lying awake for hours against the suffocating impression of being watched, unaware of the eyes upon him.

CHAPTER 2.

She woke underneath the weight of grief; truly thinking of her for the first time in a long time after her dreams reopened an old wound. She thought of her again as she got dressed; choosing a gown in her mother's signature deep red tone, hoping her father will notice the protest.

Evangeline missed her terribly; she missed her mere presence in her home. She even missed the mood swings, hysteria and scary episodes, she would live through all that again just to have her back. No matter what her mother was feeling, or how unstable she was that day, whenever she brushed and braided Evangeline's hair, she was calm and kind. Because of this, Evangeline often kept her hair in a single loose braid; a tiny way to be closer to her mother.

She could not bring herself to leave her chamber room; the pure energy she needed to get out of bed, open that door and step out into the hallway was too much and overwhelmed her. She did not even have the energy to braid her hair and left it dangling and loose; an untameable bird's nest hanging at her waist.

The box was calling her.

The forgotten one beneath her bed that lay waiting in the shadows, a monster of memories.

Leaning upside down over the side of her bed, her bird's nest blocking all light, she reached blindly in the darkness, waving back and forth until her fingers touched the corner of the box. She did not wait to open it and immediately popped the latch of the lid, opening the small box of her mother's personal belongings.

It was almost empty.

She counted five things; five things she knew by memory yet still inspected every time she opened the box. Her clothes had been given away to her daughters already, so these were her own personal affects, a meagre amount for a noble Lady.

Evangeline tried to think of her own belongings and found herself lacking, perhaps she had inherited more from her mother than she had thought.

She picked up the first item; an elaborate jewellery box oozing wealth but inside were only a handful of rings and pendants. At the bottom, a brooch with an onyx raven, covered in dust and forgotten. With a wipe of her thumb, the dust disappeared, and she dropped it back in the box. Next to the jewellery box sat a large, ornate candelabra, decorated with tiny ravens perched on vines. A silver circlet rested on a velvet pillow beside the candelabra, attached by thread to keep it in place. A wedding gift from her father to her mother, Evangeline had admired it for years, often stealing it as a child.

She left the box on the floor, pulling the writing kit out and putting it on the bed in front of her. The letters inside were useless; she had tried reading them a long time ago, but an ink pot had spilled and rendered them a black mess. What she wanted were the wax seals; a large Ravenhill wax seal made from gold and her mother's family's Rosewood seal made from silver.

There was still wax imbedded in the carving that she could not dislodge with her fingernail. Her mother's dagger was the final thing in the box that she had not pulled out; that would help clear the wax. But as she leant over the bed to reach the box on the floor, the writing kit came with her, sliding off her lap and falling to the ground knocking the box over, and spilling its contents all over the floor with a crash.

She cursed herself, jumping off the bed. Lifting the upside-down box, she jumped as something heavy fell out. An old book, falling apart at the binding had been hidden in the bottom of the box underneath a false panel. Evangeline laughed at her mother's trickery and her own ignorance. How long had she had that box? How many times had she pulled everything out to put them back in without ever noticing there was something else there?

The book was incredibly old; the cover long since disintegrated, the pages were falling out and most were completely loose. As she flicked through them, she noticed that her mother had made rough, scrawled notes along the margins, almost indecipherable. Without reading completely, Evangeline gathered it was a book about shamans, but that did not make sense. Notoriously against the occult, her mother despised shamans and passed a law banishing and outlawing them. Why would she hide a book about them?

Evangeline ran cold as she read the only line on the final page; an annotation in shaky handwriting as if written by her wrong hand and written in *blood*.

'The Nil'vetra will come for me...'

Evangeline knew one person who needed to read those words, who could help her understand what they mean: her sister Felicity. It was a bad day to find her, the morning of their father's wedding and everyone was running around, unable to pin down. Nobody had seen her for hours, and Evangeline could not find her sister's handmaiden either, who would know where she was.

She turned a corner and immediately regretted her decision, there were three hallways she could have gone down, and she chose this one. The very one her soon-to-be twin stepsisters were also in. Dressed in black just like their mother and completely identical, Evangeline could only *just* tell them apart as Vesna had the rounder face and Morana had the arched eyebrows. As soon as they had seen her, they began to whisper and giggle, and she knew immediately they were talking about her.

"Hey, catch this," Morana called out to Evangeline as she advanced on the twins. Evangeline caught what was thrown to her and screamed, dropping the burning hot coin.

"We've had that coin on the candle for ages! I am so glad that worked." Vesna was crouched on the floor tapping the coin, checking if it was still hot while her twin was doubled over laughing.

"My hand is burnt! What the hell is wrong with you?"

Vesna stepped back and joined her sister and began laughing too. Their two faces contorted into uncontrollable grins. Evangeline, embarrassed and annoyed, picked up the warm coin and threw it hard at Morana's chest but it did nothing to stop them.

"Knock it off, you savages!" With the coin not working she smacked Vesna around the head with her mother's book which did stop their laughing.

"Why are you so violent? It's not our fault you are stupid enough to fall for that."

"That was not a trick to fall for!"

"You still fell for it."

"You are not the mastermind pranksters you think you are. You do not hold a candle to Felicity and I."

"No need to be so modest."

"You mean, this candle?" Morana grabbed the candle from the windowsill and held it against Evangeline's gown before she could react. She smacked it away, panicking and patted the singed cloth as the candle wax sprayed onto the twins.

"Hey, watch it!" Vesna spat. "You could hurt someone."

"You are the ones playing with fire, back off."

"You back off." Morana shoved Evangeline back and she stumbled to regain her footing.

"Do not push me! Do not start something you cannot finish." Evangeline dropped the book with a large echoing crash and pulled her mother's dagger from the sheath in her pocket. "I will put you in the ground if you push me again."

"That is enough for today!" Evangeline was grabbed from behind, a gloved hand grasping the dagger in her own. Sir Thedamaine had crept up behind her and pulled her from the girls.

"Back off, Thedamaine!" She wrestled against his hold on her as he picked her up and dragged her down the hallway. "Let me go!"

"The loyal hound by her side once again. You need to rein her in, *dog*."

"You need to put *her* on a leash, teach her to be a good little pup."

Evangeline heard the twin's barking until they left and Thedamaine did not release her until the voices had completely gone.

"Why do they think loyalty is a bad thing? I never understood why they mocked you." Sir Thedamaine was a head and a half taller than Evangeline, one of three who were, due to her lanky height. He was a young knight, just barely older than her and had been in her father's service as long as she could remember.

"I will never understand how you think drawing a weapon on your siblings is an appropriate way to deal with situations."

"You are a knight; your job is to draw weapons."

"My job is to protect you and as of last night I cannot let you out of my sight because *you* got yourself caught out of hours on a full moon."

"Oh, I'm sorry I'm such a burden on you. But you should know, you are doing a bad job because I've been out of your sight all morning."

"I've only just started my shift, genius, and I immediately find you trying to murder your siblings."

"I was only going to slash them. Slash, don't stab."

"Just like I taught you."

"See, I do listen."

"When you want to. You just hear what you want to hear."

"And do what I want to do. I've heard it all before."

"And you want to hurt the twins?"

"They hurt me first! It was self-defence. I cannot be held accountable for my actions, so do not blame me. They burnt my hand and tried setting me on fire, and they call *me* out of control."

Sir Thedamaine took Evangeline's burnt hand and inspected the palm. "You'll be fine. Some honey will soothe that. I can take you to the infirmary if you wish?"

"No, no, I'll be fine. I'm busy anyway. Hang on, where's my book?" She had realised that she was no longer carrying it. "Oh, those little witches have stolen it, haven't they? They'll get what's coming to them."

"This book?" Thedamaine held up her mother's book and Evangeline's face lit up. "You dropped it and I picked it up."

"Yes! That's the one! You're amazing. Now have you seen my sister? She needs to see this book."

"Last time I saw her she was speaking with Lord Horus in his study."

Horus was not in such a chaotic state than his soon-to-be wife was. He had been avoiding her all morning, in his study with strict orders not to be disturbed, so of course, had several visitors. All his affairs were in order, the last thing on his list was his correspondence. He needed to sign the scrolls informing the other families of his nuptials and write personal letters to his immediate family and the Queen. He was halfway through the fifth scroll when his daughter appeared in the doorway, a dusty book clutched to her chest. *Another* daughter distracting him, will he ever finish? He was glad to see Sir Thedamaine on her tail and his fears began to subside.

She stood tall like her mother, taller than other girls her

age, and other men too, with his dear Emilia's stunning flaxen blonde hair. She was a spitting image of her mother, yet Felicity took after him; they were opposites, more often than not.

Evangeline rapped lightly on the oak doorframe and waited for the nod of approval to enter. She kept up her niceties and her manners when she needed to. She entered and slammed the book on his desk, flattening his scrolls. On the other hand, she could also be insolent and tempestuous.

"I was not finished with those, Evangeline."

"The other families do not need to know you are remarrying this soon after your wife's death, to her *handmaiden,* no less. It could open us up to civil unrest and war; the other families may wish to take our land for their own. This marriage has no political ties and only weakens our family name and soils my mother's memory."

"Are you quite finished?"

"Yes, my Lord."

"You have always been a blunt and honest person and I have admired that. I have only let three women speak to me like that in my lifetime: my wife, my mother and you. My *new* wife will never speak to me like that so I hope you have spoken all that you wish because from tomorrow you shall never speak that way about your step-mother, do you understand?"

"Yes, my Lord."

"Now, what is this that you have so passionately thrown on my desk?"

"A book."

"Yes, I can see that. What is the significance of this book?"

"It was *hers.*"

His eyes lit up and his curiosity piqued. Flicking through the pages, his eyes frantically searched every annotation, hoping to savour a piece of his Emilia. Evangeline watched him carefully, reading his emotions and taking note of the pages he stopped at. As he reached the end page and read the words, he looked up at Evangeline.

"This Nil'vetra killed her. Whatever that is. Don't you see, father?"

"*Evangeline.*" Horus rubbed his temples and closed his eyes. "Why can you not let go of your mother? I have, it is

13

time to move on."

"You don't believe me."

"The doctor did say she was recovering after the birth but with the stillborn her heart just could not take it and she died, that is all. People die every day; you need to accept it and move on."

"*Fine.* What do you make of this book? Have you seen it before? Do you know what it is about? What does that last line mean?" She asked, hoping to finish the lecture.

"It is your mother's handwriting, rushed and desperate but it is hers, no doubt. You will need to put a lot of effort into reading this, the annotations have no organisation what-so-ever and you would need to read the entire book to get some context. Looking at the state of it, you should hope that all the pages are still here. I have not seen the book before and do not know the meaning, so I cannot help you. However, your mother was not a stable woman, her mood swings could be quite severe, and she suffered nightmares and visions, this was just research on her part."

"Research?"

"When your mother could not sleep due to her 'colour storms' as she liked to call it, or the nightmares were too much to bear, she would do various things to keep herself busy. She liked to read. She probably hoped the things she saw were in this book, I do not know without reading it. I can only assume this was the last thing she did to entertain herself before the birth. I do recall, however, her whispering *Nil'vetra* in her sleep countless nights; the word she has written at the back, but I do not know what it means. She often spoke gibberish, especially in her sleep and I thought nothing of it and still do. But tell me, Evangeline, is this the best thing to be focused on right now? You have more pressing duties to attend to and so do I."

"Thank you, father. If that is all?" She picked up the book and slowly backed away toward the door.

"That is all. I'll see you at the wedding," he called out as she disappeared down the hallway.

"Can't wait," she called back in a sly, sarcastic tone.

Evangeline's search for Felicity remained unsuccessful as she was pressganged into a gown fitting by her brash and plucky intermittent handmaiden, Aria. There was no escaping her today, despite Evangeline trying, and so she stood like a mannequin while the maidens fussed with her; the temper within her slowly bubbling over.

"If you stab me with those pins one more time, I will stick them in your eyes and then you'll finally have an excuse for being blind." Evangeline had enough with being a doll and pincushion and wanted this day to be over.

"Let me do it." Aria bumped the clumsy maid out of the way and took hold of the gown. "Amateurs," she shook her head and smiled up at Evangeline whose fury had gone as quickly as it had appeared. "Your sister looked beautiful in her gown; her fitting was quicker as we did not have as much fabric to work with; you're just too tall. How can two sisters be so different in height? Different hair colour, different personalities, different attitudes."

"She was here?" Evangeline asked, interrupting Aria and trying to calculate her sister's morning schedule.

"Yes, not too long ago."

"I need to see her." She tried to move but Aria forbade her to take a step, threatening her with pins.

"Do not move a muscle or your skin gets it!"

"Alright, take it easy, we don't want anyone getting hurt now. I'll stay." They both laughed and Aria continued with the hem adjustments.

"We're almost done, you'll see her soon as it is almost time."

"What are you talking about? Time for what?"

"The wedding, stupid! Do you not know what time it is? This is why we are rushing here; the guests are already on the grounds and you need to greet them with Lady Felicity as soon as possible. You really slept in this morning, didn't you?"

"I guess I did."

"See, this is why you do not dismiss or scare aware your handmaidens, they are there for a reason and waking you up and getting you ready for a grand and formal event is one of their strengths. Next time let me help you. I am officially your handmaiden, so use me."

Evangeline was taken aback. There were things she had planned, that she wanted to do before the wedding but there was no time now. Taren would have to wait. The *Nil'vetra* will have to wait.

CHAPTER 3.

Where is she going?

Before Felicity could close the gap between them, Zorya had turned a corner and disappeared. She had pursued her from the Hazel Parlour, past the Library and the Green Room, hoping to see where she went. Zorya had no business skulking around this part of the Manor when she should be getting ready for her wedding. Felicity knew she was up to something, but what? She crept down the hallway, ear against every door to listen but heard nothing.

Turning a corner, she jumped back, hiding from the figure standing there. Peeking around the stonewall she saw a heavily bandaged Taren. He was creeping around as she was, his back to her. She smiled and using all of her stealth; crept up on the boy. On tiptoes, she whispered delicately in his ear.

"Busted."

He jumped out of his skin and collapsed to the ground, cursing and releasing a noise that resembled a muffled and strangled cat. Felicity almost bowled over laughing.

"You are silent like the night. You could have killed me!" Taren said between laughs, getting to his feet. "What are you doing down here, anyway, apart from scaring me to death?"

"I can ask you the same thing; you are not supposed to leave the infirmary."

"You're not going to tell on me, are you? Why aren't you at the wedding?"

"Let's just say I'm here for the same reason you are."

"Lost?"

"Definitely." They both laughed again. "I can't really get away with that, I live here."

"My excuse was sleepwalking."

"Oh, excellent. Innocent, plausible but what if somebody bumped into you and saw that you were awake?"

"Oh, well I would say I woke up from sleepwalking and was innocently trying to find my way back."

"Smart."

"So why are you down here? The wedding is about to begin, is it not?"

"I was on the hunt, but my trail ran cold, and I lost my prey."

"Don't you just hate it when that happens?"

"What's your excuse? Admiring the fine artwork?" She gestured to the bare stonewalls.

"I guess I can trust you. You *are* Evie's sister."

"Really? I didn't know."

"I was meeting someone."

"Evangeline?" Taren did not answer and adverted Felicity's gaze. "I doubt she will come; she woke up late as usual."

"She's nocturnal, that one." He replied, the smirk returning to his face.

"How are you, after the attack?" She asked, eyeing the bandages and regretting scaring him. "Are you in a lot of pain?"

"I'm on a lot of laudanum. Despite the pain, staying here has been the best night's sleep of my life. I literally slept all day and I'm still tired."

Felicity had never truly thought about how dangerous it was for the villagers, to live in constant fear, to be that close to death. It was safe in the Manor and she was beginning to see Evangeline's side of things.

"I think Evie is right. We are too sheltered to truly understand the danger." Felicity looked up at Taren who seemed extremely confused. "Oh, I am sorry, I forgot you are not in my head. I am just afraid. Afraid of the beast, afraid for you and the people, afraid Evie will get herself killed. Afraid my father will die soon." She bit her lip and began to stroke the fur trim of her gown.

"Easy, now. You have every right to be afraid, there is nothing wrong with it, talk to your sister, it will make her feel better knowing someone in here agrees with her."

"And you agree?"

"I did at first, not so much anymore." He trailed off. "I've come to accept my fate. If it is my time, then it's my time. But her being out there with me helps, gives me something else to fight for."

"Your own life isn't enough?" He only shrugged his shoulders, but Felicity continued. "You do not mind her risking her life? I just do not know why she is so obsessed suddenly."

"It's not sudden. She has been doing this for a while but only just getting caught. Plus, she vowed that she would bring an end to the beast before her wedding."

"She, singlehandedly, will end the beast?"

"Well, she isn't exactly going to deliver the final blow to the beast's heart, she just wanted to be a part of it. To see it end before she leaves Ravenhill. The heir's legacy." Felicity laughed but Taren continued. "She doesn't want to leave you here with it, Flick."

"Hey, if it's my time, then it's my time."

They both heard some voices down the hall and panicked, pressing themselves against the wall, listening, they crept further down the hall and turned to each other in hushed whispers.

"You need to return to the infirmary before you are punished. Head that way," she pointed to the left corridor, "down the spiral staircase, go into the second room and through the other doors. Take a right, go back up the stairs and you'll recognise where you are, the infirmary is on that floor. I will take care of them."

"Thanks Flick."

Elsewhere, Evangeline had taken her place at the main doors of the Grand Hall and smoothed her gown, steadying her feet to plant her in place as this was her position for the next hour, greeting all the guests.

"My feet are hurting already."

"Try being a knight, we're on our feet all day." Sir Thedamaine stood behind her, against the wall, on guard after he had escorted her to the hall.

Lush, detailed tapestries dotted the walls of the hall, with dried lavender vines draped across the ceiling. Pumpkins, horse chestnuts, pinecones and acorns were arranged in extravagant displays to signal the change to autumn. Most would find this wedding decoration tasteful, yet Evangeline found it all nauseating. Candles were placed all the way down each of the dining tables. The grand fireplace, behind the dais, was overflowing with burning logs. The room was the warmest it had been in years and she worried that, with all the bodies about to fill the space, the room would become unbearable. In more ways than one.

The side door opened, and Felicity came through, her eyes darted up long enough to spot her sister and then fell back to the ground as she crossed the room in a hurried scurry. The long trail of her grey silken gown reminded Evangeline of a squirrel.

"Did you even try doing any of the braids I showed you?" Felicity asked as her eyes went immediately to Evangeline's lazy single braid. Felicity had chosen her favourite style; what Evangeline liked to call "The Mermaid".

"You know I have better things to worry about than my hair, plus my arms begin to ache after a while."

"That is why you have a handmaiden, *use* her."

Evangeline shrugged her shoulders. "That's exactly what she said." Evangeline had an agreement with Aria, her work was very limited with her as she preferred to be alone and Aria was free to visit her family as much as possible. Her mother was a tailor, and her father was a cobbler, and together they owned the most successful tailoring shop in town. That reputation came with a large demand. Evangeline liked it that way; whenever she required a handmaiden, she was not able to sleep in and seeing as she hardly ever slept until the early hours of the morning, she needed that extra few hours in bed.

"I should be first." Felicity moved and stood the other side of Evangeline, so she was the first to be greeted at the door.

"Why you?"

"Did you study? Do you know their names and heraldry?"

"Of course not, but I'm older."

"By a year!"

"Eleven months actually, Flick."

"You are heir and you do not know the proper order of introduction? How have you gotten this far?"

"Just lucky, I guess."

"Tell me about it. Sir Thedamaine, you can confirm that I should be first?" She turned around to Thedamaine and he looked to Evangeline, smiling.

"She is right. The highest ranking is always last to be introduced." Felicity stuck her tongue out. "But she is teasing you, Lady Felicity."

"I sure am, of course I knew that! I've been doing this for years, Flick. I am just messing with you."

Thedamaine laughed along with Evangeline as Felicity pouted and her face reddened. The three of them stiffened as the large doors opened, the guests piling in. They were overwhelmed within minutes, one after the other with no time to take a breath. Lords and Ladies, noble families and close friends poured into the Manor, along with Guild Masters and high-ranking villagers, and business owners, too. Evangeline barely knew anyone who came but they all knew her name and took her hand, crushing it or moistly kissing it, curtsying too much, or failing completely.

"Can you move over? You're in my space." Finally, there was a lull in the current of people and Evangeline was growing impatient.

"Back off." Felicity nudged Evangeline over before the next person came through the door.

"Don't push me. Thank you for coming. We are honoured. *Move."*

"Lord Henry, Lady Anne; what a pleasure it is to see you. *Stop pushing me."*

"You pushed me first. Thank you for coming."

"What? Because you are older and the *heir,* you deserve more room? *You* move."

"Oh, there it is! That did not take long. To hells with this." Evangeline threw up her arms and left her sister at the doors alone, ignoring her subdued protests.

"Lady Evangeline, wait." Sir Thedamaine had caught her arm before she even crossed the room. "It is almost over, just a few more guests, this day is not about you." She was not angered by his words, instead they got through to her and she returned to her sister, greeting the remaining guests.

"I heard the twins talking about the hot coin trick, what a stupid prank." Evangeline loved the way her sister could brush off an argument and act like nothing had happened, in some ways they were just as fickle as each other. "I burnt Vesna's hair when I heard about it."

"You burnt her hair? When?" Evangeline whispered between greetings.

"A little while ago, I crept up behind them with a candle and held it up to her hair, it was singed before they even knew I was there."

"You can creep up on anyone, you do have a gift. I do not know how you do it."

Cadmael closed the large doors behind the final couple and Evangeline and Felicity took their seats at the Grand Table. Morana and Vesna were at one end of the table and they were at the other, somebody wanted to avoid drama at this wedding and that someone was smart.

Lord Horus Ravenhill sat at the head of the table looking over his guests, his sickly trembling distracting and unnerving. At his side, Zorya placed her hand on his, steadying him and he found his strength. She smiled wearily at him then looked to Evangeline and Felicity, throwing them a subtle nod to calm them.

Zorya had trained as an apothecary before becoming a handmaiden so she worked closely with the doctor to stabilize his sickness. Evangeline may disapprove of the marriage so soon, and the constant awareness of the possibility of an affair tainted her opinion of both of them, but at least he was in good hands.

The small band by the dais began to play and the hall broke into conversations as they waited to be called for the ceremony. Evangeline poured wine in her sister's glass and then her own, filling it to the brim, dying for a drink.

"We were much more creative when it came to pranks at their age." Felicity was still thinking of the twins. "Remember when you swapped out all the furniture in my room?"

"And you entered hoping to go to sleep but found yourself walking right into the lounge chair? You were so confused."

"We could do that to them?"

"I remember you tying a string to my chamber door and wrapping it around all of my belongings in my room so when I opened my door, *everything* fell off. That was a nightmare to clear up."

"How about when you came into my room in the middle of the night when we were kids, and told me the world had ended and everyone was dead, so we had to leave immediately before the monsters got us too?"

"That was a funny one, you really believed me."

"You even got the squires involved, pretending to be dead in the halls! How could I not believe it? You made me cry Evangeline!"

21

"Gods, that was hilarious, we should try that one, too. You used to be so gullible."

"Like the time I was stuck up the tree on the hill and you told me you would go and get help but never returned?"

"I did go to get help, I just got distracted, that's all."

"I was in that tree for two hours, Evie!"

"You saw how I got down; you should have trusted yourself."

"I am afraid of heights and I was six, I was terrified. You were horrible back then."

"I wasn't that bad."

"The wasp's nest?"

"I panicked, Flick, I didn't want them coming in the house."

"You locked me outside to get stung by the wasps *you* angered. You wanted to poke that nest with a stick, but I told you not to."

"It was fun, up until the nest fell and they all came out to attack us."

"They attacked *me*, Evie. You ran inside and locked the door behind you, leaving me to get thousands of stings."

"You'll laugh about it one day. Perhaps that should be the prank we do on the twins next; you can be on the right side of the door for once."

"It's too cold for wasps, we'll have to wait for summer."

Across the room, the doors opened. The autumn winds soared down the hall and a commotion broke out; those closest to the doors grabbed hold of their hats and their goblets while others cried out from the cold. Horus stood up and took a long look at the figures that opened the doors.

Dressed in shades of green and carrying sacks and platters stood the Forrester family. Someone at the back closed the doors behind them. The hall sat silent, the clinking of goblets stopped, the band stopped playing. The grand table watched the Forresters and finally, Duke Forrester erupted in his plummy, booming voice that carried across the large hall.

"My deepest apologies in interrupting such a grand event. I did receive an invitation but my herald, the oaf, did not pass the message onto my person and so I arrive late. In efforts to make amends, my family brings a peace offering. I hope dearly this will make up for my family's late arrival?"

"Better late than never." Horus had received them at the

door and thanked them for their generosity. They embraced in a strong hug, patting each other on the back as Zorya signalled for the servants to collect the gifts.

"Penlyn is here," Felicity whispered in Evangeline's ear.

"Oh no. Of *course,* he is here." Evangeline looked at Felicity to avoid eye contact with him. "Does he see me?"

"He sees you."

"Don't look at him."

"He's coming."

"No, he's not."

"He's behind you."

"Oh, boy." Evangeline sensed him behind her and inhaled deeply. She turned to him; he was a strapping boy, brawny and tall, well-groomed with a perfect posture. All of the people from the Forrester village were built for lumber, which did not exclude the family itself. He had dark brown hair and eyes to match; the colour of walnuts and had a strong jawline. He was shorter than her, and much younger too. When he reached her, he bent over and bowed, lingering a little too long, as if afraid to get back up.

She got to her feet and acknowledged the bow, curtsying back vaguely. He took her hand and kissed it gently. Evangeline supressed an eye roll as Felicity nudged her.

Evangeline had been betrothed to Sir Penlyn Forrester shortly before her mother's death and as a result, their wedding had been postponed several times but now her father had remarried, her own wedding was just around the corner.

"My Lady, my betrothed, you are beautiful. That gown looks positively becoming on you," he began to whisper, "I'm sorry, my mother is listening, we must keep up appearances. Manners and such."

"Thank you, my Lord." She mirrored his manners. "The gifts your family brought truly honour us."

"I had no part in that, it was my mother. I brought a special gift for you, however." He brought out his other hand he held behind his back and revealed a pendant. Three gems lined next to each other on a chain; a grand moonstone flanked by a green gem and a black gem. Evangeline took hold of it and smiled.

"How did you know I love moonstones?"

"Lucky guess. May I?" She allowed him to fasten the pendant around her neck. As she held her braid out of the way she felt his warm breath on the nape of her neck. She turned back to face him and watched him admire her but knew he did not like the arrangement any more than she did. She could not stop the wedding, but she felt at ease for knowing that the man she would marry was a nice man. Other women had it worse; she knew she should count herself lucky. "That is emerald and obsidian too, if you were wondering."

"Thank you, it's beautiful." She smiled genuinely at him.

"Now that I have honoured my Lady I must get back to my family and express my apologies to your father. Between you and me it *was* my father's fault, not his herald's. He is drunk again. Do not let him get you alone. Either of you."

"Thanks for the warning."

"Lady Felicity, always a pleasure." He bowed, lightly kissing Felicity's hand and returned to the Forresters.

Felicity immediately turned to her sister and exploded. "He is so adorable and sweet; I want him for my own."

"You can have him; I do not want him."

"But why? I mean, look at him. He's perfect."

"He will be a good political husband. I can agree with you on that."

"That is a nice necklace, though. I'm jealous." Felicity inspected the pendant closer. "An emerald for the Forresters, black obsidian for the Ravenhills and a moonstone just for you."

"Oh, isn't he thoughtful?" Evangeline asked sarcastically.

The guests followed the wedding party to the Oak Tree Hilltop. Browning, orange leaves littered the floor under the single, ancient oak called the King Tree in the centre of the clearing. Surrounded by forest, just off the Manor grounds, Ravenhills had been married here for generations and Evangeline looked around at the scene knowing full well that she will soon be married in this exact location. She was not resenting the wedding nor the marriage, she resented having to leave her home; that is what she refused to do.

A black Ravenhill ribbon was wrapped around the thick trunk of the tree, twisting all the way up. Painted wooden ravens, attached to every branch watched over the scene from their looming perches above. It was a small ceremony, but the limited seating filled up quickly; evidently this was not an event open to the public.

Evangeline barely remembered the ceremony. Her mind

was elsewhere; on her mother, on the Nil'vetra book, on injured Taren in the infirmary, on her memory of the guests; Felicity was right, she had barely studied. She had already forgotten the given names of Lord and Lady Ashton, the parents of her childhood friend who only live the other side of the lake. She desperately wanted to speak to Felicity about the book but knew she must wait. The wedding came first.

She was *bored*.

She did not approve of the marriage at all and only looked up once to see her father and his new bride during the hand-fasting. His weak and sick demeanour made him unsteady and clumsy and she could not bear to watch him fumble anymore. Zorya helped and lead the way, moving the ceremony along, not once letting any of it affect her or ruin her day, still beaming with joy.

As soon as it was over, she was the first to leave and return to the hall, she had already finished two pints of ale before Felicity and the twins took their seats. Evangeline's mood went from bad to worse when the feast began. The tables had been overloaded with food during the ceremony and now the hall erupted into feasts.

She did not eat. Could not eat. All her life she had been sensitive to sound and could not stand the sounds of people eating. She almost never ate with other people and in formal occasions such as this, she tolerated being in the proximity, but lost all appetite. With her left hand she moved the food around her plate with the fork, but her right hand was under the table; her thumb rubbing her finger back and forth until it was red raw. She kept her head down, trying to drown out the smacking, scratching, and open mouth chewing. Instead, she tried to drown herself in ale; filling and drinking and refilling again.

She wasn't the only sensitive one in the family, Felicity was too but Evangeline had noticed over the years that it was touch. She always wore fur, even in the summer some part of her gown will be fur trimmed and she stroked it incessantly. She refused to wear or touch velvet and recoiled from the touch just as much as Evangeline recoiled from sound.

Evangeline began to suspect that was the underlying reason for her mother's hysteria. She saw many hallucinations throughout her life, beginning small and becoming more and more stressful towards the end. It was possible she was sensitive to sight. Poor eyesight and the mind playing tricks on her could have been the root cause. Maybe her daughters inherited that particular strain of sensitivity?

Evangeline's train of thought was interrupted by the maid pulling her plate from under her tapping fork just as the band began to play softly and people got up to dance. She looked up at Penlyn, seeing him sitting across the room with his mother as she adjusted his collar. She locked eyes with his father, crossing the room toward her. Getting to her feet, she turned to her sister, extending her hand.

"Flick, would you like to dance?"

"No, you know I do not like dancing and I've just eaten."

"Come on, dance with me! I'm bored."

"Please, no." Felicity shook her hands, smiling, but refused to get up.

Evangeline swung around. "Sir Thedamaine, will you dance with me?" His face briefly flashed with terror then a crooked, supressed smile. He reached out his hand, but she was snatched from him and Evangeline was dragged to the dance by Duke Forrester, exactly where she did not want to be.

Unsure of what to do with herself, Felicity got up and leisurely fetched a drink across the hall, attaching herself to Mary, her handmaiden, who was hiding in the shadows. She could not even address Mary before she was preyed upon, hunted, and caught by Morana and Vesna. Felicity's drink was knocked from her hand and banged against the floor, drawing all attention to her. Cheeks flushing red, her skirt splattered with wine; she drew all the strength within her not to flee from the hall and barricade herself into her chamber for a week. The situation was made worse by Mary and a young scullery maid making a fuss of her dress as they tried to mop up the spillage, dabbing at her gown.

"Leave it," she spat, tearing her skirt from their fingers. She turned her back to the room, her rosy ears the only indication of embarrassment.

"I'll fetch you another," Mary said but was gone before Felicity could stop her.

"I do not think that is wise, getting another drink. You're obviously a spill risk," Morana leered as she slithered in front of Felicity.

"You knocked it from my hand!"

"And you spilled it," Vesna added.

"Spill risk."

"Leave me alone."

"Like your sister left you alone? Do you even have any friends?"

"*She* has the blacksmith, and the knight follows her around like a little, lost puppy. Who do you have?"

"I don't need anyone. I do not need to be escorted around the Manor like a child."

"Is that what you think friendship is?" Morana burst out laughing.

"Oh, Gods! You truly do not even know what you are missing. You are incapable of feeling lonely because you've never known companionship. Oh, I pity you." Vesna held her hands against her breast and the sickening pity in her eyes stung Felicity more than the smirking and tormenting.

"At least I am my own person, you two cannot be separate from each other; you are one being, incapable of an original thought and a shared personality of a wet sock."

"And you share your original thoughts with whom? Your father who can barely stand, let alone gather his mind up long enough to hold a conversation with you? Or your sister who would rather share a bed with a poor apprentice or risk her life than to speak to you? Or your dead mother, who let the voices in her head finally take her life?"

Morana was itching for a reaction and Felicity knew this and so refused to react to her. She shared an internal laugh with herself, imagining what Evangeline would have done if she had heard that. The entire hall would witness the Lady Heir try to claw the eyes out of her stepsister. Evangeline was so quick to anger and the twins knew this. Vesna and Morana glanced at one another before Felicity stepped forward.

"Oh, I'm sorry, did you say something?" Felicity smirked at them. "I am afraid I do not have the ear for murmurers, you will have to speak up next time. I'll assume it was nothing important." Felicity strode off quickly, but they did not pursue, and she crossed the room with a smile on her face. Meeting Mary by the dais and taking a huge gulp of the wine she was craving, she tried not to think about her loneliness.

"How did they know about my mother's mental state?" Felicity asked Mary, catching her off guard. "That was not common knowledge, the family kept it a tight secret and they did not live here before my father proposed."

"That secret was not secure, milady. I was not around when your mother was alive, but I heard rumours before I even got here."

"What kind of rumours?"

"That she saw things that weren't there, screamed at invisible spirits out to get her. Some say she was a witch that had a spell go wrong, unable to control her powers or that other witches cursed her."

"Any rumours about how she died?"

"The big one was that the voices in her head told her to kill her new-born and then herself. Another was your father killed her for being unable to revive his only son." Mary placed a hand on Felicity's arm softly and took her drink from her hand, afraid she would collapse. "Milady, they are only rumours, blown out of proportion. Should I not have told you this? Milady, what is wrong?"

"Evangeline is right." It was time to find out what really happened to her mother.

CHAPTER 4.

She pulled away from his wandering hands and lustful eyes, but he grabbed and pulled her back. He was not letting go. She flowed with the dance trying to keep her body away from his, her face away from his face, but he was strong and persistent. His eyes lingered on her breasts, his hand moving from the small of her back down to her rear.

"I look forward to the day you will come to live with me, *daughter-in-law*." The Duke savoured the words in a way that made Evangeline's skin crawl. Suddenly she had enough and stopped moving, so did he.

"You are making me uncomfortable. Please let go." She turned around and got two steps before he grabbed her wrist hard and pulled her back, she slipped and fell into his plump, disgusting body. Pulling away again, he grabbed both wrists this time.

"Don't walk away from me. I'm not finished with you."

As he jerked her back another time, she turned and forced her knee up into his groin yanking her arms free just as Sir Thedamaine reached them, his hand on his sword. Evangeline grabbed his elbow and pulled back.

"Leave it. It's over. Not here." She was whispering firmly at him as she held him back. Sir Thedamaine kept his hand on his sword and stood his ground between them. She felt the anger emanating from him and tried to pull him back again. The Duke recovered from his groin kick, furious, and lunged for Evangeline. Thedamaine was prevented from drawing his sword by Evangeline's grip on his arm, but Sir Penlyn slid in between them from nowhere. The dancers around them barely noticed the scuffle, the song playing was a fast and energetic number so nobody looked twice but if Thedamaine had drawn his sword on the Duke, Evangeline could not imagine what would happen.

"Father. Back off. Listen to me. Look at me. I mean it,

look at me. Go to mother and stay there. Do you understand me?"

Evangeline was still holding Thedamaine back, but she was the only one who saw the hidden blade in Penlyn's sleeve that was pressed deep against the Duke's gut. His words were firm and intense, and the threat had worked for the Duke turned and walked away, disappearing into the corner where he would stay all night long. Penlyn turned and nodded gratitude to Thedamaine and looked at Evangeline. She could not read the look on his face, but she saw him differently. The fact that he pulled a knife on his own father, that was something she respected. She began to imagine what a force they would make together as husband and wife and laughed to herself. Penlyn bowed slightly and left without a word. Evangeline pulled Thedamaine away and he followed her, still steaming with anger and watching the corner where the Duke sat.

"Hey, it is fine now. Look at me." She had to turn his face to look at her, but he did and finally relaxed. "Look at that; *me* calming *you* for once. What a world we live in." That made him laugh and he was back to his stoic self again.

"Sir Penlyn." Thedamaine straightened up and bowed his head slightly.

"Thank you for that. I appreciate it," Evangeline smiled politely.

"Yes, about that. May I discuss with you what just happened? There are some things I need to clear up." He was nervous and clearly embarrassed, so Evangeline tried to brush it off.

"There is no need. Let us forget and move on."

"No, please. I need to explain. Its loud in here, can we go somewhere private?"

"That is fine, but Sir Thedamaine will be escorting us."

Evangeline linked her arm around Sir Penlyn's, and he led her out of the ballroom, they went out into the central courtyard and he sat her down underneath the twisted yew tree. Sir Thedamaine stood at a respectful distance, on guard and watchful, his hand still on his sword.

"My father is an awful man." Penlyn's frank words took Evangeline by surprise. "My family knows it, my *mother* knows it and little by little, the country is learning it too. Our marriage is a political bond, and I will not pretend

30

otherwise, we both know that neither of us want this marriage, but it is a lifeline for both our families. The Ravenhill status will raise the Forresters just as much as the reverse. What I am saying is, you will be safe when you are my wife. I will protect you from him."

"Because you need my status? Because I am a bond that secures your family in the hierarchy?"

"What? No. That is not what I am saying."

"That is exactly what you are saying. You are saying that we are marrying for political ties not for love and you cannot afford for me to break that marriage over whatever your father does to me because you need my family's name."

"No, no, no. That is not what I meant. Please, let me start over."

"I suggest you do."

Penlyn inhaled and exhaled slowly, staring into the middle distance, terrified. He was too busy scrambling to find the right words to see the playfulness in Evangeline's face. She looked at Thedamaine, who wasn't looking at her but was suppressing a smile on his own face. He knew what she was doing, and he shook his head in disapproval, still avoiding her gaze. When Penlyn finally looked at Evangeline, she masked all playfulness and was back to pretending she was serious and offended.

"When you are my wife. No. I will *always* protect. No."

Evangeline was growing bored of him and interrupted. "Do not worry, I am not offended. I am teasing you. You have a lot to learn, *husband*." She stood up and headed back inside.

"Why are you torturing the poor boy?" Sir Thedamaine asked when out of earshot.

"He will be my husband, that gives me the right to torture him however I see fit." Penlyn did not follow them inside and Evangeline was glad. He bored her. She needed to be entertained and she was not afraid to admit it. She knew what she wanted and would not waste her time on what she did not like.

Returning to the party inside, she saw Felicity leave in a hurry, the colour drained from her face and her handmaiden rushing behind her. From the state of her stained dress, Evangeline assumed the twins had tricked Felicity and she could not stand the embarrassment. She felt sympathy for her

31

and thought about following, but she would rather drink.

The bar was busy, and the cupbearer was running around, filling the tankards of the burly men surrounding her father. Zorya had her own cupbearer that was not to be shared and she could not even see the bottler in the room. She refused to wait so leant over the bar and picked up the nearest jug, pouring herself a large drink. It was ale and she gulped it down until someone touched her back; a shiver running down her spine.

"Care to dance, Lady Evangeline?" It was another noble Lord whose name escaped her; though she could tell he was from the Buckley family from the antlers embroidered on his tunic.

"Apologies, but I am just getting a drink for my friend. Another time." She quickly filled up another tankard and left the bar swiftly. Not wanting to dance or talk, she crossed the room, weaving in and out of the dancers. There was a second bar on the other side of the ballroom and by the time she had reached it, both tankards had been finished. She refilled them again. "I promised a drink to an old friend." Someone else approached her and tried to talk but she lied and crossed the dance floor once again, finishing both drinks. She got away with it two more times before she felt dizzy and wanted to sit down. Outside the ballroom and down the hall was a small reading room that was barely used. As usual, Sir Thedamaine came with her but lingered outside the door.

"Oh, for God's sake, Thedamaine, please don't hover. If you must stalk me, please keep me company."

He entered the room and closed the door behind him but remained standing. "I assumed you wanted your privacy."

"What makes you think that?"

"You leave a party to sit in a room by yourself and I've seen you crossing the room several times avoiding conversations and dances, drinking two drinks all night. I can only assume you do not want company."

"Depends on the company. Please sit." She pointed to the chair in front of her and he sat, she handed him the second drink. "I have been telling people I was going to drink with an old friend. I'd hate to be a liar so, please, drink with me. That's an order," she said, half-heartedly, before he refused her. She took a sip when he did, putting the drink down when he did and lifting it back up again, mirroring him. He caught on quickly and didn't put his drink down, continuously gulping down the drink. Keeping intense eye contact, they found themselves suddenly in a drinking game.

"Damn you!" Thedamaine gasped for air, admitting defeat. "Are you a fish?"

"No, just a professional." She wiped her dribbling chin and slammed her empty tankard on the table between them, belching her victory.

"Ale is not my drink." He said between breaths, holding his heart and grinning at her.

"All drinks are my drink. All drink, every drink!" She jumped up, spinning around in victory but doubled over, her hands on her thighs. "Oh, I should not have done that! Oh, I feel sick now." She plopped herself back down in the chair. "Why did I do that?"

"Why did you spin or why did you drink?" Thedamaine asked with a grin.

"I don't know. Both, I guess." She took a breath, and the feeling was gone. "Well, that was fun. What's next?"

"Another drink?" He asked, grinning at her.

"See, I knew I liked you!" She stood up but grabbed her head, stumbling around. The drink finally hit her and Thedamaine had to steady her. "Bad idea. I know my limits." She was about to retire to bed when she saw the table by the bookcase. "Chess!" She shouted. "We need to play *chess*. Just you and me, no other players. Can we do that?"

"Yes, we can play two-person chess, but you seriously want to play chess now?"

"Of course, it's easy! Bang, bang, bang and you're done. You bring it over. I want to sit."

Thedamaine brought the chess set over, placing it on the table between them. Evangeline knocked half the pieces over trying to grab a pawn and did not do a single legal move throughout the game but Thedamaine allowed it, placing his pieces wherever and pretended she won all the same.

CHAPTER 5.

Felicity had been standing over her sisters' bed for a while, hoping she would wake up. Gossip throughout the Manor informed her that Evangeline spent the night with Sir Thedamaine, but Felicity knew for sure that wasn't true, not in the way people were assuming. Evangeline retired to bed alone, and her empty bed was proof enough. Felicity only hoped that the gossip had not reached the infirmary, worrying about Taren's feelings. She did not understand that relationship and she doubted they understood it either. Felicity knew that Evangeline could not define a single relationship in her life and was jealous that she had these relationships at all.

An impulse to smack Evangeline awake suddenly overcame her. It worked, though. Evangeline was awake, the seal broken. Moaning and groaning, Evangeline mumbled something, but Felicity did not catch it.

"You have been asleep for fourteen hours. Wake up."

"Leave me be, I have a headache. I don't feel well."

"You drank too much. Now get up, I need to talk to you."

"Can't it wait?"

"No. Get up. It's urgent and important."

"Just tell me."

"No. I need your full attention."

"Then come back later. I don't care right now."

"Fine, I'll tell you. You'll want to sit up for this."

"No, I really don't."

Felicity had no choice. "I think father killed mother."

Evangeline opened her eyes, inhaled and sat up.

"You were right. I did want to sit for that. Now you have my attention. What makes you think that?"

Felicity was surprised at how Evangeline took the accusation, she assumed she would unleash a demon of drama, but she was stoic and calm.

"He had motive. More than one actually. He killed her so he was free to marry Zorya, he killed her because she could not give him a son, he killed her because she was insane and was destroying his family's name. One of them or all of them, whichever it is, he killed her."

"But why him? Going off those motives, Zorya could have killed her too. Get her out of the way and she can marry him and gain power? But there isn't much evidence behind these motives. If he killed her for dirtying his family's name, then why would he ruin it further by marrying a handmaiden? He loved mother and she was nothing but pleasant to Zorya. If father were cruel to her or openly had an affair with Zorya or even if mother treated Zorya poorly, either one of them could have the motive."

"I don't think he did love her. At least not at the end. I could tell he had contempt for her, he hated her illness."

"You know, he does keep insisting that she died during childbirth, or from the complications with the birth and he kept passing off her illness as nothing. He could be hiding something."

"It's a hunch but things add up."

"That doesn't explain the Nil'vetra."

"The what?"

"Oh, I haven't told you! Finally!" Evangeline pulled the book out of the box and explained how she found it and what their father said about it. Felicity was confused but flicked through and stopped at the last page.

"Nil'vetra. I've seen this word before."

"Where?"

"I've seen it written down somewhere. I cannot remember."

"You have to! Are you sure you saw it written down? Father said she mumbled that word in her sleep sometimes."

Felicity cursed herself. She knew she had seen it somewhere, but where?

"Who else have you shown this to? Does Taren know?"

"No, he doesn't. Just me, you and father know of it."

"You didn't tell Taren?" That surprised her.

"I was going to but got distracted by the wedding, I actually haven't seen him since we came in after the attack. Oh, that's bad. I should go see him."

"But you saw him yesterday."

"No, I didn't. I was at the wedding the whole time, like I said I haven't seen him since the attack."

"But when I bumped into him, he said he was meeting you."

"He wasn't meeting me, or if he wanted to, he never got to me. Felicity I haven't seen him."

"He said-" she stopped, thinking over his words, replaying what happened, "-he said he was meeting someone, I assumed it was you."

"It wasn't me. Who was he meeting?"

They knew they had to find out, so they headed to the infirmary. Who would he be meeting? He wasn't allowed to leave the infirmary, so he was risking breaking the rules for someone and the only people he knew were Evangeline and Felicity.

Taren's face lit up when he saw Evangeline. "Two visitors! You've just made my day!"

"Who did you meet with yesterday?" Felicity asked, shortly.

"Meet with? What do you mean?"

"You told me you were meeting someone."

"I don't remember that. I said I was lost."

"No, you said you were meeting someone, I asked if it was Evangeline and told you she woke up late and couldn't see you, then you said you were lost."

"I didn't say that. I said I was lost. I wasn't meeting someone. I just wanted to stretch my legs and take a walk; I was sick of staring at that damn wall all day long. I got lost on my walk and ran into you."

"Taren, are you *sure*?" Evangeline studied his face.

"Yes! I would know if I was meeting someone, I took a walk and got lost. End of story."

"Perhaps your memory is corrupted?" Evangeline said, now addressing Felicity. "It happens, maybe you are thinking of something else and it just got mixed up? I mean, you did think at first he met with me, you're just remembering it wrong." Felicity knew she was right. Taren said he was meeting someone, and he was covering it up. He was lying, Felicity was sure of it.

"Maybe you're right. I misheard or something." Felicity pretended to drop the subject but that lie was forever in her brain. He was hiding something.

"Anyway." Evangeline changed the subject and put the open book on Taren's lap. Felicity tried to stop her, she no longer trusted Taren and did not want him involved. He flicked through the book, slowly, moving his lips as he read.

"The print is too small for me to read and the notes are too messy. It's giving me a headache. Can you read it to me?"

"Does it mean anything to you? Anything you read? What about this word? Ever heard it before?"

"No, I haven't." He flicked through the pages again. "What is this?" He pulled the book closer to him. "Is that fire, what is in the middle?"

"Let me see." He gave the book to Evangeline and she and Felicity looked closely at the tiny drawing.

"It's a phoenix, I think. A bird in fire? It's a phoenix."

"Wait, I saw something else, another bird. Where was it?" Evangeline flicked through the book and stopped on a page. "It's not a bird but this is a thistle." She flicked again. "There it is: a peacock." She showed Felicity and Taren, but he pointed on the other page, a cypress tree was drawn in the corner.

"These must mean something," Felicity said. "Peacock, phoenix, thistle, cypress, what else is there?"

Evangeline began at the beginning and turned each page one by one, the three of them studied each page for the small hand drawn symbols. When they finished the book, they found the following pictures: a holly leaf, a bat, a fire beacon, a cypress tree, a phoenix, a peacock and a thistle. They had folded the corner of the page at every symbol and looked at them one by one.

"They must mean something," Felicity repeated.

"Well, a phoenix means rebirth and resurrection. Holly is a symbol of the nature god of truth."

"Do they represent the families?" Taren asked, thinking. "The Forrester family have a cypress tree on their crest."

"No, it's an oak tree," Evangeline answered.

"But you could be onto something. They all have certain meanings in heraldry. I'm not positive what they are but there is a book in the library that could tell us."

Felicity convinced them to go to the library and they each pulled out a book on heraldry and studied them, comparing notes. Felicity was right, each symbol had a specific meaning in heraldry.

"The holly signifies truth. The bat represents awareness of the powers of darkness and chaos. The fire beacon represents somebody who is watchful, who gave a signal in time of danger. The cypress tree is the symbol of death and eternal life. The phoenix is a symbol of resurrection and rebirth, new beginnings and resurgence. A peacock is a symbol of immortality, also representing beauty, power and knowledge. The thistle is an ancient heraldic symbol of pain and suffering."

"There seems to be a theme here. Truth and warning of death, resurrection and eternal life." Taren looked up at the two girls. "Was your mother warning herself of her own death?"

"But what about the resurrection, eternal life and immortality?"

"She was crazy." Evangeline stated matter-of-factly. "Did she think she would be reborn?"

"Did she take her own life in order to be reborn?" Felicity asked, quietly.

"So, we've gone from accusing our own father and stepmother of killing our mother and now onto suicide. Make up your mind, Felicity."

"I'm gathering evidence and motive."

"Wait, you think your father killed your mother? Zorya, too? You think they both killed her? You actually think that?"

"It is a theory. They have several motives to want her dead."

"But your own father? You can't discuss this with me, it's treason. I don't want to be executed."

"He's not the king, it's not that bad and like Felicity said, it's just a theory."

"You two are insane. How can you sit there and accuse your father and stepmother of that?"

Felicity wanted to yell at him, how could he just lie to Evangeline about who he met with, but she held her tongue.

Evangeline did not.

"How dare you! We are not insane. We want justice for our mother's murder, and we will find out who did it. No matter who killed her, they will pay for what they did."

"Even your father? What about him?"

"What about me?"

All three of them jumped up, out of their skin. Lord Horus stood at the door of the library, his riding clothes pressed and cleaned. They hung off his body loosely now as he was rapidly losing weight and muscle. His skin a sickly grey, sunken and beginning to wrinkle prematurely.

Felicity was sweating and panting. *How much did he hear? What would he say? What would he do to them?*

"Father, what are you doing here?" Evangeline asked, a little nervous crack in her voice.

"Looking for you, so what about me?"

They didn't answer. Taren and Felicity looked at each other, terrified and then to Evangeline, her gaze was on her father and did not break.

"Taren was nervous about leaving the infirmary against your orders, but I convinced him and Felicity that he needed a walk. I said it wasn't a good idea to leave the Manor, so we came here, it's quiet. I told him that if anyone came in nobody would say anything, they don't care. That's when he said, even your father? What about him? And speak of the devil, who should walk in but you! Please don't take it out on him, I made him leave."

"You *made* him leave? She forced you out of the infirmary and into here? What, don't you like to read, son? What are these books?"

Felicity and Taren were surprised at Evangeline's quick thinking and as Evangeline showed a heraldry book to her father, Felicity subtly covered the Nil'vetra book with another, hiding it from her father.

"Teaching him heraldry, huh? Not the most boring subject, but please, teach him in the infirmary next time. *Cadmael!*" Horus yelled loudly and made them all jump again. Cadmael came into the library and scanned each of the books on the floor and then focused on Taren. "Cadmael, escort young Taren back to the infirmary then meet me in my study."

"Yes, my lord."

"You two, follow me." They bent down to pick up the books. "Leave them, come with me."

"I want to study these later, brush up on my heraldry. I want to take them back to my room."

"You can get them later. Now come on." He turned around and Felicity quickly pulled the Nil'vetra book out from the other and slid it onto the shelf between an emerald book with gold lining and a burgundy book with a leather strap. Underneath the shelf was a small bust statue of a previous Lord. Felicity would have to remember where the book was so she could retrieve it later.

They followed their father in silence to his study. Cadmael was waiting for them, already scribbling on his scroll. Lord Horus gestured to the two chairs in front of his oversized desk and the two girls sat down. Backs straight, hands on laps and trying their hardest at keeping their faces still and stoic; Evangeline was succeeding more than Felicity. They watched their father sit down and look at each of them.

"Now, girls, I leave for my honeymoon tonight. While I am gone, Evangeline will be in charge, but my wish is for both of you to share the duties, help each other out and share the burden." He paused to cough. "I have called a cabinet council to assist you both, should you require it, consisting of the Chamberlain, Captain of the Guard and The Bailiff, but first and foremost, the two of you will assist and advise each other, just like your mother and I did."

Felicity looked at Evangeline as their mother was mentioned, Evangeline did not look at her.

"I understand," she said.

This was unusual. Felicity had not been trained properly to rule in her father's name. Evangeline received the bulk of the education whilst Felicity was left alone. She was 'the spare' and she knew it. Horus was preparing for worst case scenario: he would not return.

"Wait," Felicity said. Horus was gathering his notes and preparing to get up and leave. "Please can we talk before you go? Just me, you and Evangeline?" Finally, Evangeline looked to Felicity but this time she did not turn.

"Cadmael, please excuse us." He bowed his exit and closed the door behind him. "What would you like to talk about?" Horus' voice was struggling more and more with every word. But before either of them could speak, he answered his own question. "You want to talk about your mother? Of course you do. Fine." He took a long breath. "A year ago, she went into labour with our third child, the labour was intense and difficult. She had you two so soon after each other and had three miscarriages afterwards. We did not try again for several years but she fell pregnant and made it to labour. My son was dead before he even came into this world. He didn't even take his first breath. I held him in my arms, rocked him and loved him and grieved for him. Your mother refused to hold him. She screamed and screamed, clawing into the bed, writhing in distress. I took him away and left her screaming. I told the room to leave her in peace and they did. The doctor, the midwife and Zorya all left the room. I could still hear her screams from the next room. These were not the screams of pain or grief they were screams of fear. Knowing I could do nothing, I let the doctor take my son and he left with the midwife. I stayed with Zorya. When the screams finally died down, we both entered the room, and your mother was dead."

"Dead? Just like that?"

"Did she suddenly stop screaming or did they slowly quieten?"

"It was slow. She was calming down; it was only when she was completely silent did we enter the room."

"So, what happened?"

"How did she die?"

"She died of a broken heart. Grief took over."

"But you said she was screaming in fear, not grief."

"She just lost a baby."

"And she was dead before you entered the room? Nobody else was in there?"

"No. There were four of us in the room when she gave birth and I told everyone to leave afterwards. The doctor and the midwife left with the body and Zorya stayed with me."

"You stayed in the room?"

"Yes. *No.*" He corrected himself. "Not the room Emilia was in, we were in the study, outside."

"Zorya didn't go in before you? To check on her? You didn't go in either?"

"No. What is this? Are you interrogating me?" Lord Horus' voice, cracked but steady throughout his monologue, began to crumble and his sweats were back. "If you are trying to accuse me or my wife of something I suggest you hold your tongue before I take it from you."

Felicity adverted her father's angry gaze while Evangeline stood up.

"Do not get angry at her, she is only trying to get the full story of what happened that night. You owe us that. You told us nothing. It has been a year. She is dead, you have remarried and could be dying for all we know. We deserve to know the truth, before it is too late."

"I told you the truth. Now stand down, Evangeline." Horus stood up, tall against his aching back. Evangeline did not move.

"You're lying." A forceful slap across Evangeline's face brought Felicity to her feet. Evangeline stumbled but did not fall down, she steadied herself, holding her cheek and squeezing her eyes shut to prevent the tears of pain from falling. Felicity backed against the wall, recoiling from the violence.

Still with her hand on her cheek and looking at the floor to control her emotions, Evangeline spoke again. "She was alive when you went into the room, wasn't she?" She straightened up and turned to face her father. Felicity saw the huge red mark across her face, he had even cut her skin; a small trickle of blood had been smudged from her hand. "What did you do when you entered the room?"

"I yelled at her." He had slumped from shame, but Felicity could not tell if it was shame from the slap or yelling at his wife or both. "I was tired of her insanity; she would not hold her own son because of it. I thought she was a monster. She told me it was coming for her. Don't ask me what. I don't know, I don't care. Nothing was, she was paranoid and crazy. Nothing she did or said made any sense. I sat on the edge of the bed, turned away from her. She called for me to come to her, but I refused. I sat there out of reach for hours. She died in the bed whilst I was ignoring her."

"Why didn't you just tell us this?"

"I was ashamed! I sat there whilst she called my name, she knew she was dying, and she needed me. I could have helped her, but I didn't." His voice broke into a coughing fit. Struggling for breath in between coughs, he couldn't even drink until the fit was over. Felicity worried that he would die right there. She was right though; he technically did kill her. It was closure to the story, but something was wrong. It was unsatisfactory and anticlimactic; something was missing but she couldn't put her finger on it. Evangeline remained still, her fist at her side tight and ever-so-slightly shaking, but Felicity was shaking more.

"We are done here." Horus finally recovered from his

coughing fit and headed toward the door. Neither of them moved. "Leave me be", he spat as Cadmael and Sir Thedamaine appeared outside the door when he opened it. Cadmael followed him down the corridor but Sir Thedamaine entered the room.

"Are you okay?" Felicity asked, taking a closer look at Evangeline's face.

"What happened?" Sir Thedamaine asked, also taking a closer look.

"He hit her."

"Don't touch me." Evangeline shouted and the two of them jumped back.

"Why did you provoke him?" Felicity asked, at a distance.

"I wanted to rile him up, to get a reaction from him. I wanted the truth."

"Do you believe him?"

"No. He lied to us before, he's lying again. We just need to gather more evidence. I promise you we will find the truth, but someone is covering something up."

"Yes, I am starting to think that myself. What do you think it is?"

"We'll discuss this another time. Just leave me alone for a bit." Her tone was not aggressive but still shook with emotion that was becoming difficult to restrain.

Sir Thedamaine stepped toward her. Without touching, he examined her face. "I'll take you back to your room, so you can rest."

Evangeline nodded slightly and followed Sir Thedamaine, she kept her head down and Felicity knew she was struggling to remain composed but respected her success. Felicity almost cried herself and she wasn't the one who was hit. With Evangeline and her father gone, Felicity found herself alone. Again. Overwhelmed and her nerves shattered, she wanted to get some fresh air and so headed outside.

Felicity took a seat on the bench in front of the reflecting pool, the family mausoleum on the other side. The cemetery gardens was an extremely peaceful place where she liked to sit and think. Evangeline used to have her own special thinking spot; she didn't know that Felicity knew where it was, but she did. Evangeline used to sit on the roof, there was a parapet that led to a small, secluded battlement that was badly designed for it had no access point. You had to climb out of the window, shimmy across the tiny parapet and over the battlement into the little opening. Felicity climbed it once hoping to terrify her sister, but she almost slipped and fell and realising her fear of heights, never climbed out onto the roof again. Felicity's peaceful place to think was on the ground.

The cemetery had an eerie ambiance. No matter how loud the Manor could get, noise could not reach the cemetery at all. There was no trickling water from the reflecting pool, it was still water and there were barely any birds in the gardens despite the plethora of trees, bushes and shrubs. The crypt was quite small but still held several former Lords and Ladies. Her mother's body was in that crypt lying in the stone coffin in the centre. She didn't want to go inside but would rather look at it from the outside. Eventually she grabbed a long stick and waved it slowly in the water at her feet.

"Oh, hello Felicity. I did not know you were out here." Zorya was walking up towards her, Morana and Vesna behind her.

"Hello Zorya. How are you? Are you ready for your honeymoon?"

"I am well, thank you, and yes ready to go. I am just paying my respects." She turned to the twins and her tone changed, "remember what I said?" She turned back around and kept walking, past the reflecting pool and entered the crypt. Morana and Vesna stayed with Felicity. She could feel them watching her, she kept swirling the stick through the water round and round.

"What do you want?" She eventually spat, tired of their hovering and watching.

"Lonely?" Morana asked.

"Bored?" Vesna added.

"Unlikable, unwanted, unfunny, oh I am sorry, I thought we were describing the two of you? Go bother someone else, your presence annoys me."

"Why are you swirling that stick around?"

"Why do you care? Leave me alone."

"Why are you being so moody? We are trying to talk to you."

"Since when have you ever really wanted to talk to me? Without wanting to insult me or prank me or tease me?"

Felicity got up and faced them. "What do you want from me?"

"We are trying to talk to you." Morana said, loudly and angrily. "Trying to be *nice*." She shoved Felicity back slightly, not enough to knock her off her feet but enough to push her back a step.

"You could have pushed me into the water. What is your problem?"

"Girls! Knock it off!" Zorya had emerged from the crypt and called to them. She hurried over and smacked the twins with a wallop behind their heads. "Shut your horrible mouths and get inside, both of you. You disgust me." They ran inside without another word, Zorya looked at Felicity, said nothing and went inside too.

"What a strange day." Felicity said out loud to herself when alone.

CHAPTER 6.

Between the emerald one and the burgundy one, Felicity pulled out the Nil'vetra book. The location of the symbols seemed to be irrelevant, completely at random but the themes were in the book. The book was about the occult; supernatural, mystical and magical themes. She realised that the book was originally much larger and most of the pages had been torn out, either hiding something or leaving only the necessary. One of the first annotations written said '*I am a Bridge.*' At first this meant nothing to Felicity but elsewhere in the book it explained what a 'Bridge' was. People who are able to see through the veil between our world and the next, who are sensitive to the occult are called Bridges. The spirit world and our world coexist in the same place and only these Bridges can see the spirits around us, can see them interact with our world and are usually magnets for spirits because the sight goes both ways.

If this was true, Felicity just explained the reason for her mother's visions and insanity.

She saw the spirit world.

The visions she saw were spirits.

She had said something was coming for her, was that a spirit?

The next page spoke of shamans which are a type of Bridge that choose to study the spirit world. Those who choose to learn more about the other world can bring forth gifts from the spirits themselves. These are known as the shamans. They have gifts, usually named as witchcraft, sorcery, supernatural arts, or magic and it can vary from each practitioner depending on how sensitive they are to the other side, and how much they study. Some shamans live a nomadic life that they have dedicated completely to the study of the spirit world, others live in secret with the other people of this world, keeping their gifts hidden to avoid prejudice.

Was her mother a shaman in secret?

No, she couldn't be. She was afraid of the spirit world; it drove her to insanity. Did it drive her to suicide? The passage on shamans finished with: '*Though forbidden within all shaman communities; some shamans can bring forth powers from the darkness and practise blood magic,*' but the page ended there, and the next page was torn out. Felicity thought back to the bat symbol of awareness of the powers of darkness and chaos. What did the next page say? Blood magic? She wanted to know more. There was a knock at the door to the library and Cadmael entered.

"I have come to collect you, Lady Felicity, the Lord and Lady Ravenhill will be leaving soon, you are wanted in the Grand Hall."

Felicity had shut the book when he entered and brought it with her as he escorted her through the Manor. Her mind was wandering.

"Cadmael, have you ever heard of a shaman?" She asked, hoping for a good answer.

"Oh yes, we used to have a big shaman problem a few years back, they tend to return to the village every year, trying to con some business out of the villagers before we run them out of town."

"They're here a lot?"

"Yes, we seem to be good business for them as our problems with the beast have made the people superstitious and desperate. They have profited from our tragedy and curse so return often."

"When was the last time they were here?"

"Oh, a few months now. They are due to return so Lady Evangeline will most likely have to deal with them while the Lord and Lady Ravenhill are away."

"Deal with them? We have to run them out of town?"

"It is illegal for the shaman camps to be inside our village walls, but they are smart and set up camp in the forest, just beyond the village boundaries, moving every night to avoid detection. They send some shamans into town every day, usually disguised, in order to drum up business. Our guards are on alert to detect these conmen and chase them out of town. We cannot convict them of course; we have no evidence, but we remove them from the village which is only a temporary fix. It is a shame we cannot do more because

47

they only come back the next day. If I had my way we would round up each of these shamans and flog them in the square for all to see."

"That seems a little harsh."

"Does it? They deal with poisons and curses, witchcraft and blood magic. They are frauds and scammers, hustlers and swindlers."

"Are they witches or frauds? You cannot be both."

"Trust me, they can, and they are. They do both. That's the art of the hustle; they have enough *real* power to be genuine but plaster on a generous layer of lies and deception to con you out of everything."

Felicity got the impression that she was striking a nerve. Something happened between Cadmael and these shamans, something that has made him bitter. She assumed he had been conned himself, but she had the better sense than to ask him about it. They were the first to arrive at the Grand Hall, so Felicity probed again.

"Why are the shamans illegal? Because they are fraudsters?"

"It is illegal to practise witchcraft and blood magic. I am surprised you did not know that; it was your mother's law."

"My mother passed that law?"

"Yes, she campaigned to the Queen for years to pass that law, before it was barely punished but now, with evidence and a trial, the practitioner can be executed. Though those shamans in the forest are protected by that awful nomad law. We cannot touch them. I am surprised you do not know this. I suppose you do not learn the same things that your sister does."

"Interesting." Felicity was about to ask for more information, but Evangeline and Sir Thedamaine entered the hall. Evangeline's face had bruised but she seemed to have recovered and took her place next to Felicity. Shortly behind them, Lord Horus and Lady Zorya entered, followed by Morana and Vesna, who stood the other side of Felicity.

It was time to say goodbye to their father. He would be gone for at least a month. They would have to deal with a full moon attack without him and all were worried about Evangeline. Felicity was worried that he would succumb to his sickness on the road or be a victim of a bandit attack and be left for dead, or even she, herself, may not survive the attack, despite the safety within the Manor. One thing was for certain, she was terrified she would never see him again.

Evangeline also thought this would be their last meeting, but she was worried she would never get the truth from him and he would die with a secret that Evangeline would never know. They said their goodbyes and Felicity hugged him tightly, even the twins hugged him after their mother, but Evangeline extended her arm for a handshake. With an excruciatingly strong grip and intense eye contact, her father shook her hand and left without an apology for striking her.

They all followed the newlywed couple out of the hall and watched them enter their carriages and disappear down the hill. A silence fell once the portcullis had closed, each person turned to face Evangeline, but she had gone.

"Where is she?" Cadmael roared. Sir Thedamaine looked as shocked as the rest of them then looked to Felicity. She held up her hands, not knowing where she was or even noticed she had slipped away.

"She has obviously gone to the infirmary to see the blacksmith," Morana pointed out.

"No, he was discharged this afternoon." Sir Thedamaine was looking to the portcullis.

"Well, find her then," Morana sneered.

"Yes, do your *job*." Vesna added.

Sir Thedamaine shook his head slightly and left the group which subsequently dispersed. Felicity was left alone knowing exactly where Evangeline had gone but could not care less. She wanted to follow the strings of deception; so many people around her were lying or hiding something and she was going to bring them all down.

CHAPTER 7.

"Keep them coming!" She roared as the men around her cheered and raised their tankards to her. She was racing Taren to finish her drink before him, and she was ahead. Taren stopped at three tankards, lost all colour in his face and bolted from the table, running to vomit. She cheered along with the room who roared her victory.

Evangeline had slipped away unnoticed from her father's departure, not even Sir Thedamaine had seen. After Taren had been given the word from the doctor that he could leave, they both agreed they would meet at their spot. One of them, at least. They had five places where they could slip over the wall unnoticed, today they chose the bakery. In order to escape, they had to run from the wall to the tree line as fast as they could to avoid detection and must keep running to ensure they would lose any pursuers. Evangeline had a lot of stamina and she was fast; she could run for days. Taren could barely keep up, even at full health yet still followed her wherever she took him.

As they ran through the village, Evangeline did not want to stop; it was freedom. Suddenly an impulse to keep running struck her, keep running until she could run no more. Run away from the village, away from everything so she could just be herself. The tavern sign came into view and the urge to drink overcame the urge to flee.

The locals at the Wolf and Raven tavern knew Evangeline and Taren well, it was one of her favourite places; the furthest drinking spot in the village boundaries and was right on the waterfront. Full of fishermen from the lake; tired from their shifts, locals from Birchcliffe that barely cared about her, or the riffraff that hung about near the brothels, it was a varied group of drinkers that liked her company. It was a good place to hide out for she knew not one of them cared enough to tell a village guard where she was, so she was safe to hang around.

A man sat down in Taren's chair in front of her. He pulled down his hood revealing three scars that reached from his eye passed his torn ear and into his hair where they wrapped around his skull. She knew immediately it was a scratch from the beast. The scars had barely missed his eye but ripped his ear into disfigured segments.

"I'm Nicholas. You want a challenge? You talk to me. Come on then, lets drink!" He wanted to race her.

"I already have three ales in me."

"Quitting already? Come on, just the one drink. Whoever finishes it first, wins."

"I'm not gambling with you, Nicholas."

"Why not? You have more than enough to lose."

"Whoever wins buys the other a drink."

The man lifted his tankard ready while Evangeline waited for the barmaid to refill hers. Together they flung back and drunk, she got a couple of gulps in when the man knocked the drink from her hand, causing the contents to drench a large man unlucky enough to be walking next to her.

"I win!" The cheater cheered. The large man bent over the table, dripping with ale.

"Who. Did. That?"

Evangeline looked to cheating Nicholas, he was grinning ecstatically and pointing to Evangeline. She stood up slowly.

"My deepest apologies," she said soothingly.

"How dare you...drink without me!" The large man's tone suddenly changed from restricted rage to playful glee. "Princess! So good to see you!"

"Oh, Henry! You're back, I didn't recognise you."

Henry was an old friend of Evangeline's and a former bottler for the Manor, when she last saw him he had significantly less muscles and a smaller gut. He enveloped her in a tight bear hug, lifting her slightly off the ground.

"The market's been kind to this belly."

"Sorry about the ale, my friend."

"Don't worry about it, Princess. Its rather fitting isn't it?"

"Why are you calling her princess?" Nicholas asked, interrupting their laughter.

"She may as well be a princess to us."

"But she's not. She's just a Lord's daughter."

"Woah, now, she is Lady Ravenhill."

"No, her stepmother is Lady Ravenhill, if anything she is just Lady Evangeline."

"That's exactly who I am."

"Again with the *'just'*! This is Lady Evangeline Ravenhill, she runs this town. Literally. Show her some respect."

"Her father runs the town."

"Not since this afternoon. He's out of town so she's in charge."

"Lady Regent, then."

"I don't like your tone. Starting fights, causing trouble for the Princess."

"And he cheated!" the young barmaid shouted.

"He did! Knocked the drink from her hand!" Other people were chiming in across the room.

"Get him out of here!"

"Kick him out!"

Henry grabbed the cheating Nicholas by the collar and pulled him out of his seat. From the angle, Evangeline could see Nicholas's full scar. It was deep and he kept his hair short to bring attention to it, he was obviously not ashamed of it.

"You owe the Princess an apology."

"She's not a princess!"

"Just get him out of here." Evangeline waved her hand at him and sat back down; she was bored of this. Henry nodded and pushed Nicholas from the table, lobbing him out of the door and out of the tavern. "Care to sit, Henry?" She gestured to the chair and he sat with a smile.

"It is good to see you, glad to see you well. Except, of course, for this." He pointed to her bruised face. "Let me guess, your father?"

"How did you know?"

"He always had a temper that one. Plus, you two together just bring out the worse in each other. You're too much alike, like fighting fire with fire. You need someone cool. You need fire and ice. Someone that keeps you calm."

"I guess you're right."

"He left for his honeymoon? I saw their carriages leaving earlier."

"Yes, he will be gone for at least a month while he visits the neighbouring families."

"And you're in charge?"

"I am."

"You know, I heard some rumours that you were out in the village with the beast during the last attack. I hope you're not doing anything reckless?"

"That wasn't me," she lied, sipping her newly refilled drink.

"Yes it was!" Taren had just joined them.

"Where have you been? You've missed all the fun."

"Don't change the subject, this girl was out here, in town with me and managed to escape the attack unhurt. *Her* traps worked beautifully and saved us both."

"You were there, too. You got out alive."

"Alive? Yes. Unhurt? No." Taren pointed to his back.

"To Lady Evangeline!" Henry had raised his drink high in a toast but at the same time the band started playing a loud song that was the taverns' old favourite. Nobody heard his toast, but Evangeline just shrugged and pulled Taren in for a dance. Now delightfully drunk, she danced with Taren and a few of the other men, bouncing around gleefully.

"This is my celebration, Taren. Before I am burdened with all the duties that come with taking my father's place. Now dance with me and drink with me!"

Spinning around, she ended up dancing straight into Sir Thedamaine. Not wanting her evening to be over, she laughed in his face and bolted from the dance floor, grabbing Taren's hand and fleeing from the tavern, chuckling. She and Taren ran, slipping through town and zigzagging to avoid the guards now looking for her. The sun had set, and she was now breaking curfew.

They climbed the southern hill and took refuge under the old Hangman's Tree. Listening for any guards on their tail, they waited while catching their breaths. Evangeline laid down on the grass, against the trunk of the tree and looked up at the branches. There were still a couple of old pieces of rope hanging from the largest branch.

"This is where we first met."

Evangeline had been slipping her guard since she was a child and she first met Taren on this hill, underneath this tree. *She* was underneath, he was in the tree and dropped a branch on her head. It was a small branch, but it still hurt. She cursed him down out of the tree and suddenly a lifelong friendship was formed.

"We met before that."

"No, we didn't. We became friends that day you dropped the branch on my head."

"We became friends that day but it's not the first time we met. Don't you remember?" Evangeline was blank. "*The race*? The vegetable stand?"

The memories all came flooding back to her in a wave of nostalgia. She could remember it like it was yesterday and the entire race replayed itself in her mind:

They all broke from the starting line like crossbow bolts. Evangeline knew she would win, she was tall, with long legs and a broad reach. She could take one step with every two of theirs. She was fast, yet she paced herself to a steady spot in the middle of the race, then took a sharp left turn at the last moment.

"Coward!" She heard one child shout.

"What? Follow her!" She heard another.

"Cheat!" Was the last word she could make out before they were out of earshot.

She knew these streets just as well as they did and she knew they were about to do the same thing to her and break off to the right one street ahead, leaving her behind to run the long track and lose. She ran through the bakery doors and out the back, causing an uproar. She guessed two or three children were pursuing her and followed her through the bakery, not very gracefully by the sound of it. She did not look back; she would lose her footing and her position. She ran through two streets then bounded up the stairs of someone's home, hearing one of her pursuers stop in their tracks and curse her. She hopped the staircase onto the adjoining rooftop and jumped from roof to barrel to floor and continued running, cutting off an entire street and giving herself an advantage.

Continuing through the village, weaving through alleys and hopping fences; she ended up colliding with another body. They knocked heads and fell to the ground, writhing in pain. Dizziness and nausea mingled together as she tried to process what had happened. She had run right into another racer. He got up quickly and so did she, mirroring him. He was closest to the alley she was about to run down but a half wall in front of her hid the street, she took the chance. Needing another head start, she rammed into him again, knocking him to the ground. Scrambling up and over the wall, there was a cart behind it that she did not see until the last moment and miscalculated her landing, hitting the floor hard. The pain shot up her shin and knee and caused her to hesitate for a moment, but the boy was scrambling up the wall behind her and she forced herself on. That was karma for using that cheaters move on him. She shouldn't have knocked him down.

She knew where she was; Tanner Row, she was now close to the finish line, but the boy was closer still, suddenly he broke off and she lost him. She doubted herself, had she taken a wrong turning, did he know a shortcut that she didn't? Her knee was hurting so much. Her shin cutting like knives with every step. She broke free into the High Street and weaved in and out of shoppers and traders but saw him. He was on the other side of the street, running with her, at her pace. They were tying for first place which meant she wasn't going to win. Trying to match and beat his stride, she was watching him, making sure she was always in front. He flashed between the pedestrians and carts and stalls that they zigzagged through. She was running and she was winning.

There it was: the finish line just ahead.

He suddenly stopped, she watched as he grinded to a halt, waving his arms, but she kept going, grinning wide.

She was going to win.

Turning to face forward and lock eyes with the finish line; she ran straight into a vegetable stall. She crashed horribly into it, flipping it over, snapping wood and throwing vegetables everywhere.

It was over.

She was not getting back up.

She had lost the race.

That was Taren. She never realised it was him. She was too focused on the race itself, the boy she collided with then pushed to the ground, and who tried to warn her of the vegetable stall; it was Taren.

"That *was* you!" She couldn't believe her memory; how could she not have known that? But it made sense when she thought about it. "I have not thought about that day in years! How long ago was that?"

"Got to be close to a decade ago."

"A decade later and I'm *still* beating you!"

"You can outrun us all, even the beast. I couldn't do that."

"It clawed you inside the cellar, it had nothing to do with your speed. If you had gone first I would have been caught."

Evangeline felt something shift and Taren fell quiet. Obviously, he did not want to talk about the attack, so she sat there in silence with him until he wanted to talk. She waited for him to tell her what was on his chest, but he never did. Eventually Sir Thedamaine found them. Evangeline accepted the escort back to the Manor, not wanting to run again. She found herself drifting off to sleep against Sir Thedamaine while she rode on his horse back home. Once she was in her bed, she fell into a long, deep sleep full of dreams.

CHAPTER 8.

Evangeline screamed out of her slumber, drenched and shocked. She was rudely awakened by a jug of freezing water dumped on her. She screamed, scrambling upright and saw the glimpse of a dress disappearing out of her chamber room. She raged, growling like an animal as she threw back the soaked covers and ran out of the room, following the cackling down the corridor.

"You are dead!" A few of the household poked their heads out of their doors as the three girls sprinted down the corridors and stairways. "Morana! Vesna! I will *kill* you!" Evangeline stayed in pursuit of the twins as they kept running through the Manor trying to lose her, but she was fast.

"It was time to wake up, lazy bones!" Morana called as Evangeline almost ran right into a maid, giving them a precious moment to gloat. Their mistake of stopping was all Evangeline needed. Once she finally got around the girl, she crossed the distance and tackled Vesna to the ground. She was the slowest and the closest. With a hard thump, they both hit the ground. Vesna cowered on the floor as Evangeline straddled her back, pulling Vesna's arms behind her and pressing her head firmly into the ground.

"You are dead!"

"Get off of her!" Morana screamed as she tried to pull Evangeline off. As she yanked Evangeline's braid, Vesna was released. Evangeline turned to Morana and dragged her to the floor as well.

"What is wrong with you?!" Evangeline shook Morana violently, banging her head against the floor.

"Me? What about you?! You've gone savage! Get off!"

"Someone get a leash on her!" Vesna called out, holding her head.

"What is going on here?!" A voice called as several people

came barrelling down the corridor at both ends. They stopped abruptly at the commotion on the floor. Evangeline finally let go and climbed off of Morana but stayed slouched on the floor. Morana and Vesna got to their feet, limping and groaning and playing up their injuries.

"Will someone please tell me what is going on here?!" Cadmael was centre of the mob. Instantly all three girls burst into their own accounts of what happened. They shouted over each other and then at each other when their stories did not match. Cadmael roared over them until they stopped. "Lady Evangeline, please tell me you did not attack your sisters just because they threw water on you?"

"Not *just* because of the water, they do this all the time, and I am sick of it! Someone needs to teach them a lesson."

"It was just a prank." Vesna moped. "We didn't mean anything by it."

"And we certainly did not want to be *assaulted*."

"This is all just silly childhood games to me; it would be best to make up and move on. You are all too old for this nonsense. Lady Evangeline, you are *an adult*, act like it and control your temper. You cannot attack people and expect to get away with it."

"I will punish anyone who mistreats me. In a way that I see fit. Self-defence is my right." Evangeline rose and glared at Cadmael, he was a short man, and Evangeline towered over him.

"Good heavens! Put some clothes on, you are humiliating yourself!" Cadmael averted his eyes and the twins laughed but Evangeline stood her ground.

"She is wearing a night gown, it's not like she is naked." Evangeline closed her eyes. she did not know Felicity was there; guilt, shame and humiliation flushed over her and her shoulders slumped. Sir Thedamaine was pulling off his cloak, offering it to Evangeline but she refused.

"I am not ashamed," she growled.

"You are soaking wet and it is freezing." He wrapped her himself and she stood still, not refusing his help but not accepting either.

"Good dog, you'll get a treat later." She heard Morana whisper under her breath. Vesna answered with a quick, quiet bark that both Evangeline and Thedamaine heard.

"I will have to report this. Go and get dressed, we have

duties to attend to. Now you are *finally* awake we can get to work. I suppose you will want to eat before we begin as you missed the morning feast, I will be in the Lord's Study when you are ready. Do not keep me waiting."

"Do not talk to her like that. You wait on her, not the other way around. She is in charge, not you. I think it would be best if you remembered that. You can whisper 'petulant child' and 'insubordination' under your breath all you want but you are not the Lord. You work for her." Felicity rendered the room stunned but received a nod of approval from Sir Thedamaine.

"Indeed." Cadmael pursed his lips, "I will wait for you in the hall, send word for me if you want me elsewhere. Take your time."

Evangeline turned and walked away without another word, trying to preserve the rest of her dignity. She refused to answer Felicity's questions or even laugh at Felicity's attempts to lighten the situation. Evangeline was in too much of a foul mood to humour her.

"Why don't we get them back? Let's start a prank war. I've been thinking about it for a while now and wondering why we haven't done it sooner. I've thought of great one. Want to hear it? I start by filling up a big bucket of-"

"Flick, please shut up!" Evangeline rubbed her temples. "Come back when I don't have a pounding headache and not soaking wet. Come back when I actually care!" Evangeline slammed the door behind her as she entered her chamber room, Felicity stopped behind the door, hurt and frozen.

"I stood up for you!" She shouted through the door. Sir Thedamaine stood stoic beside Evangeline's door on guard and trying to remain invisible, but he felt Felicity watching him.

"You know she needs time to calm down. She doesn't mean it, don't take it personally."

Felicity scoffed at his words. "Honestly, it's like handling volatile Greek Fire! Why do you always have to be so dramatic!?" Felicity shouted through the door again but stormed off, returning to her own room. She was met with her favourite formal gown, laid out on the bed waiting for her. It had been burnt and singed. The twins' prank again. Felicity knew something had to be done.

"You want permission to visit the village? Are you sure

you should be asking me, *I'm* not in charge?"

"I was not asking permission. You're blocking my exit." Cadmael was waiting at the Grand Hall doors for Evangeline and Felicity wanted out, so she took a page out of Evangeline's book and took a stroll through the village. She was not alone, she had asked her handmaiden, Mary to join her and Cadmael had assigned the veteran knight, Sir James to escort her. She was fine with the escort and enjoyed it. It made her feel important and powerful, people knew who she was when she had an escort, when she was alone nobody knew who she was, unlike Evangeline who everyone knew.

Felicity was more excited than she had been in a long time. When was the last time she went into town? She thought over what she would do and how she would spend this precious time. The prank will be first, she was not discouraged by Evangeline's mood and would start this prank war, with or without her sister.

The crisp and fresh day brought the winter chills that drifted in the wind. Autumn was coming, though it already felt like winter. She and Mary decided to walk down into town instead of taking horses, she wanted to savour the time. Felicity led the way straight to the lake, Sir James as a close escort. They were met by an even colder breeze drifting off the surface of the water as they came out behind the protection of the buildings.

"Are you sure we can get some? It's not too cold? Can't we just buy them?"

"Buy them? Why would we buy them when we can have fun getting them ourselves?"

"Fun?" Mary looked sceptically at Felicity. "Look me in the eye and tell me you will enjoy doing this."

Felicity remained transfixed on the water, carefully picking out the perfect spot to set up. "It may not be getting them that's fun but the reward we will get out of it. Here will do." Felicity pointed at the edge of the lake; left of a fishing jetty and far enough from the hubbub of Raven's Beak pub. Felicity and Mary crouched by the edge of the lake and got as close to the marshy reeds as possible.

"I see some!" Mary called out. Felicity followed her line of sight and delighted to see three frogs hopping along the mud bank.

"Quick! Get the bucket!" Mary scrambled up the bank and

met Sir James halfway as he passed her the bucket they had brought. Felicity rushed to pull the handkerchief out of her cloak pocket and pounced on a frog.

They spent hours around the lake searching, tracking and catching frogs, even Sir James helped by walking into the chilly water to lead them toward the girls, but they struggled to catch them. After the third frog slipped through Felicity's fingers she threw a rock into the lake in anger, growling.

"Easy there, little Princess." It was Taren. He stood on the jetty smiling down at the three of them. "What on earth are you doing? Is-"

"She's not here." Taren snapped his gaze back to Felicity after searching around for a sight of Evangeline.

"So, what are you doing?" He asked again as he made his way down to the water's edge.

"We're catching frogs!" Mary squealed, ecstatically. "But we've only caught two."

"Why are you trying to catch frogs at all? You'll be lucky to find some, it's not exactly the time of the frogs."

"Sir James told us we've come just at the right time as it is just before they start disappearing. But we just can't grab them. They're too fast."

"Is there a reason for this or just for fun?"

"Oh! It's for revenge!" Felicity rubbed her hands together and sneered.

"You're starting a prank war, aren't you?"

"Indeed, I am!"

"This is for Pain and Suffering?"

"The twins? Yes, of course."

"Wait here." Taren sped off away from the lake toward a farm, returning shortly afterward with a short, skinny and balding man and, what Felicity assumed, was his squirrely son.

"These two lovely sirs have agreed to source your frogs for you."

"What, really?"

"My boy can catch every frog in the lake for you, milady."

"Can you really, every one of them?"

"Yes, ma'am." The boy said with a smile, but his father nudged him. "Milady."

"Come along, Princess. Let the froggers do their thing. We'll leave them to it and come back in a while."

Felicity tried to protest but Taren pushed her along, so she thanked father and son and left them to it.

"You'll head back to your castle with that bucket full of hoppers. The finest frogs' money can buy." Taren said, climbing up the bank.

"You paid them?"

"Yes. People do not work for free."

"But *you* paid? Mary, hand me my coin purse. I'll reimburse you."

"Please, there's no need." Taren held his palm up.

"I insist." Felicity grabbed Taren's refusing hand and forced a gold coin into it. "Take it."

"Yes, ma'am." Taren said, imitating the boy and pocketed it. "So, what's the plan with these frogs, anyway?"

"If there is one thing the twins hate more than terrorising Evangeline and me, it is gross, slimy things like snails, slugs and frogs. With frogs being the liveliest of the three, I chose to collect a whole bunch of them, and throw them at the twins."

"Ingenious and devious. I love it. Could I recommend you lock them in a tiny room where they have no place to go?"

"Even better. So where are we going?" Felicity asked.

"Going? I was following you."

"Me? You led me away from the lake, I was following you!"

"Well, where would you like to go?"

"Could I see your workshop? I've never been inside a forge before."

"Of course. Right this way, milady."

Taren led the way to his shop, the long journey to the very next building. Felicity could see the lake from the workshop and knew Taren did not run into Felicity by accident. She would have had to pass him on the way.

"I didn't know how close you were to the lake," she told him. From his street, there was a direct, straight road all the way through the village to the Manor.

The workshop itself was quite small yet the building was large. Taren explained that his master's quarters was above the shop's armoury and Taren's tiny chamber room was above the open forge. A cramped, rotten staircase led the way to the miniscule space he called his own.

"So, what do you actually make for people? We have our

own weapon-smith in the Manor so you cannot provide us with that."

"I do sometimes. For your sister, mainly, but there are several smithy's in the village to choose from and the majority of it is sales and speciality. Your own weapon-smith and armourer likes to mass produce to provide for your army, so the quality is sacrificed. A couple of your knights come to me; others go elsewhere. I know of one who goes all the way to Birchcliffe, across the lake, to get theirs."

"But why?"

"Price, preference, convenience. It depends on the person. Sir Beckett was born and raised in Birchcliffe and knows the smithy there, grew up with him and refuses to go to anyone else. Sir Thedamaine also grew up there but comes to me, instead, so it really just depends on the person. Sir James, who do you go to?"

Felicity was always amazed at Taren's memory and acquaintanceship with the knights, but she suspected it went with the territory.

"Harris and Hartley." Sir James answered without hesitation.

"Those criminals! They charge you twice as much as the labour they actually do!"

"Still twice as fast as you."

"Woah! Easy, soldier. I am still an apprentice. I may only have a couple of knight clients, but I have a whole heap of villagers queuing for master craftsmanship for apprentice prices! Not that I see any of that profit."

"What do the villagers need from you?" Mary asked as she looked about the forge. Felicity wandered around, too, curious.

"Farming equipment, locks and keys, horseshoes, mending jewellery for the richer villagers. I'm working on all of those right now."

"Can you show me something you're working on? Please?"

"But of course!"

The fire was raging, and the forge was warm enough for Taren to pull off his cloak and jacket. As he picked up a scythe, Felicity saw the bandages behind his worn, leather jerkin from the beast attack but also noticed the numerous, small fist-sized bruises on his neck, back and arms. Taren turned to speak but knew exactly what she was really seeing.

"Its dangerous work and I am clumsy. Plus, I'm still learning. It's easy to mess up. You know, I hit the anvil and sometimes, I get hit back." He laughed weakly and put the scythe down.

That doesn't explain the bruises on his back, she thought to herself. 'Sometimes, I get hit back.' Was the blacksmith master abusing him? Or was it something else? She thought back to the lie, who did he meet with? Why did he lie about it?

"Did this take long to make?" Felicity asked, picking up the scythe and changing the subject. She adjusted her grip as it was heavier than it looked.

"Not at all. Farming equipment, for the most part, is quick and easy. I get commissioned to make it all the time so it's just second nature now."

"Is it boring?" Mary asked.

"A bit, there's no detail, no creativity. Not like swords or jewellery."

"What is your favourite thing to make?"

"Swords." He said immediately and smiled to himself as if he had just shared an inside joke.

"It was the first thing I ever made. My father taught me."

"Your father? I thought you were an orphan?"

"I am now. But when I was a kid, I had a family. A family of smithies. My father got sick and died when I was eight, then it was just me and my mother. She was an amazing woman, she had helped my father in the forge since they married at fourteen, working from sunup to sundown every day, working like a dog to bring in the coins. The day my father died she was accepted into the Guild."

"Is that true?" Mary asked, showing some genuine interest. Even Sir James was curious.

"Yes, the Blacksmith's Guild accepted her because she was brilliant and fast and had earned her reputation. Only the best were accepted in the Guild and she made the cut. I still remember some things about her. I remember just watching her work, taking in everything. That is until she clapped me around the ear to get me back to work. She raised me until her death."

"How did she die, if you don't mind me asking?"

"I don't know." Taren picked up his hammer and swung it into his hand. "I was playing in the woods like I usually did, trying to track animals to watch and observe like I usually did and came home, like I usually did. I came home to an empty house. She was gone for three days before they came for me."

"They?" Mary asked.

"The orphanage." Felicity answered. Taren nodded.

"They are gone, I'm no longer in the care of the orphanage and now I'm doing what I'm supposed to do, what I love to do. It all works out in the end."

"I guess it does." Felicity walked about the forge again, thinking about Taren's life and his mother.

"Lady Flick, if you stop there, on that back wall is my pride and joy." Felicity turned to the wall; hanging haphazardly were a variety of tools and on the lip, high on the wall were swords, daggers and knives.

"What am I looking at? This?" She grabbed a soiled and dusty covering.

"That's it, pull it."

Felicity pulled off the sheet. Once the dust settled she smiled; it was a suit of armour. She had never seen one like it before. It was like no regular armour; it was not plated or chainmail. It was scaled.

Sir James was by her side in an instant. "Amazing. What is this?"

"My life's work. Everything I have worked toward comes down to this. The way an apprenticeship works is that we get room and board and training, that's it. We make next to no money, only make things for our master. However, it doesn't always stay like that. We must make our Masterpiece. Something that shows our skill and creativity. Once it is completed and we have had enough training we present our Masterpiece to the Guild; they decide if we advance to Master or wait it out as an Apprentice."

Mary and Sir James inspected the suit of armour, but Felicity walked back over to the forge where Taren stood.

"This suit of armour is my Masterpiece," Taren continued. "Actually, it began as my mother's. We started this together before she died, and I had buried it all these years to protect it until I was ready and now I'm almost finished; I'm almost a Master. I could have my own shop, my own wage and my own life."

"Taren, can I ask you something?" Felicity took the

65

opportunity to probe him whilst they were alone and out of earshot of the other two. Perhaps if it were just those two, he would not lie to her.

"What about?" He subconsciously matched her hushed tone.

"Why are you lying to Evangeline and me? Who were you meeting with?"

"Oh, this again? Honestly, Felicity, you are paranoid, did you know that? I did not meet with anyone. Look, what happened was-"

"Is this a brothel?!" Taren was interrupted by a booming voice that entered the forge. The blacksmith master, pink cheeked with a bottle in each hand crossed the room to Taren. "Then why are you screwing me? Why aren't you working, boy? All these women in my shop taking up your time. Get back to work!"

"Sir, please, contain yourself!" Sir James puffed his chest out and stood face to face, inches away from the drunk blacksmith.

"Boy, why are you wasting time entertaining these guests who have no reason to be in here? Wasting good time that should have been spent making me money? We need to pay taxes, those high taxes that *her* family forced upon us."

Before Sir James or Taren could explode upon the Master, Felicity stood in. "We are customers, sir, Taren is not wasting your time. Lord Ravenhill has commissioned a project and we are here to ensure my father has got the right man. You see, my sister vouches for this boy constantly, but my father believes she may be a little biased, so he sent me, with no real ties to your apprentice, to decide for myself. My father would have come but you understand he is a busy man. If you remember, he is on his honeymoon at the present moment and left the duties in my care. We are, or were, examining this boy's work before you so rudely interrupted us."

"What's the project?" The blacksmith asked, a little humbled.

Felicity froze. A million thoughts raced through her head in the space of a moment. *A sword*, she thought, *no, you cannot just say a sword. Everyone makes swords. It cannot be a normal weapon, the Manor weapon-smith makes our weapons, why Taren?* She ran through a short list of weapons she knew but she kept coming back to a trebuchet but that was made primarily of wood and too large; useless. She started to panic.

"My father needs a new suit of armour." *You've said it now just go with it.* "One of our knights is already a client of yours and recommended Taren's skills. Lord Ravenhill can no longer live with the abysmal quality of the Manor's armourer, he makes it fast, but the quality is poor. My father is interested in supporting his local businesses and go where the true quality lies. Sir James here was just expressing his love for Taren's Masterpiece skill; Lord Ravenhill is a tough man to impress but if his knights approve then he will too."

The blacksmith's face lit up. "Here, Sir, let us talk business." He pulled Sir James aside, Taren started to join them but was shoved back. "You've got work to do, boy, I suggest you wrap it up." He waved his hands in Felicity and Mary's direction.

"That was quick thinking. Well done." Taren was genuinely surprised at her, but no one was more surprised than Felicity. "I do need to get back to work now before he punishes me. You should probably have a nice collection of frogs now."

"Oh yes, the frogs!" Mary was bouncing up and down, "come on, milady, let's get the frogs." Felicity and Mary left Taren and returned to the water's edge where the farmer and his squirrely son awaited them. The boy was soaking wet all over, his father damp, up to his knees.

"Thank you kindly, sir. Please take this as a gesture of my gratitude." The bucket was full of frogs of all sizes and she exchanged the heavy thing with a gold coin.

"Don't thank me, thank the boy. He's half frog himself."

Felicity looked at the boy, half her age, soggy and muddy but looked as if he was in his element.

"Thank you, Frog-Boy." She grinned and held her hand out to him, presenting the large golden coin bigger than his hand. With confirmation from his father, he took the coin and brought it to his chest. As they parted, the frog boy croaked at her and she and Mary croaked back.

"Do you want to go back now? We got what we came for." Mary asked.

"No, not yet. I don't spend much time here, let's appreciate it, while we can."

Sir James returned to them as they settled down in the town centre with a pigeon pie each. Mary asked Sir James what the master said to him, but Felicity didn't care and didn't listen, choosing to lose herself in the world around her. After taking three bites of her pigeon pie, she lost her appetite in a second and put it down behind her.

It was the height of day, right in the midst of trading time. The chorus of merchants chanting, children playing, and villagers bartering wove between the disorder of the square. Felicity sat still, a tranquil calmness washing over her.

"Look! I'm the Horned God!" A little redheaded girl shouted at her twin brother as she held two sticks on her head like antlers. Felicity watched them with a smile.

"You can't be the Horned God! You're a girl!" The young boy pointed his tiny finger at his sister, teasing her.

Ignoring this, the girl nimbly jumped on a barrel keeping the antler sticks on her head and growled at him. "I am the one and only Horned God, fear me!" Her brother dramatically threw himself on the ground, worshipping her.

As Felicity watched the children run off, her line of sight caught an old woman crossing the Market Square, walking directly toward her. Despite the bleak clouds gathering overhead, she wore a large sunhat and far too little clothing for the chilly weather. Her skin was cracked like the hard dirt in a heavy drought. The large amount of cheap and amateur iron jewellery seemed to weigh her down. Each of her fingers held a badly made ring, three thick pendants hung around her neck at alternating lengths and she wore two hideous, colossal earrings.

Once the old woman reached Felicity, she sensed Sir James stir behind her. The old woman took Felicity's hand in both of hers, grasping it firmly and looking intensely into Felicity's eyes.

"My Lady, what a precious moment it is to have you here!" Her voice was as frail and weak as her body looked. "We are truly honoured. I would like to take my chances to express my deepest sympathies." Felicity was confused. "To lose one's mother so young, it is a cruel and vicious thing that I know all too well."

"Yes, we are still grieving but we remain strong." She took the words straight from Evangeline's mouth.

"How profound! You're handling it better than I did,

Princess." Felicity did not know what she meant.

"Oh, I'm not royalty." Felicity blushed, wishing she were lying.

"In this little corner of the world, you might as well be. To us, you are."

Felicity grinned, liking this woman more and more with every word. "I am honoured."

"Your mother must have taught you to be brave? It is not your fault this village is cursed."

"Cursed?"

"We have lost so much. I lost my own family. My mother was murdered. You lost your uncle, too. I remember that first night. We lost so much in such a short time. All of those murdered on the first attack, including your uncle, then you lost your mother and unborn sibling so soon after, not to mention the festivals we lost. In my day we celebrated so feverishly, the Wheel of the Year was sacred, now this generation spits upon it."

Felicity tensed up. The conversation had taken a wrong turn. *Was she blaming us? Does she think it is under my family's rule that the beast has taken everything? She does. She believes it is our fault, as if we released the creature.* Felicity pulled her hand from the crone's grip. "We should all be on full alert this coming full moon."

"Yes, we must do everything we can to prepare, for we are cursed!" The old woman looked up as Felicity blinked from a rain drop landing in her eye. Grey and grisly clouds loomed overhead and spitted out a light mist. "There is a storm brewing," the old woman said, "we are not prepared for the rains that are coming." With that she turned and left, disappearing into the crowd.

"You are too nice." Evangeline's voice made Felicity jump and emit a tiny scream. The three of them turned to Evangeline, perched on the edge of a merchant's wagon behind them, alone. She was smothered by the huge deep purple cloak covering the plain gown beneath in the same dark purple, almost black colour. Her bright hair was plaited; hidden by the oversized hood that shadowed half her face. It was dark, it was plain, and it blended in, exactly what she wanted and exactly the opposite of Felicity.

"What is wrong with nice?" Felicity asked.

"She was openly rude to you, but you passed it off and let

her get away with it. These people will test your status and your power, don't let them disrespect you."

"I couldn't exactly say 'you need to leave now,' could I?"

"Why not? Being honest and direct is the quickest way."

"And the rudest way."

"Rude? Rude?!" Evangeline got to her feet and stepped forward. Nobody moved. "Why are you worrying about being rude when she offended our family, our ruling, our handling of the beast and everything we have done to protect her and everyone in this village?"

"You're the one who says we are not doing enough to help. I would think you would agree with her."

"She does not have the right to say that about our family. She does not know our pain."

"She lost her family, she told me, she's lost just enough as the rest of us."

"She was lying to you. An old woman who lost her mother? She's a shaman, it's what they do."

"She was a shaman? Here? There are shamans here?"

"Yes, why are you freaking out?"

Felicity was about to tell her, but she remembered Mary and Sir James and decided not to, not here.

"I'll tell you later."

"Fine." Evangeline sat down at the table, helping herself to the rest of Felicity's pastry.

"That's mine."

"I'm hungry. I haven't eaten anything all day."

"That's your fault and my pastry. Give it!" Felicity reached over the table to grab the pastry, but Evangeline held it from her reach. "Give it!" She ran around the table, but Evangeline changed hands. "Evangeline!" She whined. "That's mine!" She took a huge bite, teasing her. Evangeline's arms were just long enough to keep it from Felicity's hands as she tried to grab it. Once Evangeline stuffed the rest of it down her throat, Felicity smiled. "Now I don't feel so bad for stealing your dress and getting it wet."

"You little witch!" Evangeline had not realised what Felicity was wearing but it was indeed her dress, now getting soaked in the heavy rains. They ignored Mary's shy little requests of returning to the Manor and kept fighting. "You're dead!" Evangeline grinned good-naturedly as she chased Felicity around the table. She feigned right and almost caught Felicity before she hid behind Sir James, who stood rigid and neutral like a tree trunk.

"Get her, Sir James!" Felicity pointed accusatorily at Evangeline and urged the knight forward, but he did not move.

"You idiot, he cannot get me. I am immune." She smiled smugly, placing her hands on her hips.

"He may not be able to get you, but I can." Sir Thedamaine had appeared from nowhere and picked Evangeline up, throwing her over his solid shoulder and began walking her back to the Manor, ignoring her kicking, wriggling and laughing.

"No, Thedamaine, put me down!" She smiled as she wriggled against him.

"Ha! He caught you this time, no escaping today!"

Evangeline quickly gave in and resigned herself to the lift home. Mary and Felicity laughed as they followed behind her.

"He's smart, it's the only way he could get Evangeline back home, she's bound to have run off again." Mary whispered, but Felicity just nodded.

The walk back to the Manor was laboured, she was out of breath halfway up the hill, and her sick feeling earlier had come back, physical and thick. She ignored Mary, keeping her thoughts solely on her stomach. Just as they reached the gate, Felicity doubled over and vomited.

CHAPTER 9.

The rain fell in sheets, too thick to see through and with no chance of stopping. The courtyard was flooding, the stables were leaking, and everything and everyone was thoroughly wet.

"What's your plan? Power through the rain and go to the aviary or choose someone else, someone inside?"

Evangeline mulled over Aria's words. "Screw it. Let's go, it's only water." Aria, Sir Thedamaine and Cadmael followed Evangeline out and into the rain.

The doctor had given Felicity the 'all clear' the day before and sent her on her way to rest up. Evangeline was jealous as Felicity had been in bed the whole evening, all night and all morning long and Evangeline had been coerced into carrying out an official duty she had been avoiding for months.

One of the advantages of being Lord was being able to delegate his less loved duties to his heir, and this was one of them; the idea was to visit each and every one of the factions and departments of the household so each one is heard. Evangeline must meet with a designated member of the group, usually the senior, and listen to their whining, note down their demands and, in theory, take those demands to the Lord. She had learnt early on that they were all rejected. The more demands she took to him the more they were thrown back to her. It was more a test on herself to break those demands down into smaller bites and then take them to her father. It was a tedious task as she knew they could never get what they wanted and they usually talked and talked for hours on end, she almost never completed more than one in a day.

An upside to this was that she could visit them in any order she saw fit. So far she had met the cooks and bakers, the armourers, the treasury, the handmaidens, the governesses and the scullery maids, that one had taken hours but had the best outcome as three extra maids were entered into the budget due to their low cost.

Today, Evangeline chose the aviary, a poor choice due to the rain but she hoped it might shorten the time. She introduced herself and her entourage to the senior bird handler; Lysander McAllister, who she had learnt had been employed by her family for over forty years and in turn, his family had been serving hers for over two hundred years.

"So, what type of birds do you home here?" Evangeline was pacing the room, studying the birds in the cages and the structure itself. There was a raven high above them, perched on the rafters, watching them.

"Well, you have your doves for messages, birds of prey for falconry and hunting, fowl like chickens and ducks for food, we have the recovery centre for the injured and of course, the rookery."

"To house our mascots." Evangeline finished. Lysander nodded. "What kind of birds do you have in the recovery centre?"

"Right now? All kinds, we have a few chickens who survived a fox attack and a couple of doves. I have some local birds I found that needed help; a blackbird, a robin, a seagull and a magpie and crow who came in together."

"They are my two favourite birds. I know it is cliché for a Ravenhill to have a crow as her favourite animal, but I can't help it, they fascinate me."

"It's not cliché at all!" Aria moaned sarcastically in a droll.

"Perhaps it's fate," Lysander added.

"A curse more likely. We are an unimaginative family, unable to break away from our namesake."

"I wouldn't say it's *that* bad."

"Shall I count the ways, Mr McAllister?"

Aria groaned long and loud and Evangeline could almost *hear* Thedamaine roll his eyes.

"Oh, here we go." Aria could barely finish the sentence before Evangeline spoke over her.

"Let's start with my beloved ancestors; the family of Ravenhill who live in Ravenhill Village and reside in Ravenhill Manor that sits atop the Raven Hill. Shall I go on?" She didn't stop for an answer. "The villagers of Ravenhill like to frequent such taverns like The Wolf and Raven, Raven's Beak, and Crow's Feet, the latter of which backs onto the River Corvus which, if you didn't know, is the Latin name for ravens. Let me also add the lovely street names in Ravenhill such as Raven Street, Raven Road, Crow Way, Crow's End, Rookery Way, and Rook Ridge. Lastly, let us not forget the family crest of the Ravenhills which, of course, features, you guessed it; a raven. Which supposedly means, in heraldry terms; strategists, divine providence, watchful for friends and intelligence, which is unlikely seeing that we have the imagination of-"

"Imagination of a rock!" Aria finished. "She loves that rant."

"Are you done?" Cadmael asked Evangeline.

"I've made my point." She grinned smugly at Aria and Thedamaine, ignoring Cadmael.

"You should end it with 'we have the imagination of a raven itself' as you can't seem to get off them."

"That wouldn't work," chimed in Lysander, "ravens and crows are extremely intelligent birds."

"You're a bird handler, of course you would say that!"

"Come with me and I'll show you."

The raven that was perched on the rafters dropped down and sat on Lysander's shoulder as he exited the room, Evangeline and Aria exchanged a look of curiosity.

The four of them followed Lysander to the rookery; a large, cold room with fewer cages and more open space. The outside backed onto a large outdoor caged space, but few birds were out in the rain.

Lysander brought them to a nook in the wall where he was met with loud, excited squawking. The raven on his shoulder hopped off and perched on the cages above. Lysander stood next to a raven drinking from the water bowl on the wall. From his pocket he pulled a treat and held it up. "Mischief, Mischief," he called, and the raven turned, "say hello," Lysander said.

In a completely human voice, the raven actually spoke. '*Hello.*' The keeper gave him the treat.

"Amazing!"

"Say hi."

'*Hello.*' The raven repeated but Lysander did not treat him.

"Say hi."

'Hello.. Hello.'

"Hi." Lysander repeated.

'Hi.'

He swallowed the treat whole and Lysander pulled a chunk of meat from a sack on his belt.

"This is her favourite food. I am going to show you how intelligent their brains are." He put a few chunks on the ground and all the ravens in the room piled onto the floor. "I am going to hide this piece of meat in a spot where she cannot reach." Lysander squeezed the chunk of meat into a small crack in the brick work. It was a long crack but too small for a beak. He pulled a stick from one of the bird's nests, "they need a tool." He placed the stick on the windowsill, arms width from the crack.

The talking raven, Mischief came to his side with a whistle and the call of her name, immediately smelling the meat in the crack. With a few pecks she knew she wasn't going to be able to grab the meat alone. Twitching her head, jerkily, she looked around. Evangeline could almost see the bird's mind at work. She saw the stick, picked it up in her beak and poked it through the gap. With a few clumsy tries, she managed to free the meat.

"That is wonderful! I never knew how smart they were." Aria was beside herself with excitement.

Cadmael snorted in derision. "So, it can say hello and use a stick. Not impressive."

"Still smarter than *you,* Cadmael," Evangeline said. "So shut your mouth." The raven that had been watching them since they entered returned to its perch on Lysander's shoulder. "So, who is this raven?" Evangeline asked, looking closer.

"This is Shadow. She is my shadow. I found her a few years ago and saved her life, she hardly ever leaves my side."

Evangeline looked at the bird, it was a large raven but with curled, mangled feet. Despite the crippled feet, it was a beautifully huge, silky black bird with a large, slightly hooked beak.

"She was a crippled fledgling who I found, nursed back to health and have been stuck with ever since. She cannot fly like other birds, so it is safer for her here. She believes I am her mate, raven's mate for life, you know. Extremely loyal, intelligent beauties."

Evangeline stepped forward, closer to the keeper but Shadow flapped forward and nipped at Evangeline, she darted backwards, falling into Sir Thedamaine.

"She's very protective of me. Come here, you." He held his hand out and she flapped over to perch on it. She could fly and glide a short distance, Evangeline noticed, like a chicken, but could never fully take flight.

Evangeline pulled Lysander aside, taking his arm and walking through the rookery.

"How long have you been in our service, Mr McAllister? Forty years, was it not?"

"Yes, I am an old man of fifty-seven years and I have been working here since I came of age, around twelve years old. Before me, it was my father and his father before him and so on and so forth. We were all seniors, my mother also worked here as well as my two siblings, but I have the longest service in my entire family."

"Is that so?"

"That is correct. A fine achievement." Cadmael interrupted. "But your family lineage ends with you, doesn't it, Mr McAllister?"

"Indeed. My first wife died in childbirth and took our child with her and my second wife unfortunately did not survive the Beast of Ravenhill. I have no living children, no parents and only one sibling alive; my sister."

"Could she not take over the business?"

"No. She gets sick often, she could never take over here, I doubt she could make the journey as she lives in Hawkshead Hamlet. If I retired, the care of the birds would be in another family's hands."

"Who is your assistant?" Evangeline recalled her briefing from Cadmael earlier.

"Henry? He is my apprentice, a lucky boy with a penchant for all birds. Your mother granted me an apprentice to train when I campaigned for help years ago."

"Would you say he is ready to take over?"

"He has a little way to go but I would say so."

"What would you do if you retired?"

"Oh, I would move in with my sister and take care of her so her daughters no longer have to, I would open a lovely little inn; small and cosy, nothing too rowdy and live out the rest of my days as a landlord."

"That sounds lovely."

"That is an expensive ambition."

"Cadmael! That was rude." Aria practically gasped at her horror of his rudeness.

"That is not your place to say," he hissed back at Aria.

"Oh, shut up, Cadmael, that was incredibly rude but thank you, you have just convinced me." Evangeline had an idea.

"Convinced you?" He asked.

Evangeline smiled first at Cadmael then at Lysander, more genuinely. "Lysander McAllister, I wish to invest in your future. The family of Ravenhill will fund your lovely little inn and your relocation as a gift for your family's long service with us."

Sir Thedamaine grasped Cadmael's shoulder in warning before he could protest, and Aria jumped and clapped gleefully.

"Milady! What an honour."

"I will arrange an entourage to escort you and your belongings to Hawkshead so you may move in with your sister to live out your days in your lovely little inn. Your apprentice, Henry, will take over as Master Bird Handler, I will appoint an assistant should he require it. The funds for your inn will be a gift from the Ravenhill family and in no way be taken as a loan. My word is law Cadmael, hold your tongue." Evangeline was not looking at Cadmael but knew he was silently protesting. "Should you require anything else to aid in your retirement and relocation it will be provided to you. Is there anything else you can think of?"

Lysander stammered, gobsmacked. Evangeline held back her grin, composing herself. Cadmael was furiously scribbling on his scroll and Aria was feeding meat chunks to the birds from the pouch Lysander had left on the bench.

"Milady!" He repeated, "a thousand thanks. I just cannot express my gratitude to you and your family. This is an amazing gift to me that I cannot fathom. What can I do to thank you?"

"Nothing. Just take our gift to you and make the most of it. Take good care of your sister, run an amazing inn and have a wonderful, happy life."

He looked toward Shadow. "She will have to come with me, I could not leave her behind."

"I never imagined you would. Take whatever, whoever you need. You can hammer out the details with Cadmael later."

"Thank you, Lady Evangeline, your kindness means the world to me and might just save the life of my sister." He was violently shaking Evangeline's hand and grinning like a child at her.

She watched the crippled raven limping about the rookery and squawking as happily as any other bird around her. "May I suggest naming your inn, The Crooked Rook?"

"I love it!"

"So do I!" Aria grinned again.

Evangeline wished him well and finally felt good about herself and her family. This was a promise she *would* see accomplished. She wanted to share this good deed with her sister and after dismissing Aria and Cadmael, she went to Felicity's room. When she entered, Evangeline found her fast asleep, cocooned in her furs, she couldn't even see her face; she was just a big lump in the bed.

Not wanting to venture out in the rain to visit Taren, she decided to challenge Thedamaine to a *sober* game of chess, which turned into several games, then a drinking game because she just could not help herself.

CHAPTER 10.

The mound under the covers looked convincingly enough like her in the dark. She had stuffed clothes and boxes and anything she could underneath the furs on her bed to make it seem like she was asleep under there. In the dying fireplace light, it looked good enough, the flicker of the flames even made it seem like the heap was breathing.

Felicity had recovered from her sudden illness quite quickly. A short nap fixed it right up, but she stayed in bed all evening anyway, reading the Nil'vetra book. The next morning, she had an epiphany; she was going to sneak through the Manor unnoticed and see what she heard or found, she just needed an alibi, and a disguise.

Her handmaiden, Mary, was in on the deception, she was there as a cover to push back any visitors and she collected the disguise. Felicity pulled on the loose, plain gown, tied the apron and put on the large bonnet. It was the uniform of a chambermaid, a perfect disguise because she could wander through the Manor going in and out of the rooms without drawing suspicion. The bonnet covered her face and chambermaids were next to invisible. She would move about undetected.

She began by testing the waters, travelling through corridors, keeping her head down, always returning back to her room but eventually, after passing several people without being identified, she ventured further.

She passed behind Evangeline, Sir Thedamaine, Aria and Cadmael as they walked out into the rain. None of them noticed her.

Her first stop was to Morana and Vesna's solar. She lurked in the antechamber, hovering by the open door. Vesna was braiding Morana's hair as Morana was picking at a seam on a gown.

Felicity had brought the bucket of frogs with her.

Carefully, she pulled off the lid to the bucket, placing it on the ground, just inside the door. She then kicked it over, and the frogs were free. Before the twins even looked up, Felicity slammed the door shut which would have gotten their attention and a moment later they both screamed, noticing the frogs. Felicity had pulled a small dresser from the wall and dragged it against the door, locking them in. She then hurried out of there before anyone noticed her, savouring the screams for as long as she could hear them.

She banged the door in frustration: her father's study was locked. She thought about Taren, who would be able to pick the lock or make a new key. She could not trust him, however; something was off about him and she disliked that. Suddenly she remembered what he had said to her in his forge. He was about to explain something to her but was interrupted. Leaning against the door, she banged her head against it, irritated. She needed to find out more about him, what he is hiding but noticed that she had not seen him around. He was usually strutting about the Manor every day or every other day, but he had not been inside the Manor since he was discharged, and she only saw him the other day because she was in town. *Is he distancing himself from the family because he is hiding something? Or was Evangeline simply growing apart from him? She did admit that she only saw him once whilst he was in the infirmary.*

"What are you doing up here?" A man called to her down the hallway, she jumped away from the door and held her head down, shielding her face with the bonnet. "You have no business here; this room does not need preparing."

"Sorry." She masked her voice and ran away before he could say anything else. She did not know who it was and did not care. She just wanted to get free. Too afraid to venture out again, terrified that someone followed her back to her room, she remained in bed for the rest of the day and promptly fell asleep listening to the rain pouring outside.

The following day, she decided to wait until the evening to sneak away, under cover of darkness where fewer people roamed the halls. She heard from Mary that Evangeline had been training all day and she had already checked on Felicity in the morning, so wouldn't be visiting again.

Once more, she stuffed her clothes and belongings under the furs on her bed, covering it all. It looked like she was cocooned under the bed. No one will know. She slipped on her disguise and headed directly to Zorya's personal study, this time. It was the only room at the top of a tower and as Zorya was away, nobody would be disturbing her.

It was unlocked.

Felicity stood in the doorway taking in the room. She had not been in there since her mother had died and subsequently the room had been redecorated into purples and greys. Stood in the centre of the room was the overly large table that had always been there, Zorya had kept one thing of the old room. On the left wall was the fireplace, unlit as the room was not being used. On the right wall, two floor-to-ceiling stained glass windows sat either side of the door to the tower balcony. A small pool of water was beginning to form under the door from the rain.

There was a large dresser on the back wall, between the two bookcases. It had six large drawers, three on each side, and four, skinny drawers along the length of it. She opened each drawer and rummaged through, full of junk of no value, writing kits, official papers, or other useless scrap. Felicity started regretting her mission, until she tried opening the last drawer, which was locked. She rummaged through the other drawers again to see if she could find a little key that fit the small keyhole in the drawer.

Climbing underneath the table, she felt for any hiding spot or secret key, she hoped Zorya would have attached the key to the underside of the table for safe keeping or had a secret drawer. As she reached around the table legs, she felt something and grabbed the candle for more light. It was a latch. The table had two front legs and one long leg at the back, along the length of the table, at least that's what she always assumed. In reality, between the two back legs was a large trunk. With all her strength, she pushed the trunk out from under the table and opened the latch.

The trunk held five boxes inside, along with a gown and a pair of children's shoes. Felicity noticed immediately that the gown was her mother's wedding dress, stuffed carelessly in the trunk. She pulled it out, *why does Zorya have this? Why is she hoarding it?*

Felicity looked at the child's shoes next, old and worn and unrecognisable to her. *Whose shoes are these? Are they Morana or Vesna's? Why are they in here?*

She pulled out the first box and opened it. Empty. Felicity assumed the shoes lived in the box but were not put back. The second was heavy and filled with small apothecary bottles and jars, each sealed with wax. The third box was heavier still. The clasp was rusted and dented, and she struggled to pry it open. Inside were rocks and gemstones. Amethysts, quartz, rubies, sapphires, emeralds and lots of obsidian; all of it raw, uncut and natural.

The fourth box held bunches of letters addressed to Zorya. Each in their own envelope with the wax seal still attached but broken. She pulled a letter out at random, reading the contents but grew bored at the meaningless text. She put the box aside and would circle back to it once she had seen everything in the trunk.

The final box was lighter than the others, the only thing inside were scrap pieces of paper of various sizes and ages. She picked the first one up, it had a faded watermark: a rose. Her mother's family was the Rosewood's, was this hers? Felicity held the paper up to candlelight to better see the watermark but there was writing on the other side. She turned the paper over and dropped the box. Her blood ran cold, and her heart skipped a beat. She read it twice before dropping to the floor and pulling all the papers out of the box. She scattered the papers out in front of her, there were so many and each one only said one word on the parchment.

Nil'vetra.

She heard footsteps. Startled like a deer, Felicity froze solid and clenched every part of her body. Somebody was coming. She willed herself to move, to take cover and hide under the table or behind the door, to do something.

It was too late.

They had found her.

The door opened.

CHAPTER 11.

After waking up past noon and checking on Felicity, finding her asleep once again, Evangeline chose to do something that always put a smile on her face: sparring. Under Sir Thedamaine's education, she had learnt sword fighting, up close hand-to-hand combat and unarmed self-defence. She was also an amateur with a bow and arrow and liked to swing an axe, though she would avoid these as much as possible if provoked into an attack. The lessons began as a way to steady her temper and a means to let off steam, but as she grew older, the skills became crucial and valuable.

Armed with blunt, wooden practise swords and thick leather armour to protect from bruising, Evangeline and Sir Thedamaine started their lesson. He was not going easy on her, despite the armour, the pain of every hit shocked her and knocked her back. The plan was to include Felicity, but she still wasn't feeling better and was recovering in her room, sleeping it off. Sir Thedamaine's young squire, Oslo had joined them instead, to learn alongside Evangeline and to team up against her.

"Come on, boy. Hit her! She must learn to dodge." Sir Thedamaine urged Oslo as he hit Evangeline on the hip.

"Sir, I'm uncomfortable with this, I don't want to hurt her."

Evangeline laughed and swung at his neck, knocking him half to the ground. He was meant to dodge the attack, but he stopped to talk and that was long enough for her to hit him, "whoops."

"Whoops?!" Oslo said, holding his neck with a grin.

Sir Thedamaine roared with laughter, holding his stomach and bending backwards. Evangeline joined the laughter but swung her own sword to hit the knight in his ribs. The smack stopped his laughter and he jokingly looked shocked.

"Never take your eyes off your target." She taunted,

echoing his lessons.

Oslo pointed at Sir Thedamaine. "See?! You got hit too."

"Alright, time to take it up a notch, we are losing."

Evangeline concentrated hard on her skill, there were two against one, so had to be quick. A few hours in, Thedamaine noticed she was growing tired and changed the set up. Now, Oslo and Evangeline had to hit Thedamaine. That was the game, get one hit in and they win. At first they attacked at random, but Evangeline noticed quickly that they had to work together, utilising the environment around them. Thedamaine, proud of his students, clapped them both on the back in appreciation when they managed to knock him off his feet.

A third opponent helped the lesson in new ways. Thedamaine was able to see Evangeline's steps, skill and manoeuvres from a distance and study and correct her mistakes or praise the parts he would not have seen up close. The three of them took turns on being the spectator, learning from each other. Evangeline liked to grapple Oslo because he was smaller than her and could actually win but preferred the challenge that Thedamaine brought. He was so strong that he could lift her off her feet without any struggle and she always enjoyed their training together.

Exhausted, tender and drenched in sweat, the three of them sat under the armoury archway, cooling down in the chilly evening air but sheltered from the pouring rain and flooding courtyard. Evangeline was leant against Thedamaine's side, holding each other up. Oslo sat slouched against the opposite wall, watching the rain.

"This was a bad idea, sitting on the floor like this. We won't be able to get up." Oslo shifted his slouched position, wincing from pain and exhaustion.

"I think you're right. I may never get up." Evangeline lazily dropped her head on Thedamaine's shoulder.

"I guess we will have to stay here forever," Thedamaine added, resting his head on top of Evangeline's. "These muscles could not move even if I wanted to."

They sat in silence for a while, listening and watching the rain wash away the courtyard. It grew dark quickly and the temperature was dropping even more so. It was true, Evangeline did not want to move but her drying sweat was now making her cold, yet she powered through. She could see moving candlelight inside the Manor, A chambermaid was traveling up the corridor, circling the courtyard.

"Why has nobody bothered me?" She asked, half to herself and breaking the silence. "People can see we are finished with training yet annoying Cadmael has not weaselled his way out here, dragging me off to do some boring duty."

"I cleared your schedule." Thedamaine answered, a little cheek in his voice. "I knew you wanted to let off steam and did not want to jump headfirst into work so Cadmael has spent these past few hours sitting with Morana and Vesna trying to find them suitors."

"No way! Is it bad I actually feel sorry for him?"

"A little bit, yes."

"He's going to have a tough time finding suitors for those gargoyles." Evangeline and Thedamaine looked at each other and burst out laughing. Neither expected Oslo to come out and say that, it was a bold move by him. "Did I say that out loud?" They both nodded through their laughter.

"Did the rain put you in a trance?" Evangeline asked. "It does that to me, too."

"Has it even stopped?" Thedamaine asked.

Evangeline looked at the pools around the courtyard, it had been raining non-stop for two and a half days now, with no indication of it stopping anytime soon and she worried about the village flooding.

"Didn't we have a small flood a few years back?" She asked.

"Yes, that was about three years ago."

"Really, that long?"

Thedamaine thought it over. "Yes it was, because it was just before Lady Zorya came to work here."

"Maybe she brought the floods with her? She already brought the plague twins."

"Wow, Oslo, you do not hold back, do you? I hope you do not talk this freely around anyone else?" Thedamaine was jesting but underneath, it held a concerned tone.

"I know I can speak freely in front of Lady Evangeline."

"You sure can. Unless it's about me, then you'll have the devil to pay!"

"He already knows my name." Oslo groaned heavily as he struggled to get to his feet. "It's getting late; I'd better report back to my post before I get into trouble. Thank you for the training session." He bowed slightly and ran through the courtyard back into the Manor, shielding his face from the rain. Evangeline and Thedamaine still did not move, still leaning against each other and watching the rain stream down.

"You know, there *was* something weird about the way Lady Zorya came here."

"Really? How?" Evangeline was not in town when Zorya became her mother's handmaiden, it was during her first visit to the Forrester's home.

"Your mother, the Lady Emilia, acted strange when she first saw her."

"She always acted strange."

"This was different. I was there, in the Grand Hall when Lady Zorya entered; your mother turned white. I thought she would faint, so did a few others, it was not subtle. She worried a lot of people that day, but she ensured us all that she was fine, and they moved on."

"That *is* strange. Do you know why she acted like that?"

"Well, I think, and this is assumption here so please do not take my word for it, I think they knew each other. The way Zorya greeted Emilia, it was like they had not seen each other in years."

"Do you think there was bad blood between them? The reason for my mother turning pale? Like she assumed she would never see her again?" Evangeline added one more motive to the pile.

"But why would Lady Emilia accept Zorya as her handmaiden? If there was bad blood and something bad happened, why would she want to be in such close proximity to her at all times?"

"To keep her close, to watch her? Make sure she did not do anything bad?"

"I know what you are doing," Thedamaine said, "you're trying to determine if Lady Zorya killed your mother." He was whispering now, terrified he would be overheard.

"My father said she was there, in the room." Evangeline was also whispering now. "That is not her only motive, though, if she had an affair with my father before my mother's death then that is motive for *both* of them."

"I think we need to find out the relationship between Zorya and your mother."

"I think we do, but how do we do that with my mother dead and Zorya away?"

"Zorya may be away but her things are not. Let's go ransack her study. See if there are any letters or evidence of a previous life that they are trying to hide."

"Thedamaine breaking the rules? I've never seen this side of you. I love it!"

Evangeline stood up quite easily through the excitement and took Thedamaine by the hand, pulling him to his feet and dragged him through the Manor, to the second floor, up the tower and towards Lady Zorya's personal study. Both of their hearts were racing.

Somebody was already in the room.

CHAPTER 12.

"What is happening?" Evangeline asked, flustered and perplexed. She had terrified Felicity to death when she entered Zorya's study and found her on the floor surrounded in papers with Nil'vetra written on. Felicity explained everything she had found; the wedding dress, the children's shoes, the alchemy box, the gemstones, the letters and the Nil'vetra papers. Nothing made sense, even less so when Thedamaine explained what he knew about Emilia and Zorya.

The papers were the prime evidence and their most important lead. Scrap pieces of parchment, some old, some young, each in the same type of paper with only one word written on them. Their mother came from the Rosewood family and their crest featured a rose, the same rose that was on the back of each paper. Assuming Zorya and Emilia knew each other, either one of them could have wrote them. But why did Zorya have them? Were they addressed to her from Emilia? What is a Nil'vetra? What does it mean?

Each question only added more to the list. Like a Hydra, following one thread split into two, but they needed answers. Evangeline linked the gemstones with the alchemy bottles as they were both used by shamans, just as much as doctors and apothecaries. Felicity linked the Nil'vetra with the shamans but mentioned the torn page and missing information of the book. Evangeline and Felicity had landed on the explanation that Zorya could be a shaman, but Thedamaine brought their attention to something they missed.

The items in the box could all belong to Emilia, not Zorya. It was Emilia's wedding dress in the box. The children's shoes she could have bought for her unborn son. The bottles could have been for a remedy for her visions, the gemstones a desperate, superstitious act to ward off evil. The Nil'vetra letters branded with her family's crest with the word that was linked to Emilia *not* Zorya. But that did not explain the letters. The bunch of letters that were all addressed to Zorya, opened and read.

"What if the letters were never sent to Zorya? What if Emilia wrote these letters to Zorya but never sent them, just kept them in this trunk for years?" Thedamaine said after a brief think.

"And when she died and Zorya took over the Manor, she found this trunk, found the letters and read them?" Evangeline was sat crossed legged on the floor next to Thedamaine, knees touching, while Felicity sat across from them, leaning toward the candlelight.

"That would explain why they are opened," Felicity added. "Mother wrote the letters, addressed them to Zorya, sealed them but never sent them. Years later Zorya finds a bunch of letters addressed to her, obviously she would open and read them."

"What do they say?" Sir Thedamaine asked.

"Nothing interesting," Felicity answered. "The few I flicked through seemed like official reports on what happened. I would have to read them all to get context and see if anything else is in there. Something good."

"I think we should divide and conquer. Pick a thread and follow it. I would like to learn more about the shamans, I assume I will be dealing with them soon anyway. We saw that one shaman in town, didn't we? When they eventually turn up I will do whatever I can to learn more about them."

Felicity nodded in agreement with her sister. "I should read these letters. See what I can find, I will also finish reading the book, see what I can study from it."

"How about visiting the library and seeing what you can find on shamans or even reports on Lady Emilia's family?" Sir Thedamaine suggested. "Maybe something has been recorded about her relationship with Zorya?"

"Good idea, Theo."

"Theo?" Felicity asked, never hearing that nickname from Evangeline.

"What about the locked drawer?" Evangeline asked, changing the subject. "You mentioned there was a locked drawer that you couldn't find the key for."

Together they ransacked the office, searching in every nook and cranny for a key but never found it. Evangeline, temper rising at the frustration, pulled and jerked the drawer.

With Thedamaine's dagger she tried jimmying the lock, then the hinge but nothing.

"Don't break it!" Felicity stressed, pulling Evangeline away. Thedamaine took back the dagger immediately.

"I want to know what's inside. The answer to everything could be in there."

"But Zorya would know we were here."

"Taren could bust open that lock easily and then replace it before they come back, no problem."

"Yes, problem. Zorya will then have a key to a drawer she can no longer open, then we will be in trouble."

"That's true, I guess. So what? What is she going to do?"

"Don't." Felicity grabbed Evangeline's arm hard, the intensity in her eyes convinced Evangeline to back down.

"Fine, but *you* have to find a way to open it. I swear, if all the answers we need are in that drawer, I will kill you."

"Oh, don't be so dramatic. It's highly unlikely we will have all of the answers in one place. Like you said, we need to pick a thread and follow it. There are many threads of mysteries in this investigation, we need to follow *something* to get *somewhere.*"

The girls agreed on their investigations, even Thedamaine suggested he ask the knights what they remember about Zorya's arrival. Felicity was comfortable with her reading assignment. She loved to read and was the faster out of the two, Evangeline usually only read when she had to, but Felicity read for pleasure. Plus, she had her own investigation on the ropes.

She had hired a select few of the squires to spy on Taren and gather any information on him. Even Thedamaine's squire, Oslo was on the payroll. Though Felicity was not impressed with him because he was late for his first patrol and tried to blame it on Evangeline's training session running over. So far, they had not gathered much. He spent his days forging in his workshop and his evenings drinking in the pubs without Evangeline for she was too busy running the Manor, the duties taking up most of her time.

Felicity still did not trust Taren yet did not dislike him. He had a natural charisma that seemed to wash over Felicity; soothe her in a way. Felicity assumed that was why he and Thedamaine got on so well with Evangeline, her volatile nature was calmed by their presence and words. Felicity did not have the patience to deal with her sister like they did and praised their tolerance. She could only hope that one day she would have someone to care about her, someone she could be herself with.

CHAPTER 13.

As the month crept along, the next full moon loomed as a weight on everyone's shoulders. Evangeline and Felicity fell impatient, frustrated that their investigations were going nowhere. Evangeline could not learn more about the shamans until they appeared in the village. There were odd sightings here and there, but she had to visit their camp to learn more. She could do nothing but wait.

Felicity was the same. The letters in Zorya's trunk held no value, mere official correspondence that bored her half to death. She never did find the key to the drawer and still maintained they did not destroy the lock. Felicity would have to wait for Zorya to return, by then she would have mustered up the courage to speak to her. She had never admitted it and would never tell Evangeline but Zorya intimidated her. The pale skin, the dark hair and the dark gowns plus the ethereal gliding around the Manor; no one would guess that she used to be a handmaiden from the way she held power. She was born to it; the same way Evangeline was. Evangeline was literally born to inherit power, but it suited her, she was built for the responsibility, whether she liked it or not. Felicity knew she was not born to have power; she would not know what to do with it even if she had it. Evangeline and Zorya had more in common than they realised and that is why Felicity felt intimidated.

She was the odd one out.

Morana and Vesna, though identical twins, were still the spitting image of their mother. Black hair, pale skin, short and petite, they were miniatures of her, and Felicity assumed they looked exactly like her at that age. A thought occurred to Felicity that she had never seen their father. Horus was not the father for Zorya already had the twins thirteen years prior. As the twins looked like their mother, she wondered what their father looked like, where he was and if he was still alive. She thought about asking but decided against it as that would mean having to talk to them.

Felicity was worried about the full moon. Evangeline had been preparing all month long for the next attack, the one she would have to handle on her own and Felicity had the awful impression that her sister would be joining the knights in the attack. She had commissioned Taren to make both of them their own suits of armour, Felicity did not see why, she would be taking cover in the safety of the Manor and the armour was not necessary. It was heavy and clunky and another thing that intimidated Felicity. Evangeline loved her armour, it was on display in the girl's solar and made her smile every time she passed it, Felicity did not understand why. With the armour, stood Evangeline's short sword that she had crafted herself, with Taren's help, on the last full moon. It was still stained with the beast's blood.

Felicity stood in front of her sisters suit of armour and took hold of the sword. It was lighter than she expected, but well balanced. Though not a two-handed sword, she grasped it with both hands. She swung it, spinning around. Standing at the door was Vesna and Felicity's stomach dropped. She deflated and put the sword back, embarrassed, waiting for the insults and ridicule.

There was only silence.

Vesna watched Felicity from the doorway, wearing a black gown that was a copy of one of Zorya's. Felicity glared at Vesna, not moving, and staring her out. Suddenly Felicity moved passed the dislike and actually read Vesna's face.

She was afraid. Uncomfortable. She wanted to say something but couldn't.

"What do you want?" Felicity asked. Not aggressively but not nicely either.

Tentatively, Vesna entered and crossed the room, looking at Evangeline's suit of armour.

"Will *we* need one of these?" Vesna asked, timidly.

"No, why? Do you think my sister will put us in danger?" Felicity asked, wanting to know the true answer as she, herself, may believe that.

"No, I don't think she will but if she knows something and thinks you two need them, please could we have protection too? I know you two do not like us, but we are family now. Morana would never ask this but I ask on behalf of both of us, please can you keep us safe?"

"Evangeline and I would never knowingly put you in danger."

"She said she would kill us, threatened that we'd be dead."

"She didn't mean it that way. Look, the Manor is safe, it doesn't attack the building and does not even climb the hill, you do not need the armour. I didn't want it; Evangeline just gave me one. Trust me, we'll be fine."

"Is she going to attack it herself? I heard that she had an encounter and managed to trap it."

"That's true," Felicity confirmed.

"Did she tell you what it looked like? What it was like being that close to it?"

"She does not like to talk about it." It occurred to Felicity that she never asked. She did not approve of Evangeline's risk and did not want to give her any ideas of doing it again so never spoke of it. She began to think that was a bad idea.

"Is it true that it has a skull for a head?"

"A wolf skull, yes, but the shadowy black furry body of a monster."

"So, it's like a wolf?"

"Not really, it has the horns of a ram and long monstrous claws on its paws. We do not know what it is because it is a *beast.*"

"My mother says it is a curse."

"Really?" Felicity was curious. "What type of curse, by whom?" She thought back to the Nil'vetra papers in Zorya's study, thinking about the spirit world and shamans.

"She doesn't know. But she said that the town had been cursed for some reason which is why a beast is stalking the village. Cadmael says it's a shaman curse to drum up business and it would go away if we paid them. Morana thinks it's a shapeshifter which is why we cannot follow it to its lair."

"Interesting. What do you think it is?" Felicity asked, hoping to gather all the theories she could, fuelling her investigation.

"I have no idea. All I know is that I'm terrified of it and want to leave this village to get far away from it. Cadmael helped Morana and I look for suitors a few weeks ago but it is difficult for us. It's alright for you, you have a noble name but us? We have no luck in getting out of here."

Felicity never thought about it that way. She just assumed all suitors ran away once they tasted the twins' personalities but never thought they wouldn't even get that far. Vesna took a seat, defeated, but Felicity remained standing, unsure of what to say or what was happening.

"Can I ask you something?" Felicity finally said. After Vesna nodded, she continued, "why are you being normal with me right now? This is the first time we have ever had an ordinary conversation where you haven't insulted me, assaulted me or pranked me. What is going on?" Vesna only shrugged. "Seriously. Why do you hate us?"

"You two used to prank each other."

"Yes, when we were kids, not anymore and not in the way you do it. You're cruel and mean and always cross the line."

"Yeah, well you deserve to be taken down a peg. You have this perfect little life. Rich, Lady Felicity with the beautiful face and the family who loves her. Rich, Lady Evangeline, the heir with a love triangle and a husband. She has three men to choose from and we do not have any. We are second class citizens in this Manor and will never be equals."

"You have got the wrong idea. How is my life perfect? Either of our lives? Evangeline is *not* in a love triangle. She will be married to a man she does not love and who does not love her and so could never fully be with the man she truly loves. Her life is not perfect. You said we have a family that love us? Who? It is just me, Evangeline and my father and he is growing sicker every day. His love for us died along with our mother and now nothing is left except cold resentment and unstable aggression. If he loves us, then why did he hit Evangeline?"

Vesna grew quiet. "Our mother hits us too. You've seen it, heard it. She hates us."

"Perhaps they really are a good match."

The two of them actually shared a laugh; an awkward one but they laughed. From screaming at each other to laughing with one another. Just like siblings do, now Felicity laughed for a whole different reason.

"She must not actually hate you. I don't think my father truly hates us, just his illness is affecting him."

"Oh, no. She does hate us. We remind her of our father."

There it was. Felicity was just thinking about this and coincidentally Vesna brought it up on her own. "May I ask about your father?"

"We only know a little; she doesn't talk about him and hits us if we ask too much. He was some sort of traveller or merchant. She met him on the road and from the way she acts, he did something horrible to her."

"What did he do?"

"We don't know. She won't tell us. All we know is that she is not in contact with him anymore."

"Is he alive? Do you know his name?"

"She won't tell us."

"Oh. So, she met him on the road, was she a traveller too?" Felicity thought about the travelling nomadic shamans.

"Yes, she used to be an apothecary. Until she heard that her old friend Emilia was now the Lady Ravenhill. She begged your mother for a stable job here and the rest you know."

"They were old friends?" Felicity's heart raced.

"Yes, they grew up together in their old town. Didn't you know that?"

"No," she said. Felicity thought things over. So, they *were* old friends. Zorya must have known that her mother was a Bridge. If they were from the same town, those Nil'vetra letters could have been from either of them. There was no evidence that Zorya was a Bridge, but she could have known about it, maybe she wanted to help? Travelled with them to learn more? Came to work here to get close and help? But what about what Thedamaine said? Her mother went pale when she saw Zorya. There was bad blood or something awful went down between them.

"So, when she came here, was she still friends with my mother?"

"Not really. It had been about twenty or so years since they last saw each other."

"Any reason?" She hoped for an answer.

"Not that I know of. Grew apart? One left the town and not the other? Out of touch? How should I know?"

Felicity clasped her hands together and looked into the fire, annoyed that another lead had died. *Something* happened between their mothers.

"Somebody was killed." Felicity looked at the door to see who was speaking. Morana was leant on the door frame looking at the two girls.

"Killed?" Both Vesna and Felicity asked.

"When they were kids, the two of them had a third friend and that friend was executed by law. Under your mother's family name."

"Executed for what?"

"I couldn't find out. The records do not mention it."

"How do you know this?" Vesna asked.

"What records?" Felicity added.

"Cadmael's records, I was snooping and found them. He has records of the hierarchy's scandals. Every sordid detail that he could find out is written down in these records. You should hear the Forrester's scandals, holy hell they're bad."

"Why, what happened?" Vesna asked, hungry for the gossip.

"What about the execution?" Felicity asked, hoping to keep them on topic.

"I told you, the records do not mention why the girl was executed or list her name, just that she was friends with young Lady Emilia Rosewood."

"And Zorya? Was your mother mentioned?"

"No, but she wouldn't be, she was just a low-born in the village. Would the blacksmith be mentioned on Evangeline's scandal report when the truth about her and Thedamaine come to light?"

"There's nothing between them. They are not lovers." Felicity was growing tired of this. Morana seemed to be the one who started things, at least she could hold a normal conversation with Vesna.

Luckily, before a fight could break out, the dinner bell rang. Evangeline was missing from the feast, along with Sir Thedamaine and Cadmael. Evangeline's absence did not surprise Felicity, she hardly ate around company and these few weeks had been very busy for her, she had barely seen her sister.

Somebody tapped on Felicity's shoulder, she turned around.

"Don't freak out. Its me." Taren was filling Felicity's drink with wine, his head down. He was dressed in a cupbearer's uniform.

"What are you doing here?" She asked quietly. "You could get into a lot of trouble impersonating a household worker."

"I need to talk to you."

"Me? Why?"

"Meet me in the apothecary as soon as you can."

"Why?"

"Just go there. I will explain."

Taren slipped from the hall unnoticed and Felicity was left speechless and confused. She didn't even finish her feast, she got up and left.

The apothecary was on the same floor as the infirmary but on the other side of the Manor, it was a tiny, cold room with shelving on every wall, even over the doorway. It was a storeroom for medicines and ingredients, chosen specifically for the location, sheltered by the courtyard's yew tree shadow. Bottles and jars that stored herbs, chemicals, materials, liquids, and various other ingredients needed for medicinal purposes needed to be kept in the cold for preservation, yet it could not be kept underground for risk of frost.

Taren was already in the room; he closed the door behind Felicity after she entered. She could not decide if she was confused, curious or scared. Perhaps all three?

"Taren, what is going on?"

"I know you have had me followed." Felicity decided that she was scared. She had indeed hired people to follow him and had been for weeks.

"I have." She said, trying to muster up some courage.

"I brought you here to explain. I did lie to you and Evangeline. I did meet with someone. I wanted to explain and come clean before you hear from someone else."

"Who did you meet with?"

"Zorya."

Felicity had to take a seat. She tried to keep her mind blank for as long as she could, to hear his explanation before she thought of a million reasons why he would meet with her stepmother. Her hand found the fur trim of her gown and stroked it.

"Please explain, from the beginning," she said.

Taren told his story from when he was in the infirmary the night the beast attacked him and Evangeline. After she had left him, he laid awake for hours, the pain of his scratch not going away despite finishing the large jug of laudanum pain relief. Just before the sun rose, Zorya entered the room and stood over his bed. At first, Taren did not realise she was there, she glided over to him silently and he had been lying on his front, trying to cool down his sores. Clearing her throat, he was startled and turned around to look at her, wincing with the pain.

"Drink this." She said, presenting a small, corked bottle. The bottle was reddish brown in colour, like laudanum but he could not see the colour of the liquid inside.

"What is it?" He asked, not taking the bottle.

"It will stop the pain. More potent than laudanum and will taste better, too."

He was desperate for the pain to stop so he took the bottle, uncorked it and drank it. She was right, it did taste better than laudanum, no bitter taste at all. It was warm, he could feel it going down his throat, but the bottle was cold. He sniffed the empty bottle but smelled nothing.

"What is this?" He asked.

"Do you feel better?"

He moved around, shifting in the bed. The pain was gone. Completely gone. "Yes."

"Then it doesn't matter. It's an old family recipe. I do not give it out often."

"You should, this is brilliant."

"The effects do not last long. In a few hours, your pain will return, should you wish to have more you must meet me in the apothecary before the wedding." Zorya turned and glided toward the door. "I will not provide this for free. If you decide you want more you must do something for me."

Felicity listened to his story eagerly, without interrupting but now she had to speak up. "Well, what did she want from you?" She asked when Taren took a long pause.

"Well, you found me on my way to the apothecary and I never made it there, you sent me back to the infirmary when we heard people."

"So, you didn't meet with her?"

"When I got back to the infirmary, she was waiting for *me*. She said she would help me and if I wanted the pain relief I would have to help her. She made me promise that I would spy on her husband. She wanted me to spy on your father."

"What? Why?" A thousand thoughts ran through her mind.

"She didn't say. She wouldn't say. I tried to ask but she just told me to listen to what he said behind closed doors. See where he goes. I told her that was impossible, I don't live in the Manor, how could I hear him or follow him? She just told me to figure it out, he doesn't always stay in the Manor."

"Interesting. So now he is away, what happens?"

"She left me a supply of this pain relief and told me to find out what I could from the villagers. Be her inside man."

Felicity thought things over, that's where Zorya was heading. If Zorya really was a shaman, maybe she wanted to know what her father knew. The pain relief seems like a shaman thing, but could also just be an apothecary thing, she shouldn't just jump to conclusions. Zorya did say it was a family recipe. Thinking back to what Thedamaine said; perhaps her mother, the Bridge, created it and passed it onto Zorya?

"This pain relief she is giving you, is it making you sick?"

"No, not at all."

That threw out one theory. Felicity thought maybe Zorya was poisoning Taren, along with her father and her mother. But why Taren? If Zorya was the poisoning kind, she has motive for her mother and father but no motive for Taren.

"So, have you found anything out about my father?"

"Not really. He's not even around. I'm not sure what Zorya was looking for or expecting from me. He's a very sick man and it's getting worse. I know that he refuses to see the village doctor, apothecary or surgeon. He only sees the Manor workers."

"That makes sense though, my mother was the same. That's not exactly strange."

"I hear rumours about how he killed his wife or has the same sickness that she had, things that you have heard already."

"Yes, I know those rumours."

"But the people also say that they have passed that sickness onto you."

"Me? What?"

"People saw you vomit a while ago and these things just snowball out of control."

"Really? I vomit once and now I'm crazy like my mother or deathly sick like my father? Honestly! I just ate something bad or something else. I'm not sure. I'm fine now."

"I know that but once these rumours start they cannot stop."

"Wait a minute, why didn't you just say this to us in the first place? Why did you lie?"

"Because she told me not to tell you. She didn't want you finding out anything bad about your father."

"So, she expects or knows something bad? Or she is trying to pass the blame onto him? Maybe she knew you were going to tell us and tried to get us to suspect him instead of her?"

"Felicity, I honestly think you are wrong about Zorya. She's not evil, she's not a killer. Listen, she helped me. Why would she do that if she were evil? What could she gain by helping me?"

"She gained a spy. Look, she hates her daughters, Vesna told me so and I've seen her contempt for them, it's cold and cruel."

"So, she hates those scabs? If that makes her evil then we all are."

"It's not just that. It's the whole picture." Things started to add up and pile on top, painting her as the suspect. Felicity needed to think. The shamans needed to come to town so they could learn more about them and they needed to find out what happened between Zorya and their mother. "Are you going to tell Evangeline this?"

"Yes but I wanted to tell you first as you were the one spying on me, trying to take me down." Felicity let out a tiny, awkward smirk. "But are we good now?" He asked. "Because I like you, I hope we can be friends. With Evangeline temporarily crowned as queen around here, I'm going to need someone to talk to."

"Oh, so I'm just your last resort?"

"Quick wit! I love that. You are your sister's sister. Look, if you ever get bored, come by the forge and I'll help you make your own sword, or you can try hammering out some steel or we can just get a drink together."

"Maybe I will. But I don't drink like my sister."

"Nobody drinks like your sister."

"How about this: I will stop my people spying on you if you tell me everything you find out about my father *and* you spy on Zorya for us?"

"How am I supposed to do that?"

"Figure it out, you're a big boy."

"Holy hell, I'm being blackmailed into being a double agent."

"I'm not blackmailing you, but I will find out all your dirty little secrets, Taren."

"We've all got dirty little secrets, Princess Flick. What happens in the dark comes out in the light."

CHAPTER 14.

One more day before the full moon. It would attack tomorrow night and there was still so much to do, and it was *still* raining. It had been the wettest month the village had known for years. Hardly a day went by where there was no rain.

Evangeline had given herself a headache from rolling her eyes too much. She was sat in her father's chair in the Grand Hall, arms crossed and bored out of her mind. She did not want to be there. She had things to do, things to prepare. She wanted to check on the progress of the fortification of the village walls and rebuilding of the houses and businesses damaged in previous attacks. She could check on the blacksmith cellar where she could see Taren, but these duties had to be done. She did not like to be bored but sat through Cadmael's lecture with a perpetual eye roll.

"The constant rain and storms have caused some panic in both the village and the Manor. The courtyard is flooding, roofs are collapsing, and there are leaks everywhere."

"Some people are even homeless now because of it."

"Homeless?" Evangeline perked up and started listening, focused on the concern and anger in Aria's voice.

"Those who live at the bottom of Orchard Hill are getting the worst of it. All the rain is flooding down from the top and those houses are swimming in it."

"Yes, that is the truth, but they knew that was an issue when they moved in. It happens most years."

"Wait, what are you saying? They become homeless whenever it rains?"

"When it rains enough to flood them out, yes. Usually they live with it, but this month has forced them out of their homes."

"Why haven't we done something about this? Why has nobody brought this to my attention before? Why now?"

"Your chamberlain refuses to talk about it because of the class of people who live there. These people are too poor to live anywhere else and nobody who has money wants to live in houses that are flooded every few years. You have never been told about it because they will not help the poor."

"Miss Aria, do hold your tongue." Cadmael's chest puffed and the disgust on his face just infuriated Evangeline. "Those bold opinions should not be voiced by a handmaiden."

"Shut up, Cadmael." Evangeline rolled her eyes once again but turned to Aria, "Aria, I will help the poor." Her frown softened finally.

"Lady Evangeline, the law states that taxes are to be used for such circumstances, extra funding will not be necessary."

"Do not lecture me on the law. Obviously, the taxes are not reaching that area, and something has to be done. We must fix this once and for all. Take me there, I want to see for myself."

Evangeline was rendered speechless at what she saw; the houses were sad and pathetic; they could have been abandoned years ago yet the poorest of the village 'lived' in these waterlogged shacks. Orchard Hill was one of three hills in the village: the other two being Raven Hill, where the Manor stood, and Windmill Hill. The manor's hill had the forest that shielded the village from its floods and Windmill Hill was too small to make a difference, it all streamed into the lake anyway. However, Orchard Hill was large and situated in the poorer end of the village, despite the popular Orchard Inn at the top of the hill that catered to everyone; rich or poor. Nothing prevented the rain to gather at the bottom, flooding everything.

She waded through the waist-high flood water to see for herself just how bad the houses were. The house she entered was falling apart and mouldy, the roof had even caved in from the rain. Sir Thedamaine and Aria joined her to see the damage, yet Cadmael turned his nose up at the filth and refused to enter.

When she could not bear to see anymore lest she grow insane imagining living in such degrading conditions, she followed Thedamaine and Aria out of the flood and looked into the eyes of each of the villagers who lived in the houses. They were from all walks of life; beggars with nothing to their name, except their flooded home, the elderly who could barely stand, adults who have lost everything, young families wasting away and children with no more joy in their eyes.

"My friends," she called to them. "A complete reconstruction on these houses will be arranged for you all, free of charge so you may have a basic necessity in life; a shelter that keeps you warm and dry. No longer will you live in squalor wading through an ocean every year. Until this construction is complete you will be sent to foster families like my own, noble houses in Ravenhill or Birchcliffe, who will house you and feed you in exchange of your service, to the best of your abilities. You do have a home in Ravenhill, and you forever will. Please see my chamberlain, Cadmael, to find your new homes."

"So how will you do it?" Thedamaine asked her as she turned back to the houses once the villagers had left. They were both soaking wet from top to bottom now, the rain seeping through their cloaks down onto their sodden legs.

"Stilts," she said. Her knees were starting to quiver so she wrapped her cloak tight around herself. "I saw it in a book once, eastern construction or something. We will raise the houses off the ground and build into the hill itself, so the rain falls down underneath the house keeping it dry. Perhaps a moat as well? Lure the stream of water from the hill to the lake. The stream by The Wolf and Raven could be extended to here.

"Excellent, I'll tell the crew."

Evangeline stood in front of the dilapidated houses, shivering from the cold, drenched to the bone and savoured the grateful faces and genuine smiles she received from the villagers. Tomorrow the beast would attack once more but she helped people today and that is what she must focus on.

Back at the Manor, Evangeline had convinced Felicity to take over some menial duties for the rest of the day and by convinced, she had straight up tricked her sister and escaped. She managed it when Thedamaine finished his shift and a new knight took over her guard.

The Wolf and Raven pub was as busy as ever and Evangeline noticed a few prostitutes hanging around, moving away from her as if she had the plague, afraid her status would put them in danger. Evangeline did not care. She wanted a drink.

"Care for a rematch?" A man said behind her as he bumped

her shoulder, spilling her drink. It was Nicholas, the man she had met before and cheated during the drinking game.

"I do not play with cheaters," she sneered at him, shaking the drink off of her hand.

"Your father is a cheater. He cheated on his wife with that maid, now he's married to her. Though I would cheat too if my wife were crazy. I would not cheat with that, however. That's the first rule of infidelity; always cheat on someone better than the person you are cheating on, otherwise it is just pointless." He paused for a moment, waiting for a response but Evangeline kept drinking. Sipping her ale one gulp at a time. "Oh, what am I saying?" He continued. "You would know all about infidelity, you little *whore*, you have the smithy and the knight, and a husband. Oh, you're not married yet, are you? Just be careful when you're around your father-in-law, I've heard just how awful he can be. Nothing you're not used to, though."

Evangeline had finished her drink and looked Nicholas in the eye. His facial scars from the beast gleamed in the light, pink and bumpy. He smirked at her, raising an eyebrow. With her left hand, she struck Nicholas around the head with the metal tankard, dropping it. She then grabbed his hair and smashed his face down onto the bar and finally kicked him off the chair. He squirmed on the floor, holding his bleeding nose and she left him there, taking a jug of ale, flicking a gold coin into the barmaid's hand and moving to the other side of the pub. Nobody around her reacted, in this place, on this side of town, it happened often, and nobody cared.

"I see you're enjoying yourself." Taren had followed her from the bar to the booth where she sat.

"I am, thanks for asking." She smiled at him. "And thank you for coming to my aid and rescuing me." Her sarcastic, jesting tone put a smile on his face.

"You do not need me to rescue you, you just proved that. I see you haven't been neglecting your training. Is that what has kept you so busy?"

"I've been running the place, Taren. Doesn't leave me much time to run around with you."

"Yet here you are in the pub drinking without me."

"You're here, aren't you? Or are you a ghost?"

"You didn't come and get me."

"I knew you'd be here."

"There are five pubs in town, I could have been anywhere."

"Oh, please, you love this place. You've been hanging out here every night this month."

"How would you know that? You've barely left the Manor."

"Felicity told me."

Taren rolled his eyes and tutted. "You know she's been following me, right?"

"Serves you right. Are you going to sit down?" Evangeline asked, annoyed by Taren just standing in front of her.

"That depends. How long will you be here? Are you going to ditch me?"

"Oh, grow up, Taren. You're trying my patience. Just sit down and have a drink with me while you still can. I cannot sit here all night, not like I used to."

The two of them drank together and Evangeline could not help but sense the atmosphere between them change. It was thick with uncomfortable awkwardness. She sensed he had things that were left unsaid but underneath there was fear.

She returned to the Manor gone midnight contemplating Taren. Unable to sleep and not tired, she began to think about the full moon. This time tomorrow the beast would be attacking, and she wanted to help. In any way she could.

She balled up another piece of parchment and added to the large pile. Bent over her desk, she scribbled notes as fast as she could write; twice she had spilt ink over everything. Now she had gone off on a tangent, abandoning her strategy and began to list the many threads of her investigation. She listed the main mysteries: who killed her mother and why? What is the Nil'vetra? What is the beast and how can they kill it? What happened between her mother and Zorya? What is Zorya hiding? What is her father hiding? Is Zorya a shaman? What is the importance of the shamans? There were so many questions. She began to draw lines between them, connecting mysteries to conspiracies until her page became a bird's nest of tangled lines.

She realised she had gone off course and tossed the paper into the fireplace, bringing forth the next tower of books to read. Opening the first book, her mind wandered back to the investigation. Thinking about the shamans and hoping she could meet them and learn more. She cursed herself for remaining distracted. *Read. The. Book,* she commanded herself, banging her head against the pages with every word.

"Have you slept at all, my Lady?" Sir Thedamaine was at the door, straight-backed and smiling. She raised her head up from the mountain of paperwork on her desk, pleased to see him. Leaning back in her chair; the first time she had done so since she sat down; she stretched, raising her arms up above her head and interlocked her hands on the back of her neck.

"Says the guard who never sleeps. You know all about overtime, you ended your shift only a few hours ago. When was the last time you slept?"

"Good point." He nodded, smiling. Evangeline looked at him, slightly rocking in her seat. She squinted, studying him. Thedamaine stood like a board and returned her gaze, patiently. With a short inhale, Evangeline shot to her feet and crossed the room. She poked her head out of the door, checking both ends of the corridor and closed it behind her.

"I need your help," she breathed, standing close against him.

"Anything, my Lady."

Evangeline returned to her desk and Thedamaine followed her into the room. "I have filled my head to the brim with strategies, war stories, tactics and formations. We need a plan of attack to draw the beast out of its hiding hole, surround it and kill it, but all of these books have gotten me nowhere, fast. They ramble on without giving any useful information, it is driving me crazy." Thedamaine opened his mouth to speak but Evangeline continued on. "I am Heir, I will run this Manor one day and I need to know this stuff. What if my home is under attack or my family gets called into battle by the Queen? What if the Manor is under siege or one of the families decides to widen their ruling by usurping my power? I will need to rally my troops and give them a battle plan; I cannot send them in armed with sewing needles and a demure smile."

That got a laugh from Thedamaine, but Evangeline did not notice. She picked up a large book, the cover worn away, and shuffled through the pages. "I need a simple list of strategies. Things like the pincer movement, wedge formations, encirclement; every strategy, formation and tactic there is to do with battle, so it is there in front of me.

But this is all rubbish!" Evangeline swept the papers off her desk, sending them flying across the room. "My head is so full of terminology and jargon and I do not know what any of it means!" She collapsed in her chair, throwing a leg over the arm and huffing loudly. She blew a loose strand of hair out of her eyes and rolled her neck back. Thedamaine, feeling safe that her rambles were over, collected some papers at his feet and flicked through them.

"What have you got so far?"

"Lists, research, nothing solid." She waved her hand as she spoke, remaining slumped on the chair and her head back.

"I think you are over thinking this too much. The truth of war is that most of the time the head of the family is not the one who strategizes, they are the face of the battle, they have an idea of what to do and how to go about the attack, it is the war general, captain of the guard or the strategist's job to put these ideas into motion. Now I understand that you want to have all the information to sound serious to your father, but he knows you and will understand that you mean business. Looking at these formations you have planned yourself, you are really onto something." He put the rest of the paper on the table and read over one crumpled sheet. "This sounds like an entrapment and envelope manoeuvre if you want to label it. Can you elaborate?"

"It will not work." Evangeline lifted her head long enough to glance over the paper. "That one all rests on the beast attacking the Manor."

"What makes you think it will attack the Manor, it never has before?"

"I know but I hoped the majority of the village taking refuge within our walls was enough temptation to draw it here."

"It is an extremely dangerous plan. Where would our forces be? At the edge of the forest cutting off its escape like a decoy?"

"That would put everyone in even more danger. I was thinking of putting the villagers in the courtyard so the beast has to go right through the Manor where we can trap it and kill it."

"What is preventing the beast passing right through and getting to the courtyard where its prey is herded together?"

"The competence of my men will prevent it from

advancing any further than the Banquet Hall where we will swarm in from the surrounding rooms, trapping it."

"We can use machines and weapons to slow it down and prevent it from getting through."

"Anything to slow it down. Plus, the troops will be concentrated in one area, not spread about the village, this will give us a higher chance of killing it."

"It is a risky plan, it could go very wrong very fast but as long as we flank successfully and protect the courtyard, there is a chance."

"So, it is a flanking manoeuvre? I wasn't too sure."

"Of course, you are coming at the beast from both sides, advancing from the surrounding rooms and trapping it."

"Will it work?"

"That's hard to say. We will have to go over everything."

As the night crawled along, their minds began to tire. They had moved their strategizing to the lounge chair, almost as long as a bed, with enough room for both people and their mountain of research. They spoke only to voice a new part of the plan or to point out a flaw. Blanketed in scrolls and parchment, Thedamaine spoke up after a lengthy silence to find Evangeline asleep, her head resting on the arm of the chair and a piece of paper stuck under her cheek. He stood up sluggishly and hesitated, mulling over the situation; should he leave or wake her up? Should he touch her or just call her name? He beamed at her peaceful sleeping face and without thinking, he crouched down in front of the chair and whispered her name. Gently, he placed a hand on her arm, and she shot awake instantly, gasping loudly. Thedamaine bolted upright and stepped back, frightened and embarrassed.

"Easy, easy. You fell asleep." He suppressed a smile; the piece of paper was still attached to her cheek and it hung there as she blinked herself awake. It fell off as she came to her senses.

"Oh, thank you for waking me." She cricked her neck. "That was not comfortable, at all."

"Would you like me to get you into bed?"

She flung her head around to him, grinning widely and burst out laughing. Realising what he had said, he stammered, averting her eyes.

"I-I meant would you like help, or y-you should get into bed. It is late, you need sleep." He ended up sounding authoritative and commanding to overcome his stammer.

She was still grinning as she stood up, "Thedamaine has to get me into bed." She laughed in a singsong as she hopped past him, winking and jumped underneath her covers. She swore she saw the corners of his mouth curl, but he turned around too quickly to be sure.

"Is that all, my Lady?"

She did not answer immediately, wanting to see if he reacted but he composed himself. Defeated and disappointed, he was dismissed, and he left wishing her a good night's sleep. Evangeline dropped her head on her pillow, unable to tear the grin off her face.

CHAPTER 15.

The village was in complete lockdown. Houses, buildings and businesses were boarded up and protected. Each of the blacksmiths in the village, including the Manor's weaponsmith had been making spears and spikes and fire traps all month long in preparation of tonight's attack. Equally funded by the Ravenhill treasury and the people's taxes, Evangeline spared no expense. She wanted to do *something*.

Evangeline patrolled the streets along with her large entourage; four knights accompanied her plus Sir Thedamaine, Aria, Cadmael, and even Taren. Felicity wanted to join as well but she had been feeling under the weather and remained in bed, resting. Evangeline was wearing her suit of armour in case the beast attacked early. She wanted to set a good example for the people. Be better than her father. She was armed with her sword and her mother's dagger.

As usual, it was still raining, and the group were soaked but Evangeline had things to do and a little rain would not stop her. Her patrol took her through the entire village, checking that everything had been properly boarded up with proper blockades that protected her people within. She checked the village walls and ensured the watch towers were stocked up and ready. Traps had been set up on every entrance into the village, as well as several spots in town and one at the bottom of the Manor hill.

Aria was fascinated with the traps and enjoyed seeing them tested. She always amused Evangeline as she was easily impressed with almost anything. Cadmael had been uncharacteristically quiet the entire day, which surprised Evangeline considering how much money she had spent in her father's absence. Equally quiet, was Taren. He had joined the group when they had arrived in town and Evangeline invited him along in order to kill two birds with one stone. She could spend time with him and complete her tasks for the day. She assumed his presence would arouse at least one comment from Cadmael, but she received only silence.

They congregated outside the Raven's Beak pub after making their rounds of the village. Near the centre of town, with the lake on one side and the river on the other, it was a great place to take a breath and rest. The pub canopy shielded them from the rain as they caught their breaths, but Evangeline was craving a drink. The pub was closed, the owner safe inside its locked and barricaded doors and they only used the outdoor seating as a resting point. Being next to the pub and her nerves becoming more and more restless as the day drifted on, she needed something to calm her down.

"I want a complete guard on the village infirmary all night long," she said after a lengthy silence and contemplation. "I also want the opportunity to bring any injured people into the Manor walls to seek help from our doctors and surgeons."

"We can arrange that." Sir Avery nodded; he was the knight in charge of the patrols and counter attacks and had earned himself the title, almost losing his life several times and incidentally lost an eye. The three other knights, Sir James, Sir Morris and Sir Morgan nodded too whilst Cadmael scribbled on his scroll.

"Only if it is safe to transport the injured person," Aria added. "You cannot always move someone who is injured because it could make them worse."

"Good point, thank you Aria. I want the village infirmary protected to prevent attacks on the already injured and the healers that are treating them. Should they be overwhelmed, any injured people, who can be transported safely, can seek refuge in the Manor walls. However, that should be a last resort, purely because transporting them opens them up to another attack. The option is there if needed."

Evangeline had gone over her strategies with Thedamaine the night before, but both agreed her plans were too risky. She could only double up on the protection and add more traps to the village. She hoped this was enough to maintain her status. She knew she would not kill it or prevent its attack, but she wanted to show the people that she had done something. They were superficial changes and only minor advantages, but it was something and that is what she promised.

She had to do something, and she did.

They returned to the Manor just before the evening feast. Cadmael and the knights disbanded, and Taren had split from the group just before they reached the hill. There was one more thing Evangeline had to do before the day was up, she took the package from Aria's arms and knocked on the mahogany door. She entered, alone.

Vesna was stood by the fire braiding Morana's hair who was sat in the chair, writing something. They both looked over at the door as Evangeline entered.

"These are for you." Evangeline said, placing the package on the table.

"What is it?" Vesna asked, leaning away from it. Morana took a poker from the fireplace and delicately tapped the package.

"It's not a prank." Evangeline spat, her patience already thinning. She removed the wrapping and revealed two plain daggers.

"She's here to kill us!" Vesna jumped back, hiding behind the chair Morana was sat on.

"Look at her, she's all dressed up, these are for us, while she has a sword. She wants an unfair fight."

"Listen to me, you human blister, these daggers are for you, just in case the beast attacks. They are for protection. Now, I doubt you know how to use them so they must only be used as a last resort, hopefully you never need to touch them."

"You just want an excuse to kill us, if we are armed you can pass it off as self-defence and get away with murder." Vesna remained cowering behind the chair.

Morana took hold of one of the daggers and grinned. "Next time you attack us and pin us down, I'll be ready for you."

The corner of Evangeline's mouth curled, and an eyebrow slowly raised. She stepped forward, a hairs width from Morana and towered over her. "I dare you," was all Evangeline said. Morana held the dagger at her side, it trembled. Evangeline was wearing armour, but her head was unprotected. Morana kept her gaze and her fist clenched around the dagger.

In a flash of clinking metal, Evangeline unsheathed her

sword suddenly and Morana screamed, hitting the floor, cowering. Evangeline only unsheathed her sword and stood there, watching Morana roll on the floor terrified and trembling. She did not hurt Morana, did not even touch her with the sword but the sudden movement had shocked her. Vesna skidded over to her sister, checking if she was hurt but found nothing. When they both looked up, Evangeline had left the room, leaving the daggers with the twins.

"I admire your will power." Sir Thedamaine laughed as they travelled down the corridor.

"I thought you stabbed her when you pulled out your sword." Aria was almost jumping up and down as she followed them.

"I didn't hurt her; I didn't plan to. All I did was unsheathe my sword and it was enough to scare her. I didn't know she was going to drop to the floor like that, I assumed she would just jump back."

"Why didn't you stop her, Thedamaine? You usually do when she gets violent, or just before she does."

"Perhaps I wanted to see what she would do."

"But what if Morana had actually attacked Evangeline, your job is to protect her."

"If Lady Evangeline could not block that blow from an unskilled weakling whilst wearing a suit of armour, I have failed as a teacher and mentor."

"I think even Aria would have been able to block it."

"So, Thedamaine are you going to start training the twins now?"

"Oh, Gods, no. They can go to someone else."

"I'm not sharing, anyway." Evangeline took hold of Thedamaine's arm. "He's a good teacher, he's all mine."

"There's no one else I'd rather teach."

CHAPTER 16.

Felicity had spent the day in and out of sleep, in her own bed after a burning hot bath that left her body pink and sore. She wanted to sleep off her sickness, but the fear of the attack kept waking her up.

The fifth time she awoke was to the sound of the bells, finding her room in darkness, the moonlight struggling through the window against the streaming rain. She loved the position of her bed; she could see the moon and it always brought a smile to her face, however tonight it just terrified her. The full moon shone as a beacon of death above, glaring into her window, crawling into her room with a ghostly light.

There was some kind of fruity beverage on her table beside her. She lifted it to her nose and sniffed; she could not distinguish the smells. It was in an apothecary tonic glass; she assumed the doctor left it there for her to drink once she awoke. She did. Thick liquid flowed down her throat like pure honey. There was a concoction of ingredients she could not hope to list. As she felt it hit her stomach, her blood ran cold. She had just enough time to bend over the bed, pick up the pot beside her and vomit into it. She placed it back onto the floor, pushing it under the bed a little.

She pulled her knees up to her chest and hugged them, feeling alone and uneasy. The fire was dying but she could not bring herself to stand up. Pulling the furs from the foot of the bed up and around her shoulders, she scanned the room and listened to the pouring rain.

She wished she and Evangeline still slept in the same rooms as they did growing up, they each had their own room that backed onto each other. Whenever Felicity wanted her sister in the middle of the night she would throw something big and bulky at the wall and Evangeline would come in. She could not do that now; she was down the other end of the corridor and on the opposite side. She would have to shout ever so loudly for Evangeline to even know she needed her if Evangeline was even in her room at all. That was not helping her settle down. There was not even a guard patrolling the corridor.

She was starting to shiver and becoming weak and shaky, which always happened after she vomited. *Just get up, walk to the fireplace and throw another log on it, or leave the room and find someone.*

Her head snapped from the window she was staring out of to her door; it was pulled to, a gap shining through. There was someone coming down the corridor, she heard the creaking floorboards. They were trying to be quiet, sneaking. It wasn't a knight; she could tell instantly. *Evangeline?* She was going to speak aloud but her internal voice just couldn't come out.

"Who's there?" It was barely a whisper, but she finally managed to speak, and the person stopped walking. Felicity sat frozen on her bed, still hugging her knees, cocooned in furs. She clenched her eyes shut as the person crept into her chamber room.

"Flick?" It was not Evangeline. Felicity smiled, unclenched and relaxed on her bed.

"Taren! You scared me half to death!" She threw a pillow at him. He caught it and came into her room, sitting on the edge of her bed. He was soaking wet, but she hardly cared.

"Well, my job's only half done." She threw another pillow at him. "I had to get you back for scaring me at the wedding. How did the frogs go?"

"Quite well, they were terrified, I kind of feel bad that Evangeline wasn't there to see it."

"Well, she can prank them herself next time. Are you sick?" He frowned as he searched her face. "You look pale, what's wrong?"

"It's nothing serious. Did you break into our home to visit Evangeline?"

"Oh no, I was hoping your stepmother was back so we could continue our secret love affair."

"She's moved onto someone better looking." Evangeline was at the door and it scared both of them. "Someone who can truly satisfy her needs. A *bigger* man than you, Taren." Taren laughed sarcastically and Evangeline brushed her hand against his back as she passed him. As she entered the room,

Sir Thedamaine appeared at the door with his back to them, on guard as usual. "You do know he's joking, right, Flick?"

"I think so."

"She's sneakier than you are."

"Practise makes perfect." Evangeline said in her best imitation of their mother. "How are you feeling?"

"Better, I just can't sleep now."

Evangeline held the back of her hand on Felicity's forehead while Taren helped himself to lighting the fire. A flash of lightning momentarily lit up the room and a roll of thunder shortly followed. Evangeline was still wearing her suit of armour but was inside the Manor, so Felicity felt better knowing she was safe.

"Lucky for you, none of us can sleep."

"Will you stay here with me?"

"Of course, we will, Flick. All of us. Together. Sir Thedamaine, please join us and close the door behind you."

Evangeline crawled onto Felicity's bed and sat next to her, under the covers. Taren laid on his side at the foot of the bed, holding himself up with his elbow whilst Thedamaine took a seat next to the bed by the window.

Evangeline could not help but beam with joy, her heart glowing; everyone she loved was in the room with her and safe within the Manor walls. Her father was far away, safe from the attack and her people were as protected as they could be.

Felicity jumped at another lightning bolt outside. "How did that poem go? The one about the beast that you made up to try to frighten me."

"I succeeded in frightening you, Flick."

"You did not. How did it go again?" Felicity asked.

"The lightning will flash, and the thunder will smash,
But the monster will only sit,
Waiting for you to come to it.
The monster will keep where your fears will seep,
And start to creep when you fall asleep."

Evangeline sped up with each line.

"The monster with the poison claws who rips at all the doors,
That moves silently across the floors,
And gallops on all fours,
Covers your face with its large paws,

118

Clamping down with its large jaws,
And eats you as it roars!"

She ended the poem with a roar and grabbed Felicity, making her jump out of her skin as an unfortunately, or fortunately timed, depending on how you looked at it, loud thunder crash frightened them all at once.

"That was good." Thedamaine clapped. "You'll have a great career as a bard."

"I'll be sure to tell my father that."

"Why don't we tell stories, like the old days?"

Evangeline smiled at her sister. "Like when we were kids?"

"Story time? My favourite!" Taren sat upright on the bed crossed legged and leant against the bed post waiting for Evangeline to begin. Evangeline could not tell if he was teasing her or genuinely wanted to listen, she began either way.

"I've got one. Across the land, in the frozen mountains, cut off from the world lived a lonely Countess. She was young and beautiful, her fame reached all, but her beauty held a deadly secret. In her castle not one man was found, she only surrounded herself with young women, girls as young as six but never older than fourteen. Tales were told far and wide of the Countess with the divine beauty and the youth that took your breath away. But-" she paused for suspense and Felicity leant forward, Taren sharp eyed, Thedamaine just smiled, "-the young girls were going missing. As they reached fourteen years they started to disappear. As these girls were orphans, taken in by the Countess, not many people noticed but once the orphanages ran dry, the Countess ransacked the towns. She instilled a law that every young girl was to 'go to finishing school with the Countess'. Many were never seen again. People began to talk; these were the villagers' children! Somebody had to do something! But nobody came to help, many tried to confront the Countess themselves but disappeared just as their daughters before them."

"What happened to the girls?" Felicity asked.

"Well, word of this got out to the nobles of the neighbouring village. A few of their daughters had been abducted and they all suspected the Countess. So, they banded together and managed to contact a group of assassins who agreed they would send one of their own into the castle to find their daughters."

"Did they find them?"

"The young female assassin gained entry to the castle, for she was the perfect age and beauty and every day she sent messages to her assassin friends. This is what she found out; the Countess treated the girls like living dolls. She dressed them in pretty gowns the younger girls sewed for her, she made up their faces and was forever brushing their hair."

Felicity sunk back into her pillow but jumped as another flash of lightning lit up the room and the thunder rumbled the Manor.

"But," said Evangeline in a burst, "that was not all she was doing. The Countess loved to bathe her girls, she would wash off the dirt and makeup, and brush their hair, nice and clean. Once they were done she would drain the water and slit their throat, filling the bath with their blood."

"I knew it!" Taren clicked his fingers and shook his head. Felicity gasped then laughed at her outburst.

"She would bleed them dry, filling the bath to the brim, then she would remove the body and bathe in the blood herself. The blood gave her youth and beauty; it was her Elixir of Life. She did not stop there, however. She needed more. Once the body was bled dry she would hang it in the cellar to dry out and cook the flesh, feeding it to the rest of the girls to infuse them with the Elixir of Life so she may harvest more and more. She kept going."

"What else did she do?"

"If a girl had seemingly lost their beauty overnight the Countess would beat the girl to death, sometimes forcing the other girls to join in. If a girl talked back to the Countess, said no to anything she asked or was too talkative, her mouth would be sewn shut and she would starve to death. If the Countess merely felt like it, she would torture her girls; sticking needles under fingernails, burning genitals, cutting off breasts or removing eyes."

"What happened to the assassin?" Felicity asked.

"Was she killed also?" Thedamaine added.

"The assassin was only there for a reconnaissance mission; to observe and report back what she had seen but could not sit by and watch any longer. She vowed to free the girls, every one of them. She tried to take out the Countess and free the girls herself."

"Did she do it?"

"She was so close."

"Crap."

"The girls were almost out, she almost freed them all but there was a traitor among them. Somebody talked to the Countess, so the assassin and the girls were recaptured. But help was coming!"

"The assassins!"

"That's right. The assassins stopped hearing from their agent on the inside and assumed the worst. They joined forces with a group of mercenaries and a collection of knights from the noble families. Together they stormed the castle. Assassins and mercenaries have seen some terrible things in their lifetime, even causing some, and knights have been to war but what they saw that day haunted them forever. Bodies were littered everywhere. Corpses of young girls with body parts cut off, missing eyes, bite marks and flesh ripped from the body. Bathtubs filled with blood on every floor. Girls hanging from hooks in the cellar, still alive, maggots crawling in their flesh. Girls chained up, unable to move, smothered in their own excrement. They found the Countess in her chamber room bathing in the blood of an unknown girl in a state of tranquillity. Her body, her face and her hair smothered in the thick, red blood; her 'Elixir of Life.'"

"So, what happened to her? To the Countess?"

"She was tried and found guilty of the murder of over five hundred young girls."

"I hope she was given the same treatment as those girls."

"She was sealed into a windowless tower to await her death in solitary confinement. She was given enough food and water to sustain her through a high hole just bigger than a fist and that was all we heard from her."

"So, she's dead?" Felicity looked sick, even more than she did before.

"Has to be." Thedamaine answered.

"What happened to the assassin?" Taren asked.

"Her body was never found."

"Damn, that's good. Queen of bedtime stories, you are." Taren exhaled and smiled.

"You'll even give *me* nightmares." Thedamaine was leaning forward, his elbows on his thighs.

"She wasn't a very good assassin if she didn't assassinate her target," Taren pointed out.

"She was a junior assassin, still learning. She was only there to report." Thedamaine retorted.

"That was brilliant!" Felicity cheered. "What's the next one?"

"Next one?"

"Oh, I have one!" Taren held his hand up. "Not as horrifying as Evie's but I got a good one." He climbed down from the bed and moved the candle from the bedside table and put it on the chest of drawers. "This one-" he pointed to the wall in front of him and they watched, "-is about-" he crept forward, his shadow growing, "-the Shadow Man!" A lightning flash lit up the wall and his shadow was gone. They looked from him to the window flash, and back to him, but he had vanished and made them jump as he appeared from behind the bed. "The Shadow Man travels in the darkness, clinging to the shadows of this world, sneaking along from one to the other until he finds his prey. He is quiet and subtle; he will creep up on you before you've even realised it. When you are walking through the streets and your shadow starts to gain on you, that's the Shadow Man crawling his way to you."

"That's just the street lanterns and the moon moving your shadow, not the Shadow Man!" Evangeline protested.

"No, no, it's him alright."

"You've got it all wrong," Felicity said. "The Shadow Man is good! He is a guardian."

"A guardian?" Evangeline asked.

"Yes, he is a good luck charm, watching over you while he feeds on your shadow and that alone, protecting you from the darkness and what lurks within it."

"Isn't *he* what lurks within it? Feeding on your shadow?" Thedamaine added.

"It is payment, he doesn't hurt you but while he is there nothing else will ever hurt you."

"*I* was telling the story!"

"Sorry Taren, go ahead."

"No, it's dead now."

"You told it wrong."

"Hey! The Shadow Man is evil!"

"He is good!"

"Evil!"

Evangeline watched Taren fight childishly with her sister and heard the playfulness underneath. She shook her head at Thedamaine who looked equally done with their childish games. He was enjoying the show, just as Evangeline was.

"Do you have any stories, Theo?" She asked, trying to change the subject. He thought for a moment.

"Have you heard about the legend of the Bone Queen?"

"I haven't!" Felicity squealed excitedly, "tell me."

"I'm not much of a storyteller and I only remember the main details, but there once was a queen that was convicted of murdering her husband, the king. She was found guilty by the royal court; they called her a monster and a murderer though she maintained that she was innocent. She did not murder her husband. She lost everything, her home, her family, her status and power. Even her dignity was stripped from her as her people stoned her half to death. Bloody, bruised and close to death, she was imprisoned in the dungeon and left for dead. For a final punishment, the word murderer was branded on her chest, just above her breasts."

"Seems a little harsh." Taren said.

"Did she die?" Felicity asked.

"No. She recovered from her injuries and punishment and broke free of her shackles, escaping the dungeon. She began hunting down the thirteen members of the court who had sentenced her to death, one by one. The first she killed was a notoriously hated man who was found poisoned to death in his chambers. A death ambiguous enough to avoid suspicion, he had many enemies and any one of them could have murdered him. It was only when she turned to the beloved King's Aid, a kind and long serving member of the household did the court first suspect that they were being hunted."

"Oh, they're in for it now."

"Taren, stop interrupting." Evangeline spat.

"The queen killed her accusers in slow, painful ways and tormented them by showing herself in small doses enough to frighten them. She would appear in the shadows at night or in the distance, enough for them to wonder if it were a dream or a trick of the mind. She slowly began to own her nickname; for she wore the bones of her victims upon her person, always wearing a corseted gown that showed off the brand on her chest. Lurking in the shadows and stalking her prey, she let her intentions be known and wanted the court to know just whom was after them. Half the remainder of the court were terrified of this looming threat, but the rest were still to be convinced, passing off the rumours without a fear, certain the others were paranoid."

Taren opened his mouth to speak again but Evangeline kicked him under the covers, and he held back, Thedamaine continued.

"One year after her husband was murdered she tracked down the final accuser. After being tortured and tormented, he still did not reveal who really killed her husband, so she skinned him alive and ate his flesh. With the royal court all dead and her accusers punished and murdered, she was unsatisfied with the results, so she turned to the villagers who stoned her and murdered them one by one. Now she is a legend, a slave to her bloodlust. She travels from village to village murdering everyone in her path, hoping one day to find the one who poisoned her husband and started it all."

"She became the monster they already thought she was." Evangeline thought hard over the story.

"They already thought she was a murderer so she reckoned she might as well become one." Felicity shook her head. "That's a good story."

"Is it true?" Taren asked.

"It's a legend," Thedamaine answered. "Might be based on some version of the truth."

"There probably once was a queen that was falsely accused and murdered her accusers but everything else is most likely exaggerated and dramatized. I think I have heard of it before." Evangeline tried to think of when and where she had heard the story and who had told her but could not recall. Lightning flashed once again, lighting up the room briefly and a few moments later thunder rolled overhead.

"It is really coming down. I won't get any sleep tonight," Felicity mentioned.

"I won't get any sleep because I'll be thinking of the Blood Countess." Taren shivered dramatically.

"The Blood Countess and the Bone Queen, what a terrifying combination."

"Do you think it's bad down there?" Felicity asked after a moment's silence. She was looking toward the window, and everyone knew she was referring to the beast currently attacking the village.

"I don't like to think about it." Evangeline said.

"I'm just grateful to be here." Taren added. "Last month's attack was terrifying. I do not know if I could go through it again." Taren reached into his back pocket and pulled out a bottle, sipping it, Felicity knew it was the pain relief that Zorya had given him. It was as if the mere memory of the attack was enough to bring back the pain. She remembered her father was now addicted to laudanum due to his illness. She hoped Taren was not addicted to this pain relief, though he had said that Zorya would provide more if he spied for her. Perhaps she knew it was addictive and that is how she secured spies? How many did she have? A network of spies that told her everything, saw everything? Could some of those spies murder for her? If they are addicted to a substance and she withheld that substance, their desperation could force them to kill for her, keeping her hands clean.

The four of them remained in Felicity's room all night long. Only Taren and Felicity managed to fall asleep. Taren bundled himself up in some furs on the floor by the fireplace like a dog, and Felicity slept in her bed cocooned like she always was. Evangeline was just glad Felicity had a chess set in her room.

Thedamaine had never been fond of chess but it was soon becoming his favourite pastime. Evangeline was a great chess player, she always studied Thedamaine as he made his move, enjoying his concentration face. Nine times out of ten she won the game, never knowing that he let her win each time, in truth she was a terrible chess player; Thedamaine just loved to see the joy in her face.

Down the hill, villagers were dying.

CHAPTER 17.

The smell of smoke lingered long after the blaze had died. Whilst Evangeline, Felicity, Thedamaine and Taren were playing chess or sleeping, the villagers were burning in their homes. Trapped inside because of the lockdown; it kept the beast out but the smoke in. They had not yet found the source of the fire but that was not the priority.

Evangeline walked the length of the village infirmary, looking directly at the faces of those who had died. The fire seemed to have limited the beast's attack, yet it still managed to kill. A grieving father sat beside his young son's body. He couldn't have been more than six years old; his clothes burnt and skin blistered. An elderly couple looked as if they were sleeping in the bed, yet their motionless bodies and soot covered skin revealed the truth. Evangeline could barely see the next dead body; it was surrounded by knights. They parted to let her through. Sir James had been killed by the beast. His stomach had been torn open and he bled to death on the cobblestones opposite Taren's forge. Evangeline could not help but wonder if she had been in the forge like last time, she could have helped him, saved him. Or even Taren himself could have been there to help. If either of them had been there, they could have been killed themselves. Evangeline looked at his bloodied face, she knew his family. He had a wife and child, in the next village, safe from harm. His son was on his way to become a squire, following in his father's footsteps. Evangeline touched Sir James' boot in a final goodbye. There were more dead to see.

She moved on, corpses of all ages and walks of life littered the room; on the beds, on the floor, even leant up against the wall. Twenty-three people had been killed, the rest were injured, grieving or both.

Evangeline dreaded reaching the end of the room. She took a breath and readied herself, approaching the bed with the man and woman. Thrown across the two of them, Aria was sobbing desperately, grasping the hands of her mother and father who had both suffocated in the smoke that engulfed their tailoring shop.

Evangeline placed a gentle hand on Aria's shoulder, but she shook it off, ignoring Evangeline and sobbing harder. Thedamaine shook his head and Evangeline understood, leaving Aria alone to grieve.

Cadmael was also going from corpse to corpse, collecting information on the dead from their relatives. It was a hard job and Evangeline respected him for it, for it was a perfect job for a cold, insensitive man.

"How are you feeling?" Thedamaine asked. He was standing close to Evangeline, to avoid being overheard in order to get the truth from her. She could not lie to him even if she wanted to. She leant against the back wall, inhaling deeply and he knew something was wrong. She couldn't speak, though, she had to steady her breathing first, compose herself. Reading this, Thedamaine turned her around so she was facing him and the wall, the room would not be able to see her face, would not be able to see any weakness. That is what she feared and so she looked only at Thedamaine, ignoring the room, ignoring the dead, the grieving and the injured and focused on Thedamaine's hazel eyes.

"Tell me what you are thinking." He added.

"I am thinking that their blood is on my hands." Evangeline was grateful that Thedamaine did not jump on that immediately. He waited for her to keep going and she did. "I have failed them. I tried to do a better job at protecting them than my father did, and it has turned out even worse. I condemned these people to death, they were trapped in their homes, suffocating from smoke or succumbing to the flames.

"First rule of leadership: everything is your fault."

Evangeline actually laughed at his audacity. "Are you trying to make me feel worse?" Her smile forced a single tear out of her eye, but she brushed it away.

"The fact that you think this is your fault proves that you will not fail them again. This is simply a consequence of war, an unfortunate accident in difficult times. You did not fail anyone but because you think you did makes you better than your father."

"I need some air." Thedamaine escorted her outside but the restlessness and claustrophobia grew inside of her. She wanted to run to clear her head, feel the cold breeze on her face as she sprints away. "Can I be alone for a moment?" He hesitated but obeyed, staying by the infirmary door and waited for her. Evangeline went around the side of the building and crossed the alleyway. Just ahead of her was the treeline to the forest, the village wall's gate open and inviting her to run.

As she reached the end of the alley, a whistle to the right startled her out of her thoughts and grounded her to the spot. Nicholas was sat on the half wall behind the butchers, his elbow on his knee, his other leg swinging.

"Hello Nicholas." She said, trying to remain polite.

"Hello? That's what you say to me?" He jumped down from the wall and marched toward her, she took a step backwards but remained tall and composed.

"What do you expect me to say?" She asked, knowing she was treading dangerous waters, her heart pounding.

"How about you're *sorry*?" He took another step forward and she jumped back. Her eyes darted to the side, aware that Thedamaine was close by. "Go ahead, cry for help. They'll always save you."

"Please back away." She was firm, using the courage inside her but he didn't move.

"Oh, I get a warning this time. I'll give you one shot; trust me, you will not catch me off guard again." She tried move around him suddenly, but he blocked her. "No, no, he won't come for you. Your boyfriend is downtown; my men are distracting him, and they just told him you've run away."

"Your men?" She asked, humouring him.

"Some followers with a common goal."

"Following who?"

"Not you. Not your father. You think you're above it all, with the whole population on your side ready to do as you command. They call you *princess* and treat you like royalty but not me. Not us. You deserve to be taken down a peg or two. You are not better than us and we will expose you as the failing fraud you are."

"That's enough now. Let me go." Rooted to the spot, afraid any movement will invoke violence, her voice began to crack. Was he bluffing? Was Thedamaine still there, at the front of the building? Or was she alone? If she called for help, would she be saved or punished?

"You failed us, *Princess*. Your people died under your watch. What are you going to do about it? You're not fit to rule us any more than your dying father. We will all die if your family remains in power. This is all your fault."

"We are doing everything we can."

"No, you're not!" He screamed at her and spun on the spot, backing away from her. If Thedamaine was still there, he would have heard that and checked on her, but nobody came. If she ran, he could catch her. She could not see a weapon on his person but that would not stop him. She was not particularly strong, but she was fast, and she would need a head start to get to safety. If only she had brought her sword or dagger with her, something to give her an edge.

"What good are you doing?" She asked, aggressively, finding her courage. "My soldiers are fighting it; you are cowering from it. I hide in my Manor; you hide in your homes. You're no better than me."

"You're safe! We're not! The beast is your family's fault."

"Then why does it attack the village and not the Manor? Where my family lives? If my family binds the beast to this place then why does it not come for us?"

"Because you cower behind those walls! Come down from your fortress, let it take its revenge and it will stop."

"What makes you so sure?" She asked, taking a step forward.

"Only one way to find out." His hands reached out and lunged for her, Evangeline bent her knees, dodging his lunge and straightened up like a bolt, ramming her head into his chin. It hurt her just as much as him as she felt her teeth smash together. Quickly, she kneed him in the groin, but he grabbed her leg before she could turn and run. As she hopped to steady herself, she jabbed Nicholas in the throat. Gasping for air, the shock of it stunned him for a moment, just long enough to free her leg.

She turned to run but was immediately grabbed from behind, a dirty hand covering her mouth and pulling her out of the alley and around the back of the building, hiding from view. She was thrown against the wall, her head smacking the brickwork. Through her blurring vision, she could only make out Nicholas' scars.

Evangeline struggled against him, he could not cover her mouth and hold both her hands at the same time, though he tried. He smacked her head against the wall three more times before she stopped struggling. With his body completely pressed against her own, she was pinned up against the wall, the stench of stale body odour leaking into her nostrils. With one large hand finally managing to hold both of her own up above her head, he slowly started removing his hand covering her mouth.

"If you scream I will smash your head into the wall until your skull cracks open and I can spit on your brain."

She nodded and Nicholas removed his hand from her mouth, grabbing hold of each of her wrists and holding them both up above her. His feet were planted strongly on top of her own, his pelvis and torso pinning hers against the wall. He was not looking at her, if he were, she would immediately spit in his eyes and head-butt him. Instead, his mouth was at her ear, his breath on her neck, reeking of port and blood.

"I should sacrifice you to the beast and then we'll all be free, but we have time. We have a month until it feeds again, and I can do whatever I feel like in that time."

"Please don't do this." She was whispering, her eyes slowly leaking and unable to stop it. "Do you want money? I will pay you whatever you want."

"Does it look like I want money?"

"Everyone wants money."

"Do you really think you can buy your way out of this?"

"You can have whatever you want. You can travel far away from here, from the beast, and start a new life with all that you wanted."

"I want to see you get what you deserve."

Nicholas rearranged himself again, grasping both of her wrists in one of his own hands. She struggled against him, writhing and jerking against his strength.

"Please don't. No. No!" She shouted through her struggle and he smashed her head against the wall again, she fell limp. Dizzy, sick and tired. Her lack of struggle loosened his grip ever so slightly and that was enough to yank her left hand free. She immediately jammed her fingers into his eyes and pressed into the soft eyeballs. Nicholas screamed as he pulled his head back as far as it could go. His free hand waved blindly at her head and caught on her hair which he yanked downwards. She kept pushing her fingers in his eyes and, as he tried to wriggle free, his feet slid off hers but before she could knee him in the groin again, he used his weight and momentum to swing her over his hip and throw her to the ground. The air left her body at once and she struggled to breathe but she jabbed his throat again, kneed his groin and punched his jaw as hard as she could, as quickly as she could.

He was off of her. She scrambled to her feet but jumped back as his hand reached for her ankle. She stomped on it hard. As he rolled with the pain, she took off finally and ran.

She got what she wanted. She wanted a run. She wanted to feel the wind in her hair, and she got it.

Outside the tanner, a man was beginning to attach a small cart to a black and white horse. Evangeline ran past the man, bumping into him and knocking him down, stopping him from attaching the cart. She jumped on the man, using the momentum to reach the stirrups and threw herself up and onto the horse, galloping away.

"Oi!" The man shouted. "She just robbed me!"

Evangeline did not stop. She galloped hard through the village, causing a few accidents and several injuries but she did not stop.

As she burst through the Manor doors, she collapsed into Thedamaine's arms. Unable to walk through the shock, he carried her to the infirmary, roaring at the doctors to help, screaming to the other knights to go out and search for the culprit. She awoke with a start in the infirmary bed, gripping tightly the forearm of the person who woke her.

"Evangeline, shush. It's fine. You're in the Manor infirmary. You're safe."

"Felicity." Evangeline exhaled and laid back down.

"Are you going to tell me what happened?"

"I was attacked, let's leave it at that."

"No, we need more. Who attacked you? Why? We need to bring them to justice. Evangeline, Sir Thedamaine is furious, if you tell him he will-"

"Kill him, I know." Evangeline hardly stopped to think about the consequences of her actions but when her mind told her not to do something, that was usually a good sign that she should not do it. She thought about what Nicholas had said to her, about his men, the followers. If she executed him, who knows what would happen? She needed the people on her side and murdering one of their own would be the straw that broke the camel's back. She had already failed at preventing deaths in the attack, she was on thin ice and had to think before she acted.

"Evangeline, are you listening to me?"

"What?"

"Is there anything you can tell me?"

"Fine, but you have to keep this to yourself, promise me?"

"I promise, go on."

"He said something that stuck with me."

"Who's he?"

"Don't. Just listen. He said that the beast is our family's fault and that if we came down from the Manor and sacrificed ourselves to it, then it would stop."

"Do you believe that?"

"Well, in a way, yes. When I was in Taren's cellar, I was in the village not the Manor that night. It could have attacked anyone in town, but it chose us, because I was there."

"It could be a coincidence."

"It chose us out of everyone in town that night. It cannot be a coincidence."

"So, what if it is true. What's your angle? Is your plan to sacrifice yourself to stop it?"

"No." Evangeline thought things over. "We just need to find out why it is bound to our family. It cannot be mother, it attacked before she was murdered, and it would have stopped when she died."

"She must be involved somehow. Too many threads link back to her."

"All I know is we need the shamans to come back to town. I need answers from them. Zorya, too."

"Ok, fine, we wait for the shamans to appear, we wait for father and Zorya to return, what do we do in the meantime? What are we going to do about the man who attacked you?"

"I do not think it is a good idea to do anything right now."

"Are you serious? Why not?"

"Just humour me, please. It's a delicate situation and I don't want to tip the scales."

"I have no idea what you mean."

"Promise me you will carry a weapon with you at all

132

times? Taren can provide you with a dagger of sorts, or our weaponsmith," Evangeline corrected, seeing the discomfort flash on Felicity's face. "I do not know what is going on with you and Taren, but you need to figure it out because you are acting weird, *he's* acting weird. I barely see him anymore. Look, I don't care what it is just protect yourself."

Felicity did not answer but nodded in agreement and left Evangeline alone to her thoughts, her memories and nightmares.

CHAPTER 18.

"Just let me think!" She had been training for hours, now exhausted and beaten, she couldn't think straight. As she peeked over the hay bale she was cowered behind, she was hit on the head by a large potato, two more missed her along with a rotten tomato and apple. Thedamaine stood with his entourage of squires with barrels full of various things to throw at her. Thedamaine's training was the best; Taren sharpened her melee skills but Thedamaine tested her brain.

"You must not think! You must know!"

"I'm stuck, I cannot get free. It's not a fair fight." She hated herself for saying that.

"Life's not fair, adapt and overcome it. When life cheats; you cheat!"

Evangeline was lost in thought when her vision suddenly focused on the hay bale and the string holding it together. Quickly, she drew her dagger from her new ankle strap and cut one of the strings. Before it fell apart she flung it across the courtyard and a rain of straw blinded the bombardment. Darting to the left, she slid across the floor, low to the ground. She took cover behind the well, then the chicken coop and then the other hay bale before she did the same thing. The straw covered their line of sight and she turned tail and bolted through the doors back into the Manor. Keeping low to the ground to avoid being seen out the windows, she ran around the courtyard and burst through the doors right behind Thedamaine and his 'army'. With a kick to his legs, she held her dagger under Thedamaine's chin with her left hand and pulled off his helmet with the right.

"Hay."

Half of the squires burst into laughter, the others cursed and moaned.

"She cheated!"

"She's not supposed to leave the courtyard!"

"When life cheats, you cheat." Evangeline echoed.

"Lady Evangeline wins this match. Game over, boys."

They quickly dispersed in a chorus of whines, laughs and tired yawns. They had been throwing objects for hours. Evangeline withdrew from Thedamaine, feigning a struggle to put her blade back in its sheath.

"You scared me half to death!" He joked. "I did not expect that at all."

"Is that so?"

"Honest." He held his hand over his heart.

"That was a hard one." She said, rubbing her head where the potato hit her.

"The lesson or the potato?"

"Both!" She hit his arm playfully and they burst out into loud laughter. "When is the next lesson?" She asked, a little more seriously.

"Evangeline, these training sessions will not stop the nightmares."

The smile dropped from her face, her arms wrapped around herself and she turned her back to Thedamaine. Evangeline barely slept before but now, when she closed her eyes or someone touches her when she is not expecting it, she relives the moment. The sweating, the heavy breathing, the pounding heartbeat, the sheer panic that rises up inside her like a volcano; it was all too much.

She needed to do something.

Her mother's dagger now hung at her waist and her ankle strap hid her new blade. She no longer ran off alone, terrified she would be attacked once more. She was becoming afraid of the villagers as well. Nicholas had sewn the seed in her that there were people that wanted her, and her family overthrown or dead. She did not feel safe. These training sessions were the only thing that made her feel better, at least for a short moment.

"Have I ever told you about my mother?" Thedamaine asked. He sat down on the yew tree bench and leant forward, his elbows on his thighs.

"No." Evangeline took a seat next to him and listened, curious.

"She suffered through a lot of trauma. Nightmares, panic attacks, she had them all. She was an incredibly unstable woman. My father was a knight like me and was often away on duty. Growing up I thought I chose to become a knight to honour my father and follow in his footsteps but eventually I came to realise that I only chose that life to get away from my mother."

Evangeline tried to watch Thedamaine's face, but he was fixated on the floor ahead, still leaning over.

"It was awful. The hallucinations, the visions, the voices, the mood swings, the violence; I could not take it anymore and so every chance I got I left."

"The visions?" Evangeline whispered to herself, Thedamaine did not hear.

"I hated being around her, so I avoided her. I had not seen her for just under two years when I got word that my father had died. He did not survive the Siege of Blackfire, and I had to return to inform her. When I got there, I found her dead."

"Was she murdered?" Evangeline asked, hoping to follow a new thread; the similarities were piling up.

"I don't know. The cause of death was never determined, but when I found her; she had clawed her own eyes out."

"Holy hell. To stop the visions?" She asked.

"Yes. That is what I think."

Evangeline and Felicity were forbidden to see their mother's corpse when she died. Felicity always believed that was the root of Evangeline's conspiracy, she never had closure, but Evangeline began to think that perhaps they were shielding them. Preventing them from seeing the gruesome end to their mother. If Thedamaine's mother was also a Bridge, saw the spirit world just like her mother, perhaps they both died the same way?

"So why did you come to serve a family with someone just like your mother? Did you not have a choice?"

"No, I chose to come here. I was supposed to serve the Ashton family but when I heard the rumours about your mother, I transferred here."

"But why? How could you be around my mother? She must have reminded you of yours?"

"It was a way to right my wrongs."

"You've always been a protector."

"That's the point: I didn't protect her. I didn't save her. I neglected her."

"You can't save everyone, Theo."

"I'll sure as hell try." He finally looked at Evangeline, leaning back against the tree and smiled at her. "I'll learn from my mistakes and protect the ones I care about."

Evangeline rested her head against the tree, the tiredness from the training creeping up on her. In an impulse move, she placed her hand on Thedamaine's. He looked down at it and then at her.

"Evangeline!" Somebody was calling her name from across the courtyard. Evangeline jerked upright, the sudden sound and call of her name startling her. She snatched back her hand from Thedamaine and grasped her dagger, ready. She heard the doors swing open and slam, the footsteps smacking against the stone. It was Felicity. She was running across the courtyard to them both while Cadmael and a knight that Evangeline could not place stood just inside the Manor, watching Felicity.

"What is it?" Evangeline asked, afraid of the answer.

"Good news!" Felicity answered, almost bouncing with joy, "father's dove has returned."

The dove was a symbol to inform the household that the Lord and Lady were soon returning home. Usually signifying that they would return within the week. Evangeline shared her sister's joy and requested an audience with the household at once.

"This is excellent news," Evangeline announced after her speech, "we shall all pray for his, *their*, safe and quick return. You all know your duties. Dismissed."

The room emptied quickly and as usual, Cadmael and Sir Thedamaine remained behind. They sat at the long table on the dais, waiting for her to join them. Felicity took a seat as well, joined by her handmaiden, Mary and Sir Morgan, who had taken up the personal guard on Felicity. Aria was still away downtown, grieving for her family, preparing for the funeral, handling the tailoring shop and her life without her parents. Cadmael had pushed to recruit a new handmaiden and Evangeline cursed him outright.

Neither Evangeline nor Felicity were listening to Cadmael's lecture. Felicity's mind was too busy going through the million questions she needed to ask her father and Zorya. Evangeline was bored and had been carving a tiny hole in the dais table with the tip of her blade. Once she had enough, she stabbed the table with a grin on her face after making everyone jump.

"That's quite enough for today, Cadmael. I have things to do. You are dismissed." She waited for him to bow and leave the room before addressing the others at the table. "I want to celebrate," she announced. "Everyone here is invited to an intimate dinner and drinks with me tonight." She looked at Thedamaine. "Drinking is not optional." She smirked at him.

Evangeline often ate alone but she wanted to celebrate her father's imminent return in a way only the Lady of the Manor could. She chose to host the dinner in the Upper Dining Room, the smallest of all banquet rooms but, by far, her favourite. It was called the Homestead by Evangeline and Felicity for its cosy and warming atmosphere and burgundy tones in the decoration. The scorching, full wall fireplace filled the room with a sleepy heat, the other wall was covered by an elaborate tapestry depicting the brave knights in battle against the beast. It was well designed, the beast in great detail. After seeing the beast up close, she praised the work; the ram horns, wolf skull, furry body, long claws; the beast monstrosity clear as day in front of her. The knights were battling it with spears and swords, shields and fire. Evangeline knew from her briefings with the guard that fire was the only thing that kept it at bay. When she and Taren took refuge in the Manor, the trebuchet's burning firebomb was the thing that drove it away and from the look of the tapestry, the beast was retreating from the growing flames. Fire did not stop it, of course, but it was the furthest they had come. All they could hope for is to slow it down. Evangeline vowed one day she would have this tapestry removed and replaced by a new one depicting her family's victory.

Evangeline was studying this tapestry when her entourage entered the room. She smiled at the sight of her friends dressed finely for her. Felicity wore her favourite red fur-trimmed gown that she loved to stroke, inadvertently matching Evangeline's black lace gown with the red corset. Mary's simple emerald gown seemed to be the most elaborate gown she owned, still a nice change from the scruffy handmaiden gowns she was used to.

Sir Thedamaine and Sir Morgan surprised Evangeline the most. Sir Morgan, a newly appointed knight, who possibly struggled to grow a beard, looked his age outside of his armour. Squires became knights at twenty-one, so he was the same age as Evangeline but with the loosely fitted garments, fresh face and the expression of a startled cat, he looked significantly younger.

Evangeline saw Thedamaine and had to look twice to take in the sight. An elegant gentleman that could be passed off as a king. The majority of knights seemed much smaller when out of their armour but Thedamaine remained muscular and brawny, Evangeline suspected he still wore his light armour underneath his suit just in case. She could not stop smiling and struggled to keep her composure; taken aback at this complete change.

Felicity and Mary sat down immediately, breaking bread and pouring drinks. The kitchen maids had set out a nice spread for them and it was waiting for them, the two knights took their place by the door watching.

"Sir Thedamaine, Sir Morgan, I have invited you to dine with us, as friends. You may have noticed Sirs Morris and Beckett outside should we need them but please sit down, you are my guests tonight."

The knights sat down opposite each other and remained just as still and tense as normal. Evangeline looked around the room, nursing a chalice of wine as Felicity passed around the bottle. A Ravenhill family shield and ceremonial swords hung on the wall between the two large windows on one side and a large metal Raven with a rose in its mouth was mounted on the other. Evangeline smiled at this.

Finally taking her seat next to Thedamaine and opposite Felicity, she filled her now empty chalice with the good wine she requested from the cellar. The kitchen maids were dismissed, she only wanted her friends in the room with her. The candles on the table were lit, melted into old wine bottles and the chandelier was flickering above. The fire covered the room in trembling shadows and the sun was beginning to set, she could not help but grin.

"Care for some wine, gentlemen?" She held the bottle between the knights next to her. They shook their heads in protest. "Please, you are off duty, when was the last time you had any fun?"

"What is this word, *fun*?" Sir Morgan grinned, elbowing Felicity who grinned at him.

"Is this new training?" Thedamaine added.

"Yes!" Evangeline laughed. "Training is in session; you better learn quickly!" She filled their chalices.

"*Please* teach us how to have fun, Evie." Felicity held her hands together in a prayer and Evangeline threw a bread roll at her head which bounced onto the floor.

"I could have eaten that."

"Here's another one."

The next roll fell straight into the fire as Felicity had moved her head out of the way in time. The room laughed loudly and began to eat. Evangeline gorged herself on boar, mushroom pies, spiced pears, vegetable potage, cod, and knot bread, drunk enough already to tolerate the noise of eaters.

Evangeline and Thedamaine reached for the honey cakes at the same time and knocked their hands together, Thedamaine retracted his hand and let her take one first but she insisted.

"Did you hear about the frog prank, Lady Evangeline?" Mary asked, pulling apart a bread roll.

"I did hear about that, yes. I approve, it was a good one."

"What will be the next prank?"

They looked toward Evangeline, but she remained quiet, thinking. "I have not thought of anything," she admitted. "I have nothing planned, you're the ingenious one."

"It's your turn next."

"Technically it's the twin's turn to retaliate, then it will be Evangeline."

"If they have not acted already."

"I do not want to think of those two." Evangeline lifted her chalice, "to Lord Horus Ravenhill, may he return safe and sound."

The rest of them lifted their chalices and sounded off to Lord Ravenhill's name.

"To father!" Evangeline and Felicity shouted.

By the time the sun had fully set, the food savaged and the fire starting to simmer down, the table was comfortably drunk. Evangeline spilled some wine as she fumbled with the bottle trying to fill up her chalice. Giggling, she buried her face in her hands, leaning into Thedamaine; too drunk to stay sitting up and too heavy to move. Felicity picked up the wine bottle and moved it from Evangeline's reach. She felt Thedamaine's hand on her arm, holding her up and grinned.

Felicity was speaking to her, she was saying words, and her mouth was moving. Thedamaine's grip adjusted and she leant back more, she was spinning, better to lean on him then fall on the floor. Felicity was still speaking to her and Thedamaine, he was talking too, his chest vibrated deeply with his words and she bounced as he laughed. Mary was wearing Sir Morgan's helmet and it swallowed her head up, balancing haphazardly as she moved it away from Felicity who tried to take it and wear it herself.

She was so tired. She just wanted to sleep but it was all so funny, she couldn't sit up. There was a warmth around her that kept her safe and made her so sleepy. Feeling the numbness all throughout her body, collecting in her hands and feet, the weight of it pulled her down. The swaying wouldn't stop, she just wanted to sleep. Just to sleep.

"Evie, wake up." She groaned and swayed and fell to the ground.

"I thought you had her?"

"She is heavy. I thought you had her?"

"You were helping me. You know I cannot do this alone, it's inappropriate."

"You could literally carry her by yourself and you are always inappropriate, why is it different now?"

Evangeline felt a support give and she slumped and stumbled.

"You are on your own."

"What? You are going to leave her? She needs protection."

"I am only here helping you bring her to her room because you asked. I am in no condition to protect anyone, not while intoxicated. Once she is in her room, you will get her into bed, and I will call the next guard to watch her."

"You cannot switch off, even when drunk."

"And you are a mean drunk, where is this anger coming from?"

"Help me with this door, please?" Evangeline fell completely to the floor.

"You dropped her. You are not very good at this; she is going to get hurt."

"I asked for help, Thedamaine!"

Evangeline heard a door open and was lifted onto her jelly legs again. The double support was back, and she was lifted with ease and landed with a soft bounce.

"Take care of her, I am off duty."
"You are never off duty, Thedamaine, not for this one."
Evangeline fell hard into a drunken sleep.

CHAPTER 19.

Cedarwood and pine, lilies and lavender. Crackling wood and tinkling wind chimes. The sight and smells took Evangeline's breath away. She did not expect much from the shaman camp and was shocked to see its beauty. Lit up by candles melted to the tree branches above, or the handful of campfires outside each of the highly decorative caravans. Even the tents looked inviting. One word came to mind when she gazed around the camp: nature. Dried bunches of flowers and herbs hung from string zigzagging through the site. Animal bones and skeletons were arranged in ornate displays. Effigies stood guard around the boundary of the camp like watchful sentinels.

The sun was setting, and Evangeline had planned to sleep off the alcohol still lingering from the night before but when Taren appeared with news that he had found the shaman camp, she slipped her guard and abandoned all plans in order to follow him.

"I do not like this place." Taren said, still with the pout on his lips he had since he appeared in her room that evening.

"Why? I think it looks great. Oh, hello little dog." A scruffy tan hound came up to her and sniffed her shin, she petted its head, and it ran off.

"I do not know why you wanted to come here. These people are all frauds and con artists. Do *not* believe what they tell you."

"You're free to leave, Taren. Thank you for bringing me here but if you don't want to stay, you can go."

"Trying to get rid of me already? Why don't you want to spend time with me?"

"What did I say? You don't want to be here so you can leave but I am staying."

Taren was in a terrible mood and it was starting to annoy Evangeline. They hadn't spent much time together recently and she felt guilty that she did not even *feel* like seeing him. She did not invite him to her celebratory feast, and it occurred to her that perhaps she had hurt his feelings.

However, Evangeline was here for a reason and that reason was to speak to someone and get answers. That was her priority. There was not many people around, which surprised her. In the centre of the camp was a large circular tent with thick supports and a large light source within. She could hear music and people inside, so she moved toward it. Taren pulled her wrist back, stopping her.

"Let's go in this one," he said, pulling her toward the closest caravan on the left.

"What? Why not the tent?"

"This one is closer." He did not wait for her and entered.

"Wait, Taren. What are you doing?"

"It's fine, come on."

Evangeline followed him to the caravan. There was a long rug that ran down the steps and created a path and entry way to the caravan. Potted plants and flowers decorated the steps and a tall vase full of shiny black stones sat by the door.

Taren knocked on the open door and a small, stocky woman appeared from behind a curtain. She was wearing a ram skull atop her head and a necklace of bird skulls. Her short, greying black hair cut roughly, stuck out alongside the magpie feathers.

"Come in, come in." She took hold of Taren's wrist and Evangeline's hand and pulled them both inside.

"What can I do for you two? Love spell? Unrequited love? Reconciliation? No, not for you two. Let me see, let me take you in." She was circling Taren like a vulture and her prey. "Oh, *you* need our help. You've got a sickness in you, boy. Only we can clear that up. For fifteen coppers you'll be good as new."

"Girl!" She suddenly locked eyes with Evangeline and appeared at her side in an instant. Evangeline stepped back instinctively, aware of the dagger at her waist. "You've got bad energy weighing you down, this effects every relationship you have and will ever have. You will never be free or truly happy without our extensive treatment. Only six instalments of twenty gold coins and you'll reach your full potential."

"You have *got* to be kidding?" Evangeline asked, it was

clear the shaman was a fraud, just like Taren said.

"Oh, no. I see it now. The smoke is clearing." The shaman went on, looking back and forth between Taren and Evangeline. "Oh, this is bad." She stood closer to Evangeline, inspecting her eyes and Evangeline frowned but held her ground. "Your blood is cursed." Evangeline's eyebrow twitched and her heart pounded just a little faster. "Oh, fate has a plan for *you*!" The shaman grinned hungrily.

"She's not cursed!" Taren spat. "You're just trying to manipulate us into giving you money, but it doesn't work!"

"Ah, but boy, you already know about *your* curse, you know all about that. You can feel it and I can see it."

"So, now he's cursed too?" Evangeline asked sarcastically, starting to regret coming.

"There is an evil inside of you, a great vengeance. But do not worry! We can fix that. We are curing a man right now, same infliction. We've had him here for several new moons now."

"And you still haven't fixed him?"

"It's a difficult curse. You'll know soon enough."

"So, if we don't pay you, he'll be cursed?"

"He's already cursed. Soon it will take over." She moved closer to him. "But you know that. You can already feel it."

"I do not know what you are talking about." Taren said in a monotone, looking to Evangeline.

"So, what is his curse?" Evangeline asked, humouring the shaman.

"I'm *not* cursed!" Taren shouted.

"Can you not see it, girl? It's clear as day. Oh, this is a funny one. But I promise I can remove it, for a price."

"You just said you haven't cured the other man yet."

"He came to us too late, if we start work on you now, boy, it will all be over."

"You're lying."

"Of course, she's lying, Taren. There's no curse."

"Do you want me to tell her, boy?"

"Tell me what?" Evangeline was growing tired of this charade, her patience thinning. She was about to leave when another woman blocked her path, appearing at the door to the caravan.

"Willow! Get out. This is my space." Without a word, the stocky shaman left the caravan with a smirk on her face, lingering on Taren.

The new shaman girl walked around the table in the caravan and took a seat. She was tall; even sat down, her head towered over the long-backed chair and her long red hair hung at her hips.

"I apologise for Willow's rude presence. I did wonder why all the birds suddenly stopped singing. Please pay no attention to her, she is not like the rest of us."

"Is she not a shaman?"

"Oh, she is but she represents the very worst of our kind. They give our people a bad name. You have most likely formed an opinion of us based on people like her. But enough about that, my name is Sienna how can I be of service to you?"

Evangeline looked around. There was not much to see, it was a bit like an apothecary. Ingredients, herbs, plants, animal pelts, bones, gemstones and other things dotted about among the silks and tapestries. Taren leant on the door frame watching Evangeline with a deadpan face, but Evangeline ignored his presence. She thought about what she would say and ask but she was just curious about everything and did not know where to start.

The shaman, Sienna, was a little older than Evangeline, perhaps Thedamaine's age. She was holding a shiny black rock in her hand, like the ones in the vase by the door. Her other hand waved the smoke above the candle beside her.

"What do you do here?" Evangeline asked finally, easing in slowly.

"How about a taste of what we can offer?" Sienna put the rock down and pulled out a deck of cards. "Have you heard of tarot cards?"

"Really? This is what you do? You're going to tell our fortune with a deck of cards?"

"I can give insight on your past, present or future, or all three. The cards will represent and signify things related to your timeline. This I do for free. Do you want to see?"

"Why not?" Evangeline said, taking a seat on the other side of Sienna's table. Taren stood by the door, inspecting a wolf skull hanging from the ceiling of the caravan.

Sienna began shuffling the deck, as she did she watched Taren, never breaking her gaze with a stoic expression. Evangeline noticed this and could not help but wonder why.

146

"Please shuffle the deck," she asked, now addressing Evangeline. "You need to touch them for them to work and it also shows you that these cards are random."

"The cards may be random but the meanings you make up on the spot."

Neither Evangeline nor Sienna replied. Evangeline returned the cards once she had shuffled and peeked at a few to be sure. Sienna took the cards. On the left she flicked three cards face down onto the table, then three cards in the centre and three cards on the right. She held her hand out over each pile.

"Past, present and future. Three cards each. Shall we start with the past?"

"The easy one, yes. Everyone knows her past."

Sienna flicked over the first card on the left. Evangeline immediately saw the skull head and bloody picture. She laughed out loud.

"Death?" She snorted in derision, unable to believe the audacity. "Right out the gate. Now that is an easy one. Taren who has died in my past? Do you know of anyone?"

"Well, no I don't. No one significant in your life has died."

"The death card signifies *change*." Sienna stressed, drawing their attention back. "It simply represents that a stage in life is coming to an end and from this ending new experiences will evolve."

"Okay, fine. My childhood came to an end. Next one."

"The Queen of Swords." Sienna announced as she turned over the second card with the redheaded queen holding a sword upright. "There is a focus on sadness."

"Of course there is sadness in her past. This is ridiculous." Taren remained standing, running his fingers through his scruffy hair in frustration.

"There is also perception." Sienna continued, ignoring him. "This card represents widowhood, female sadness, embarrassment, absence, mourning, separation and intelligence."

"Wow, all that?" Evangeline was being sarcastic but could not ignore the curiosity.

"Queen of Pentacles. Reversed." The third card was upside down.

"Another queen, is that good?" Evangeline asked.

"The reversed queen signifies evil, suspicion, suspense, fear and mistrust."

"Not a good card, then?"

"What a shocker. Already sentencing you to death."

"This is my past, Taren. She's not dooming me yet. Lighten up, now we get to see my present."

"The Fool. You are at the beginning of your journey. It is important to trust your own judgement and plan for the future but do so wisely. This is not a good time to make binding commitments." She turned over the second card in the present pile. "The Devil. This card represents limitations, powerlessness, violence, force, failure, disaster, death and ominous events."

"That's obviously about the beast. How profound!"

"Enough, now, Taren! Shut it. Stop interrupting, you're getting on my last nerve."

"You must reflect on the situation, ask others for advice and work towards solving difficulties cautiously."

"I like to think I have been doing that. I have been consulting with the court when I make decisions. What's the third card?"

"The Tower. Reversed."

"Another upside-down card. This can't be good."

"This card in its reversed position represents oppression, imprisonment, tyranny and ongoing depression."

"I was right."

"There is a fear of change and a need to avert disaster. You may feel dominated by someone or something and feel powerless to fight back." Evangeline heard Taren tut behind her, she shushed him before he could speak.

"You should concentrate on the future and on ways to redress the balance of power. This card indicates that the time has come for a new start."

Evangeline smiled. She was now a believer and was eager to learn what her future cards held. "So, my present is the beginning of my journey and I should trust myself but also ask for help and advice as there is death, violence and failure. There is also oppression, tyranny and depression and so I need a new start?"

"Do you wish to see your future cards?"

"Of course."

"Two of Wands. This card indicates a need for

independence and solitude. It is about planning, decisions and taking risks. You may feel the need for separation in order to feel in control of your destiny. You should assert your independence and not allow others to deny your freedom."

"She does that now, anyway. Don't give me that look, Evie, you're already extremely independent and love your solitude. You've already separated from *me*."

"What is with you today? You're very aggressive *and* needy; it's not a good look on you. Please, carry on."

"Wheel of Fortune. Reversed. This represents bad luck, uncertainty and decline. You may find changes occurring in one area have a negative effect on another. However out of chaos a new start will emerge."

"So, a lot of change and separation in my future? And the last card?"

"The Chariot. There will be a time of solitude and questioning oneself. This card represents change, providence, and triumph. You must take control of the situation while remembering the importance of compromise."

Evangeline looked at the nine cards individually, going over the meanings and what they represented. She wanted to memorise them, to prove them right or wrong. Either way, she wanted to know if it was true.

Sienna brushed a delicate finger over each of the cards in a single swipe. "Together these cards tell us that you are experiencing life-changing events that will have long-term effects. There are important lessons that you must pay attention to in order to progress and succeed.

"That was interesting. Thank you." Evangeline smiled and Sienna blinked at her then almost smiled back.

"You have questions." Evangeline could not be sure if that were a question or a statement but either way she agreed with Sienna.

"Can you tell me what a shaman is?" Evangeline asked, "please?"

"My people hold the gifts to wander between the two realms. Our world and the next. We have the gift of sight and can see the spirit world just as clear as the world you see."

"How?" Evangeline asked. "Are you born with these gifts?"

"Yes we are, but it takes practise to see it clearly. It is not like normal sight, at first it is a sense, a feeling and over time we come to see what is really there."

"What do you do with this sight?"

"We ferry the dead, heal body and soul and retrieve trapped souls."

"How do you do it?"

"Through rituals, incantations and ceremonies."

"Can you see the future?"

"The future is indefinite, ambiguous and unclear. Multiple strands of fate make it almost impossible to see what the client wants to see; therefore, we prefer to stay away from divination as much as we can."

"They say you put curses on people, use magic and witchcraft against us, is that true?"

"We are a proud people. We have the gifts of the spirit world and only those who study its power will be granted the gifts of a shaman. But with any power there are those who seek to use it for themselves. My people have rules and binding laws and those who break those laws are punished dearly."

"How?"

"That is not for you to know."

"Fine." Evangeline did not press the subject. "So those who are born with the sight can see the spirit world but if they do not choose to study it they are not granted magic?"

"If they do not embrace the gifts it could have disastrous effects for them. Like your mother encountered."

Evangeline saw out of the corner of her eye Taren stand up straight. He was no longer leaning on the doorframe pouting but alert and interested. She, herself swallowed and counted to five in her head to compose herself.

"She was a Bridge." Evangeline confirmed. Taren stepped forward slightly.

"You know more than you tend to admit. Why not ask the right questions? You may get the answers you came to seek."

Heavy, metal footsteps climbed the steps to the caravan and in the doorway stood a tall knight. Sienna sprung upwards and Evangeline got to her feet, assuming the knight was there to bring her back to the Manor, but it was nobody that Evangeline recognised, none that worked in the Manor.

The music flowing through the campsite had stopped, all muffled voices suddenly silenced and even the forest chorus had ceased. The knight stood there bold and brash. His helmet shielding his face from emotion so Evangeline could not read him.

Something was wrong.

Dressed in combat plate armour, his gauntleted hand grasping the helm of his longsword, he watched Sienna. Nobody said a word. For a moment time stood still in a four-way standoff, each afraid to make the first move. At the sound of a woman's scream everybody moved at once. The knight unsheathed a dagger at his side, deciding against the sword in these close quarters. He lunged for Sienna who recoiled back, cowering from the attack. Evangeline leapt forward between the two and was forced to stop the blade with whatever she could; her own hand halted the dagger in the air for she was too slow to unsheathe her own and had to act. The blade cut into her skin as she pushed back, blood already bathing her arm. At the same time her other hand pushed Sienna back further out of harm's way and Taren sprang into action too, ramming his full weight and momentum into the knight, colliding into the iron pole securing the caravan. The impact knocked the knights helmet off just as he hit the floor with a sickening crack. He did not get up.

Taren did not stop to take it in, he grabbed both the girl's arms and dragged them out of the caravan into a flurry of smoke, flames and panic. The campsite was on fire, knights on horseback mowed down shamans here and there. Bodies trampled by horses, some of whom were still alive and crawling on the floor as the hooves crushed and flattened their bones.

"What is happening?" Sienna squealed, her hands pulling her hair.

"Why are they doing this?" Evangeline could not wrap her head around what she was witnessing. These were her family's knights committing this atrocity but why? Under whose authority?

A knight grabbed a yielding woman by her hair, pulling her to her feet and unsheathed his sword in a large swing, savouring it, Evangeline bolted toward him. She yanked his sword arm back hard and twisted it. His other hand dropped the woman and Evangeline yelled at her to run, she scrambled away. The knight knocked Evangeline to the ground easily and kicked her before she got to her feet, then pursued the fleeing woman. Taren skidded to the floor beside Evangeline and helped her up. He prevented her from taking out her dagger, they both knew it was useless against the armoured knights and her injured hand had crippled her.

"We *must* get out of here." Taren led the way but was met by flaming tents, collapsing caravans or murderous knights at every turn."

"Where's Sienna?" Evangeline asked, looking around for her. She had vanished in the smoke, lost in the panic.

"Come on. We have to get to safety!"

"We cannot leave her here! Sienna! Sienna! Where are you?"

"This way!" Sienna forced Evangeline around, grabbing her by the forearm and leading her. Evangeline took Taren's hand with her own, forming a chain to prevent losing one another. The three of them weaved and zigzagged their way through the tornado of tragedy, but something stopped Evangeline.

A small, fenced area housed a handful of horses, each tied up and unable to get free, rearing up in fear. Caravans on each side were up in flames, the fire getting closer to the wooden fence, threatening to lick its way to the trapped animals. Evangeline ran to the fence, slipping Taren's grip who did not want to let her go.

"Evie, *don't!*"

She unlatched the gate and cut the ropes, struggling against her bloody and painful palm. Guiding them away from the heat of the fire that was closing in around them, she got them free, Taren and Sienna steering the horses to safety once clear. When the last horse was out of the fence she returned to Taren and Sienna.

"They can't help themselves; somebody has to be there for them!"

"Come on, before you are killed." He took her arm again, holding her close to him.

"They can't hurt me!"

"It's dangerous thinking that way. Now how do we get out?"

"Follow me!" Sienna roared over the chaos. She ran into the fenced area where the horses were stabled and hopped the fence with surprising grace. "Come on!" She pressed, waving them toward her. Taren boosted Evangeline up and over the fence and climbed over after her, rushing to beat the flames creeping up on them. Sienna took them through the tree line. In the darkness and the commotion, it seemed to Evangeline like a random trail through the foliage, but Sienna knew exactly where she was going and finally led them into a clearing with an abandoned ruin of a windmill. They climbed the stairs and took refuge at the top, with a perfect view of the smoking campsite now burning to the ground.

CHAPTER 20.

"Thank you for saving my life." Sienna said as she wrapped Evangeline's bleeding palm with a strip of cloth torn from her own gown.

"Thank you for getting us out of there." Evangeline sat cross legged on the floor of the ruined windmill in front of Sienna as she was bandaged.

"You did not have to save me, or the horses or the other shaman."

Evangeline did not know what to say, it did not occur to her *not* to save them. The shamans had done nothing wrong, nobody deserved what had happened to them and the horses could not save themselves.

"I could not stop it. I swear I had nothing to do with what happened, if I'd had known, I would have done something. I *swear* I was not behind this."

"I believe you."

"Do you know who did this?" Taren finally spoke up, still leaning on the windowsill watching the smoking embers of the camp.

"The Ravenhill family have been at war with my people for many years now."

"But I don't understand. Nothing makes sense. What just happened was completely illegal. It is law that shamans have complete immunity outside the boundary of the village. The mass slaughter and destruction of your camp is an atrocity I do not think my family could have caused. Those *were* Ravenhill knights and with my father and stepmother on their honeymoon nobody had any power to be able to pass that act."

"Does it strike you odd that it happened on the very same day that you visit the camp for the first time? Or that Sir Thedamaine was off duty all day for the first time in months? The only knight close enough to you to have told you this plan?"

Evangeline, listening to Taren's words, got to her feet as Sienna had finished. Taren turned to face her, and Sienna got to her feet too.

"What are you trying to say? That someone conspired behind my back?"

"I'm not saying that."

"Why not? You have this big secret that you are hiding from me."

Taren, startled by Evangeline's words, exhaled briefly. "I don't have a secret."

"You're spying for my stepmother. You admitted it to Felicity. Is she behind this?"

Evangeline stepped back, grasping the wall to steady herself. Lightheaded and heart racing, the realisation had just occurred to her. Threads were coming together. *Nicholas.* Nicholas told her that he had followers who wanted her family out of power. Zorya has Taren and who knows how many others spying on her father but for what reason? It must be to get him out of power. Zorya married him to gain power. Zorya killed her mother so she could become Lady Ravenhill and now she is undermining the Ravenhill name. Undertaking genocide in the Ravenhill name to make Lord Horus Ravenhill and his daughter look bad so the people turn against them. Evangeline knew in her gut that her father would not return from his honeymoon. There would be an '*accident*' on the road. Zorya will return without him. She was sure of it.

Evangeline slumped to the ground in her realisation. Sienna joined her on the floor and placed her thumb and two fingers on Evangeline's forehead, the touch completely calmed Evangeline, as if removing all emotion from her soul.

"What did you do?" Taren asked, noticing her complete overturn of emotion.

"Just calmed her down. Cleared her mind. I specialise in emotions. I can sense them in other people like noise, as if you were shouting them to me."

"Sounds annoying."

"A little. I tend to drown it out, like a noisy crowd."

"Wait, so you can control emotions, too? You just calmed her down."

"Yes. I sense emotions and can manipulate them too." Her

tone changed. "I can also sense when people are lying."

"I wasn't lying."

"Yes you are." Evangeline said, quietly and calm. "You have something you are holding back. Something that is making you irritable and aloof."

"She is correct," Sienna added.

"Why did Zorya ask you to spy on my father? Do you know of the conspiracy to remove my family from power?"

"What? No! I swear."

Evangeline got to her feet and crossed the distance between them. "You're lying."

"No, I'm not. Ask her, I'm not."

"I don't need to ask her. How long have we known each other? How long have we been best friends? I can tell when you're lying. You *know.* You are involved. You're part of the conspiracy."

"Evie, no."

"Stop lying!"

"That's not it."

"Then tell me. Tell me everything. Your side of the story, I want to hear it."

"I can't tell you."

"Why not?"

Taren did not answer. He rubbed his eyes and ran his fingers through his hair, holding his head. Evangeline turned away from him to avoid looking at his quivering eyes welling up.

"He wants to keep you safe." Sienna finally said, both looked at her.

"From what?" Evangeline asked, still avoiding Taren, who did not answer. "This is a complete betrayal that I cannot forgive."

"No."

Evangeline finally turned and faced Taren. Despite the tears and devastation in his eyes, she powered through, fuelled by rage and shock. "Stay away from me and my family."

"Evie, please."

"I want you to leave right now. Get out of my sight and stay away. Go. *Now!"*

Taren ran his fingers through his shaggy hair once more and turned around. He descended down the windmill stairs and Evangeline watched out of the window as he disappeared out of sight and out of her life.

"You are lucky I was here beside you as you made that decision." Evangeline almost forgot Sienna was in the room.

"You kept us calm?"

"I did."

"What I wouldn't do for your gifts. I have trained my whole life to be as stoic as possible but if I were you I would not even have to try. It's an amazing thing."

"You keep surprising me, Lady Ravenhill."

"Why?"

"Your attitude to shamans, your actions, your views. It's against everything I was ever taught. You saved my life; you saved my sister's life." Sienna exhaled a little laugh, "you even saved the horses. They are a currency for my people and are more valuable than you could know." Her tone changed, becoming serious and firm. "Listen to me, my people are sworn to never speak to a Ravenhill. We are forbidden to answer your questions."

"Why? What happened? Why can you not answer my questions?"

"Because that is what you came for. I could foretell your tarot cards because that is not what you wanted but I am forbidden to give you what you want, and you want answers."

"Why are you forbidden?"

"The curse."

"What curse?"

"That is what I cannot tell you."

"Fine. I think I understand. I came to you with a select few questions, you are unable to answer those questions but can answer any others?"

"Correct."

"Being a shaman is complicated."

"It is indeed."

"You have a lot of rules. Many things are forbidden, like blood magic?"

Sienna smiled. Evangeline was trying to pry for information that she was allowed to know. She tried to tiptoe around certain questions, hoping one answer was connected to another.

"Should a shaman practise blood magic they are banished from the community and their souls are branded with evil.

Any shaman that makes a deal with the Darkness and practises this blood magic must pay the ultimate price."

"What price is that?"

"Their soul belongs to the Darkness. A debt that must be paid in full."

"So, a shaman makes a deal with the Darkness, selling their soul in exchange for gifting them the powers of blood magic? The Darkness then comes and collects that soul?"

"That is correct."

"What does that mean for the shaman?"

"Once the debt is paid they will spend eternity in the Abyss."

Evangeline so desperately wanted to ask about the Nil'vetra, but she knew she would not receive an answer. She tried an alternative route. "What is classed as blood magic?"

"Sacrifice, assassination via magic, resurrection, binding, necromancy, sometimes all of these at once."

"Resurrection?"

"Yes. It is possible, although extremely difficult, for a shaman to resurrect a body. As this is blood magic, a sacrifice must be paid in order to bring back the dead."

"What kind of sacrifice?"

"Life. Someone must die for another to live."

Evangeline thought for a moment. There were so many possibilities from this. In frustration, she punched the wall with her injured hand, forgetting the slash. Crying out in pain, she kicked the wall instead, angered at herself and the situation. More questions, no answers. She could feel herself welling up in rage, but it washed away in a current of calm.

"Take it easy." Sienna said in a half whisper.

"You can control emotions without touch?"

"Yes, but it is not as fast or strong."

"Well, that's amazing. I wish I had your gifts."

"I think you are the first Ravenhill to refer to our powers as a gift instead of a curse."

"I do not understand this feud." Evangeline was mainly speaking to herself and, at first, did not notice Sienna's internal struggle but then Evangeline remembered what Sienna said about the curse forbidding her. "You don't understand it either?"

"No." Sienna breathed, her words now a struggle. "I do not agree with my people's beliefs. Everything we know is wrong. Everything that they have done is wrong."

"What have they done?"

Sienna took Evangeline's wrists and looked her in the eye, desperate and scared. "Please do not judge me on my people's actions just like I do not judge you on your mother's."

"Why? What did my mother do?"

"I cannot speak of it."

"Why not? Please you have to tell me something. I want to end it. Let me right her wrongs."

"This is wrong. What they are doing is wrong." Sienna had gotten to her feet and stepped away from Evangeline, now talking to herself. Evangeline listened anyway. "Be careful," Sienna turned back to Evangeline, "what happened at the camp tonight will have terrible repercussions on both sides. This horrific crime will have a vast retaliation."

"What do you mean?"

"I promise I will try to stop it."

"Stop what?"

"If what you have told me is correct and I can tell when people are lying, you wish to end the war between our families and right the wrongs?" Evangeline nodded at Sienna. "Then we are on the same side. I must go back to camp and take stock of what we have lost and see what good I can do."

"I will go with you. I can help you rebuild."

"No. It is too dangerous for you now. Return home and remain safe."

"I promise I will bring whoever's behind this to justice." Evangeline said after a brief hesitation. "I will go back and get to the bottom of this."

"Go now. I sense a danger rising. The shamans are angry. I will be punished for this but good luck."

Evangeline knew it was time to leave, despite being overloaded with questions and confusion. She left with a final apology on behalf of her family and tried to make sense of the evening. Running through the thousands of questions she had.

Evangeline returned to the Manor with an audience waiting for her. News of the attack had reached the household before she did, yet nobody had known where she was, Thedamaine and Felicity smothered her with questions and concern, afraid she had been attacked again and once again without protection. She brushed them off, hoping to get to the bottom of what happened.

Taking a seat at the dais, Felicity and Cadmael joined her at the table, along with her advisory court, Sir Thedamaine taking watch. Before she could begin, the doors burst open and Evangeline's breath caught in her throat. The room thick with tense silence.

He was the last person she expected to see.

CHAPTER 21.

"Father?!"

"Lord Horus? What a surprise. It is good to see you."

"Shut up." Horus entered the room, striding over with rage and purpose, sneering at Cadmael. Felicity was taken aback at how well he looked. The colour had returned to his face, strength straightened his back and a new purpose drove him forward.

"Who authorised the attack on the shaman ca-"

Lord Horus' hand smashed the tabletop shocking everyone. He snapped his head toward Evangeline beside him. His voice low but firm, exactly where Evangeline got the talent from.

"What did I say?" Horus asked rhetorically. Evangeline was stunned into silence. "It is my turn to speak. I will have no interruptions." He was addressing the table now, but his head subtly tilted toward Evangeline. "Under my orders, just after sundown, the shaman camp was burned to the ground."

Evangeline leant forward; mouth open, ready to speak but managed to hold her tongue. She closed her mouth, leant back and crossed her arms, ready to listen.

Felicity tried to make sense of it all. Her father returning early making a seemingly miraculous full recovery. The sudden ferocity and animosity to everyone. This was not the same man who left her, nor was he the same man before his sickness. Zorya was in the room but hardly anyone had noticed her. She stood at the door watching them all, dressed in black as usual and just as pale and beautiful. Nothing seemed out of the ordinary for her. It was just Lord Horus. Felicity searched her father's face for any tell, listening to his words.

"For too long we have been at war with those witches and abominations. They are crimes against nature, a diseased tree that needs culling. The time has come to remove this disease root and stem. They are a curse on this land, and I will stand for it no longer. They come into my home, curse my wife, my family and my land. Well, we fought back, years ago we executed their leader, here in our land, not theirs."

"The beast is *your* fault." Evangeline breathed, just loud enough for the table to hear. Horus stopped his monologue and froze.

"I beg your pardon?" He was still calm but there was no ignoring the rage in his voice.

"You executed their leader? You have committed nothing but atrocities in our family's name. Out of fear. You cowardly scab." Evangeline stood up, the scrape of her chair grating on everyone's ears. "You do not understand their power, so you murder them for it."

"They cursed us!"

"You murdered their leader! Of course, they will retaliate. This is your fault. Everything that has happened. All the deaths are your fault. Yours and mothers. You are both cowards, hiding behind your swords murdering anything that frightens you. You could be studying them, working with them, their powers are a gift that could be shared with us but you're just afraid. You see them as a danger when you should have seen them as an ally."

"They are our sworn enemies."

"Because you made them! You're a disgrace. You burned down their camp and slaughtered their people, breaking your own laws. Your wife's laws. Your knights are sworn to be the champions of the right and the good against injustice and evil but what you have done is an *unjust evil*. They ran their pledged swords through the shaman's hearts in your name and are now stained with evil because of you."

"You were there." Horus stepped forward, closing the gap between him and Evangeline. Felicity could not tell if it was a statement or a question. Either way, it was not good. "You were there! What have you done?!" The entire room exploded into action. Horus grabbed the scruff of Evangeline's dirty cloak and shoved her across the room, slamming her hard against the wall and shaking her violently. Evangeline tried to push him off as Sir Thedamaine and Sir Morgan did the same. Horus' elbow came into contact with Thedamaine, spraying blood as his eyebrow was split open. At the same time, everyone at the table had shot upwards, chairs toppling over and people scrambling. Felicity, afraid of getting hurt, just watched in astonishment as her father successfully managed to brush off both knights, pull back his arm and punch his daughter in the face, knocking her to the ground. For a split moment everyone stopped moving then moved at once. Thedamaine and Felicity were at Evangeline's side. Sir Morgan, Sir Constantine and even Cadmael grabbed Horus and pulled him away, he struggled against them, screaming.

"What have you done? You have doomed us all. You were there. You were there!"

"You're a coward and a thug and you deserve to die!"

"Evangeline!" Felicity cried out, "do not say what you cannot take back."

"Enough!" Horus roared. "That is enough." He repeated in a calmer tone. Zorya was at his side now shushing him with her hand on his cheek.

"Evangeline, you have disobeyed and disrespected me for the last time. You have no idea what dangers you have inflicted on us by visiting that camp. Constantine!" He cried out, Sir Constantine, Horus' personal guard tensed up at attention beside him. "Take Evangeline to her quarters and lock her in. I want her door bolted from the outside and her windows inside to be boarded up. There will be no escape attempts. Felicity too. She will be locked in her own quarters for good measure."

"Felicity did nothing wrong." Evangeline said, calmly yet still quivering with rage and pain.

"Sir Thedamaine. You will not go near her. You shall no longer be Evangeline's guard. You have failed one too many times. Tomorrow you will leave the Manor and your time in my service will come to an end."

"No. Don't do this." Evangeline stood up, crossing the gap once again to her father but Thedamaine pulled her back. "Do not dismiss him. It is not his fault. Do not blame him."

"He was charged with keeping you in the Manor. He failed. He must go."

"Do not dismiss him. *Please*." The last word was a whisper that only Thedamaine heard as he took her other arm in comfort. Evangeline's heart pounded and she could no longer contain herself. She desperately wished for Sienna to be there or to have her powers. She needed something to calm her. Evangeline hated feeling her emotions, it made her look

163

weak and most of the time did not work because the constant repression was pent up and erupted into rage that she could not control. But now, struggling against the pain and shock of being punched by her father, the knowledge of what he has done and now taking away Thedamaine. She could not handle it. She craved to cling to Thedamaine and never let go but afraid any movement would break her composure. She refused to look Thedamaine in the eye, knowing for sure that would break her. She smashed her hands over her eyes to force the tears back in.

Do not cry.

Felicity took Evangeline's hand, but it was torn from her as Constantine grabbed Evangeline and yanked her forward.

"Get her out of my sight." Horus spat. "Lock her in and make sure she cannot get out. Felicity is to be taken to her own quarters and locked in. Thedamaine, you are off duty from here on and will be officially dismissed tomorrow. I want a guard outside their rooms all night long. No one close to them. If they get out, whoever's responsible will be severely punished."

Evangeline kept her eyes on Thedamaine until the last moment. Eventually she was alone. Her window had been boarded up by the carpenters and they finally left her room. The click of the lock on the outside of her door was the last sound she heard.

Finally, she broke down and cried.

CHAPTER 22.

She woke, shivering, in the dark of the night, the autumn wind rattling the windows. She slid out of bed, added another log on the fire and walked over to the window seat, cocooned in her fur blanket. Through the slats that boarded her window, not a single star could be seen through the thick cloud, but the large crescent moon peeked through brighter than usual, bathing the forest in moonlight. Most of her view of the town was blocked by the forest but what she could see was quiet, barely any lights shone at her, it was late, and she was bored.

She went to the door, but it was still locked, putting her ear to the oak and listening, she heard no armour knocking together to indicate a fidgeting knight. She sat back down on the edge of her bed, with nothing to do and nowhere to go, she was useless. There was no way she could go back to sleep now and no way of leaving her room.

Her sobs had tired her out and she fell asleep soon after calming down. Now she was awake; puffy eyed and confused. Felicity had their mother's book so Evangeline could not pass the time reading it. On the dresser were her embroidering patches and Ancestry Compendium, two things that could pass the time, but she did not have the patience for either. She was restless and in pain. Her cut palm was bleeding again and her eye was definitely bruised. Her chest was tight and sore from the knight's kick in the camp and serious fatigue had set in.

In the small antechamber before her bedroom, stood her suit of armour. Once bringing her pride and protection, it now just reminded her of Taren and his betrayal. The short cloak had black leather feathers to tie in with her Ravenhill name, another thing that used to bring her pride but now was tainted. There was no avoiding it. Taren was involved with the conspiracy. All the arrows pointed to it. Everything came back to this secret conspiracy. Zorya had her spies everywhere and planned to overthrow the Ravenhills and get the people to turn against them. However, her father was doing that himself. He didn't need help doing the wrong thing.

It was time to speak to Zorya.

But she was trapped.

An awful weight contorted her stomach as she thought of Thedamaine. Taking a seat on the lounge chair they shared when they discussed strategies only made her feel worse. She had to do something. He must not be dismissed. She needed him.

She heard a ruckus outside her door. Down the hallway were men's voices, heightened and loud. She heard armour and many footsteps. Next she heard her father shouting; barking orders that she could not hear.

The Manor shook and rattled. An explosion of burst metal and wood with roars of men that reverberated up the staircase to Evangeline's chamber. She was not sure what was going on, she could only guess. She kept pacing from the door to the window, trying to work out what was happening. Had the conspiracy reached its peak and now the people were rebelling against them? Were they storming the Manor to overthrow and assassinate her father? Would she be safe in her room or a sitting duck?

She bashed on the door, kicking it, shouting to let her out but nobody was there, they were all down at the doors and on the grounds. Unmistakably, there was a fight happening in the Manor so Evangeline, forcing herself to do something, changed her clothes and put on her suit of armour. As much as she could put on herself. She armed herself, her sword hanging at her waist, her mother's dagger on her belt and her third blade, usually hidden on her ankle strap, had no hiding place in a suit of armour and so was tied haphazardly to the belt, for easy access. If Nicholas came for her, she would be ready.

The life drained from her as she heard the long howl penetrating through the Manor. A woman screamed followed by a crash of metal on stone. Evangeline hugged the wall.

"Impossible." She breathed. It was impossible. The beast could not be attacking. It was not a full moon; it had never attacked like this before. The beast had never reached the

Manor before. Everything was wrong. Her room shook once more, and some dust fell on her head. She knew she could not stay there. She needed to get to safety. Banging on the door, she tried to force it open. She flung herself at the door as hard as she could but only injured herself. She tried to pry open the lock with her dagger, but it did not work for it was locked on the outside. Her window was boarded up and she was not strong enough to break free.

She could do nothing but listen. She could hear the hounds barking incessantly in the grounds, the aviary squawking in fear, crossbow bolts firing, crashing and screaming and she heard her father. He barked his commands loudly, they powered over the knight's commands whom she heard spread out through the Manor.

All she needed was one person to hear her and unlock the door, so she banged and banged, screaming until her voice was hoarse.

She jumped from the door when a crash against it frightened her. Through the noise of the commotion, she could not tell what it was. As she pressed her ear against the wood, she looked down at the floor. There was something coming into the room under the doorframe, pooling and flowing; it was blood.

"Anybody out there?" She asked, it was half a whisper. She repeated it, loud enough to carry to the outside.

"Evangeline?" A voice carried back, pained and groaning. She was not familiar with the voice.

"Who's there?" She asked, ignoring the blood seeping into her room and pooling around her feet.

"Eva- Lady Evangeline." He corrected himself. "It's Oslo."

"Oslo? Thedamaine's squire? Are you hurt?"

"Yes, milady, please help me."

She heard the pain and fear in his voice as it cracked. "Let me out and I'll help you."

"I cannot reach, I'm pinned down. Please it hurts, please help me."

"Can you not call for help? Where are the others?"

"They have followed the beast somewhere else, I'm on my own. There is no one out here, please help me."

Evangeline sensed that he had started crying. He was so young and frightened. She heard his weeping as it grew louder; he could not supress it anymore.

"You are not alone. I am here with you, just the other side of this door. What are you planning on doing tomorrow?"

"What?" He was confused. She was distracting him from his pain and the possibility of not seeing tomorrow.

"What will you be doing tomorrow? After a battle like this one, most of the household are off duty to see their families. Will you go to see yours?"

"Yes. I will. I haven't seen my mother for six years."

"What does she do? Where does she live?"

"She's a tanner; she lives in North Rockcliffe where I was born, but she will be moving here soon to be with me, she just purchased a shop on Stone Street next to the bridge on east side."

The river Corvus, snaking off the lake, ran through half the town separating it into two sides, those born on either side claim the other is the poor side and their own is the better. Taren came from the west side and often mentioned how lucky he was not to be born on the poorer side; Evangeline did not see any difference; both had their redeeming qualities. Both had the same amount of filthy brothels and criminals, the west side had hard labour, like the blacksmiths, stonemasons and glass blower but the east side had the majority of the merchant shops, tailors, cobblers, grocers and potteries. West side had the Manor, but east side had the infamous Old Vineyard Inn.

Rockcliffe was a tiny sister village run by the vassal liege Lord Stafford. It was one of the most northern villages before the forest disappeared into the mountains; Evangeline had only read and heard about it; she had never visited.

"Was she proud to see you be a squire?" She asked, trying to get his attention back to her and not the pain.

"Oh yes, she did everything to get me here. After my father, two brothers and sister died from the flu, she wanted me to have the best life." He groaned and spluttered; Evangeline hoped the talking was helping.

"Do you like training with Sir Thedamaine?"

"Yes, he is kind and honourable yet strong and loyal. Everything a good knight should be." His voice was fading. "He is the knight I aspire to be."

Evangeline stayed by the door, sitting in the pool of blood and listening to Oslo talk about his future and his family.

She spoke up frequently just to let him know she was still there and to keep him talking. After a while when the pain was fading, Oslo's voice had completely trailed off despite Evangeline's questions and probing. The Manor had calmed as well, a full eerie silence fell.

"Oslo?" She called. "I think it is over." She listened but there was no reply on the other side of the door.

CHAPTER 23.

Felicity panicked and screamed. Roused from sleep by her door smashing open and Mary tearing her from her bed, urging her to run. A crowd of people flowed past her on the landing of the stairs. Her first thought was of her sister, but she was swept away in the mess and chaos. Mary grabbed her arm and pulled her along.

"Milady, you must get to safety."

"No! Evie's still in her room."

"You are in danger."

Felicity tried to resist but she relented when Evie's own handmaiden, Aria had pulled her along as well. She was about to turn the corner toward the south stairs when she heard her father's voice on the floor below her.

"Father!" She shouted, leaning over the railing of the balcony.

"Felicity!" He was in his armour and carrying his longsword with a mace on his back. She thought of her own suit of armour waiting for her in the solar, never been used. It was too late for that. "What do you think you are doing? Get out of here, now!" He barked, barely stopping. Felicity was about to answer but he disappeared into the next room.

She started toward her sister's room but stopped and turned around but changed her mind and swung around once more. She did not know for sure if Evangeline was still in her room. *Maybe someone let her out? No one would have forgotten her. Do not risk your life for something you are not sure about.* With a bit of uncertainty, she decided to free her sister or at least check, she *had* to know. She started to run down the corridor but was shaken to the ground, grabbing the railing to steady herself. A howl of the beast made her jump and she panicked when she heard the men's screams. She did not move, frozen in fear.

The ground moved beneath her feet and this time the floor

cracked and it spread up the wall until the ceiling dropped debris on her head. It was raining crumbled stone and Felicity could stand it no longer.

She left her sister.

Afraid she would be crushed, she sprinted back the way she came and down the southern staircase. She did not stop when she got to the bottom but continued down to the lower floor where she heard voices. She followed them down into the cellar, squeezing herself through the crowd of people.

The entire household was cramped in the cellar; maids, cooks, handmaidens and the higher service positions were sat between the aisles of the cellar. The men were sat closest to the door so they may slip out if called upon.

Felicity chose to sit next to Mary and Aria who were holding hands, heads together. As she sat down, Mary took her hand.

Felicity looked around; at least half of the servants were still in their underdress tunics, the others who slept in the colder parts of the Manor were still wearing their day clothes. Vesna and Morana had made their way safely into the cellar, looking out of place yet still terrified. They quivered with every shake of the Manor, every bang or explosion. Felicity gestured toward them and Vesna pulled her sister through the crowd. Zorya was not in the room, she did not escort them, they were alone and scared and finally looked their age. Felicity reached out and took Vesna's hand who took Morana's. Aria connected the chain and they sat in a close circle clenching each other's palms.

She thought of her sister, trapped in her room and how she abandoned her. She was afraid, she did not want to get hurt or be anywhere near the fight. The beast had never attacked the Manor before, nor had it attacked on a night that was not a full moon. She remembered the first time it hunted. It was a blur, a few years ago. She was shielded from most of the attack, just as she was now but her mother and Evangeline almost lost their lives that day. Her uncle had been killed and it was the first time she saw her father cry, but it was not his last. He cried when his son was born with no heartbeat and cried once more when his wife and her mother died.

Felicity was starting to well up. She had not missed her mother more than in that moment. She looked up at the ceiling to hold back tears but felt Mary and Aria looking at her, she looked back and noticed the entire cellar was watching her. They were looking to her to lead. Her tears dried and she sat up straight, she put on the half smile her sister had mastered and sat quietly until, one by one, the room stopped looking at her, several groups following their example and holding hands in their own circles. She had successfully calmed the room even though she was screaming inside.

Her mind flicked to her stepmother; she was the ruling power in father's absence, but she was not in the cellar, neither was Cadmael. A passing thought entered her mind and she worried that they may have been hurt but she did not have time to dwell when the ceiling to the cellar shook and dust rained down on their heads. The air in the room became thick with fear and anxiety. Felicity squeezed Mary and Vesna's hands to stop herself from shaking as she watched the two young squires by the door. One was holding his hands over his ears; she was sure he was crying. The other was hugging his knees, rocking back and forth.

Suddenly Felicity shot up, breaking the circle. A realisation and panic washing over her. She pushed her way to the cellar door and cried out, screaming for someone to come down. She ignored Mary and Aria's questions until a knight, Sir Morgan came barrelling down the stone steps. He had lost his helmet and was bleeding, the blood dripping from the cut above his brow down to his chin. His armour was dented and bloody and his poleaxe had furry flesh covering the blade.

"Morgan! Help my sister. Evangeline is not here which must mean she is still trapped in her room. Please get her! Bring her here, to safety! Please!"

"Do it!" Aria barked from across the room when the knight hesitated. He finally nodded and sprinted back up the stairs. "She could be out of her room and trying to fight, you know what she's like." Aria was now addressing Felicity with a hand on her back.

"Is that supposed to make me feel better?"

"She didn't fight it before." Mary added. "When it attacked the blacksmith's and she was there, she ran. She ran straight back here. Do not worry, Lady Felicity. Sir Morgan will free her, and she will come straight here."

"When will it end?" Felicity breathed to herself, still

listening to the roars of man and beast, the shuddering and creaking of a Manor under attack. She was worried about her sister, her father and herself. The howl of the beast caused the hairs on her arms and the back of her neck to stand on end.

Another knight came down the steps. It was not Sir Morgan and he was alone. He searched the crowd for Felicity, others had stood up and she was lost in the bodies, but she pushed her way back to the door.

"What is it, Sir? Is it my father? Did you find my sister?"

"No, my Lady, I have come to request more men. Your Lord father has commanded all able men to join him in the battle."

"Oh, I see." She knew what that meant. They were losing. She turned around and was surprised to see the castellan, bailiff and the marshal already standing, waiting. She nodded and they called the men to follow. The herald, chancellor, reeve, cooks, stewards, carpenters, porters and the falconer left the cellar. In a rush they were out the door, the knight was last and closed the heavy door behind him, sealing the women and children in the cellar.

Felicity was scared. The ceiling still shook, and the dust was falling. Mary and Aria were sat on the floor now holding hands with the handmaidens. Vesna and Morana held each other's hands, eyes closed. The cleaners and scullery maids kept to themselves but were still huddled together. Felicity had a chance to get Evangeline out of her room, but she had missed it, choosing to be a coward instead.

Living can be a cowardly thing to do.

CHAPTER 24.

"I'm in here!" She screamed, banging on the locked door. Someone was calling her name, their footsteps smacking the floor with the clink of metal. She jumped back from the door as it unlocked, narrowly avoiding it swing open and bang against the wall. Sir Morgan was gesturing her to him, leaning on the railing and glancing fearfully down the mezzanine to the ground floor. She knelt down next to Oslo just outside her door, gasping at the broken support beam that had collapsed on top of him. His eyes were open, and face had drained of all colour.

"You must move! Come on!" He pushed her hard making her hand slip on the drying blood on the floor. "Get up!" He barked, gripping her arm and yanking her upwards. His hand cupped her back and she finally felt safe. No longer trapped.

As the floor shook beneath their feet they began to run yet stopped still as the doors below burst open and the beast appeared, locking eyes with them above. Evangeline moved first and pulled Sir Morgan along. He did not protest and sprinted along with her. Sir Morgan was one of the youngest knights, a relatively new recruit and unproven in battle. The two of them steadied themselves as another quiver of the Manor walls almost knocked them off their feet. Evangeline clamped her hands over her ears to drown out the beast's long, ghoulish howl. She turned, afraid to look; it had leapt from the floor below and now came for them.

Sir Morgan stopped and unsheathed his sword which rattled with fear in his grip. They exchanged a look that Evangeline answered with a nod, continuing sprinting down the corridor leaving the knight alone with the creature. She told herself not to look back, but she did and regretted it, witnessing the beast clamp down on the knight and rip into his neck, pulling flesh and armour out within its jaws.

She had clenched her eyes, hoping to cleanse them of the

grotesque sight but she almost tripped as she ran; her foot had caught a dead knight's cloak. Running down the corridor, it was littered with corpses, debris and blood puddles. Dodging the obstacles, she wondered where all the soldiers were. The beast was there, just behind her, pursuing her on four monstrous legs and she was alone, running from its jaws.

It occurred to her that she did not know where she was running. She must get to safety but where was that? Where was everyone else? The beast had never attacked the Manor before so there was no contingency plan or rally point. They would need a safe place, secure and well-constructed. Easily guarded and locked. Would they have risked crossing the grounds to converge in the crypt? Cramped into the cellar? Did they flee into the forest? Or did they just scatter in the wind to be picked off like flies?

She was running faster than she ever ran before, the adrenaline fuelling her legs but as she turned a corner, her foot slid out from under her, skidding on blood and falling hard on the ground. Her body kept going, sliding on the floor, her feet smashed straight through a post in the railing, but she was stopped dead by her ribcage smacking into the next post and her forehead hitting the third. A guttural exhale was all she could muster as all the air burst from her lungs. With most of her body hanging over the balcony, she clung to the balustrade afraid to fall but forced to let go as the beast caught up with her. Cutting through her armour like butter, the elongated claws sliced her forearm from elbow to wrist.

She landed in the atrium on the ground floor and finally heard men's voices somewhere in the Manor. A shooting pain went up her back that tingled in her toes and her arm was streaming blood in a large slash; only one claw caught her. The beast's howl echoed through the Manor once more. Evangeline scrambled upright, supporting her back and headed toward the closest doors to her, bursting her way through. It was a dead end, the oratory had one door in and one door out.

Her path was blocked by the monster crashing down to meet her. She backed up, slowly, arms extended, forced into the room. With each drop of blood hitting the floor, the beast's ears twitched. The creature was low to the ground, eyes locked on her. The long snout of the wolf skull head pointed directly at her; the curled ram horns ready to be used as a battering ram to further tear up its prey. Only its head was a skull, the body covered in bloody, matted fur that walked on two legs but galloped on four.

As she backed up, she bumped against something, terrified to break eye contact with the beast, she felt the heat behind her. The oratory had a large wall to wall fireplace and in front of it, a large oak altar table full to the brim with candles. Crossing the room in a single leap, the beast lunged for Evangeline, she bolted like a hare to the left, leaping at the last moment, but the beast kept going, falling headfirst into the altar, smashing it to splinters and following through into the lit fireplace behind it. The candle wax splattered everywhere but its fur went up in flames as it scrambled in the embers of the fire. At the same moment, Evangeline tore a sconce off the wall above her and hurled it into the fireplace at the beast. Pitch and wax drenched the beast even further and ignited in the flames.

Evangeline listened to its tortured screams as the oratory doors swung open; a cluster of knights, including her father, clambered into the room, chasing the noise and chaos. A human shield around her formed in the instant it took for them to notice her. An encirclement to protect her and cover the beast. Evangeline fell into her father's arms as he cradled his daughter and pulled her from the room to safety. Rubbing her face and gathering her nerves, she merely wanted to sleep or cry or both, but she looked into the eyes of her father; beaten and bloodied and froze still. She did not react to his hug or his quivering hands on her face.

"It's gone. There's nothing more we can do." A man shouted, entering the room.

"We can follow it!" Somebody else said. "Follow it back out to the village, to its lair and kill it!"

"No!" Her father shouted, turning around to face his knights. "We have lost too many tonight. It's over. Constantine!"

"Yes Sir?"

"Sweep the Manor, I want the injured and the deceased in the infirmary. I need a rundown of our losses."

"Yes Sir."

Horus tried to pull Evangeline to her feet, but she could not move. She only closed her eyes. She was grateful that he did not urge her. She felt him touch her arm, her hands and her leg but she did not react. The room fell quiet and he said something, but she heard nothing. Horus sat beside her, and they waited.

Shocked at the sudden noise of something entering the room, they were both frightened and alert, jumping to their feet to defend themselves but it was only Sir Constantine.

"My Lord, the dead are being transported now."

"How many guards did we lose?"

"Seven knights."

Seven. Evangeline knew there were only ten in the Manor. Such a high number, lost. A team from the village would have come to aid once they knew but it was a huge blow to their forces.

Evangeline bolted from the room, slipping her father's grip, her heart pounding furiously, her gut liquefying and eyes full of tears.

Where was he? He would have come got her. He would have freed her. He would have protected her. *Seven.* Only one thing would have stopped him. *Seven.* She had not seen him. *Seven. Where was he?*

Pools of blood littered the floor with large voids where the bodies had been moved. She had been sat in that room with her father longer than she realised. She did not pass his body on her way to the infirmary as she sprinted through the ruined halls.

She fell through the doors and grinded to a halt as she was met with a sea of broken, bloodied people. Flooded with the injured, dead or frightened, she tried to scan the room, her eyes flitting to each person around her, unaware if he was still in his knight armour or off duty clothing. She lingered on the bodies in the beds, desperately pushing her way through, rushing around the room, searching for him.

Her eyes darted immediately to the cluster of knights gathered around a bed in the centre of the room. Her hand instinctively touched her heart and she leant against the wall for balance. She bolted again, crossing the room and barged her way through the knights, stopping at the foot of the bed.

Deep cuts ripped down the side of his neck, teeth marks clamped down on his skull and torn armour from his chest revealed the shredded stomach. Body drenched in blood, the bed sodden with it, the sight of the mangled corpse only brought relief to her. It was not him.

Sir Morris was dead. Sir Morgan was dead. Five more were dead. She stepped back from the gathering, her hands running through her bloody, tangled hair, loose from its braid. She needed to find him.

The infirmary doors opened with a slam. Evangeline elbowed her way through to see the door, gasped and ran, zigzagging her way through the sea of people. Crossing the room, she threw her arms around his neck and hugged tightly. Sir Thedamaine had run toward her as well and the force of his hug as they collided lifted her off the ground.

"I thought you were dead!" Evangeline finally pulled away, taking his head in her hands and searching his face for injuries. His eyebrow split open from her father, a superficial scratch on his neck, a layer of blood and dirt smothering his skin. Bloodied and bruised, he was beaten but not broken.

"I'm sorry I was not there. I thought I was too late. When I came for you, you were gone and Oslo-" he trailed off, looking away but Evangeline pulled him into a hug once again. He held her so tightly she could hardly breathe but she squeezed just as hard. Frozen in the embrace.

"Evangeline!" Felicity had entered the infirmary and threw her arms around Evangeline's neck, breaking her hug with Thedamaine who moved several steps back, suddenly aware of the situation and the people around them. "You're alive!" Felicity squealed. "When I heard about the fire, I thought it had got you. You actually hurt it!"

"Evangeline, Felicity. I am glad to see you two are unhurt." Zorya entered the room next, the twins piling in after her, all untouched and as glamourous as always. Felicity was dirty and slightly bloodied, Evangeline assumed it was splatter from someone else as she could not see any serious injuries except a minor cut on her cheek. Felicity urged Evangeline to perch on the edge of the nearest bed, sharing it with Sir Constantine who was sat on the other side, his broken arm in a sling. Zorya came up to them and placed a delicate hand on Evangeline's cheek. An act that completely threw Evangeline. "It's over now, you may breathe." Zorya said, quietly.

"You're lucky to be alive." Vesna added, at her mother's side. Morana was still at the door, arms folded and watching the room.

"Thank you." Evangeline replied, looking to both. It was as genuine as she could muster; breathy and unbelieving yet grateful.

Zorya removed her hand with almost a smile, squeezing Felicity's hand briefly and turned to Vesna.

"Fetch the surgeon. Evangeline is injured. She needs immediate help." Vesna nodded and disappeared into the crowd. "Felicity, will you remove what is left of the gauntlet? That cut will need stitching."

Evangeline held her arm out for Felicity, it was beginning to hurt now, the adrenaline wearing off. Everything hurt. Her palms were red and sore from the sconce, saved from burning by the bandages covering her bleeding palm. There was a piece of splintered wood sticking out of her ankle from when she went through the railing. A large bump on her forehead and a bruised, possibly broken rib from hitting the railing as well. Bleeding cuts on her head from falling debris. Shooting pains in her back from falling from the balcony. Everything hurt but she did not think about it. Her eyes were on Thedamaine. Longing to hold him again.

"Let me get some bandages." Felicity said, leaving Evangeline with Zorya.

Zorya looked behind her, at Thedamaine then back to Evangeline, who noticed and met her gaze. "I convinced your father to keep *him* at his post and in the Manor."

"What?" Evangeline asked, gobsmacked.

"Sir Thedamaine will remain a knight in the Manor and at your side."

"You convinced him?"

"Yes."

"Thank you." Evangeline meant it and smiled.

"We all need a little bit of happiness in our lives, don't we? If we do not have that one life raft, we will be lost in the current forever. Doctor." She announced once he appeared at her side with the surgeon.

"Yes, milady?" He answered, almost as bloody as his patients.

"Ensure Lady Evangeline is seen to, *immediately,* she has a reunion to get to."

CHAPTER 25.

Evangeline slipped out of the infirmary at the first opportunity, once she was stitched, bandaged and full of laudanum, she crept out unnoticed. She returned to her chambers, fetched a wet rag and began to clean up Oslo's blood on the floor just outside her door. His body had been moved but the blood and debris remained.

She struggled to lift up the beam that had crushed him. A small puddle of blood remained just underneath, and she had to move it to get to it. Forced to use her arms instead of her hands, she groaned with pain and struggling strength. It was not moving. Then she felt it shift. Thedamaine was beside her, lifting it up, he moved it and leant it against the wall. She smiled and cleaned up the rest of the blood. Once she was finished, they looked at one another; their silence deafening. Evangeline went inside her chamber room, leaving her door open. Thedamaine followed and closed it behind him.

"My life has been," she paused, gathering her thoughts, looking at her boarded-up window, "out of control lately and recent events have made me realise what is most important to me." She looked to the floor. "I was scared of losing my life, of course." Evangeline turned around and faced Thedamaine. He was across the room, eyes down. "But," she continued, her heart pounding, "thinking I had lost *you*," he finally met her gaze, she saw his shoulders rising up and down rapidly, "it almost broke me."

Evangeline could not read the expression on Thedamaine's face until he suddenly crossed the room toward her. She gasped slightly and took a step toward him, but he stopped in his tracks. There was a desperate rapping at the door. Evangeline stood still, looking at Thedamaine, waiting, but he avoided her gaze, glancing over to the door. She finally exhaled deeply and yanked open the door to see who was knocking.

"What is it?" She spat. Felicity barged into the room.

"We need to talk." She said seriously.

Evangeline remained at the door, staring into the empty doorway, thinking about what would have happened, almost happened. Thedamaine appeared beside her and the two of them stared intently at the other as he slid past her out the door, a hairs width apart. The butterflies in her stomach contorted her gut in the split moment they lingered but then he passed, broke the gaze and stood guard outside. Evangeline slowly and reluctantly closed the door.

"Are you even listening to me? *Evangeline!*"

"What?" Evangeline answered, unable to mask the irritability in her voice. She had not heard a thing Felicity had said when she entered the room.

"Please don't ignore me. I'm trying to talk to you."

"Fine." She broke from the door and focused on her sister. "What is it? Start from the beginning."

"You really need to stop running away from everything."

"What am I running away from? I ran away from the beast and managed to escape with my life."

"No. You're running away from fights, confrontation and things that overwhelm you. That's what you do, you run. Now you're running away again, ignoring me, trying not to listen to what I am saying."

"I am listening."

"No, you're not. You're hearing but not listening."

"Please can we not do this now? Can I just have some time to recover? I am really hurt. I almost died. *Twice.*"

"No. We need to discuss what happened. The investigation. What happened at the shaman camp? What have you found out?"

"Felicity, please." Evangeline glanced at the door, grabbing her head, running her palm over her eyes. "I need to figure things out."

"No. We need to figure things out. We are in this together. We are sisters. It is our mother, our father, our family. Together."

Evangeline had no choice but to put Thedamaine out of her mind. It was harder than she realised. She had opened up and let him in. There was no closing that door once she had opened it.

"Listen to me!" Felicity was punching her open palm to get Evangeline's attention back; she had drifted off again. "Fine. You talk. From the beginning. What happened at the camp? What did they say? How was it burned down? What have you found out?"

Evangeline inhaled slowly and fully then exhaled it all. She began. The shamans, Sienna, Taren, the knights, the slaughter, the flames, the empath gifts, the secret, the conspiracy, the betrayal, the curse, the questions. She explained everything. Finally, Felicity was silent.

She did not know where to start. Her first thought immediately clung to Taren. There was enough evidence of the conspiracy proving that it was behind everything. Zorya wanted power, she wanted to be Lady Ravenhill. She visited her childhood friend, killed her, married her husband, gained power and hired spies around the village to watch the family. She armed a rebellion, undermining the Ravenhill name so they would eventually revolt and overthrow them.

Taren, a spy in the rebellion, knew of the plan but did not tell them of it. Yet something was off. It did not sit right with Felicity.

"Why would Taren spy on father when he was not even here?" She asked.

"You don't understand. He wasn't spying on father; he was spying on *us*!" Evangeline replied. She was sat on her bed, sharpening her dagger with a whetstone hoping to keep herself calm.

"What if he wasn't? What if he was pretending to and feeding false information?"

"What are you basing this on? Why are you on his side? You were the one who didn't trust him in the first place. You had him followed. You found out the secret."

"There's something about him. Something not right."

"That's what we are saying, Flick. He's a spy and a traitor trying to overthrow our family."

"But he loves you. You two are best friends."

"An act. It was all a rouse. He lied to me for years. Our friendship was not real."

"Again, you're hearing but not listening. You two had a real bond."

"Oh, shut up, Flick. You're obsessed with him. You are romanticising my relationship with him because you're in love with him yourself."

"That's not true!"

"It is." Evangeline was calm, still sharpening her dagger. "Perhaps you don't see it yet, but you will. It just takes a little time. Trust me."

The silence dragged on, only cut by the scraping of the whetstone and crackling of the dying fire. Eventually Felicity sat down on the floor, her back against Evangeline's bed.

"So, it was Zorya all along?" Felicity whispered, ignoring the last conversation.

"It all leads to her." Evangeline followed suit, gathering all the threads of the investigation together in her mind.

A sharp knocking at the door made them both jump. Felicity stood up and opened the door, stepping back when she saw who it was. Evangeline, who had put her whetstone down at the sound of the door opening, kept her hand gripped on the hilt of the dagger.

Zorya glided into the room.

Sir Thedamaine took a stand in the doorway, reading their faces and readied his hand on his sword.

"I bear no ill will." Zorya purred, glancing from Evangeline to Thedamaine. Felicity had come to her sisters' side and Evangeline took a step forward, covering her. "I am here to help. I promise." Nobody moved. "Perhaps this shall be my peace offering?" Zorya gestured to the doorway and for a second Thedamaine was confused but flicked his head to the right and immediately unsheathed his sword at what he saw in the hallway.

"Where did you come from? Who are you? Stand back!"

"I will not hurt you." The voice replied. Evangeline could not see who was in the hallway, who had appeared and surprised Thedamaine, but she recognised the voice and went to the door, poking her head out.

"Sienna? What are you doing here? It's fine Theo, I know her. Stand down."

Thedamaine sheathed his sword and stepped aside, letting Sienna the shaman enter Evangeline's room. He entered the room after her, alert yet uneasy, once again surprised by a sudden danger and took his place beside Evangeline.

"How did you get here?" Evangeline asked.

"We have gifts." A sly smile curled around Sienna's face

and seemed to Felicity to be an inside joke that she was not in on.

"Why are you here?" Felicity asked, short and firm.

"I was invited." Sienna looked to Zorya and they exchanged a lingering look.

"You two know each other?"

"We do."

"So, you *are* a shaman?" Felicity asked, confirming her hunch.

"I was, once. That's not who I am anymore. What happened tonight has confirmed the worst and now we know we must end this."

"We need your help, both of you." Sienna continued.

"End what?" Felicity asked.

"Help with what?" Evangeline added.

"The two of you will break the curse. Tonight."

CHAPTER 26.

"You need to trust me."

"How can we when you-" Felicity trailed off, not wanting to reveal to Zorya what they were accusing her of.

"I know what you think I have done. It is not true. I did not kill your mother."

"Then who did?" Felicity asked, humouring her.

"We do not know," Sienna replied.

"We? What do you have to do with all of this?" Evangeline asked.

"Zorya and I have been working together trying to stop this and to find your mother's killer."

"I came here to stop the beast, break the curse and protect your mother." Zorya closed her eyes briefly, when she opened them, they stared into the fire. "I failed. In every way."

"What happened between you and my mother?" Evangeline asked, bringing Zorya back. "When you were children?"

"Your mother had a friend who was also a Bridge. Her powers and strength scared your mother and so she exposed her to the world. Your mother's family sentenced her friend to death and burned her alive in the village square."

"What did you do? You were her friend too?"

"I eventually found my peace with it."

"She betrayed and burned your friend alive, yet you still came and found her years later to protect her?" Felicity asked, not buying the story.

"You expect us to believe that you did not kill her?"

"She was my friend, I loved her. She did not deserve this curse. No one does. Which is why I want to break it."

"And you?" Evangeline asked Sienna, "what is your tie to this curse? Why do you want to break it?"

"Because it is wrong. I want the war to end, the bad blood

185

between our people settled with. No more deaths." Sienna thought for a moment, reading the unconvinced faces in front of her. "Shamans could do so much good in the world, but we hide away manipulating people, fuelled by greed."

"Let me think for a moment." Evangeline said, sitting down on her bed, rubbing her forehead. Her body ached and cried out in pain, everywhere hurt and now her brain did too. Her eyes hung heavy and her shoulders slumped.

"The beast is the curse, isn't it?" Felicity asked, bringing some answers together. "Father said your elder was executed here in the Manor. A consequence of that heinous act was cursing our land. Our people did not stop it, we were not there, we did not stop it. That is why the village is cursed and not just the family."

"A wrong that needs to be right. We executed the shaman elder; we were cursed; the beast attacked every full moon. We slaughter and burn down your camp, the curse was doubled; the beast attacked outside of a full moon." Evangeline counted on her fingers as she listed.

"The beast could attack *every* night, now." Thedamaine added.

"That is what we are afraid of." Zorya replied. "It is why we need to break the curse, tonight."

"How do we do that?" Felicity asked.

"In order to break the curse, we need to first find out what binds the curse."

"Curses are sorted into three classes: hexes, spirit binds or blood pacts." Sienna counted three fingers as she listed them and held up one. "A hex can be broken by the right incantation but can take years to break."

"This is what I have been doing since I got here." Zorya added. "I needed to get close to your mother and father in order to find any object, word or subject matter to help break it. So far my search has come up empty."

Evangeline immediately thought of several words and objects that could be relevant but held her tongue.

Sienna held up two fingers. "A spirit bind is a spirit or soul unable to move on and has been bound to a person or place. In order to break this bond, a shaman must take the journey into the spirit world in order to find the spirit and break the bond. This is extremely difficult and dangerous as we must first find the person or place that has been bound and then make the perilous journey to the spirit world."

Both Evangeline and Felicity thought immediately of the elder's spirit latching onto the Manor.

Sienna held up three fingers. "A blood pact is the most difficult one to break. A shaman must tread the line between Light and the Darkness, careful not to cross over into blood magic. A blood pact is based on revenge and is connected to a bloodline that will require a full ritual to break. All parties connected to the curse will need to be in the ritual. This includes you two. Not only will the shamans make the journey into the spirit world but you two will be as well. This is a dangerous ritual at the best of times but now we do not have the support of our people."

"Why not?" Felicity asked.

"I am no longer one of them. I left them to pursue the good."

"If you left them why are you still afraid of blood magic? You no longer risk banishment as you already abandoned them." Evangeline tried to recall what Sienna told her in the windmill.

"Banishment is not the only risk," Zorya answered. "You lose your soul. You become a shell. You are forever indebted to the Darkness and must live in fear waiting for the day it will come for you and take you to the Abyss for all eternity."

"That seems like a large price to pay for a little blood magic." Thedamaine responded.

"Faced with desperation, it is your only choice." Zorya countered.

"If this is all true," Evangeline began, "how do we know what ritual to perform? It could be all three of the curses. I know plenty of things that meant a lot to mother. The Nil'vetra for sure was important to her. Have you tried that for the incantation? The elder's spirit could be the bond and easily bound to the Manor or the village itself. The beast, if that is the curse, did not stop when mother was killed so it's not all about her. It could be bound to the bloodline which means we are both cursed." Evangeline had thrown the Nil'vetra into the sentence to see if it would rise a reaction, but no one moved. Sienna and Zorya were as stoic as before.

"*What* is a Nil'vetra?" Felicity finally blurted out. "Why did she think it was coming for her? Why did she write it over and over again on pieces of parchment in the trunk in the Lady's Tower?"

"The Nil'vetra is an ancient name for the Darkness. The embodiment of revenge and retribution. It is sometimes used as a name for shamans that practise blood magic as it means 'no death' in the ancient shamanic language."

"Someone was coming for revenge?" Thedamaine suggested.

"The elder?" Felicity added.

"Her childhood friend, even?" Proposed Evangeline.

"How do we know that someone was after her?" Felicity said, addressing Evangeline. "Blood magic can be an assassination, Sienna said so herself, to you. She was a Bridge, so was her friend. Can a shaman or a Bridge be killed by normal fire?"

"Yes, we can die a mortal death, but blood magic can bring us back." Sienna answered.

"Mother could *be* the Nil'vetra. She could be the one who practised blood magic. It could have easily been her just as much as her friend."

"The Darkness came for her soul." Evangeline finished. "That is what came for her. You're a genius, Flick!" Felicity smiled as Evangeline turned to Sienna. "Fine. I believe you both. For some reason I trust you. It's time to end this and break this curse. I'm in, whatever you want me to do, I will do it. No matter the risk."

"Hold on," Felicity's smiled dropped, "you have only just met Sienna and you trust her? Just because she told you she knows when people are lying? Zorya is a shaman, maybe their powers do not work on one another? She abandoned the shamans and wants to help us for no real reason, and you trust her? Zorya we know nothing about. Our mother murdered their best friend and now she's suddenly fine with it? Mother betrayed her but she wanted to protect her? She also wants to break the curse for no real reason. She married our father for power and to get close to him to try and break the curse. We are supposed to believe that? If what you said is true and we do perform this ritual, what is stopping you from 'accidentally' ensuring that we do not make it back alive?"

Zorya stepped forward and looked to both sisters. Evangeline got off the bed and took a step forward, joining her sister.

Footsteps advanced down the hallway, heading their way. Thedamaine, on his feet immediately, swung open the door with his sword ready, looked into the room at Evangeline then sheathed his sword.

"If you do not trust me," Zorya began, "then you must trust him."

Taren entered the room, bloodied, beaten and burnt.

"Taren? You're involved with this?"

"I need you both to listen to me. Trust me, trust Zorya. She wants to help. That's all she's ever done is protect us and help us."

"The curse is connected to you? Isn't it?" Evangeline finally began linking it all together. "That's why you're here. When the beast attacked the forge, I was right, it chose us because we were there, but it was not after me. It was after *you*. The curse is bound to you. That's why it didn't attack the Manor. It was bound to you. But why? What connection do you have to my mother? To what she did?"

"It's not about her." Felicity said, watching the floor. "The curse is bound to the bloodline. It must be a blood pact. Mother is dead but her blood is still around. In you and in me."

"She's right." Sienna said. "The curse is a punishment. It is not there to kill the bloodline. It's there to punish it, torture it. The curse has connected itself to something that means a lot to you and has chosen Taren as a host."

"This is the secret I have been hiding from you. I promise that's it. We must perform the ritual tonight, so the curse is broken."

"We have to free you." Felicity said, stepping toward Taren.

"Now *you* believe them?"

"Please, let's do this. Let us free him. Please?"

"I need some air." Evangeline ran from the room, Thedamaine followed. She had to get some air after what she had heard. Doubled over, afraid she would vomit, Thedamaine cupped her back, struggling to take in the news himself. She could not believe it, yet she did. Things were starting to add up, finally. She straightened, looked up at Thedamaine and pulled him into a tight hug. He squeezed her into comfort, settling her nerves yet she only replayed what had just happened. What she had found out.

"Taren is cursed." Evangeline said to Thedamaine in their hug. "The beast is the blood pact and has bound itself to him. We must perform the ritual to break the curse."

"You wanted to destroy the beast. That was your goal. If there is an opportunity to end this, are you going to take it?"

"What do you think I should do?"

"Do as they say. Perform the ritual."

"Really? But it could be dangerous."

"If it works, you could save a lot of people."

"And once it's over, then what? The Beast of Ravenhill is dead. The curse is broken. What happens then?"

"Then we find out who killed Lady Emilia."

"Indeed. That question has not been answered yet. This doesn't end with the beast. That's only one side of the coin. We have to delve deeper. This is all connected to the shamans and I will find out the truth from them. One way or another."

CHAPTER 27.

Hundreds of candles littered the floor and surfaces, lining both sides of the staircase down to the crypt. Despite the flames, the ghostly chill in the air still rattled through to the bone. In the main hall a single stone sarcophagus held the decaying remains of her mother, the Lady Emilia Ravenhill. In the rooms snaking off the main hall hid the Ravenhill ancestors. They would only have their mothers' body for four more years before custom and tradition would take her away and lay her to rest with her own ancestors. She would be taken home to the Rosewood crypt to lie with her father. Evangeline thought ahead, glad she would eventually return here after spending five years in the Forrester crypt too far from her real family.

Stone ravens lined the room, high on the walls as little sentinels, watching over the dead. Evangeline advanced further into the crypt, passing her mother's resting place into the circle opening behind. Four tall candelabras stood in front of the stone beams that arched overhead, casting dancing shadows lighting up the room.

Evangeline immediately noticed her mother's belongings laid out in the centre of the opening. The trunk in the Lady's Tower had been emptied and its contents brought down. She finally knew the reason why Zorya was keeping them, for the rituals. The items were arranged strangely, outlining a long rectangle void in the floor.

Zorya and Sienna had already set up for the ritual before Evangeline and Felicity had even agreed to it. Perhaps they knew the ritual would take place no matter what. Evangeline had been told to meet them in the crypt for the ritual, but she was the first one there.

She was alone. She dismissed Thedamaine, knowing that any dangers she would encounter could not be stopped by him and he agreed, slowly coming to terms that he could not protect her at all times.

Between the flickering shadows, ghostly chill and the vast echo with her every step; she hated the crypt. It was coming up to a year and a half since her mother had died and so much had happened, she just wanted to talk to her about it all. Evangeline looked around.

"What an awful place to rest forever." She said aloud.

"It's not so bad." A voice replied, carried down the steps. Evangeline recognised Felicity's voice but also heard at least two other sets of footsteps coming down into the crypt. She peered out from around the pillar and watched them all jog down the steps. Sienna, Taren and Zorya followed Felicity until they all stood in the circle opening.

"Remember, this place is only to hold the vessel for your soul. Your body rests here, your spirit moves on." Sienna added.

"Not all spirits move on." retorted Zorya with an uncharacteristic smile. "That is why we are here."

"True again. Taren, you know what to do." Sienna held out her hand, gesturing to the items on the floor. Taren, nodding, stepped into the void and laid on the floor, the items forming a border around his body.

"You've done this before?" Felicity asked, she did not wait for a reply. "You should have told us this earlier."

"It doesn't matter." Evangeline answered. "We're doing it now. So how does this work?"

"We need to perform a ritual that allows you two to enter the spirit world. This brings the entire bloodline into the spirit world and Zorya and I can then work to break the curse."

"How will you do that?"

Zorya and Sienna looked at one another. "Your blood will show us the way." Sienna said with an exhale.

"Blood?" Felicity asked, horrified. "I thought blood magic was forbidden. Are you going to sacrifice us?"

"No. We need to carefully tread the line, it's difficult but we can do it."

"We just need a little blood." Zorya held up a black dagger. "Please trust us, the sun will rise soon, and we need the moonlight to guide us."

"Fine, just do whatever you need to do."

"Please take one of these." Zorya stood in front of

Evangeline and handed her a bowl, inside was a handful of small bones.

"That's disgusting! Whose bones are these?"

"They are your mothers. They are finger bones, stripped of flesh. We need them for the ritual to link body and spirit."

Evangeline shook her head and delicately took a bone.

"Please hold out your hand." Zorya continued, pointing to her left hand that took the bone. Evangeline presented it. Using the black dagger, Zorya sliced Evangeline's palm cutting bandage and flesh, avoiding her previous wound and creating another. Evangeline winced but stood her ground, focusing on the pain and watching the blood seep out. "It needs to be fresh blood." Zorya added, as if answering the room's questions.

Felicity did the same, she took a bone with her right hand and had her palm slashed. They both stood there, dripping blood as Sienna came to them next.

"Please take one of these, in your other hand." Sienna presented a vase full of shiny black stones, the same kind she had in her caravan. "These are obsidian. A very powerful and important token of the spirit world. Forged in the fires of hell, obsidian is a good luck charm and a homing beacon. See the sharp edge?" The small stone's jagged edge was indeed sharp and as Felicity ran her finger over it, she felt the edge. "Obsidian is versatile, and a lot of shamanistic tools are made of it. Zorya's knife here is obsidian which is why there was minimal pain." Felicity agreed with that statement and looked down at her incision. It was a completely smooth cut. "This obsidian is the most important tool for you two as it will bring you back to this realm. Do *not* lose it."

"What if we do?" Evangeline asked.

"Do not lose it." Sienna replied.

The four women took their places around Taren as he laid on the floor surrounded by Lady Emilia's belongings. The four of them held a finger bone in their bleeding hand and a piece of obsidian in their other.

"You will each make your journey *alone* into the spirit world. This will be a shock to the system for the spirit world reveals itself differently to each person, reflecting on your fears, your knowledge, your personality and for shamans like myself and Zorya, your proficiency."

"Proficiency?" Evangeline asked.

"Our speciality. My heightened sense of emotions were targeted and attacked."

"My skills for illusion were used against me." Zorya added. "Your mother's sight was amplified. She saw the spirit world much more clearly than the rest of us. Where we saw a delicate veil between the two worlds, she saw both as clear as the one you see now. This is what the spirit world will do when it reveals itself to you. Be careful."

"Let us begin." Sienna said.

"Wait!" Evangeline called out.

"Yes, wait! We don't know what we are doing. I have questions!"

Sienna and Zorya held out their hands over Taren, extending to Felicity and Evangeline. The two of them presented their bleeding hands that dripped onto Taren and the shamans grabbed hold of their hands, keeping the bones between them. Carefully keeping the obsidian in their other palms, Evangeline and Felicity copied Zorya and Sienna and held each other's hands completing the circle, immediately bringing a gust of wind down into the crypt, blowing out all of the candles.

"What do we do?" Felicity screamed.

The winds picked up and roared passed their ears. The crypt, now in total darkness, was beginning to freeze.

"When you see the raven, cut yourself free." Sienna's words over the winds were all Felicity heard but she had enough. Trembling, wide-eyed and close to hyperventilating, Felicity was too afraid to carry on and let go of Sienna and Evangeline's hands. As soon as she did, she was blinded by a bright light. When she opened her eyes again, adjusting to the light; the crypt had gone, she had entered the spirit world.

CHAPTER 28.

She could not see more than five steps ahead of her through the thick, grey fog. She looked around but saw nothing. Nothing but fog. The ground was covered in pine needles and dead grass and that was all that she could see.

"Evangeline?" She called out, to no answer.

She clasped her hands together to settle herself, but she realised her hand no longer hurt. The cut from the obsidian blade had healed completely, as if it did not happen. She was no longer holding the bone either, but her left hand still clamped down tightly onto the obsidian.

The fog was all around, Felicity could not see what was ahead nor if anything were coming toward her. That thought unnerved her, so she stepped forward and kept walking, always scanning around her, looking over her shoulder.

She hesitated when a dark object appeared through the fog. She could not make it out, so she tentatively advanced on it. It was small, shin height and sticking out of the ground. As it came into view, she realised it was a tombstone and jumped back, afraid of what was written on it.

Curiosity pulling her forward, she crouched down and took a look but was only met with a worn, mossy stone, too weather worn to read. She continued on, and noticed a few more tombstones dotted about, just barely poking through the fog.

"A graveyard?" Felicity said aloud, preferring to hear her own voice to cut through the dense silence.

Of course, it is. Her own voice replied. *You're in the spirit world. Spirits, death, graveyards.*

As she progressed through the graveyard something new materialised through the fog. This was not a tombstone. It was taller than her and gave her a fright as it came into view. Her startled face was looking back at her as she advanced on a large mirror.

Felicity peered around the mirror, but the immediate surroundings looked the same. She took a chance and reached out, touching the mirror. As soon as her finger touched the surface everything exploded into colour; the fog immediately dispersed and the ground she was walking on replaced with a vast wildflower meadow.

She jumped out of her skin when she turned back to the mirror, she was no longer looking at her reflection but a tall, blonde and very familiar figure.

"Mother?" Felicity placed her free hand on her heart and stepped closer. Her mother smiled on the other side of the mirror and began to speak. "I can't hear you." Felicity said as she watched her mother's mouth move. She thought for a moment, just watching her mother. "I miss you." She said aloud. Her mother rested her own hand on her heart and gently smiled, knowing what her daughter said.

"I don't know what to do, mother. Do I keep going or stay here?"

She placed her hand on the mirror and Felicity did the same, placing her hand on the same place, only touching the cold surface of the mirror. "I'll stay here, then."

Now what? Her own voice asked. Felicity looked around, still with her hand on the mirror. It was so silent, there were no birds singing nor a breeze in the air. The wildflowers around her did not sway in the wind and the clouds were not moving. She realised she had been turning the obsidian over and over in her left hand since seeing her mother, so she brought it up to her face and inspected it.

Felicity was startled once more when her mother began banging on the mirror and pointing at the stone. She held it out to show her and saw the desperation in her mother's eyes. She ran her finger over the sharp edge of the obsidian.

"When you see the raven, cut yourself free." There was no raven, but Felicity was looking at Lady Emilia *Ravenhill*. Perhaps that was the symbol that she needed to follow Sienna's instructions. Her mother was still knocking on the mirror's surface and pointing at the stone, so Felicity took another chance and touched the edge of the obsidian against the surface of the mirror and scraped down.

She shielded her eyes from the sharp pieces as it completely shattered before her. As she straightened up and opened her eyes, she was alone again, stood in the centre of the Ravenhill Manor Courtyard. Dark and grey, grisly storm clouds hung overhead, threatening rain. Perched all around were hundreds of ravens, as she looked up they began to squawk and screech at her. Some flapped their wings as they squawked, and a few began to swoop down to her. She jumped back from their beaks, screaming with every swoop.

Every door was locked. Whichever one she tried to escape refused to open. She was trapped outside with the ravens and now they were beginning to peck her.

She panicked, realising that both hands were empty. The obsidian was gone. She ran back to the spot where she appeared, failing to dodge the swooping ravens and searched the floor in case she had dropped it, but it was gone. She had lost it.

Did she use the obsidian too soon? Was that her only chance to get back home? *When you see the raven, cut yourself free.*

Well now is the time to cut yourself free!

The squawking was too much for her to bear and the swooping and pecking terrified and pained her every time. Her hands clamped down over her ears and she fell to her knees. She screamed for the ravens to stop as she squeezed her head. She felt four more ravens hit her body as they swooped down but then they stopped. The squawking stopped.

She opened her eyes and looked up; they were still there but just watching her. Some were circling high overhead, but they stopped. They listened to her.

"What is going on? Evangeline? Where are you?" She whispered to herself. "Is this real? Was the meadow real? Was mother real?" She remained on her knees in the courtyard surrounded by the ravens and began to stroke the fur lined trim of her gown. She needed some way to calm herself for she was beginning to think she had been tricked. Things were not as they seem. "Did I set something free that should have remained trapped?" She took a long breath. "I am in the spirit world." She confirmed to herself. "It has revealed itself to me as something familiar. These ravens are spirits and identified an outsider. That must be it. They stopped attacking because-" she did not have an answer for herself.

Finally, she stood up and walked toward the doors to the

Manor, this time it opened for her. She entered and headed toward the Grand Hall. As she walked through the halls, she noticed everything was black and empty. All the furniture was missing, the walls and floors black, if she did not know her home that well she could have gotten lost, but she knew where she was going. She did not know what to do but she had to do something. The blood pact must be broken, perhaps she could help?

The Grand Hall would have been where her mother and father met the shaman elder. She opened the large doors but just like the halls; the room was empty, all the furniture missing and not a shot of colour anywhere. She entered the room, looking up, expecting to see a raven but the room was empty.

"Evangeline?" She whispered once more, knowing it would not work. She thought harder. *Why am I here? To break the curse. Break the blood pact. Free Taren.* Taren. *He is the one now bound to the curse. The infirmary.* She headed there next. *He took refuge here after being attacked. He was injured, that was when the curse was bound to him.* Once again, the infirmary was empty.

Felicity had a sudden urge to go into her chamber room, something was pulling her there. She climbed the stairs, hurriedly marched down the hallway and entered. On the floor in the centre of the room, with nothing else around it, sat her mother's Nil'vetra book, open on a page.

CHAPTER 29.

Evangeline was blind. She knew the ritual had begun the moment Felicity let go of her hand, the winds immediately stopped, and everything turned black. When Sienna warned her the spirit world could reveal itself in strange ways, she did not expect it *not* to be revealed at all. Her own voice was the only thing she heard but there was no reply. She could not see her hand waving in front of her face, no matter how wide she opened her eyes. Afraid to move, she stood frozen, trying to wave her hand or cover one eye to adjust to the light but it was not about the darkness. It was sight. Her eyes were not working.

All she had was her inner voice. *You cannot see. Calm down.* She snapped her finger next to her ear to ensure she could still hear, and her voice was not her imagination. She heard it. *You can hear. That's one thing. What about touch? What do you feel?* In her left hand, grasped tightly was the obsidian stone. She felt the three large smooth sides and one small side, like an arrowhead. It was sharp but comforting. The smoothest side calming her down as she stroked it.

Her right hand was empty. Completely empty. Her bandages had gone on both hands, too. With her thumb she felt the surface of her palm and felt the smooth, uncut skin. *Strange. You're in the spirit world. Perhaps you are dead? Dead people do not have wounds.* Dead people do not need weapons either for she found her belt missing. *Let's get this straight: you are unarmed, blind and stuck in the spirit world. What do we do?*

"When you see the raven, cut yourself free." She said aloud. "I am blind! How am I going to see a raven?" *Do not panic. Take a breath. Count to ten. Do it. One. Two. Three. Four. Five.*

"Evangeline?" The outside voice scared her to death, and she screamed, wincing. The voice was right next to her, so she waved her arms, hoping to touch someone but felt nothing. Tentative steps moved her on, slowly but still connected with air.

"Who's there? Who are you?" There was no answer. "Are you a spirit?" She asked, more calmly this time. "Spirit world, show yourself."

"*Evangeline.*"

"*Evangeline.*"

"*Evangeline.*"

"*Evangeline.*"

"*Evangeline.*"

More voices than she could absorb began to whisper in her ear, saying her name over and over, calling her. On the left, on the right, in front of her, behind, far away and up close. Her heart began to race, and she cupped her hands over her ears, keeping the obsidian in her palm. The voices did not stop, they were *in* her head. She slumped to her knees and fell forward but as her hands extended to break her fall, they did not touch the ground but something else instead. She winced, startled by the foreign object at her fingertips but reached out again and felt it. She ran her fingers along the edge and over the top of it.

It was a book.

She scooted forward, dragging her knees closer to it as she picked it up and got to her feet. From the feel of the naked binding and the missing front cover, she knew it was the Nil'vetra book. Which could only mean she was in Felicity's room. Felicity kept it in the trunk at the foot of her bed, but this book was on the floor. Evangeline reached out again trying to feel for the trunk or bed but felt nothing.

"You're not in Felicity's room, you're in the spirit world, idiot." Hearing her own voice made her realise the voices had stopped. As soon as she touched the book, they had gone silent.

"*Open the book.*" Evangeline screamed loudly at the ethereal whisper by her ear, she dropped the book, and the obsidian, cursing herself. She had stumbled backwards slightly at the voice but scrambled forward, dropping to the floor and searched for the obsidian. Her hands waved back and forth, combing the empty floor. She tried to recall the sound of the stone hitting the ground and work out where it fell but she could not. She searched and searched, in circles around the book, trying to find it again but it was gone. She was blind and she had lost it.

"*Open the book.*" The whisper repeated. Evangeline was prepared that time and only jolted a little. She had no choice but to humour the whisper, so she slowly returned to the book, picked it up and, at random, opened it to a page near the centre of the book.

"Now what?" Evangeline asked, annoyed at herself and the situation.

As soon as the words came out of her mouth, a white light blinded her again. She kept hold of the book this time as she stumbled against the light. Her eyes slowly began to adjust as the light went out. She was no longer blind.

She *was* in Felicity's room.

Felicity was there, too.

CHAPTER 30.

"Is it really you?" Felicity asked, sceptical of Evangeline standing in front of her.

"Yes. And you?" Evangeline squinted at her sister who nodded in agreement, yet neither were convinced the other was real. "How did you get here?" Evangeline asked, scanning the room.

Felicity exhaled and frowned, shaking her head in disbelief as she spoke. "I broke a mirror. A mirror in the middle of a graveyard in the fog. Which turned into a meadow and then I appeared in the courtyard."

Evangeline chuckled and relaxed. "At least my experience was not as weird as that."

"What happened to you?"

"I was blind, and I heard voices, then I found the book." She looked down at the book she was holding and confirmed it was indeed the Nil'vetra book.

"Voices?"

"They said my name over and over, they were calling me. Then I heard a whisper. This was different."

"Different? Did you know the voice?"

"I do not think so but now I think about it, it was familiar."

"Familiar? Who was it?"

"I cannot place who it was. It was a woman, I know that."

Felicity thought it over and had a hunch. "Do you think it could have been mother?" She asked, putting their experiences together.

"What? No. It can't have been. I don't think I even remember what her voice sounds like."

"Evie, I saw her. She was in the mirror, but I could not hear her. You might have heard her but not seen her. We are in the spirit world, it has revealed itself to us and her spirit will be here, somewhere. I think she is trapped."

"I guess that makes sense but how would I know it is her?"

"*Evangeline.*" The ethereal whisper appeared at Evangeline's ear again and she jumped back, screaming. The shock startled Felicity as well and she jolted out of her skin.

"Would you *stop* doing that?!" Evangeline roared into the room.

"I didn't do anything. Why are you screaming?"

"Didn't you hear it?" She asked, scanning the room, looking for the voice.

"Hear what?" Felicity asked, confused and frightened, but she put it together. "You heard the voice again? Was it her? *Mother?*" She called out. "Are you here?"

There was no change to the room. Both Evangeline and Felicity looked around and waited, but nothing happened.

"What is going on?" Evangeline finally asked, her hands beginning to shake. She held the book close to her for something to cling to.

"Can you hear her?" Felicity asked, Evangeline shook her head. Felicity looked at the Nil'vetra book in Evangeline's arms. She had entered the room, seen the book open and as she had touched it, she was blinded again with Evangeline appearing before her, holding the book.

When she had touched the mirror, the graveyard changed into a meadow. When she touched the book, Evangeline appeared. Felicity looked down at her hands, thinking.

"Where is your obsidian?" Evangeline asked.

"I lost it." Felicity said, matter-of-factly. "I might be stuck here."

Evangeline burst out laughing and kept laughing, releasing the pent-up stress within her. She laughed so much, her legs began to buckle, and she stumbled.

"Don't laugh at me!" Felicity spat.

"I'm not, I swear." Evangeline breathed between laughs. "Look," she opened her left palm showing her empty hand, "I lost it, too. We are both stuck here." She was still laughing. "I dropped it while blind and it disappeared, it's not in the room so it's gone forever. Sienna said that is how we get back and we have both lost it. We have no way to get back home."

"Why are you laughing?"

"What else can I do? I think I am about to lose my mind. No wonder mother went crazy, this place sucks!"

"Did you say my name before, when you were here alone?"

"What? Why?"

"I'm trying to work something out. Think, did you say my name, out loud?"

"No. Oh, no, I think I did. Maybe."

"While you were here, in this room?"

"Yes."

"You called me here. I felt an urge to come to this room, it was you. We connected because of this book."

"Where are you getting this from?"

"I'm using my brain, Evie. You should try it for once."

"Well, then use it to get us out of here. I want to go home. I don't like these voices."

"Pass me the book, please. I need to hold it."

Evangeline passed the book over and Felicity took it, expecting something to happen but nothing did. She looked to Evangeline for any ideas.

"Open it." Evangeline said, remembering the voice.

Felicity turned the first page but immediately the book shuffled its pages, turning them on its own. It finally settled on a double page spread that Felicity recognised. At the bottom, the passage finished with: '*though forbidden within all shaman communities; some shamans can bring forth powers from the darkness and practise blood magic.*' She had read the book several times and knew that the next page had been torn out, there was nothing else on blood magic but still she turned the page and there it was, the torn-out page, back in the book. They began to read.

'*These shamans are forever indebted to the darkness and must give up their soul for the gift of blood magic. They are known to take on the title of the Nil'vetra, their spirits forever chained by the Ghouls of the Abyss. The veil between the realms will be burnt before them and the Abyss will slowly take over, poisoning their spirit. Ghouls and spectres from the Abyss will slowly creep through, calling the Nil'vetra to them, they will become a magnet for the Darkness until finally the debt is paid and the Abyss takes them to live eternity in the Void. Punishment and torture are mere dreams to what the Void holds for the Nil'vetra.*'

As Evangeline and Felicity finished reading, shivers ran down their spine, sending a chill down to the bone. The sound of rattling chains crept up on them. They looked at one another and took each other's hands.

"Mother?" They both said in unison. They slowly turned around to face the clinking of metal chains, holding each other tightly at the sight before them.

Together they stared upon the petite figure bound in chains and surrounded by writhing skeletons, clawing their way toward her. Their mother, stretched toward them, held back by the chains at her wrists and legs. Her red eyes bled down her face, a dirty veil laid across her blonde hair and a crown made from bones sat upon her head.

Felicity stretched her hand out toward her mother's face, but Evangeline pulled her back, pointing at the skeletons now facing them. Felicity fought against her sister's tugging, just wanting to feel her mother again but Evangeline kept dragging her away, very aware of the skeletons creeping toward them.

"Stop!" Felicity shouted, yanking her arm from Evangeline's grip. "She's trapped. Maybe this is what we need to do."

"You can't know that! Read the situation, this is dangerous."

Felicity reached out again, stretching toward her mother. "I. Just. Need. To. Reach. Her."

Evangeline grabbed Felicity around the waist and pulled her back, away from the skeletons a hairs width from her arm. She twisted Felicity away, causing the book to fly out of her arms and crash to the floor. The two girls scrambled to the ground to pick it up, but the book closed on impact with the floor and the vision of their mother bound in chains disappeared, filling the room with a waist-high fog.

"No!" Felicity cried, running to the spot where her mother was. Everything was gone, the skeletons, the chains and her mother. She flung around to face Evangeline, "why did you do that?"

"I couldn't risk it."

"Risk what? I could have helped her. I just needed to touch her. Then everything would have been fine."

"Why? What makes you think you know what is going on here?"

Felicity looked down at her hands again. "Let's work this out together." She looked up at Evangeline, "why are we here? What do we need to do? What does it all mean?"

Evangeline stared blankly at her sister but allowed Felicity to take the book from her hands. "This book is the only thing that we have found that is from our world. There is a connection to this book. Perhaps this is the object that has been cursed? But wouldn't Zorya have broken the hex already?"

"No." Evangeline added. "She has never had this book in her possession. I found this book in mother's box that I took from her room the day she died. This book was secret even to me, Zorya must not have known it existed."

"So, this book is the key. What do we do now?"

"I don't know."

"Can you still hear the voices?"

"No."

"What if we go into the courtyard? Its where I first got here."

"Need to start somewhere, I guess."

Felicity let Evangeline exit the Manor first, afraid the ravens would attack again but the courtyard was empty. No ravens, only the fog that seemed to have filled the entire Manor grounds, inside and out.

"Can you hear anything?" Felicity asked. Evangeline shook her head and shrugged her shoulders. "Those voices must be important. What do they want to tell you? Are they calling you somewhere? Do they want something?"

"I don't know, I can't hear them."

"*Listen* to them."

Evangeline relented and closed her eyes, exhaling in disbelief and boredom. Felicity remained silent, watching Evangeline intently, observing the changing expressions in her face. From boredom, to stillness, to a flicker of an eyebrow, a twitch in the crease in her forehead, a subtle tilt of the head, a sharp inhale, she opened her eyes.

"The crypt." Evangeline commanded. Felicity smiled and agreed, following her sister across the bleak grounds, through the dead, dried out gardens and down the cold, stone steps. Felicity's hand unconsciously found her sister's as they advanced into the crypt. There were four dark figures standing in the main hall and as Evangeline and Felicity descended the stairs, the figures separated, each going into one of the four rooms that snaked off the main hall.

Together they followed the first figure into the closest

room but as they entered, they found the room empty, except for one thing. A single skeleton sat on the floor against the back wall; its skull removed. Evangeline and Felicity exchanged a look but before they could act, they were both startled by the sound of undulating flames and wood crackling in the next room.

There was no dark figure in the second room either, only a charred body burning at the stake. Felicity wanted to see the other two rooms before confirming her hunch and Evangeline followed suit.

The third room did have a figure standing in it. Dressed in the black cloak with their back to them, hiding all features, they merely stood like a statue until the cloak slipped, draping onto the floor and several falcons took flight around the room. The bird's feathers began to fall out as they flew above the girls and one by one, dropped dead around them. When the last bird landed with a thud, they immediately sprung to life and swooped toward them, squawking and screeching, talons arched, ready to attack. Felicity screamed as Evangeline pushed her out of the way with her right hand and batted the closest falcon to the floor with her left. Evangeline and Felicity swiftly exited the room, dodging the attacking birds which did not follow them out.

The fourth figure stood in the centre of the fourth room, also dressed in a black cloak but this time was facing them. A familiar face which unnerved them and froze them to the spot. The candles beside him cast a large shadow projected onto the wall but that shadow did not reflect the human it was connected to. Taren stood tall and still against the shadow of the beast.

"Taren?" Uttered Evangeline, stepping toward him.

"This is it." Felicity said when Taren did not answer. "The connection. The key. The beast is connected to Taren, we must break it."

"So, what was all of that?" Evangeline asked, gesturing toward the other rooms.

"A skeleton without its head, a burning body. Those are the horrors of her past. Don't you see it?" Felicity asked. "Mother and father executed the shaman elder here in the Manor, it must have been a beheading, hence the missing skull. The burning body is mother's friend she betrayed, that friend was burnt at the stake. She is trying to show us things, she is guiding us."

"And the birds?" Evangeline added.

"I don't know. I can't make sense of them, but it is not the first time I was attacked by birds tonight. They must signify something."

Evangeline glanced down at the Nil'vetra book. "What about heraldry? There are symbols in the book that have heraldic meaning, what do falcons symbolise?"

"Let me think, falcons used for the hunt, a search for power, it's a symbol of a desire for knowledge, also meaning vision and courage. If you connect that to the other rooms, these are all visions. The falcons symbolise the shamans themselves. Shamans have a desire for knowledge and search for power. The birds were flying free then died at our feet and then attacked, representing our family's relationship with them."

"These are all visions of the past, leading to Taren and his connection to the beast. We sever the connection; we break the curse."

"We break the curse, we free Taren and end the beast!"

"Exactly, Flick! So how do we break the curse?"

Felicity thought for a moment then looked up at Evangeline, smiling. "Like you said, we must right the wrongs."

CHAPTER 31.

"Tell me what you are thinking, Felicity. I cannot help you if you do not tell me."

Felicity ran from the fourth room into the first, looked at the beheaded skeleton and ran into the next room, the fires still blazing, melting the figure burning at the stake. She stepped forward, closer to the fire, reaching out and watched the flames withdraw from her fingers. Grabbing Evangeline's hand, she pulled it forward and the flames recoiled from her, too, but she jumped back.

"Watch it." Evangeline said through clenched teeth. She was not rubbing the hand that touched the fire, she was rubbing the other, the one holding the book. The fires retreated from their empty hands but clung to the Nil'vetra book, burning Evangeline's hand that held it.

"Interesting." Felicity whispered, her mind hard at work, running through several theories at once. Evangeline merely stood still, watching her sister pace up and down, running between the four rooms, counting on her fingers and stroking the fur trim of her gown.

Finally, Felicity came to a stop in front of Evangeline, grinning from ear to ear, her hands together at her chest. Evangeline remembered that look from when they were children just after Felicity had set up a prank. She was excited and had just figured it out.

"Let me guess," Evangeline began, "we have to right the wrongs by fixing the visions? Bring the skeleton its head and put out the fire?"

The smiled dropped from Felicity's face in shock. "Yes. That is exactly what we need to do. How did you know that?"

"From watching you, stupid! *You* figured it out, I can just read you like a book."

"The book!" Felicity pointed down and took the book from Evangeline's hands. "This is the key; we agree on that?"

Evangeline nodded. "This is also the only object from our world that has followed us here and is the only thing that affects that fire. What if we burn it?"

"Woah, wait a minute. You cannot burn it. It's important. We still need to decrypt mother's notes."

"I really think this is what we need to do. We need to put out that fire and I believe this is how we do it."

"We cannot risk it." Evangeline stepped forward and reached for the book, but Felicity jumped back, spinning out of her sister's reach. Evangeline lunged again but missed Felicity. "Give me the book, Flick."

"No. Trust me, I know what I'm doing. This is what we must do."

"How? How do you know that?"

"It feels right. Trust me." Without waiting for any further reply, Felicity threw the book into the flames. Evangeline reached for it, hoping the fire would withdraw from her hands again but she recoiled from the heat and could only watch it burn.

As the book slowly burned to ash, the fires burnt out with it. As the flames turned to smoke, the vision of the charred figure blew away too, the body and the stake turning to ash.

"Fine." Evangeline said, "you know what you're doing."

"The spirit is now at rest. Did you feel the relief?" Felicity looked around, "the spirit world just got lighter."

"Now the skeleton?"

The two of them returned to the first room and crouched down in front of the beheaded skeleton, looking around at the empty room. The walls of the dead in the real world were bare and empty in the spirit world and this thought unnerved them.

"We need to reunite the skeleton with its head?" Evangeline asked, not knowing where to begin.

"That's what I'm thinking," agreed Felicity. She delicately reached out and placed a hand on the rib cage as she closed her eyes, when she opened them again she was in the meadow. The same meadow of wildflowers that she saw when she touched the mirror in the graveyard. Something was different, however. There were trees around her. She wondered if they were there before and she did not notice, or they were new. She was in a forest. *The* forest.

She stepped forward but her foot collided with something

as she kicked it. At her feet sat the missing skull. Felicity blinked and was back in the crypt.

"What did you see?" Evangeline asked, a hand on Felicity's arm.

"How did you know I saw something?"

"The way you acted; it was like you were dreaming."

"The skull is in the forest; we must go and get it."

"Where in the forest? Without someone who knows the way, and without following the road, we could easily get lost out there, it's huge."

"I know. I remember getting lost on a hunt once when I was young."

"I remember that. It took the knights hours to find you, but they eventually did. You were smart, you knew to remain put and they would find you. So where in the forest is the skull?"

"I don't know, Evie. It's in a wildflower meadow, in a large opening. That's all I know."

Evangeline thought for a moment and listened. The crypt was strangely quiet now there was no crackling fire yet still she listened. She was waiting for that tiny signal, that confirmation that they were not alone. The voices were terrifying at first yet now they comforted. They guided her to the crypt and now they were guiding her to the forest.

She knew where she had to go.

Felicity followed Evangeline up the stairs of the crypt, knowing better than to question it. She knew for definite they were on the right track and were doing the right thing when they exited the crypt and found themselves directly in the meadow in the centre of the forest. The treeline surrounded them, a summery blue sky above and just before them, laid the skull. Evangeline urged Felicity to pick it up and she did, turning to return to the crypt but Evangeline halted her.

"Wait. This is wrong. The body is in our grey, dark crypt and the skull is out in beautiful nature. Shamans worship nature, they use the land for their rituals. Their caravans are full of herbs, plants, flowers, bones, whatever they find. We shouldn't be reuniting skull with the body, we should be bringing the body to the skull, where it belongs."

"I think you're right." Felicity placed the skull back on the ground and they returned to the crypt, bringing back out with them the skeleton. Felicity carried the bones up the stairs delicately and crossed the meadow to meet the skull. She placed the body on the flowers. As Evangeline picked up the skull, Felicity crossed the arms and placed a sprig of forget-me-nots in its hands. Evangeline placed the skull at the tip of the spine to ensure bone connected with bone. The two of them stood up and watched the complete skeleton disintegrate into dust before them.

Evangeline and Felicity turned to face the crypt once again and were welcomed by a warm glow of candlelight inside. They descended the stairs once more, very aware that the crypt looked exactly like it did before the ritual began, as if they were back but they knew they were not for thousands of ravens and falcons watched them as they advanced into the crypt. Seeing both birds together, calm and vigilant, eased their minds completely. Back in the main chamber, Taren was laid in the centre, eyes closed and unresponsive.

"What do we do?" Felicity asked. "Is he real? Is he a vision? Taren? Can you hear me?"

"Everything looks the same, we are back where we started but no Zorya or Sienna. We have no obsidian and no book."

"Is this a vision before the ritual? Our blood is not on his chest." Felicity pointed at his clean shirt, the blood that dripped on him as they began the ritual was no longer there.

"Perhaps that is how we get out of here? See the raven, cut yourself free. We need to complete the ritual by completing the circle. We started the ritual by drawing blood, we need to leave the ritual by doing the same."

"How are we supposed to cut ourselves free? We have no obsidian."

"They say shamans and Bridges see the spirit world like a veil over our own. Perhaps we are in neither world but in the veil itself." Evangeline reached down and felt Taren's hands. They were both grasped shut but she prised one open and inside was a piece of obsidian. She looked at Felicity and threw it up in the air toward her. Felicity caught it and smiled. "You go first," Evangeline said, gesturing to the stone. "In case it is only one per customer."

Felicity hesitated for a moment but sliced her palm with the stone then gave it to Evangeline. She avoided dropping her blood on Taren until Evangeline had managed to cut herself, too. Together they held their bleeding hands over

Taren's body, standing in the same spots they began in. The blood dripped onto his chest, but nothing happened.

Once Felicity took hold of Evangeline's free hand, a bright light blinded them both.

They were back.

CHAPTER 32.

Taren sat up suddenly, gripping his chest. The chronic pain since being wounded by the beast was gone, the grip on his heart relieved, his soul had been freed. He scrambled to his feet, cheering and laughing as he flung his arms around Felicity and Evangeline.

"You did it!" He roared, light and giddy and unbelieving.

"We did?" Evangeline asked, laughing along with Taren.

"You did it!" Taren repeated, letting them go and looking at them, searching their faces and bodies, taking them in. "You set me free! How did you manage it?"

"It was all Felicity." Evangeline said, gesturing to her.

"Felicity? You saved my life." Taren took Felicity's reddening face in his hands and planted a kiss on her forehead. Evangeline grinned at Felicity's blushing cheeks as Taren hugged her again but shook her head when Felicity didn't hug back, shocked frozen at the situation.

"What happened?" Taren, Felicity and Evangeline's cheery moment was shattered at the sound of Sienna's fearful question. "What did you do?" She asked, short and fearful but equally curious.

"We righted the wrongs and set the spirits free." Felicity said proudly.

Zorya and Sienna exchanged a look between them that could not be read by the others. Zorya stepped forward and placed a hand on Taren's chest. She whispered some incomprehensible language as she closed her eyes and when she opened them, they glowed yellow for a moment.

"You did it." She said. "The connection is broken."

"How?" Asked Sienna, "what did you see?"

"We saw visions. The horrors of our mother's past. We put them to rest. She guided us."

"She guided you? How? How did you know it was her?"

"We saw her."

"What?" Sienna asked, dumbfounded.

"You saw her? You actually saw her." Zorya stepped forward, close to Evangeline and Felicity, desperation in her eyes. "What did she look like? Did she say anything to you?"

"Yes, we both saw her. At first, I saw her but didn't hear her, but Evangeline heard her and didn't see her. Then when our visions connected we both saw her."

"You two connected?" Sienna asked.

"You actually saw each other? And you shared the same vision?" Zorya added.

"Yes, we were together, why? What does that mean?" Felicity asked, trying to understand.

Sienna and Zorya exchanged a look once again and neither Evangeline nor Felicity could read it, but their own exchanged look confirmed their confusion.

"Did we do something wrong?" Evangeline asked, knowing they were hiding something.

"The entire spirit world was fractured the moment the ritual began. We could not break the curse ourselves; something was stopping us. Something powerful. We thought we failed until we returned but it turns out it was you two. *You* broke the connection."

"Why is that?" Felicity asked.

"We don't know." Sienna breathed, her hand on her chin.

"Is it done, though?" Taren asked. "Is it over?"

"If my calculations are correct and my interpretation is true, the beast will not attack again." Zorya looked to Sienna.

"You are correct. The connection is broken. Gods only know how you did it, but you have done it. It is time to spread the word."

The four of them emerged from the crypt, squinting at the break of dawn cracking through the gardens. A chilly winter breeze swept over them.

"Thank you for your help." Evangeline said, holding out her hand to Sienna. "You have no idea what good you have done for my family and my people."

"I am glad I could help." She said, shaking Evangeline's hand.

"What will you do now?" Felicity asked. "Go back to the shamans?"

"No. I am a rogue now. I have been banished from my people for helping you and will not be permitted to return."

"You could stay here with us. Be our shaman consul?"

"No. There are answers I need to find. I must go and search for knowledge. You will not need me again."

The three of them watched Sienna leave without a fuss. Next was Taren, who suddenly felt exhausted and thanked the girls once more before leaving them to return to their father. Taren did not want to be near Lord Horus, whom he disliked and needed to process what happened alone. Evangeline knew exactly what he meant and wanted to leave too but had to remain by her sister's side.

"He is inside, my Lady." Cadmael said as the three of them reached the Lord's study. "He's been in there all night, asked not to be disturbed."

"Step aside." Zorya commanded. Cadmael complied and allowed the three of them to enter.

"Father?" Felicity was the first to notice his body behind the desk, laid face down on the floor, motionless. The three women ran to his body. Felicity took his hand and tapped his shoulder, trying to wake him up. Evangeline pulled him over onto his back, placed a finger under his nose and then her head on his chest, checking for breathing.

"He is alive." Zorya said, standing over him. She turned to the cabinet by the window and removed some vials and bottles. Felicity watched her pierce his finger, drawing blood and let it drop into an amber vial. She poured another vial into the first and sniffed the vapours.

"He has not been poisoned."

"Then what is wrong with him?" Felicity asked, tears in her eyes.

"Cadmael!" Evangeline roared, "What happened? Who has been in this room? When was the last time you checked on him?"

"I do not know what happened. He asked not to be disturbed and I respected that command. He retired up here after leaving the infirmary shortly after you did, my Lady, and he has not left the room. Nobody has gone in or out."

"It's his sickness." Zorya whispered, a hand delicately placed on his chest. "It has returned." She moved her hand from his chest to his face and cradled it gently. "I will do what I can to keep it at bay whilst I find a cure, but it will take time."

"I thought he was better?" Felicity asked. "He was better

when you returned. What is wrong with him?"

"He *was* better. I do not know what has gone wrong. I've missed something." Zorya stood up and took each of the girl's hands. "I promise I will help him as much as I can but there is not much you two can do right now. You have both had such a long day, please get some sleep."

"What about the beast?" Evangeline asked.

"I will give the news. Despite this," she looked down at Horus and back at them, "some good has come from tonight and I will ensure that the people know it. Please get some sleep and recover from the events of tonight." Zorya let go of their hands. "Cadmael, no one is to disturb these two at all today, do you understand? Leave them be. Everything is to go through me."

"Yes, my Lady."

Felicity led Evangeline from the tower, eager to take up the offer of sleep. "He'll be in good hands, Evie."

"I hope so." Evangeline replied, her eyes drooping. The walk back to their chamber rooms was silent, the night weighing heavily on their shoulders. Felicity parted ways with Evangeline and retired to her room, falling asleep immediately, still in her clothes but Evangeline remained at her door, afraid to enter.

The armoured steps of a knight advancing on her down the hallway excited her, but it was only Sir Constantine. She craved to see Thedamaine but also wanted to sleep.

"Constantine." She called out before she realised. He turned round and faced her.

"Yes, my Lady? How can I help?"

"Is Sir Thedamaine still on duty?"

"No, my Lady. I just passed him in the Knight's Quarters, he is asleep."

"Thank you." He carried on walking down the hallway, leaving Evangeline alone. She barely slept and because of that, Thedamaine slept even less. She could not disrupt his sleep just because she wanted to see him.

Stood in front of her door, finally alone and safe, the laudanum started to wear off, the pain of her many injuries finally returning as if being in the proximity of shamans temporarily cured her.

She entered her chamber, opened a bottle of wine and filled a goblet, mixing in the small bottle of laudanum she had hoarded in her room. On her bedside table sat an unopened letter branded with the Forrester seal. She already knew what it said and cast it into the fireplace, burning it.

With the beast gone, there was nothing to delay her wedding.

CHAPTER 33.

Felicity waited outside her father's chamber door gathering the strength to go inside. She had not seen him for days as he was bed ridden and catatonic. With Evangeline shut up in her room and Zorya splitting her time between doctor and Lady of the Manor, Felicity was running out of places to be happy and people to talk to. Taren had been her only saviour in the seven days since the ritual but even so, she only met with him twice. There had been no beast attacks so far, and Taren spent his free time drinking in taverns, somewhere Felicity did not feel comfortable.

The door swung open and Felicity jumped, torn from her thoughts. Zorya stood in front of her; hair ratty, her black dress filthy and coal smudged on her face. Felicity had never seen Zorya look so terrible before and the sight rendered her speechless.

"For God's sake, Felicity, just come in. I cannot take you hovering like that." Zorya stepped aside and Felicity entered the room.

"I didn't know you were here. Weren't you just in the Grand Hall with Cadmael?"

"I am a shaman, have you forgotten?" She swept across the room and stood behind a pot above the fireplace, stirring it swiftly.

"Right, illusion. I remember, that is your proficiency." Felicity scoffed at herself, finally realising how Zorya disappeared before the wedding when she was following her. Advancing into the room, she saw her father in his bed and went over to his side. "How is he doing?" She asked, reaching out to touch him but stopping when he began to fidget and thrash.

"I have induced sleep. Deep slumbers like this are good for healing and slowing down time and that is what I need right now." Thrashing more violently, Zorya came to his side and placed a damp rag on his forehead, soothing him. "I am not afraid to admit that I do not know what is wrong with him, but I will care for him until I cure him." Still holding the rag on his head, she looked at Felicity and smiled slightly. "I promise you; I will fix him."

Felicity swallowed a large lump in her throat as she looked down at her father. Despite the thrashing and the fidgeting, he already looked dead. All the colour and strength that had returned to him was long gone, leaving a sickly, frail man in its place. So much had happened so soon, how could she lose her father, too?

Spontaneously, afraid doing nothing would bring the tears, Felicity threw her arms around Zorya's waist and hugged her tightly. She held on for dear life, squeezing out all emotion inside her.

"Thank you." Felicity said. "Thank you for helping him. Thank you for helping us with the ritual. Thank you for saving Taren. Thank you for protecting us. Thank you for everything."

Zorya held her hands up just above Felicity's body, unable to process what was happening. She stood frozen, taken aback whilst Felicity hung on. Finally, she slowly lowered her hands, lightly tapping Felicity's back. Felicity still did not let go and hugged tightly, not knowing this was what she had needed for months.

Zorya did not pull away until Felicity let go and when she did, she had to wipe away a single tear that had materialised out of nowhere. "You have a special touch." Zorya uttered, hiding a smile and turning back to the pot.

Felicity wrapped her arms around herself, chuckling lightly at those words, remembering the ritual. "Do you miss her?" Felicity asked.

Zorya's back was to Felicity but she stopped stirring the pot and looked up. "Yes," she said and began stirring forcefully. "I miss your mother every day. She was my best friend, my confidante, my sister in bond. We shared a connection that she refused to accept but I encouraged. Where I studied my powers, she locked them away. Refusing to accept the voices only made them louder. Turning away the spirits only invited more to her. She was the link, but she severed it."

"The link?"

"All shamans can see and hear the souls of the dead. Some more than others. They gravitated toward her because she was a link between worlds. The spirit world has many names; Underworld, Helheim, Yomi, Xibalba, Duat, Nav, Iriy, all telling the same story. Your mother was born to be a ferryman, the beacon of hope for a lost soul or newly deceased spirit but she refused this burden and was taken from us."

"Is that why she was killed? Can she ferry the dead now she is one of them? No more avoiding the task?"

"No. She was killed via blood magic. Something strong I had not seen before. I could not stop it and did not see it coming."

"The shaman elder would have been strong. Although mother would have been killed instantly, surely? If the elder used blood magic to kill her, why did she die years later? Can you assassinate via blood magic and delay the death?"

"No. An assassination is almost instant after a long ritual, but that is not the only way you can kill someone." Zorya stopped stirring and turned to Felicity. "One can be offered as a sacrifice to the Darkness and that sacrifice can be taken at any time. It is down to the mercy of the Nil'vetra."

"A sacrifice in exchange for resurrection?" Felicity asked, half-rhetorically.

"Correct. A shaman may commit blood magic and perform a resurrection, offering a sacrifice to the Darkness."

"If you choose to resurrect someone else, can you sacrifice yourself?"

Zorya stepped closer, a small frown contorting her brow. Placing a delicate hand on Felicity's cheek, she shook her head subtly. "Trust me." Zorya breathed. "It is not worth the trouble." Dropping her hand and changing tone, she returned to the pot once more and kept stirring. "Shamans have the ability to resurrect themselves too, you know? Only if you know how."

"Really? Interesting."

"It is only a temporary measure though; I suspect you know that. Resurrection is selling your soul to the Darkness and eventually you'll have to pay the piper. You must only hope that you have done enough good to make the most of your new life before it is taken from you." Zorya pulled out the metal spoon from the pot and hung it over the fireplace.

With her fingers, she gestured for Felicity to come over and she did. "Watch this." She said, pointing into the pot, a light air of excitement in her voice.

The pot was filled with a clear, bubbling liquid. Inside was a little whirlpool from the stirring and as Felicity watched it spin, the liquid turned black so suddenly that it made her jump.

"What was that?"

"That means part one is done."

"Part one?" Felicity asked, assuming that process had been long and difficult and now more work was to be done.

"Now we must let it cool completely. Would you like a drink?"

"Of that? No thank you. Tell me what it is first."

"Not that. A real drink. Wine, ale, beer, rum? What's your poison?"

"Um, wine?"

"Wine it is." Zorya reached up and pulled a bottle of wine from the top of the wardrobe and picked up four goblets from the chest of drawers. She uncorked the bottle, sniffed it and began to pour, slowly filling them one by one. Felicity opened her mouth to ask but Zorya answered for her. "We are about to have company." She nodded toward the door just before someone knocked on it. "Enter."

The door creaked open slowly and Vesna popped her head around, the smile dropping from her face as she saw Felicity.

"Oh, you have company." She said, closing the door again.

"Please join us." Felicity said, opening the door herself. Morana was just behind her, hidden from view. She passed her goblet to Vesna and picked the third off the table, handing it to Morana as she entered.

"We can come back later." She said, reluctantly.

"Nonsense." Zorya replied. There was a table and four chairs by the window and Zorya sat down, gesturing to the other chairs. Both equally uncomfortable, Felicity and Vesna took a seat and sipped their wine. Morana remained standing.

"Where's Evangeline?" Vesna asked, awkwardly.

"Last time I saw her she was playing chess with Thedamaine, too drunk to move the pieces."

"How did she take the news?"

"The usual way. She's hiding, hoping it will go away."

"I have spoken to the Forresters," Zorya began, "there is

nothing else we can do, not with your father incapacitated."

"Out of the jaws of one beast and into the belly of another."

"Vesna, what are you talking about?" Asked Morana, her patience wearing. "What are any of you on about? She's got it easy, it's us you have to worry about. Evangeline can run away with her husband whilst we are here forever looking over our shoulder hoping the beast will not return."

"Morana, enough with the attitude, just enough." Vesna hissed, slamming her goblet on the table.

"What is your problem?" Felicity asked, growing tired of the difficult child. "Why are you so angry?"

Morana looked to her mother who only tilted her head at her daughter. Felicity remembered all too well the silent communication that a mother mastered. Knowing exactly what her mother meant, Morana exhaled deeply and took a seat, dropping herself in a slump incredibly similar to Evangeline. Felicity chuckled.

"I'm just scared." Morana muttered. "I guess it's easier to be angry. It's a good mask."

"Anger lies at the surface. More often than not anger is just masking something else. Passion, fear, regret, grief." Zorya was staring into the fire, her eyes glazed over and remained lost in thought.

"Do you think we will be safe?" Vesna asked. "Is it really gone?"

"Only time will tell." Felicity began. "The coming full moon will soothe all our fears, you'll see. We just need to wait it out."

CHAPTER 34.

The next full moon came and went in a blink of an eye without a single beast attack. The entire village was celebrating the victory, including the Manor, everyone except Evangeline who remained in her room, with an eternal drink in her hand.

"Evangeline! Open this door!" Felicity's constant pounding at the door finally broke Evangeline. She unlocked the door and swung it open, pushed out of the way when Felicity barged her way through.

"I want to be left alone." Evangeline emptied the last of the wine in her goblet and took a swig.

"I have respected your wishes for a week now, but you refuse to come out of your room and will not see any of us. Not me, not Taren, and you barely even speak to Thedamaine. This cannot all be down to what I think it is?"

"I do not have to explain myself to you. My mental state is none of your business."

"Evangeline, put down the wine and talk to me. You know this ends tonight, there is no avoiding it."

"I'm not going." Evangeline finished the goblet and immediately opened the wine bottle on the chest of drawers.

"You're the guest of honour! The ball tonight is celebrating *your* wedding. You're the bride, you have to go. You know this. Give me that!" Felicity snatched the bottle from Evangeline's hands, but Evangeline continued drinking from the goblet. "Listen to me, drink will not postpone your wedding. You have two days. Tonight, is the celebratory ball, tomorrow is the preparations and after that you will be married. There is no avoiding it."

"Why are you here?" Evangeline asked between swallows of wine, "it's bad luck to see the bride before the wedding."

"That's for the groom and for the day of the wedding, not for the world as soon as the date is set. You have locked

224

yourself away drowning yourself in wine and misery."

"I don't even like wine."

"This pathetic pity party ends now. Why are you shutting us out?"

"I am close to a nervous breakdown and because I am aware of this, I can control it-" Evangeline snatched the wine bottle back off of Felicity, "-and control it I shall." She smiled as she drank from the bottle.

"This is not controlling it." Felicity took the bottle again, straight from Evangeline's mouth, causing her to spill a little down her chin. Felicity turned around and put the bottle down behind her, out of Evangeline's reach, when she turned back around, Evangeline had materialised another bottle. Felicity took this bottle, too, putting it down behind her but once again, when her back was turned, Evangeline had found another stashed bottle. "Where are you getting these? Give it to me."

"You will not win." Sir Thedamaine was stood in the doorway watching Felicity wrestle the bottle from Evangeline's hands. "She has bottles hidden everywhere in here."

"Theo!" Evangeline suddenly let go of the bottle and Felicity fell to the ground. "You know me so well. I've missed you."

"Whose fault is that?" Felicity grumbled as she got to her feet.

"Why are you here, Felicity?"

"You need to get out of this room. If you want to drink, why not come to a tavern with me and Taren before the ball?"

"Are you two an item now?" Thedamaine asked innocently.

"What? No! I'm not in love with Taren."

"That's a goddamn lie." Evangeline mumbled under her breath as she opened another bottle of wine she had fetched from behind the books on her bookcase.

"Right! That's it." Felicity lunged for Evangeline but Thedamaine caught her, pulling her back. "Let me go! Let me just *break* her arm!"

"Please do," smirked Evangeline, "then maybe I'll feel something."

"I thought *she* was the violent sister." Thedamaine said, still holding Felicity back. "What has gotten into you?"

Felicity stopped struggling as Evangeline stepped toward her. "Maybe recent events have effected *both* of us? It's hard isn't it? All this change? The beast is dead, but father is on his death bed, barely leading at all, bedridden for days. Zorya is the ruling power now; there is no changing that. I'm about to get married and move away and neither of us have been the same since the ritual. I know you've had the nightmares, too. They're making you angry, trust me, I know, but you are smarter and better than I am so don't let it control you. Me? I've gone down a different route." Evangeline jumped on the bed, spread eagle, gulping down the wine straight from the bottle. "It's far too late for me." She added, taking a breath.

"I don't understand why you suddenly care about your wedding. A political marriage has always sat fine with you before. What has changed?"

A thick silence fell over the room as Evangeline did not answer Felicity. Eventually, Evangeline sat up, corked the wine and left the room without a word. Thedamaine followed Evangeline down the hallway, silently, leaving Felicity alone.

"What?" She said aloud to the empty room, rendered bewildered at her sister's chaotic state. "Well, I got her to leave her room, so problem solved."

Felicity left Evangeline's room and returned to her own. Zigzagging around the stacks of books she had collected in the last month and a half, received as gifts from Sienna and Zorya, after days of pestering.

When they had returned from the ritual, the Nil'vetra book was missing, as if burning it in the spirit world had erased it from theirs, so Felicity had written everything she remembered in her red notebook and it was the foundation on which she built her new investigation.

Evangeline was correct, Felicity was having nightmares. Every night since the ritual, she dreamt of the beast, the mirror, her father, Taren, even Sienna. She knew her thoughts and fears were being targeted in her nightmares; she was afraid her father would die, she was afraid the beast would return, her thoughts lingered on Taren and she desperately needed answers from Sienna. The nightmares were only figments of her imagination fixating on fears and thoughts, so did not think twice about it.

Almost every waking moment Felicity spent reading and

studying shamans and magic, seeing everything in a whole new light. She wanted to know everything. *Needed* to know. Why did she and Evangeline connect in the spirit world? Why did they both have visions of their mother? Was she really guiding them?

Felicity thought back to Sienna and Zorya's reaction to this reveal, neither of them could believe they had both seen their mother. Felicity needed to know why.

She opened one of the shaman books and began to read:

'An extremely powerful shaman, bound to the powers of blood magic, also known as a Nil'vetra, has the ability to mutate and amplify a curse, however once this curse is mutated, it can only be broken by parties involved.'

Felicity spoke out loud to herself, preferring to hear her thoughts in order to organise them. "Sienna and Zorya were shocked when they realised that we broke the connection, this must be why. The curse was amplified when father attacked the camp which meant that only me and Evangeline could break it as we were the parties involved."

She still did not know the true reason behind his attack on the camp, she could not believe that it was just because he hated them. Perhaps he assumed they killed his wife, and he could not act until he was better? But how did he get better? And why was he sick again?

Felicity had a sudden epiphany and rummaged through the books trying to find a specific one. Two stacks fell to the ground as she carelessly pulled books from the bottom, buried underneath a pile, she finally found it: The Healer's Guide to Alchemical Magic.

'When two opposing shamans are battling against each other's magic, the effects can severely harm a mortal stuck in the middle. These effects can manifest in physical deformities, mental state decay or serious fatigue as their life force is drained. When a shaman is trying to break a curse of another, the person involved can suffer serious consequences. Should this process be prolonged over a long period of time, the mortal in question will continue to suffer indefinitely until the curse is broken or the mortal dies.

There are several remedies that can stabilise the effects, but these are temporary and minor. The following remedies may help the situation: ... '

Felicity stopped reading and thought for a moment. Her

father's sickness was beginning to make sense. Zorya confirmed she had been trying to break the hex since she arrived here, that in itself contributed to his sickness.

"Serious fatigue as their life force is drained." She said aloud, writing it down in her notebook. "That does make sense. But why did he get better and then was sick again?" She rubbed her eyes, trying to think. The constant nightmares had ruined her sleep and sleep was the one thing she knew she was good at. Her eyes opened, "Zorya must have thought she broke the curse, made him better and then returned from their honeymoon." Felicity betted herself that they did not actually go on a honeymoon at all but perhaps to the shaman camp to break the curse. That would have been why he attacked it, he found out he was kept there. "The curse was amplified when he attacked the camp, which is why he was sick again and why Zorya and Sienna came to us, to break it."

Something was still gnawing at Felicity's mind. Something was not quite right with the situation. If the curse was making her father sick, what was it doing to her?

CHAPTER 35.

She had been staring for an eternity. The harmless presents laid out on the trunk at the foot of her bed stared back, waiting for her to open them. Waiting for her to finally confirm she will be married. The celebratory ball was only hours away, she had to open the presents then and there. No more avoiding it.

With Zorya taking over the rule of the Manor, there was nothing to distract Evangeline. The voices she heard in the spirit world refused to let her sleep but when she did, the attacks she had narrowly escaped returned to her in her nightmares.

She was afraid.

"Refusing to open them will not delay your wedding." Sir Thedamaine entered the room and closed the door behind him.

"What will?" She asked, quietly. She picked up the first gift and angrily tore off the paper. Inside was a silver chalice with a raven and oak tree engraved on the side.

"At least you'll get good use out of that." Thedamaine said with a smile. Evangeline laughed and threw it across the room, tossing the box it came in and refusing to read the attached scroll.

The next gift was an embroidery hoop. Thedamaine was the first to laugh and did the honours of throwing it into the fireplace.

Evangeline opened three more gifts; she rolled her eyes at every reveal but Thedamaine made her laugh each time. A gown she would never wear, a writing set she would never use and a book on the Forrester family archives she would never read.

When Evangeline thought she was finally finished, Thedamaine presented a final box. This was different. He held the box close to him and was looking down at it, not at her.

"You have one left, my Lady."

She took it from him and placed it on the trunk, he remained by the wall behind her, watching her open it. It was an ordinary wooden box, secured by a black ribbon. Inside was a beautiful pewter chess set. Evangeline inspected it closer, it was Ravenhill versus Rosewood. Most of the pieces were the same on both sides but the pawns on one side were little ravens and the other side were roses. Each rook was a detailed miniature of Ravenhill Manor atop its hill.

She picked up both bishop pieces. They were both young girls, one with her intricate braid and reading a book and the other, taller, with a simple braid, sword at her waist and drink in her hand. They were miniature pewter versions of her and Felicity.

Felicity may look like a Ravenhill, with her brown hair, tanned skin and dark eyes but nobody could doubt she inherited the Rosewood intelligence. Her bishop was on the Rosewood side. Evangeline inherited the rare blonde hair and pale skin of a Rosewood, but she was truly a Ravenhill through and through.

She noticed that each chess piece sat upon a black stone pedestal, both sides sat on smoothed obsidian, but the Rosewood side was snowflake obsidian, she could tell by the white speckles.

Looking closer, she could tell that both kings were her father and both queens, her mother. Evangeline marvelled at the detailing. The heavy pewter pieces, the obsidian pedestals, her family and home in miniature; it would have cost a fortune, but it was perfect.

This was not a wedding gift. If it were, it would have been Ravenhill and Forrester. Evangeline knew in her gut this was a leaving present. A memento. An inside joke.

She picked up the Ravenhill knight piece; an armoured knight rearing on his steed and an accurate Ravenhill shield in his hand. She put it to her mouth then held it close to her heart.

"Thank you, Theo, for the gift."

"How did you know it was from me?" He asked, faintly.

"Only you could have done this." Evangeline smiled down at the chess set, placing the knight back in the box. As she let go, she was immediately reminded of her future and the smiled dropped from her face. "How do I get out of this?" She asked, "I have two days left."

"You cannot stop this." He replied, knowing what she meant. "You can either go kicking and screaming or with your head held high. I *know* you will be able to handle this."

"And what about you?" Her voice was barely more than a whisper and she had not turned to face him, still looking at the chess set. Thedamaine stepped forward, just behind her and placed a hand delicately on her upper arm, grazing the skin.

"I will be beside you every step of the way, so please don't push me away. This world is a lonely place, don't make it any lonelier."

"I thought if I withdrew from you, it might hurt a little less. I just wanted to protect you for once."

"We've both been trying to protect the other," he whispered, "perhaps that should stop?"

Evangeline turned to face him, reaching up and sliding her hands around the back of his neck and kissed him tightly. He returned the kiss with relief, but stopped, pulling back. Evangeline kissed him again, encouraged his every move and led the way.

CHAPTER 36.

Evangeline got dressed in silence with a ghost of a smile on her face. Deciding against a braid for once, she kept her wavy mess of hair down, only half tied up to keep it out of her face. She chose the black lace gown with the dark red corset, purposely ignoring the emerald green gown laid out for her. Thedamaine helped her with the corset, brushing a finger down the skin on her arm, giving her shivers and bringing the smile forth.

She headed to the door, picking up a bottle of wine on the way but Thedamaine stopped her, raised his eyebrows and presented the silver chalice she received as a wedding gift. She sighed with a smile and filled the chalice with the wine. He dropped his shoulders and smirked, taking the bottle from her and handing her the chalice. She took it and exited the room, Thedamaine followed, leaving the bottle.

The Manor had been completely redecorated for the upcoming wedding and for the celebratory ball. Black and green *everywhere*. Evangeline refused to look at any of it. She advanced through the Manor, ignoring people she passed and came to a halt at the closed doors of the Grand Hall. The music within and ruckus of the crowd stopped her in her tracks. She could not bring herself to open the doors and enter. Her feet would not move, her arms would not move. She could not move.

Thedamaine took her by the hand and led her away from the Hall, down the corridor and into the small reading room parlour that they had their first game of chess in.

He closed the door behind them and took the chalice from her hand, placing it on the table next to the chess set. Wrapping his arms around her, she buried her face in his chest and hugged him tightly. Neither said anything and neither let go.

Evangeline's head was in Thedamaine's chest, but she was

looking at the chess set beside them, she wasn't aware he was, too.

"In a few short months, you have gone from just another knight in my father's guard, to my babysitter, to my bodyguard, to my confidante, best friend and now ... the love of my life."

Thedamaine took Evangeline's face in his hands, "you've always been mine," and pulled her into a kiss.

It was exactly what she needed to convince her to enter the ballroom. With Thedamaine behind her, wine in her hand and a smirk on her face, she opened the doors, and the celebratory ball began.

"Care to dance, Lady Evangeline?" Lord Ashton from across the lake was the first to ask the question once the formalities were over.

"My apologies, I promised a drink to an old friend." It worked before, it worked again. Evangeline grabbed a second drink from the bar and went from one side of the room to the other, dodging and weaving in and out of the guests, not wanting to talk or dance. Finishing both drinks before she reached the dancefloor.

"Will your poor old friend ever get a drink?" Thedamaine asked, stopping her at the wall by the window. "You've been drinking his drinks at two events now!"

"I knew you'd notice that." She looked down at her two drinks, both were empty. "Perhaps it's time to put down the drink and dance?" She held out her hand to him and he took it, leading her to dance.

Felicity, on the other side of the room, took the risk and stood beside Vesna, alone against the wall. Morana was nowhere to be seen and Vesna seemed to feel naked and exposed without her twin at her side.

"Where is Morana?" Felicity asked, unable to mask the awkwardness in her voice.

"She's helping my mother, they are at your father's side, tending to him."

"Oh." Felicity's awkwardness only amplified. "Do you not wish to help?"

"I was not allowed. Too many hands only mess things up."

"I am sorry my father took precedence; he truly is a burden."

"He is my father too, now and I do want him to get better."

"Do you think he will make it to the wedding?" Felicity had not seen him in days, not since the strange night she shared a drink with those three.

"I hope so. A father should be there when his daughter is married. But I am worried he will not make it. That is why Morana is there, to help speed things up."

"Does Morana help your mother often?"

"Sometimes. It is rare that mother requires help but when she does she does not like me joining."

"Why is that?"

"Morana is better at it than I am. She is a fast learner."

"What is it that you help her with?" Felicity was trying her hardest to see if Vesna knew who her mother was, if they knew she was a shaman and if they were shamans themselves. It had suddenly occurred to her that she did not know how the powers of a Bridge came to be. If they were passed down and inherited or chosen at random. Perhaps they skipped a generation? Felicity began to imagine Evangeline's children struggling with the veil between worlds.

"We help her with her remedies. She is a healer by trade. Before she became a handmaiden she was a travelling apothecary. We follow her instructions and mix some liquids or add some herbs, I really didn't pay attention, you're asking the wrong sister."

"Would you say it is a bad sign when she asks for help?"

"Yes. It does not look good."

Felicity left Vesna's side without any further replies. She wanted to wait for the celebration to be over before she visited Zorya again, afraid she would only receive bad news of her father, but she had to go see her.

She was about to exit the room when she was stopped in her tracks. Coming through the doors at that exact moment was Taren, dressed finely and smirking directly at her.

"What are you doing here?" She asked.

"What? I'm dressed the part; do you not want me here?" He replied, brushing off imaginary dust on his jacket.

"You'll get in trouble; you're not supposed to be here."

"Felicity, relax." Evangeline was at her side, linking arms with Sir Thedamaine. "I invited him here. He is an official guest."

"Are you sure?" Felicity asked, not trusting either. "I do not want to get into trouble."

"Oh, unclench," Evangeline frowned, "Zorya signed it off herself. It was one of my demands."

"It is true." Thedamaine confirmed, his word was the only one Felicity trusted.

"Are you really going to turn away your date?" Taren asked, bowing to Felicity and presenting his hand. "I apologise for being late but the envoy that provided this costume took his sweet time." He looked at Evangeline, eyebrows raised and a scrunched nose.

"You're my date?" Felicity asked rhetorically, trying to understand.

"Yes, Felicity. For God's sake, no one is tricking you." Evangeline grabbed Felicity's arm and dropped it on Taren's hand. "Take his hand, dance all night, do whatever makes you happy."

Taren began to lead Felicity away, but she pulled back, whispering in Evangeline's ear. "I do not understand."

"Just go with it, Flick." Evangeline grinned after an eye roll. "This world is lonely, don't make it any lonelier." Evangeline turned away, staring up at Thedamaine and Felicity followed Taren across the hall.

"I do not like to dance," she said, trembling just a little.

"That's why I got these." Taren presented two goblets of wine and passed one to Felicity, she took it and swallowed almost all of it but stopped herself.

"Why didn't you tell us about the curse?" She asked, her mind still on her investigation.

"Zorya made me promise. She didn't know how you two would react and needed to ensure she could break the curse without any dangers. She thought it was better to keep you in the dark just to be sure."

"She was protecting herself just as much as us."

"That isn't always a bad thing. Live today, fight tomorrow. She would not be able to break the curse if you two had sentenced her to death."

"I guess that makes sense. The pain relief she gave you, was that really what it was?"

"Yes and no. It did stop the pain but only because it kept the connection at bay. She couldn't focus on both curses at the same time."

"Both curses?"

"Yes, your father. He was connected too, I thought you

knew this? Did she not tell you?"

"The honeymoon. They did not leave town at all did they? They were here, in the shaman camp. All that time Zorya was trying to break the curse."

"Yes, the shamans helped him, but he betrayed them."

"He attacked the camp, and they amplified the curse, but his connection was broken."

"Mine wasn't. It mutated." Taren smiled, washing away all the seriousness in his face and body. "But you saved my life and freed me. I owe you one, Felicity." He looked around at the room, scanning the dancers, he lingered on Evangeline laughing with Thedamaine and smiled, turning back to Felicity. "Would you like me to teach you how to dance?"

"What? No. I do not dance."

"It's fine, Flick. No one is looking at you. Now make like your sister, down a lake-full of wine and you will no longer care about anything. Trust me."

Felicity needed answers but she could not end this night. She had time, the answers she needed could wait but this night belonged to Taren.

CHAPTER 37.

She glared intensely at him for several minutes as neither said a word. He was beginning to feel uncomfortable, glancing at the door but she just stared, reading his face and revelling in his discomfort.

Evangeline, sitting at her father's desk, demanded a meeting with Sir Penlyn the day before their wedding to ensure the union was accepted on both sides.

"Do I unnerve you?" She asked finally, crossing her legs and leaning back in her chair.

"A little bit, yes." Penlyn admitted.

"How old are you?" She asked, already knowing the answer.

"Sixteen."

"I am significantly older than you are. Five years is a lifetime for a marriage gap. Does this bother you?"

"No." His lack of formalities pleased Evangeline, the charade was finally over. She leant forward again, the intensity in her eyes returning.

"Right. Well, I called you here today to come to an understanding. With age comes experience. I know for a fact that you are not the Forrester heir and so have not been trained in leadership and ruling. I, on the other hand, was raised to rule and rule I shall. Whether that be Ravenhill or Forrester, I no longer care but I will have power. Now our arrangement is unfortunate but necessary and so I propose a political marriage in the eyes of the people. Now you may have your mistress or mistresses or even a stable boy or two, I do not care but I will demand respect. You will treat me as your wife in public with fondness and compassion and I will do the same. These are my demands. However, they are not one-sided. Present your counteroffer and we can come to an understanding."

Penlyn's eyebrows had raised throughout the speech and

now he struggled to find words. "I admire your boldness in admitting you want power. It makes me want to admit that I have no clue what I am doing or how I can impress you. To be frank, I just want to go hunting, see some tournaments and joust. I am the third brother; I do not care for politics and the day-to-day."

Evangeline got up out of her seat, walked around the desk and stood in front of Penlyn. She held out her hand, looking down at him. "Do we have an accord?"

"Do what you want, just keep me out of it." Penlyn took her hand and they shook on it. He broke first and left the room, bowing a little before exiting. Evangeline returned with a subtle nod. Once Penlyn had gotten out of earshot down the corridor, Sir Thedamaine entered the room.

"You picked your husband well." He said with a grin.

"I do know what I am doing, Theo." She smiled at the door. "I'm going to enjoy tearing that boy to pieces."

"Are you planning a little hunting accident a few years down the line?" He was joking but Evangeline thought it over then shook it off.

"No! I'm not a cold-blooded murderer."

"Are you sure?" Thedamaine said with a laugh.

"How well do you know me?" She asked, slyly, placing a finger on his chest. "Would you be my assassin?"

Thedamaine moved his face closer to hers, "you do not need one." They connected in a kiss, only pulling away when they heard footsteps coming down the hallway.

"Aria, Mary, do come in. What can I do for you two lovely ladies?" Evangeline met them at the door and pulled them inside.

"You're in a good mood, milady." Aria said as she frowned a little.

"The wonders of alcohol and a new purpose."

"We are here to take you to your dress fitting." Mary added.

"Is that not tomorrow morning?" Evangeline asked.

"Well, previous experience with you teaches us that you may either sleep in or disappear completely, so we are planning ahead. There is no avoiding this."

"Yes, Aria. I am aware of that. Do what you must. Take me wherever you need me. Just get it over and done with." Evangeline left with the handmaidens, Thedamaine still trailing behind her. "Where is my sister?" She asked, suddenly aware that she had not seen her all day. "Is she still with her date?" She added, whispering in Thedamaine's direction.

"Lady Felicity was in the study."

"Still with her nose in a book?"

Felicity had left the study and was knocking on her father's chamber room door, hoping to gain access. Zorya had been tending to him continuously for two days now and had not left the room herself. Felicity was worried. After some time constantly knocking on the door, it unlocked and swung open.

"Yes Felicity?" Zorya looked exhausted. Pale, sick and grey, the constant toll of shaman remedies was taking effect on her.

"Is he alive?" Was all Felicity said.

"Yes. The constant slumber is keeping the sickness at bay. It has amplified and I am not sure why."

Felicity entered the room and went to her father's bedside. He was cold to the touch, with clammy skin and twitching as if he was suffering through a nightmare.

"Will he make it to the wedding tomorrow?" After Zorya did not answer, Felicity continued. "Please, Zorya. He must make it tomorrow. For Evangeline. Promise me?"

"Fine. I will lift the slumber, but I cannot promise he will make it. I will try my hardest, but I cannot guarantee how far he will reach without collapsing."

"Perhaps if you lift it just before the ceremony then there is a higher chance he could make it?"

"I will try my hardest."

"Thank you." Felicity held his cheek, bent down and kissed him on the forehead. "What is wrong with him?" She asked.

"The curse has taken its toll on him."

"I read that the physical effects of breaking a curse will stop once the curse is broken. Why hasn't it stopped?"

"I do not know. It is new to me."

Felicity turned to Zorya. "Why didn't you tell us about his curse?"

"To protect-"

"Protect us, I know." Felicity finished.

"Your father's curse was broken so I did not need to tell

you. I had to involve you in the boy's, so I had no choice but to tell you. I did not expect you to work most of it out yourself, however. You are a smart girl, Felicity. Do not lose that. Keep studying, you may find something about yourself you did not know was there."

"Like what?"

"If I have to tell you, you will never know. Now please, let me sleep. We have a big day tomorrow."

"Wait. Tell me. What do you mean?"

"I mean your sister is getting married and it will be an early start and a late finish."

"No, that's not what I meant. Please can we talk a little bit longer? I still have so many questions."

"Please, not now. Wait until after the wedding. I must save my strength and my power to fight his sickness and prevent this mutation."

Zorya pushed Felicity out of the door and closed it behind her. She heard it lock and knew there was no opening it again. Resigned to having to wait for answers, Felicity returned to her room and buried herself in books hoping to discover something important. Something to explain everything. Eventually she fell asleep, her head on a book and dreamt of the spirit world, her mother guiding her along the way.

CHAPTER 38.

The wedding was held at sunset upon the Oak Tree Hilltop. An orange setting sun lighting up the red, orange and yellow autumn leaves that covered everything in an amber carpet. A short walk away from the Manor grounds, it was inside the hilltop forest; an open clearing with a single, giant and ancient oak tree as its centre point; the King Tree, where Lord and Lady Ravenhill had married and where Ravenhills had been married for generations. Two cloth ribbons were tied into a large bow around the thick trunk: black for Ravenhill and green for Forrester. Hundreds of candles covered the branches of the tree, melted to it by the yellow wax. On either side of the tree sat two altars made from individual tree stumps. More candles littered the altars, along with orange dahlias, snapdragons and bunches of holly, rowan and blackthorn.

The benches had been made from forest trees, carved into seats for the audience and arranged in a semi-circle around the King Tree. At the centre, just in front of the tree was the wedding arch. Crafted from long, flexible birch wood, woven into an ethereal arch, wrapped in willow vines and topped with elderflowers.

Candles suspended from string hung from the treetop canopy around the edge of the clearing. Wreaths and vines made from lavender and wheat wrapped and hung from the trunks around them. Garlands of elderflowers suspended over the wedding, draped from one side of the tree line to the other.

Temporary canopies and marquees had been erected for the occasion, two on each side for the gifts, feast tables, further seating and the Ancestor's Altar. They had been crafted from wood of the forest and completely covered in elderflowers and dahlias.

The clearing filled up quickly, Ladies Anne and Caroline

Ashton chatted away enthusiastically to Duke Forrester near the front with Cadmael sitting patiently in silence. The highest of the household took their seats behind the Lords and Ladies, the Governess, Bailiff, Reeve, Castellan and Chancellor. The rest of the benches were taken up by various nobles and liege lords from the village and neighbouring lands and villagers invited by the Lord himself which tended to be strictly guild leaders.

Sir Thedamaine and Sir Constantine stood at either end of the wedding arch by the tree line, the rest of the knights standing like sentries around the semi-circle benches. The harpist and lutist had been playing their tranquil tunes since the first guest arrived. The two minstrels entertained the crowd until the ceremony began; juggling, contorting, cracking jokes and simply making the audience laugh.

Felicity chose her seat on the end of the row, with Vesna at her right. Along the bench sat Morana and Cadmael. The two empty seats by the aisle were awaiting the Lord and Lady Ravenhill. Felicity looked around and spotted Taren at the back of the audience giving her a little wave and a smirk. Zorya was the last one to a seat, and whispers ran over the crowd, aware of Horus' absence.

"Where is he?" Felicity mouthed to Zorya.

"I am sorry. He will not make it." Zorya shook her head and faced forward.

"What do you mean?" Felicity whisper screamed, trying to get Zorya's attention. "Will not make it to the wedding or will not make it at all?" *As in dead?*

The audience stood and turned around as the harpist announced the start of the ceremony. Felicity could not think of that now. Appearing from the canopies on either side, Penlyn Forrester and Evangeline Ravenhill came together and walked the aisle hand in hand. They took their place under the wedding arch and faced each other, still holding hands. Together they untied the bow around the King Tree and brought their family ribbons to each other's lips. They began the handfasting with the groom wrapping his green ribbon around their clutched hands, the bride did the same with the black, intertwining the two colours and becoming one.

A silence fell over the wedding, not for respect but from fear. The band had stopped playing and the audience had frozen. The bride and groom turned to face their audience, their hands successfully bonded, all at once every candle was extinguished from a single gust of wind.

Evangeline squeezed Penlyn's hand as she realised something was very wrong.

"Get back!"

"Everybody move!"

"Move!"

The knights all shouted over each other as they clamoured toward the wedding arch. Some of the audience got up screaming and ran, others froze in fear. Evangeline turned toward the treeline past the thick oak tree and jumped back, still shackled by the hand.

The beast had returned from the dead, peering through the tree trunks, one huge paw out in the open in a prowl. The entire wedding party erupted in terror as the candles relit themselves and then exploded into a ring of fire, blazing the treeline and completely surrounding everyone, trapping them in the open.

Thedamaine and Constantine grabbed hold of Evangeline and dragged, pulling her back from the wedding arch. Penlyn was taken too, by his father, pulling him away from her and the danger but they were still tied together, and she slipped from the knight's arms. The Duke let go of his son just as the beast pounced. Evangeline watch in horror as it ripped apart Duke Forrester's throat, blood splattering the leaves beneath. She lunged for Penlyn, who sat on the floor, screaming at his father and pulled him back, out of the way of the beast. She finally tore off the handfasting ribbon, pulled his face to look at hers and yanked him to his feet, running with him as the knights attacked.

She and Penlyn were separated as they tried to take cover under the closest canopy that collapsed on them. Evangeline jumped free, scraping the skin off her arm. She tried to get to her feet, but her long train was caught under the debris. Pulling the dagger from her hidden leg sheath, she ripped the thick, dark dress cutting off the entire train and trailing skirt until she was free and mobile.

As she ran for safety, she tripped over a body, slipping in wet leaves; its head crushed under a wooden beam. From the clothes and figure, she knew immediately it was Cadmael and screamed at the sight, scrambling away. She glanced up to witness the beast leap onto young Morana's body, breaking underneath its weight.

"Felicity!" She screamed as loud as she could, it did not have much effect over the flames, roaring beast and terrified screams of the wedding party around her. She screamed again but nobody answered. On her feet, she looked around, struggling to see through the smoke. People were running all around her, dodging the flames that was surrounding and trapping them. She could not see Felicity, nor Taren, nor Thedamaine.

She did see Zorya.

In the centre of the chaos, Evangeline grabbed Zorya's arms, forcing her to look in her eyes.

"Help us!" Evangeline screamed, Zorya only shook her head slowly.

"I cannot! I failed! I do not know what happened. The curse was broken, I felt it."

"You are a shaman, use your power; help us!"

"I can't! I have failed. I've killed us all."

"How did this happen? You said the curse was broken. Taren's connection was severed."

"It was. It is! I did not see this coming, I missed something. The curse is mutated beyond my power."

"Mutated?" Felicity had slid across the leaves at Evangeline's side, behind her was Taren, armed with a dagger he had hidden on his person.

"What are you two doing here? Get to safety!"

"Zorya," Felicity began, "the curse has mutated? How? We broke the curse."

"I failed you. Your father..."

"His curse is not broken. You thought you did break it, but he got sick again."

"What? Father's cursed?"

"Yes, the beast is also connected to father."

"No." Zorya breathed, looking at the girls with tears in her eyes. "The beast *is* your father."

CHAPTER 39.

"How is that possible?"

"We saw father battling the beast. When Taren and I escaped the forge, you, Cadmael and father came and met us. He could not be the beast."

"The mutation." Zorya whispered. "His attack on the camp transformed him."

"Your magic slowed the transformation, but when he awoke, he transformed." Felicity said, Zorya nodded slowly.

Evangeline stood up and faced Taren. "And you? Are you a beast?"

"My curse was broken, Zorya confirmed that."

"How can we be sure?"

The beast was attacking some knights, backed up to the burning forest and began tearing out the burning trees by the roots, throwing them to get to the knights. "Evie!" Felicity screamed and pushed Evangeline out of the way of a tree trunk.

"We've got to get out of here." Taren roared.

"We're surrounded." Evangeline took Felicity by the hand and dragged her away, trying to find a way out of the opening and back to the Manor. She ran headfirst into Thedamaine, smacking her forehead into his armour and falling to the ground.

"Taren get Felicity free. Keep her safe." She roared, her hand on her bleeding forehead. Thedamaine helped her to her feet, his eyes watching for the beast.

"Come on!" Felicity screamed, refusing to follow Taren and pulling on Evangeline's other arm. She took her by the hand and dragged her.

Taren and Thedamaine led the way, weaving in between guests, flames and bodies. Thedamaine, using Taren's help, picked up a broken section of a canopy wall and threw it against the flames creating a walkway through but it did not last long enough and burst into flames before they could reach it.

Zorya ran up toward them, covered in blood and raised her hands, with a twitch of her fingers the fire parted, just wide enough for a body.

"Go. All of you, through there. One by one. Hurry, I cannot hold it for long. The curse is too strong."

"What about you?" Felicity asked, "your girls?"

"Too late. I cannot go near fire. Go! Hurry!"

Evangeline went first, followed by Felicity, Taren and then Thedamaine. Just as his body passed the flames, they connected again, trapping the rest of the wedding party inside, the guest's screams all they could hear.

The four of them ran toward the Manor and piled through the doors, closing and locking them behind them. Thedamaine stayed by the door, sword unsheathed, listening. Taren was bent over panting. Felicity dropped to the floor to catch her breath and Evangeline paced up and down, thinking.

"Flick, you're bleeding." Evangeline skidded on the floor to Felicity and pressed down on her rib, a piece of splintered wood poking out of it.

"So are you. We all are."

"This is nothing." Evangeline said, pointing at her head. "*This* needs pressure."

"Don't take out the wood." Taren exclaimed as Evangeline touched it. "The bleeding may worsen, leave that for the surgeon."

"Wait! Evie! I figured it out!" Felicity pulled on Evangeline's gown.

"What? Now? Figured what out?"

"Yes. The falcons in the spirit world. They don't represent the shamans. Remember, the visions on the left of the crypt represented the horrors of the past but the visions on the right were the two curses. One with Taren and one with father."

"But we didn't see father there."

"Because we didn't include him in the ritual!"

"But how do falcons represent him?"

"*Horus*, named for the ancient God with a falcon head. It was too literal for us to see."

All four of them screamed in terror as something hit the

Manor doors. The beast had followed them. They scrambled to their feet and sprinted down the corridor just as the doors buckled against the weight and broke in half.

Evangeline, the fastest, led the way, heading toward the Courtyard. It was gaining on them fast. Her father; the beast. Trapped in the curse.

Suddenly she stopped, looking down at her hands.

"What are you doing?" Taren screamed at her.

"Evie, come on!" Felicity ran toward her, but Taren held her back.

Thedamaine tried to shield her from the beast, now several steps behind them but Evangeline ran around him, slipping his grip. Struggling against all better judgement, Evangeline ran straight at the beast, slit open her own palm with her dagger and dodged the attack, sliding on the floor, her hands outstretched. Her left hand, covered in Felicity's blood and her right hand, covered in her own, touched the beast's fur, connecting with its chest.

Evangeline scrambled backward as the beast recoiled, writhing in pain, shedding fur and contorting before them.

"What did you do?" Felicity asked, watching in horror and shock at the transformation before her.

"I completed the ritual."

The fur turned to skin.

The fangs turned to teeth.

The paws turned to hands.

The beast turned to man.

Evangeline cradled her father's head in her arms as he sobbed desperately, twitching and shivering. Felicity, still in shock and pain, rested at the end of the corridor, Taren putting pressure on her wound and Thedamaine bandaging her.

"I am sorry." Lord Horus wept. "I have caused so much death, so much tragedy. It must be stopped."

"It has stopped now, father. The curse is broken."

"No. Only with my death will it end."

"You don't know that. The ritual is finished. Our blood has freed you."

"Please, Evangeline. Please end this. Just end it. Please don't let me change back."

"You won't change back. It's over now."

Lord Horus cowered at his daughter's feet, gripping her

legs with all the depleted strength he had left.

"You must do what I could not. Get justice for our crimes. I thought I was saving you and Felicity when I did it. I thought I was ridding the world of an evil, but I was wrong. The wrong person was killed."

"What are you talking about?"

"I killed your mother. I thought it would stop the beast and kill the monster, but I became the monster instead. So now it falls to you. Promise me. Stop this madness. I can see everyone I killed, now. All that death and murder. I do not want that blood on my hands anymore. Please end it."

"I don't understand." Evangeline glanced over at Felicity who was out of earshot, when she looked back, her father had grabbed the dagger she was holding and pulled it to his chest.

"You must kill me. Please."

"No. I can't. The ritual is complete."

"I cannot live with the death. Bring justice to our people and defeat the beast once and for all."

Evangeline straightened, took one last glance at Felicity to ensure she was looking away and ran her dagger, her mother's dagger, through her father's heart.

"What have you done?!" Felicity screamed, jumping to her feet and sprinting down the corridor, falling to her knees at her father's side. Taren and Thedamaine followed, gasping at the sight.

Evangeline stood up and took a step back, holding the dagger at her side, her father's blood dripping on the floor. Thedamaine placed a hand on Evangeline's shoulder and tried to look in her eyes but she only stared into the middle distance.

"Evangeline? What did you do?" He asked firmly.

"It's what he wanted." Evangeline said, deadpan and detached. "It's all over now." She began to walk but Taren stopped her.

"Why did you do that? The curse was broken. There was no need for murder."

"*He* is a murderer. There was too much blood on his hands. Now we have justice for all those killed by the beast and my mother."

Felicity got to her feet as Evangeline began to walk. "That was cold-blooded murder. I will *never* forgive you for this."

"I did what had to be done."

CHAPTER 40.

Lord Horus' stone sarcophagus sat beside his wife's in the crypt, Evangeline stood beside it, a hand on the cold top. Felicity had not spoken a single word to her since it happened nor should she, coming to terms with what she had done.

"I told you I wanted to be left alone." She whispered as Sir Thedamaine came down the stone steps.

"You should not be alone, not after what has happened. Plus, it is less about what you want and about what you need. I still need to protect you from danger."

News of what Evangeline had done spread quickly through the Manor and the town. The rumours of a rebellion against the family were no longer rumours but a real threat.

Vesna, Morana, Cadmael, Aria, Sir Constantine, Duke Forrester and his eldest son, the entire Ashton family; so many had perished in the attack. Zorya was missing, her body not found but Evangeline doubted she would see her again. Felicity would not speak to her and Taren avoided her. Thedamaine did his job and nothing more. Evangeline thought of all of this as she stared at her father's resting place and felt nothing.

More footsteps came down the stone steps, Evangeline looked up, saw it was Penlyn and looked away.

"When is the funeral?" He asked, walking around the sarcophagus.

"In a month." She replied. "It gives enough time for family and guests to arrive and pay respects." Penlyn opened his mouth to speak but Evangeline cut him off. "I do not care for your opinion so keep it to yourself."

"It's not an opinion, it's advice. *May* I offer some advice?" Evangeline nodded. "Talk to your people. Directly and in person. Hearing your side of the story from your own mouth will definitely settle some rebels. It will humanise you. Seeing the grief and emotion in your face and voice will help your case. That is, if you do feel."

"Excuse me?" Evangeline faced him and straightened up.

"I have not seen you cry or regret your actions at all. That is only proving their point."

"I only did what he asked."

"The fact that you did it at all is what people cannot believe."

"And you think me greeting them in person is a good idea?"

"I do, yes. Perhaps if we did it together?"

"We are not married. We are not together."

"Look, my father is dead, and you saved my life. I owe you a huge debt. We may not be married but I still see our families as one. Perhaps together we can save them both? A union may help smooth relationships with the people."

"My answer is no." Evangeline took off up the stairs but stopped and turned back. "Ask my sister, she always had a thing for you." She continued and left the crypt, returning to the Manor.

Standing outside of Felicity's door, she heard voices and as she raised her hand to knock, the door swung open. Felicity, seeing Evangeline, tried to slam it again but Evangeline placed her foot in the door, preventing it from closing. Felicity used all of her strength to push the door and crush her foot but Evangeline, the stronger of the two, burst through.

Taren was standing by the window, dressed in riding clothes, his cloak hiding the sword and dagger at his waist. For a moment, the three of them did not speak. Evangeline looked at Felicity then at Taren then back to Felicity as she stomped toward her. Felicity pushed Evangeline against the wall, wrapping her hands around her neck and squeezed. Taren stepped forward but Thedamaine got there first, jumping through the open door and pulling Felicity's hands out of the strangle.

"That's enough!" Thedamaine roared, stretching his arms, separating the two. "What's done is done! There is no going back. Evangeline explained why she did it so you must accept that. And Evangeline, you must accept what you have done. You are in denial or shock; you must take responsibility. What you have done is not justice. You two are family, you're all each other have left, treasure it."

"Stay out of this Thedamaine." Felicity spat, pulling away from him. "She killed my family. What I feel is not up to you. I am entitled to grieve and blame and get angry." Calming a little, she turned to Taren. "Perhaps I should leave with you."

"You're leaving?" Evangeline asked, rubbing her throat.

"Yes. Tonight." He adverted her gaze and rubbed the hilt of his sword.

"Why?"

"I cannot stay here. It's not safe."

"The curse is broken. The beast is dead. There is no more danger."

"I cannot know that for sure. Your father was not aware he transformed into the beast until you broke the curse, I do not want to put you in that position again."

"What position?"

"He doesn't want you to murder him, Evie." Felicity said.

"The curse is broken."

"There's only one way to be sure. I'm going to find Sienna, maybe she will help me, perhaps Zorya is there, too."

"And you want to go with him?" Evangeline asked, looking to Felicity.

"I haven't decided."

Evangeline walked toward Taren and searched his face, looking for the blacksmith boy that was her best friend. A stranger, afraid of her and judging her looked back. "Please don't leave." She said quietly. "I need you here."

"This is something I have to do. To protect you, Felicity and myself."

"He's not safe with you around." Felicity sneered, a hairs width from Evangeline.

Evangeline walked out.

"Is that how you want to leave it?" Thedamaine asked when they were down the corridor.

"Of course not. He's my best friend, I don't want him to leave. I've never been without him before. If he has to leave I want to say goodbye. A proper goodbye."

"Then why didn't you?"

"I do not deserve it."

CHAPTER 41.

She had taken Penlyn's advice and directly addressed her people, taking their audience in the town square. Flanked by Sir Thedamaine and Penlyn himself, witnesses to the event, and surrounded by all the knights in her arson, Evangeline made her case.

"My people, Lord Horus is dead, it is true. The beast is no more. I am here to confirm to you that they were one and the same. A dreaded curse placed upon my family, revenge for the heinous acts my mother and father committed against the shaman community. They brought war to our streets, killed our families, our friends, our people; all for nothing but prejudice. By my hand I have ended this war and freed us from the evil on both sides."

"Patricide!" A voice shouted from the crowd. Evangeline carried on.

"By my hand I have brought justice to all those that fell to the beast. I have brought justice to the one that murdered my mother, Lady Emilia Ravenhill. I have brought an end to this tragedy and death, once and for all."

"Treason!" Another voice came from the crowd, louder this time. Once again, Evangeline continued, ignoring the whispers in the crowd.

"My father was not aware of his actions until the curse was lifted and his guilt overwhelmed him. He could not live with what he had done and so forced my hand. He was executed in order to atone for his crimes."

"Murderer!"

Buzzing with rage, objects began to fly toward them, and the uproar grew deafeningly. Sir Thedamaine raised his shield up in front of Evangeline before something hit her. It fell to the ground, rolling just ahead. It was a rock. A *rock*. Somebody had thrown a rock at her. Thedamaine saw it too and stepped closer to her, keeping his shield up high and his cloak held around her.

"Line of defence!" He barked at the soldiers around him. The words were echoed through the knights, as they formed a shield around her and Penlyn. Thedamaine was starting to pull Evangeline back and away from the crowd when she heard a unison of knights yell "loose!"

Thedamaine's shield was held high so she could see the floor in front of her. She saw the row of arrows that rained down over her head to land, sticking up on the cobblestones in the arms' reach between her and her people, a warning. Jumping back with fright, the closest of the villagers pushed against the crowd, causing a shockwave all the way to the back which only ricocheted to the front, full of fear and rage.

The mob rushed her. As one they closed the gap between them and her, trampling the arrows underfoot. They were pushed from behind and rushed forward to avoid more pushing. Evangeline felt the sheer weight of the crowd as the mass of bodies engulfed and crushed her. From all directions she felt people pushing on her and people pushing on them.

The flow of the crowd had separated her from Thedamaine, she couldn't see over the heads around her. Evangeline lost her footing as she was pushed into an opening behind her and she stumbled on someone's foot. Still being pushed, she fell backward into someone, her full body weight leaning on them. She could not do anything. She could not stand or push back; she was at the mercy of the mob. Eventually, the poor body that Evangeline was leaning on dropped to the floor. Seizing the opportunity, she found her feet, trampling on the bodies underneath.

She stepped on hands and faces to return upright. Some of those on the floor had gotten up and started ramming into everyone around them to gain space. Evangeline took an elbow to the face and knocked heads with another in the same hit. There was more pushing against her now, but she sensed something in the crowd, hearing a stir. She looked up and just a few steps away, between people's scared faces, was a knight, not Thedamaine but another, she could see his helmet a head taller than the others. She watched in horror as the knight swung his shield around knocking back the villagers with power. This caused another shockwave in the swarm that reached Evangeline with rib-crushing force.

There were too many people.

She could not breathe.

The horde enclosed around her every time she inhaled to take a breath. She was very aware of the dagger that was sheathed on her leg. *No.* She thought, she could not use that, would not use that.

She thought about where she was standing before she was swarmed and where she was headed in the wave. If she just went with the flow she could get out of the market and out of danger, that's where people were headed, don't fight the current.

She cried out as her head snapped back from her hair being yanked out. She looked to see the culprit disappear into the invisible ground, between people's bodies, tons of feet trampled the hair puller's body.

If you stay in this ocean of bodies you will be dragged to the depths. Get to higher ground. The stairs! If she could make her way diagonally through the crowd she could reach the stairwell. She could take refuge on the first floor of the market and get free.

Trying not to push too hard against the current, she cruelly and desperately elbowed her way around people using all of her body's strength to reach the store fronts. She regretted her decision immediately as she was rammed hard into a pillar. The people behind her were pushing her into the hard stone. It was worse on the edge, there were fewer places to go and people had to shove against the mass to avoid being crushed.

Evangeline could not push back and gave up on the stairwell. As her body was flattened against the hard pillar she looked up toward the sky for salvation. The pillar was one half of the arch midway through the market square, and she could climb it! There were notches in the decorative woodwork all the way up the pillar. She began the ascent, her knuckles white with the strength to hold on, to not be pulled back into the stampede below. Once her legs were free and she was in the open, she moved quicker. She hoisted herself up carefully, balancing her feet on the lips of wood around the walls of the pillar and gripping tightly so not to fall.

A final heave dropped her over the railing and onto the balcony of the first floor. Lying on her back, wheezing breathlessly, she took a moment to appreciate the vastness around her. Before she could even catch her breath; a new fear encased her. Screaming and thrashing, she fought against the hands that seized her ankles and pulled them, fighting against the roaming fingers and weight on top of her. As his hands reached up between her legs, she let go of the railing and pulled the little dagger from her hidden ankle sheath. She swung it upwards from his chin and felt it slice diagonally through his face, bouncing off his nose and loose skin but had it knocked from her grip as she was punched in retaliation.

Scrambling to her feet, two more men pursued her around the first-floor balcony and followed her into an open shop where she met the first with an iron stew pot in the face, he stumbled backwards into the second who lost his footing. Evangeline sprinted as fast as she could and rammed her full weight into the second distracted scarred man who tumbled over the balcony, disappearing in the current of bodies beneath.

From this height she could see Thedamaine; his eyes had followed the man's fall from the balcony but in the split second before he could look up and Evangeline could scream his name, she was dragged from the edge, a filthy hand smothering her mouth and nose; blood leaking into her open mouth.

The bloody man dragged her into another shop and the door closed behind them. With her foot, Evangeline pushed hard off of the door, sending them both flying through the room and against the opposite wall. His grip on her dropped as he hit the wall and she jerked her elbow up in a strike against his chin, freeing her. Spinning in a daze, she grabbed a poker from an ashy fireplace and, without thinking, stabbed it through the man's eye.

She was grabbed once more from behind and she jumped forward pulling the poker from the bloody mush and brandished it ready to strike.

"Stop. Stop! Put it down. It's over."

Evangeline dropped the fire poker with a frightening clank and fell into Thedamaine's arms as she sobbed. He held her tightly as he looked at the bloody mess she had made, *forced* to make. He wrapped what was left of his cloak around her and wiped her teary, bloody face with the edge. Enveloping her tightly, holding her with as much support as he could give off, she convulsed with sobs into his chest. He rested his head on hers, strangely grateful that he had lost his helmet in the riot. He held her for an eternity, until she was ready to let go.

CHAPTER 42.

"Are you sure about this?"

"Yes. It's what I have to do. I need to know more."

Felicity knew exactly what Taren meant. She needed to know more but could not leave, not now, not yet.

"What about your apprenticeship? Your masterpiece? Your parent's legacy?"

"Blacksmithing has been my everything but now that part of my life is over. I am cursed."

"But what if the curse *is* broken? You're leaving for no reason."

"If there is any possibility that I could be putting you in danger, either of you, I cannot run that risk."

Felicity smiled slightly. "You're protecting yourself just as much as you're protecting us."

Taren mirrored Felicity's smirk, "live today, fight tomorrow."

"Where will you go?" Felicity asked.

"I'm leaving with the shamans, they are looking for Sienna just like me, they can lead me to her."

"Is that safe? Sienna was banished for helping us."

"She helped *you*. They have no quarrel with me."

"Do you have to leave now?" She wanted to go with him, get as far away from her murdering sister as she could, but she had business here. She could not leave her father, not before she said goodbye.

"If I don't leave now and the curse isn't broken I could transform and kill you all. It's too dangerous. Also, the shamans, what's left of them, are leaving tonight. If I don't go with them then I'll never find Sienna. Look, I know it's difficult but trust me, it does get better."

Felicity smiled, knowing that Taren had lost parents too, but the smile soon dropped from her face, his parents weren't murdered by his sibling.

Felicity and Taren backed away from the Manor main doors as they were pushed open. Penlyn Forrester fell through with a bloodied face, bent over, holding his ribs. Behind him several knights came through, blood splattered and stressed. Sir Thedamaine limped through the doors, supporting Evangeline as she clung to his chest covered in blood. Felicity backed up against the far wall watching them all enter, her eyes lingering on her sister.

"What happened?" Taren asked, taking Evangeline's face and looking in her eyes.

"They rioted." Penlyn said beside them, a scowl on his face. "It was a stampede, bodies crushed, people killed. *Savages.*"

"A riot? How?"

"We were doomed from the start. Just the sight of her face angered them." Felicity agreed with Penlyn's words, knowing how her people felt. "We had no choice but to push them back but that only made things worse."

"How did you push them back?" Felicity finally said from the shadows, knowing where this was going.

"Line of arrows." Evangeline answered, matter-of-factly.

"Whose idea was that?" Taren asked, looking to Sir Thedamaine.

Evangeline looked up at Thedamaine, but Felicity stepped forward. "It was yours." She spat, addressing Evangeline. "You told them to rain arrows down on your people?"

"Not on them, between us and them, as a warning to stay back."

"No wonder they turned on you. They don't feel safe, no one does. You deserved to be trampled. You deserved that riot. You deserved everything that happened to you."

Thedamaine stomped his foot as he stepped toward Felicity, pointing his finger. "That's enough. Stand down."

Felicity smacked his hand away. "Do not tell me what to do. How dare you. Who do you think you are? You are just a knight. You mean nothing. Just because you are *screwing* my sister does not give you the right to rule over me."

The room fell silent. Penlyn shifted on his feet. Evangeline looked between Felicity and Thedamaine, seeing the anger on both their faces. With neither of them backing down, Evangeline placed her hand on Thedamaine's arm. "Time to go." She said, pulling him away.

"Go? No, you're not going anywhere." Felicity jumped, blocking their exit. "You need to face this. Stop running from everything."

"Felicity, let me pass."

"No. You need to hear this. You caused that riot, that happened because of you."

"Felicity, move." Evangeline's tone was calm, but she was no longer clinging to Thedamaine. Stood in front of Felicity, towering over her, she stared into her eyes without blinking, one eyebrow slightly raised.

Felicity did not back down. She glared back; the sight of her sister covered in blood just reminding her of what she had done. Between the blood she could see the minor scars and blemishes from the previous attacks and a new wound, splitting open her eyebrow. Splattered on her gown was someone else's blood, Felicity could tell immediately. The gown was also ripped and torn showing Felicity that something else had happened; a struggle, separate to a stampede.

"How many more people are you going to kill?" Felicity asked, meeting Evangeline's eyes once more. The question did slightly shock Evangeline, Felicity saw the brief flash of alarm in her eyebrows and made her blink.

Evangeline, surprised that her sister had put that together, thought over her answer carefully, however reading the subtle relief in Felicity's eyes, she knew she would be able to pass without further delay. Felicity had said what she wanted to say, and so Evangeline said nothing, stared ahead and passed Felicity with Thedamaine on her arm.

"When will you realise that by killing the monster you became one?" Felicity's words were the last thing Evangeline heard as she advanced through the Manor.

Felicity returned to her chamber room in a foul mood. After saying goodbye to Taren and ignoring Penlyn, her thoughts still lingered on Evangeline. As she entered her room, she pushed over a stack of books that was in her way, with the books falling everywhere, she picked one up and threw it across the room, then another, smashing a vase. She entered her boudoir, where a large jug of cold water sat. With shaking hands, she gathered some water and splashed it on her face, wincing at the temperature shock. As she closed her eyes, she saw Vesna, reliving her death that Felicity had witnessed.

Vesna cradled her twin's body in her hands. Morana's spine broken and mangled, her head cracked open, Vesna did not flee from the attack. The beast, leaping onto Morana's body as a steppingstone, bounced off of her and mauled Lady Ashton, tearing her stomach open. Caroline Ashton, Lady Ashton's daughter was killed next as Felicity had watched. She, Evangeline and Caroline had played together often as children, taking their row boats out on the lake, swimming and sunbathing. The beast took Caroline from her too. Lord Ashton, coming to the aid of his wife and daughter, had his throat slashed by a claw that tore into his chest. But the beast was not finished. It came back toward Morana's body, seeing Vesna there. Vesna, too late to move, reached out for Felicity, screaming her name. These are the screams Felicity hears at night.

Her friend's and family's death at the hands of her father. Her father's death at the hands of her sister. There was a new monster in her life, a monster that betrayed her.

CHAPTER 43.

Light steam undulated out of the copper tub, the warm water inviting her in. She had sent Thedamaine to his own bed in the middle of the night, forcing him to take the night off and rest for once, undisturbed by her nightmares. She wanted to be alone, knowing that some things she just needed to combat by herself, in complete solitude, yet she could not go back to sleep without him.

With sleep eluding her she just wanted to bathe; submerge herself in water and float until sunrise. She did not want to go to sleep, even if she could. She only wanted to wash the world away, wash away those bad thoughts that clung to her mind and soul like flies to a corpse.

Apart from a handful of knights patrolling the grounds, the Manor was asleep and that was exactly how Evangeline liked it. She was at her best after dusk and felt free when everyone else was asleep.

The water was beginning to cool; it was almost time to get in. She got out of her nightdress and took off her jewellery, placing them on her bureau but before she pulled off her under-slip, a thought occurred. She would read a book in the bathtub; the time would pass much quicker that way and she might be able to escape into it.

Returning to her chamber room out of the boudoir, undoing her braid, she stopped as she got to the centre of the room. Her skin rippled with goose bumps, a shudder shot through her body and her breath caught in her throat. She had only lit two candles in her chamber, one by her bed and the other next to her by the boudoir door. The rest of the room was in flickering shadows and lurking within those shadows were three black figures.

Before she could scream a large, calloused hand cupped her mouth and pulled her against a man's body. The man behind her held her tight as two other men appeared from the shadows. She did not know who they were, why they were here or how they got in, only that she was in danger.

She did not struggle; afraid fighting back may encourage more violence. The man holding her smelled of port and stale body odour. The huge man on her left eyed her body, hungry for her flesh. The man on her right was irritable, twitching around like a pigeon. The man holding her moved his face into Evangeline's neck, sniffing deeply and she turned her head to see, already knowing who it was, *Nicholas*. Her heart fell out her stomach, she was unarmed and barely clothed.

Nicholas let out a satisfied moan and looked to his henchmen for gratification. Their faces cracked into sickening grins, pigeon man still twitching while the hungry one kept his eyes on Evangeline's body, at her thin, sheer slip.

"I would have had you at the riot if you hadn't knocked me off the balcony."

Evangeline did not realise that man was Nicholas, she was too terrified to take anything in and did not see his face long enough to realise, his scars would have given him away, but she did not even see it. Oh, if she did she would have killed him! Why did she dismiss Thedamaine?

"Don't scream, *Princess*, and it will be a breeze." Nicholas moved his hand from her mouth. She screamed for help but barely finished the syllable before he rammed his fingers into her throat, the same thing she did to him in the alley. The scream and her breath fell right out of her body, she collapsed, gasping for breath, coughing and panicking and unable to take a breath at all.

"How did you get in here?" She coughed once her throat finally opened.

"We convinced one of your guards to come over to our cause. Once he was on patrol we waltzed on in here. All two hundred of us."

"Two hundred?" She doubted the numbers; they would not be able to count them but still assumed a high number of them got in the Manor. She thought about the sheer mass of people at the riot mere hours ago.

"You thought it was just us three? No. There are many more storming your castle as we speak, Princess. I hope your sister does not struggle too much."

She bolted. Ran toward the door to save her sister, the

pigeon man was too slow, caught off guard from her sudden movement but the hungry one was quicker. He caught her just as her hand reached the door handle. His thick arms wrapped around her stomach and squeezed as he pulled her back, lifting her off the ground. She struggled and fought against his hands as he pushed her across the room and was caught by Nicholas turning her around and held her forcefully by her arms, burrowing his head in her neck once again.

Acting quickly, Evangeline rammed her fingers into his eyes, feeling and hearing them squelch. He roared from the pain and backed off, letting her go and grabbing his eyes, stumbling. Before the other two could react, Evangeline picked up the lantern by the boudoir, full of wax from the candle burning all night, and threw it at the pigeon man. As the hot, liquid wax drenched his face, gluing his eyes shut and scorching his skin; he dropped to the ground. His hands shook; squealing like a little girl as his eyes burned.

The hungry man was next. With two out of three temporarily disabled, she had to think fast, he seemed faster, stronger and smarter than the other two and his hunger blurred her ability to think. With her ankle sheath dagger lost in the riot and her sword and dagger in the antechamber she was unable to get to, she had no weapons that she could reach.

Arms outstretched and growling, he lunged at her, but she dropped to the floor in a crouch. Dodging the lunge, she extended her body upwards, tensing her neck and rammed her head into his chin. She heard his teeth clink together, as did hers, but when he raised his hands to cover his chin and block his sight, she drove her knee between his legs as hard as she could. He cried out in such pain that Evangeline smiled. As he bent over in agony, she took a running start and rammed into him, shoulder first. The momentum carried him backwards and he stumbled, unable to gain his footing, tripping on the curtain at his feet. His heavy body smashed through the glass window and fell to the ground beneath. Dazed and injured, she had no time to recover.

Nicholas was coming for her. She started toward the door, leaping over pigeon man who was rolling on the floor clawing at his eyes full of candle wax. Nicholas managed to get a grip on her dress, not wanting it to tear and reveal her nudity she stopped and gave in to his grasp. He picked her up and plopped her on her bed. She bounced away from him, trying to scramble free but he pulled her back. He punched her in the face and climbed on top of her. Trying to ignore the pain, she fought against his weight that crushed her. His legs were on hers, his hands waving trying to control her struggle; she was pinned. Every time she had an opportunity to escape he hit her again and managed to overpower her.

Evangeline kept fighting against him, but he was strong, so strong, every grasp on her threatened to break the bone. Wherever she pushed, he pushed back twice as hard. She couldn't get free. She couldn't free her body to run to safety, she couldn't free her arms to hurt him, and she couldn't be free of him. Her energy was draining, her will breaking. With another punch to the head that dazed her, she let go. She lay there and stopped fighting, listening to the ringing in her ears.

He reduced his grip on her arms and went toward his belt. Her arms were free, his weight on her legs lightened. In an act of desperation, she shoved her fingers in his eyes once again, bending backwards under the pressure. She jabbed him in the groin which knocked his balance and she managed to push him off. She was free.

She did not have time to get to the door; she was on the wrong side of the bed. As soon as her feet touched the floor she sprinted to the other side of the room, to the boudoir. She pulled the door open, got inside and slammed it but it was jammed. Something had blocked the door.

In a burst, the door shot open smacking Evangeline on the forehead, reopening the wound from the riot. She fell to the ground and rolled around from the pain. Nicholas was on top of her again. As she flailed her arms she searched around for a weapon, anything. She knew that was the only way to stop him, but she was in the middle of the floor, nothing but the copper bathtub was around her.

She had managed to turn around and scrambled across the floor on all fours like a hound, toward the door. Nicholas grabbed her ankles and pulled. Her bare skin scraped the floor as she was dragged backwards, her thin slip rolling up to her stomach. She started to scream but Nicholas quickly punched her, she continued, he hit her again. Blood ran down her face, her body drenched in sweat and she ached everywhere.

She swung her leg upwards, kicking him in the face. He roared, spitting out blood and teeth. She got to her feet and ran to the door; he caught her and launched her back across the room, but she hit the bathtub. With a hand on the back of her neck and the other on one arm, he bent her over the tub and dunked her under. She was submerged in the now ice-cold water. Thrashing for her life, pushing against his weight to come up for air, she managed it, shooting her head up out of the water and gasping deeply. Nicholas climbed in the tub, pulling her in, too and put his weight on her shoulders and head, submerging her entire body as the water splashed out over the top of the tub. In her struggle she had managed to turn and face him, and she could see his evil face through the rippling water.

Her air was running out, her mind blurring. All at once she stopped struggling and went limp, her world fading. She closed her eyes, succumbing to the darkness.

He slowly let go. She half floated in the tub half sat, her hair flowing around her, the water pink from her blood. He let out a breath he did not realise he was holding and looked away.

Evangeline shot upwards, throwing her body weight at him and pushed him out of the tub. He recoiled back, falling off the edge and onto the floor, hitting his head hard with a deafening crack. Evangeline seized hold of him, picked his head up and smashed it against the marble floor again, and again, and again.

She picked his whole body up this time. Struggling to remain upright against his weight, the wet floor and her disorientation. She threw him down into the tub, another thud echoed as his head hit the copper bottom; the pink tinged water turning deep red. She held his head under what was left of the water, her hands clamped around his throat, constricting like a snake and sat on him to keep him submerged. He did not struggle as much as she expected but she did not yield. She sat there for what felt like hours, long after the last movement beneath her, never letting go, never getting up.

She sat.

She waited.

Eventually she did let go and climbed out of the tub, crossed the room and leant against the wall. Her knees gave out and she slumped to the floor, never taking her eyes off of the bathtub. She could no longer see Nicholas' body from the floor, but she kept imagining and expecting him to shoot up like she did and finally finish the job. She no longer had any fight left in her, if he attacked now, that would be the end.

Evangeline waited.

She waited for Nicholas to rise up and kill her. She waited for death to take her. She waited for anybody to come in and find her, to save her. She waited for sleep and she waited for relief.

By the time they found her, her eyes had glazed over, and she was near catatonic. Unresponsive and in shock, she would not move or talk on her own. Somebody covered her and picked her up, she thought she heard her name once, but it still did not pull her back.

She was taken to the infirmary and induced into sleep by a large amount of laudanum in order to heal from the attack and the many before it. She had no memory of this, completely unaware that Thedamaine was in the next infirmary bed.

CHAPTER 44.

"You should be resting." Sir Thedamaine looked up, wincing at the pain of any movement. Felicity limped into the infirmary, bandages on both hands running up her arms and a black eye almost swollen shut.

"You should be too."

Felicity perched on the edge of the infirmary bed next to Thedamaine. They both stared down at Evangeline's sleeping body, still and calm. Neither of them had healed from the attack yet. Thedamaine, thrown through a ground floor window, with a broken arm and sprained ankle, was rendered next to useless as a knight and spent his days sleeping and worrying about Evangeline. Felicity, beaten to the point of torture, had been stuck with the aftermath. While her sister slept, she was forced to punish the knight that allowed the rebels into the Manor, coerced into executing the survivors of the raid, and had to live with those decisions that she was never supposed to make. With her father murdered, Zorya gone and Cadmael dead; she was the only one left and it was all *her* fault.

"The doctor said she will recover." Thedamaine said, half to himself.

"Shame." Felicity purred, emphasising the word.

"Please do not say that. She is your sister."

"She killed my father."

"She killed her own father, too."

"The curse was broken, all arrows pointed to it, his death was unnecessary." Felicity glared down at Evangeline, watching her eyes shake in her slumber. "He was our father," she continued. "How can you just murder family like that?"

"I think you're having trouble seeing her point of view. You two had very different relationships with your father. To you, he was your role model; someone you looked up to and idolised. To her, he was her abuser."

"That is no excuse for murder."

"Isn't it? You could argue that she was ridding the world of an evil. Protecting you, and herself. That's how she sees it."

"Be honest with me Thedamaine, do you agree with what she has done?"

Thedamaine thought for a moment. He was a knight. He killed for protection. "No," he admitted, "but she can still come back from this. I am sure of it."

"She has killed, what? Four men now. Severely maiming two more. That doesn't scream out-of-control monster to you? Does that sound like a good leader? Someone you are happy to stand beside?"

"Lord Horus' death was a mistake, she will soon come to realise that, but the others were self-defence, that is all. You cannot blame her for these. You have no right in calling her a monster when you do not know what it takes to survive."

"Look what she's done. She has ruined everything and taken everything from me. Soon you will see what she has become."

"She didn't take everything." Thedamaine added, thinking for a moment. "She found out who killed your mother."

"No, she didn't." Felicity got off the bed and stood in front of the window, looking out over the horizon. "There is more to that story than meets the eye. My time with the shamans is not over. They are hiding something from me, and I *will* find out what it is." She turned back around. "First I must clean up the mess she started."

CHAPTER 45.

On the new moon, Evangeline woke up uncomfortable and restless; the bed beside her had been used but now vacated, the rest of the room empty and deserted. She wanted to get out and move. Shuffling about the Manor, she was not fully strong on her legs yet, her home seemed like a stranger's. Confused and disorientated; the candles illuminating the hallways shook the walls and objects making her dizzy and sick, she expected more figures to appear from the shadows, terrified of every corner. She took a left and walked as far as she could until she reached a stairwell; she went up then took a right all the way down to a dead end and turned back. She was lost in her own home.

With more twists and turns and trial and error, a few times completely turning around and going back, she reached a tower. The spiralling stairs gave it away although she had no idea which tower it was. The Lord's Tower? The Lady's Tower? The Armoury? The Library? She could not remember how many towers were in the Manor. As she climbed the spiralling stairs, stopping numerous times to catch her breath and steady herself, she was not as fit as she once was, she started to hear voices. She could count three, one was female. As she reached the door she found herself unable to enter. She had to sit and rest, panting and sweating. Lowering herself to the floor, she listened to the voices inside.

"Things have only gotten worse since it happened. If we do not do something now, I fear we will pass the point of no return. As much as I hate to admit it, we do not have the resources to survive a siege. If a neighbouring liege Lord wanted to act on this weakness we will all be powerless to stop it, even with my numbers."

"Is there any way to stop this? To undo what has been done?"

That was indeed Felicity speaking, Evangeline knew it,

despite her disorientation. After a short silence she was about to get up and walk in, but the first person spoke again.

"She must step down." Evangeline's heart caught in her throat and her mind cleared a little. She sat and listened; her ears perked to hear everything.

"That is not necessary. She just needs time." As the mist settled in her head, she realised this third voice was Sir Thedamaine, hoarse and pained. "Look, I do not condone her actions. What she did was wrong, but she is on a slippery slope. With the right help she could still turn this around. She has only lost her way, she needs to calm the people, rectify the mistakes and get a grip on the situation."

"I am afraid that course is lost. If she tries to right her wrongs there may be another riot. A second mutiny may be in the horizon if she slips up once more."

"Will there be a revolt no matter what we do? This is her fault; they are mad at her. I believe the time has come to put an end to Evangeline's reign, she must step down."

Evangeline was numb, she knew she should be angry with Felicity's words, but she felt nothing, she just had to listen more.

"We need to act now, we are vulnerable. Do you want another mutiny? A siege on your home? More lives on your hands? What happened to her to happen to you, or worse? A stepdown on her part may be enough for the rebels to back down long enough for us to clean up this mess."

Evangeline opened the door slowly and stepped inside to see the three shocked faces: Felicity at the Lord's desk, in her spot. Penlyn, standing by the desk, leaning on it before she walked in. Thedamaine by the window, his arm heavily bandaged and his face covered in scratches that Evangeline knew from experience was caused by shards of glass. He stepped toward her with a limp but stopped.

Evangeline's voice was slow and calm, as if she were talking about the weather. "You are conspiring against me." There was no anger in her voice at all, no accusation. Her eyes were wide and blank, and she felt nothing.

Penlyn stammered, looking to Thedamaine for help. He backed away from the desk, his hands raised in surrender as if Evangeline were going to shoot him, but she only spoke calmly.

"Felicity should take over all duties and be the sole ruling power. I recommend you form a small cabinet council due to your inexperience; it is common; even the Queen has one. I used one on occasion, you were on it, so was Thedamaine. Try to gather whoever is still alive with the experience you need, if you are lacking, the Forrester family should provide the rest. Although I suggest forming a formal alliance with them to ensure future loyalty. A marriage to secure the bond will suffice."

Evangeline did not care about her duties. Not anymore. She did not care that they were conspiring against her. What did it matter? They wanted to take her power from her but what power did she have left? Penlyn, the boy she intimidated into agreeing to give her all power when they were married was now conspiring to remove said power from her. Felicity, the spare sister who never once suggested she ever wanted to rule was now usurping her title. Sir Thedamaine, the person she cared for the most, who had always had her back and knew her inside and out, judged her actions.

"You want me to step down and remove my title? Take it! I'm done." Evangeline turned tail and left the tower. Descending the stairs, she knew Thedamaine was pursuing her.

"Evangeline! Evangeline, stop. *Evie!*"

"I'm not stopping, Theo. You want to talk? Then walk with me."

"You're running, not walking."

"Don't you listen to Felicity? That's all I do."

"Evie! Listen, you have been in recovery for a long time, I was too. The attack took its toll, but things have happened that you do not know."

"I no longer care, Theo. I'm done."

"We have had seven attacks on the Manor since that first raid." This almost stopped Evangeline, but she kept on going, her mind beginning to return to her. "Luckily, we were ready but tensions out there are high."

"Theo, stop. I no longer care." She had reached the foyer of the Manor, heading towards the main doors.

"I think you do; you just cannot handle it."

"I am going for a walk to clear my head, that's all."

"You can't! It's too dangerous." Evangeline heard his limping jog as he caught up with her, grabbing her arm to stop her.

"I need air."

"I cannot let you go. Not without an armed escort and proper clothing. It is freezing out there."

Evangeline thought for a moment. She was wearing a thick, long-sleeve gown with a short skirt and breeches underneath, something quite similar to what she wore as a child; convenient and useful, handy for exploring and climbing. Not suitable for a Lady on a stroll but as she had just been stripped of power, it seemed perfect to Evangeline. The main doors opened, and a few handmaidens entered, smothered by their large fur cloaks, cowls and shawls. Evangeline reached out and snatched the cloak off of Mary the handmaiden's shoulders, flinging it on herself. Mary's mouth dropped and began to protest but stopped when Evangeline glared at her.

"There," Evangeline said, smiling, "you're armed and I'm warm. Let's go."

"No, I'm injured, I'm in no fit state to protect you."

"*That's* a shame." Evangeline took off in a run, slipping out of the closing main doors, leaving Thedamaine inside. She stumbled a little, shocked by the cold winter air. It was snowing and she had not expected it.

She ran around to the stables and burst through the doors, startling the horses and stable boy inside. He was saddling up a black horse, adjusting the saddle pad embroidered with the Ravenhill crest. She pushed him out of the way, and he recoiled into the tack room, hands up, avoiding the fuss. Evangeline jumped on the stool, hopped onto the horse and galloped out of the stables and out of the Manor grounds, passing Thedamaine on her way.

CHAPTER 46.

She galloped as fast as the horse could go, the frozen air finally waking her up. The snow, at speed, fell like a blizzard, rendering her almost blind as she wove through the village. She had barely reached the river before Thedamaine had caught up with her, chasing her down on his own horse. It occurred to her that a horse was not the right choice. His limp prevented him catching up with her, but a horse evened the odds. He only had one good hand at the ready and that was all he needed. Still, Evangeline laughed, double clicked her tongue and galloped faster, stroking the neck of the black mare.

"Evangeline, stop!"

She had reached the boundary of the village, the gates to the forest just ahead. In a clearing, just beside a fountain of a mermaid, she urged the horse to stop and turned around, facing Thedamaine on his gelding. Laughing, she slid off the mare and headed toward him as he dismounted too, careful of his limp.

"You caught me, Theo, good job, but we're not done yet. Let's take a ride in the forest, just you and me."

"What? Look, we need to go back."

"No, no, let's go, run with me, Theo." She took his hands and pulled but he resisted, a grim frown on his face."

"Evie, you're being a little manic. I think this urge to run is a coping mechanism, you're not quite sure how to handle what's happened to you and what you have done."

"Enough of that!" Evangeline growled, turning away. "Just be with me." She purred, turning back.

"Look, I am with you. We can handle it together. Just me and you, but the only way out is through."

"That rhymed." Evangeline grinned in a singsong, resting her head on his chest. Thedamaine straightened, reaching for this sword with his good hand, looking around and shushing her. Evangeline tensed up, hearing it too. She instinctively reached for the dagger on her belt, or her sword, or the ankle sheath. Nothing. She had come straight from the infirmary, with no weapons. Her heart dropped once again.

Why are you so stupid?

This is your fault.

Thedamaine and Evangeline turned, looking down the alley to their left hearing a whistle but Thedamaine flicked round suddenly behind him, unsheathing his sword with a scrape of metal just before a man tried to slit his throat. Evangeline dodged the second man, alerted by Thedamaine who had heard them coming.

Swinging his sword, Thedamaine caught the first thug's arm. As he dropped his dagger, Evangeline lunged forward, catching it. With the thug's attention on his wounded arm, Evangeline leapt onto him, he collapsed to the ground as she speared the dagger into his throat and sliced. The chaos frightened the horses, which both reared and ran off, one into town and one into the forest, disappearing in the shadows.

The second thug had his own sword which clinked against Thedamaine's, but Thedamaine was losing. His right arm was bandaged and unusable and he was barely competent with his left. Evangeline got up off the thug as he bled to death and bent over, grabbing a handful of grit and snow from the cobblestones, chucking it into the second thug's eyes, blinding him. Thedamaine jumped back as she stabbed the man several times in the stomach.

There was a third man, running at them from the alley on the left, screaming and brandishing his own sword. Evangeline looked at Thedamaine who did not react, still watching the thug writhe on the ground, gripping his gut that was bleeding profusely. She snatched the sword from his hand and parried the third man's attack with it. Stepping forward and using the dagger in her other hand to push his sword behind her back, it enabled her to run her sword through his face.

Evangeline stood over the third man, the sword standing upright in his skull as he lay on the ground in the snow, dead. Standing on his chest, she yanked it free, wiped the blood on his cloak and handed the sword back to Thedamaine, but he did not take it. Rolling her eyes, she held onto it and looked to the second man, still spluttering blood and writhing on the floor. She stood over him.

"Mercy!" The man coughed, using all the voice he had left. "Please!"

Evangeline raised the sword but Thedamaine stopped her. "Don't!" He yelled, looking her in the eyes.

"He attacked us. He deserves to die."

"He yields. He has called for mercy."

"He *attacked* us." She repeated. "I'm supposed to let him live so he can attack me again? No, I'm ending this."

"This is not justice. This is no longer self-defence. This is wrong. Look around you, Evie, you do this and you're proving you are the monster."

Still holding the sword in her hands, Evangeline listened to the dying man bleeding out before her. She had stabbed him many times, piercing organs and slicing deeply. Thedamaine slowly lowered his hand, letting Evangeline decide.

CHAPTER 47.

The sword came down on his chest, piercing his heart and killing him instantly. Evangeline pulled the sword out and dropped it on the ground, beside the dagger.

"What have you done?" Thedamaine roared. "Why did you do that? He cried mercy."

"This is mercy. I gave him a quick death."

Thedamaine grabbed Evangeline's shoulders and shook, tears welling in his eyes, rage fuming on his face. "Evangeline look at me! This is cruel, cold-blooded and wrong. You have just proved you are the monster they already think you are. I told you not to come here. What is wrong with you?"

Evangeline, seeing the tears in his eyes, felt hers coming too. She looked down at the men, lingering on each of their bodies.

"I had to protect myself," was all she could say, unable to look at Thedamaine, unable to take his rage.

"No. You have lost all definition of right and wrong. This is a slippery slope, and I will no longer stand beside you as you refuse help." He turned his back to her, but she grabbed his arm.

"Please don't do this." She sobbed into his back, clinging to him. "I can lose everyone else but not you. Please don't." The snow was starting to stick to her clothes, her fur cloak was more snow than fur and she could see the snowflakes on her eyelashes, but the tears kept falling, her heart breaking.

She wanted to run.

Thedamaine broke free of her grip, backing away and walking up the road toward town. Away from her.

"Please, don't leave me! I can't lose you!"

Thedamaine did not reply. Evangeline watched him limp up the main road, sobbing and wailing, until he was out of sight. Wiping the tears from her face, Evangeline saw the blood on her hands and screamed in rage and frustration. A long caterwaul echoing out.

She bolted.

She sprung off like a hunted deer, disappearing into the treeline of the forest. She ran without a thought, her legs pumping fast and wide. Still sobbing and screaming, she ran through the falling snow that blinded her as she powered on.

She ran as far as she could manage, not slowing down until she ran out of breath. She had always been a good runner; fast and resilient, her endurance one of her proudest traits. But considering her lack of exercise recently, she surprised herself at how far she had come.

She finally slowed to a walk and then came to a stop by a large oak tree and sheltered underneath its branches where it was snowing the least. Her gasping sobs cut through the silence of the forest as she rocked back and forth on a large, cold rock. She wrapped her arms around herself, feeling exposed and frozen, but through the tears she noticed the oak tree's hollow trunk big enough for her body. Wiping clean her face, she stuffed herself into the trunk, it was big enough that she could curl up comfortably but too small to stretch out. She did not want to stretch, curling into a ball, sobbing, trying to keep warm.

It was slightly warmer in the tree trunk, sheltered from the brisk winds and snow. She wept into her knees and thought about going back but she could not make the trip. She did not want to, they would find her in the end, they would rescue her from her weeping spot like a sad fairy and bring her back home, her tail between her legs.

She sat in the trunk for a while, eyes closed, weeping and waiting for rescue, between the exhaustion from running and the puffy eyes from crying; she accidently fell asleep. Eventually she woke up, her eyelashes almost frozen shut. She had to pry them open with force and struggled to crawl out of the trunk with her frozen and seized up limbs. She fought against the pins and needles in her foot so severe that she felt she had a stump. As she stepped forward she tripped and fell in the snow.

Lying in the snow waiting to retain the feeling in her foot, she thought about Thedamaine and his knights and why they hadn't found her yet. Had they passed her while she slept and completely missed her? Or were they really looking for her at all? How long had it been? It was pretty dark and dull around her; it couldn't be dusk already? It was winter, she was in the forest, it got dark early, but it did not mean she had been out there for hours with no one able to find her. She ran far but that was nothing to a horse searching for her, she couldn't be far from home and it shouldn't be hard to find her.

A pang of anxiety jolted through her and she hastily got to her feet. It was time to go home, now which way was it? Which way did she come?

Do not panic. Find your tracks.

But there were no tracks, her footsteps had been filled in by the falling snow and every tree around her looked the same. She found this place through tears and snow; there was nothing to show which way she had come. She had forgotten the way.

She was lost.

It was a gamble. She would either be walking toward home or away from home. She had always been terrible with directions; she never needed the skill; she was a noble woman and had always been led by another. She tried to recall a map of the land, there were several neighbouring lesser villages surrounding Ravenhill led by Lords and Ladies of the Court and retired Knights and the highest nobles, but she had no clue where they were and how far from her home. She did not even know what direction she was going in; she could be extremely close to two villages but walking directly between them and will never reach sanctuary. Maybe she will walk all the way to the Forrester Manor and be a complete shock to her almost mother-in-law?

After what seemed like hours of walking, the snow never letting up, the winds still whistling past and no sign of life around her, she let her mind blur as her legs walked on their own, taking her forward.

She whipped her head to the right as tiny footfalls and a crack caught her attention and brought her back. She froze still, locking eyes with a red deer, its large antlers almost forming a circle. He stared at her, slowly chewing the grass in its mouth as she refrained from moving. She smiled but the buck's ears twitched, and it bolted off, revealing the view behind it and Evangeline could not help but gasp. *Sanctuary.* She ran toward the building; a water mill, derelict and run down. She stopped at the front door ready to knock but the state of the door made her hesitate. It was hanging off its hinges and lodged open, a fallen pillar stopping it from closing. She knocked anyway and called out. Nobody answered her and she squeezed through; the door wedged from the other side.

Evangeline looked around, the roof had caved in on one side of the building and most of the walls had missing slats. "Lots of natural light," she said aloud to herself, forcing a smile. The building was almost as cold as the outside, it did not provide much shelter, but it was better than nothing. She shivered. "Well ventilated," she said, still forcing the smile. In the middle of nowhere with nothing around, perfect for a lost girl. "Excellent privacy, what's not to like?" The forced smile dropped from her face as the tears threatened to fall again.

There was a single, rotting bed in the corner of the mill, thankfully under the small bit of roof that gave cover. She pondered over the choice; sleep through the night in that disgusting bed in the freezing cold, hoping she will not freeze to death in the night, or continue on walking blind in complete darkness with no weapon or destination, hoping she will not freeze to death or die of exhaustion?

CHAPTER 48.

She woke with a start, rousing from a dreamless sleep. Not even a single nightmare. She fell asleep in the stinking, cold bed almost instantly and just as instantly woke up again at sunrise, practically frozen to the spot. Her bones ached with every movement, struggling to stand up off the bed.

Adjusting to the light and regaining feeling in her limbs, she looked around the mill, hoping to find something. Food, clothing, weapons, a map, anything. The mill had been abandoned many years ago and nothing remained. A few pieces of rotting furniture dotted the room; a broken chair, an empty trunk, a sturdy table but nothing of value.

She followed the stream by the back of the mill, hoping it would take her home. She tried to recall whether the river started at the lake or ended there. She might hit ocean; she might hit home, or she might just reach a dead end. Whatever happens; the only way out is through.

Exhausted and cold, her mind turned off, leaving her legs to move her forward on their own. She needed food. The stream and snow gave her enough water to keep her going but her rich lifestyle did not prepare her for starvation. As she advanced through the forest, she passed many berry bushes but forced herself not to try any. She did not know which berries were poisonous and would not risk it. She had no weapon so she could not hunt, not that she knew how, neither did she know how to set traps or snares.

She tripped on a rock buried in the snow and fell to her knees, her energy gone. Debating whether or not to get back up again, she thought of home. Were they looking for her? Was Felicity worried? No, Felicity hated her. Thedamaine hated her. Her people hated her. Taren is gone. Zorya is gone.

Get up. You're not dying here. Listen.

She raised her head, noticing a quiet rattling in the distance. It was difficult to hear over the stream, but something was there. She managed to get to her feet and stumbled forward. It was rattling of wood.

Evangeline staggered through the trees, supporting herself on the trunks as she passed but the noise was getting louder, she was getting closer. She could see something through the trees, it was heading her way. *A cart!* Moving as fast as she could, she almost missed it but lurched out of the trees, waving her hands.

"Stop! Stop!" She yelled, her voice cracking. The cart almost hit her as she had jumped out at the last minute, terrifying the horse. It was a merchant cart and the driver tried to steady his horse, preventing it from rearing off into the treeline.

"What's the matter with you? You scared us half to death! Get out of here, girl." The merchant gripped his reins again, but Evangeline threw herself against the side of the cart to stop him.

"Please don't go. I need a ride. Please will you take me home?"

"Oh, no. I'm not falling for this. I stop for you and I get robbed. I knew I shouldn't have taken that shortcut. Always stick to the beaten track. I promise I do not have anything of value in here."

"Please don't leave. I'm not here to rob you. I'm lost, I just want to go home, please. I've walked for miles; I haven't eaten and I'm so cold. Please."

The merchant growled low and loudly. "Fine. Damn this soft heart. Where's your home?"

"Ravenhill village."

"Oh, no can do, I'm afraid. I'm on a tight schedule. I'm heading to Greystone and cannot afford any deviations." Evangeline ran her fingers through her messy hair, tangled and fallen loose from her braid. "Look, maybe I will take you to Ravenhill *after* I reach Greystone, but I have to deliver or it's my neck, trust me, you do not want to cross my client. If you want the ride, you're welcome to jump aboard."

"How far to Greystone?" She asked, unfamiliar with the name.

"We'll be there by sundown. Look, I have a cloak you can use and I'm sure I can spare a bread roll."

That was enough to persuade Evangeline, she hurried to the other side of the cart and jumped on. The merchant clicked his tongue, and the horse began to trot. After he pulled a fur pelt from the back and handed her one of his stale bread rolls, she hungrily scoffed it down and cocooned herself.

"Thank you," she said genuinely.

"Don't ever have kids," the merchant said, "they make you so soft."

They sat in silence for a while as Evangeline violently shook from the cold and slowly warmed up. Eventually she looked back at his cart, trying to see what was under his sheet.

"Name's Arthur, I'm a furrier by trade. I live out in the Elseways, just south of Greystone. Here I am trying to make my monthly delivery on time but my wheel breaks so that sets me back a day. Ol' Grim told me about the shortcut past the Steppingstone, that might bring back some time, but of course, it's Grim, he's sent me down a dangerous route, just for kicks. Who do I meet on this shortcut but a desperate lost girl, covered in dried blood whose been through hell and just wants to get back home."

Evangeline had not heard of the Elseways before, she never really did listen too well during those lessons. She looked down at her clothes. The man sitting next to her does not know that she murdered three men just yesterday, more before that, and her own father. What would she tell him? If he asked who she was? Would she tell him the truth? Maybe that would convince him to take her home? If she confirmed that a large reward would be paid on her safe return, would he honour it? But what if he sided with the rebels? By now word of her disappearance would have reached the village, what if the rebels had put a bounty on her head? Dead or alive. No. Just dead. No, they would most likely want to kill her themselves. Evangeline pulled the cloak's frozen hood up over her hair and wrapped the fur pelt tighter around herself.

"Not a talker, huh?" He continued, "that's fine, I'll talk for the two of us, nay, the three of us, isn't that right Calypso?" His black and white mare nodded her head and whinnied upon hearing her name.

CHAPTER 49.

Arthur kept to his word and talked the entire way to Greystone. He did not seem to notice or care that Evangeline nodded off a few hours in. When she awoke, he was still talking, now droning on about the folly of men in search of mermaids.

The smell of the sea was what awoke Evangeline, she had not encountered that divine salty air for years, but it occurred to her that she had reached the coast. Ravenhill village was inland, how far had she walked?

"Have you ever been to Greystone, girl?" Arthur asked as the town came into view. "I doubt it. It's been off the map for years; this little seaport town is favoured by pirates and smugglers. Stick with me, girl. I won't hurt you, but I can't speak for the rest of these scum."

Arthur's cart weaved through the town. As Evangeline looked around, she could tell immediately that the seediest part of Ravenhill was still ridiculously upper class compared to Greystone. Prostitutes on every other corner watched her as she passed. Men brawled on the street, urinated on walls and every one of them was armed, even the women. Cutlasses, daggers, a pistol here and there. This was a town of murderers.

Arthur came to a stop outside of a large tavern on the seafront. Several ships were anchored at sea and the docks were full of fishermen and merchants, selling to the sailors tying up their boats.

"You'd better come in with me. First drink is on the house." He climbed out of the cart and began to take his wares out of the back. Evangeline came to his side and helped pull them out. "You're just full of surprises, aren't you? Here, take these crates and follow me." She followed Arthur into the tavern, carrying the crates that were much heavier than they looked. She placed them down by the bar,

283

following his lead and looked around. The tavern was full of men and women, drinking, laughing and singing sea shanties.

Arthur leant over the bar and whispered to the barman, "tell The Bell that Skinner is here with the goods." The barman left, leaving a tankard which Arthur took and drank. He waited, seemingly forgetting Evangeline was there, standing awkwardly by the door.

"Welcome lost lady."

Evangeline's voice caught in her throat and she almost collapsed. "What?!" She blurted out. How could they know who she was already?

"I *said,* welcome to The Lost Lady pub, what can I get you?" It was a girl, around the same age as Evangeline, carrying several empty tankards in each hand. Her olive skin and accent foreign to Evangeline.

"I don't have any money." Evangeline said, quietly. The girl walked onwards.

"Then I can't serve you."

"Nerissa, be nice." Arthur grinned, elbowing the girl as she went behind the bar. "Give her the Lady's special. Look at her, she's been through hell."

"She yours?" The girl, Nerissa, asked Arthur as she put down the tankards and began pouring a drink.

"Hitchhiker. Picked her up in the middle of the forest if you can believe that. I'm giving her a ride to Ravenhill."

"Ravenhill?" She leant forward on the bar, lowering her voice. "Are you sure that's wise?"

Despite them talking about Evangeline right in front of her like she wasn't there, she leant forward too, hoping to hear any news.

"What? The beast is dead isn't it? That news got to me ages ago."

"No, now it's full-on rebellion and revolution. They *hate* the one in charge, the Lord's daughter, I forget her name. Assassination attempts, sieges, storming the Manor, everything."

"Really? Hey, girl, is that true?" Arthur turned back to Evangeline, when she didn't reply he gestured for her to come over and she did. Taking a seat at the bar, Nerissa placed a tankard in front of her.

"I cannot pay for this." Evangeline said.

"This is the Mermaid's Tear, our special drink. First one's

on the house."

Evangeline drank. It was delicious. Thick yet strong and nothing she had ever tasted before. She kept swallowing until the entire drink was finished and immediately wanted another one.

"I think she likes it." Arthur said with a smile.

"Or she's just very thirsty." Nerissa replied, the absence of a smile.

"Oi," Arthur elbowed Evangeline lightly, "I'm not going into the belly of the beast by taking you to Ravenhill, am I? I'm not getting involved in some silly town feud."

Evangeline shook her head.

"I heard its almost over anyway. The Lord's daughter was attacked and has not been seen since."

"Is she dead?"

"Haven't heard. Either dead or fled."

"Well, they should be happy. If she was the problem, she's gone now. Rebellion over."

"That's if she even is dead. We don't know, but if she's not, she will be."

Arthur took a long sip of his drink, looking around but swung back and slammed his palm on the bar. "Why's he keeping me waiting?"

"Who?"

"The Bell. I've got his delivery."

"The Bell's not here."

"What? I told your boy to go get him."

"Oh, Jack? He's having you on, mate, making you sweat it out to spend some money here."

"Are you kidding me?" Arthur jumped up off his chair, nearly spilling his drink.

"Calm down, Skinner. I can take delivery." Nerissa gestured to him and Arthur picked up the top crate of furs and placed it on the bar. Nerissa covertly lifted the top pelt, reaching inside.

"The goods all here?" She asked under her breath.

"You have my word."

"Alright, take them out back."

"Hey, girl, you stay here with Nerissa, she'll take good care of you. I'll be back."

"Oi!" Nerissa yelled as Arthur left with the crates. "I'm not your babysitter."

Evangeline sat in silence, highly aware of Nerissa's eyes on her as she poured herself a drink. When she left to tend the bar, Evangeline watched her. Clearly a pirate, Nerissa held herself high with such swagger, she commanded the room. With her chin-length dark brown hair, dark eyes and olive skin, her exotic appearance was appealing to all and it was clear that everyone in the room loved her. Her breeches were long and dirty, and she had a dagger sheath belted around her thigh. A short cutlass also hung at her belt with a golden hilt. Her small black corset kept her waist thin and her breasts high, something she was not above utilising when fishing for tips.

Evangeline looked down at her empty tankard, running her finger round and round the rim. In the corner of the tavern, a man with a large, feathered hat was ripping into a chicken. Evangeline heard him tear the flesh and smack his mouth, but she could smell it. Desperately hungry, she tried to ignore the delicious smell, but it was not working. When she was just about to leave to get some fresh salty air, Nerissa returned to the bar and leant over, now smoking a cigar, squinting through the smoke.

"What's your name?" She asked, staring at Evangeline.

"Evelyn." She said, thinking of the first name that popped in her head that wasn't her own, not unique enough, but she said it and now had to run with it. "Evelyn Smith."

"Smith, huh?" Nerissa nodded slowly, puffed on the cigar then blew smoke in Evangeline's face. "That's a lie."

"Excuse me?"

"You expect me to believe you're a common smithy? No chance."

"My father was a blacksmith."

"That's a lie. Your clothes give you away, girl. Rich, noble clothes on a smithy? Sure, they've been through hell but you're highborn."

"No, I'm not. I stole these."

"Another lie. They fit perfectly. Highly unlikely for an unusually tall girl such as yourself. So, let's see, fake name, highborn girl, in a right mess and headed back to Ravenhill. Oh, who could she be?"

Evangeline jumped off the bar stool and backed out of the tavern, she ran around to Arthur's cart, but it was empty, even the horse was gone. Where was he? She needed to go, right now. She tried to walk around the tavern but could not find him anywhere.

Returning to the entrance, Nerissa was leant against the wall, one leg up on the brick, a bottle in her hand and her cigar smoking.

"Why are you going back?" She asked, keeping the cigar in her mouth.

Evangeline stopped rushing, froze and looked at Nerissa. "It's my home."

"Is it?" Nerissa asked after taking a puff and exhaling smoke. "Is home where people try to kill you, hate you and want you dead? Where no one wants you around and blame all their problems on you? That doesn't sound like home to me."

"You live in a place where everyone has weapons and brawl in the street. A place full of pirates and smugglers. Are you telling me no one is trying to kill you here?"

"Ahh, I see Arthur's opened his mouth. This is just a sea town where pirates take off their boots and have a drink. You see there are few places left in this world where pirates can do that freely. That's what we are here, free. No lord or lady bossing us about in their towers, no sheriff or knight keeping the peace, if you can call it that. Just free people having a drink and sailing on. Any skirmishes that arise are quickly dealt with, no judgement. Something I think you need."

Evangeline stepped back, "you don't know me. You don't know who I am or what I've done."

"Evangeline Ravenhill killed her own father to spare her people and her family. She ended the blood curse on him, ridding her town of the Beast of Ravenhill. Sounds like a hero to me. Her people don't see it like that though, do they? They see her as a murderer and a monster. And hearing the rumours coming from your village about the attacks on you, perhaps you did kill. From the state of your clothes and the look in your eyes I think I know my answer. They see a monster? I see a survivor."

"Why are you saying this?"

"I'm telling you; you have a choice."

CHAPTER 50.

"You have a choice."

Those words echoed in her mind as she laid in the soft, foreign bed, staring up at the ceiling. She had barely slept a wink. Arthur could not make the journey to Ravenhill without resting his horse, so in exchange for a bed for the night, Evangeline was forced to agree to help Nerissa tend the bar and serve drinks for the day. Sent to bed with half a loaf of bread, a bit of cheese and another Mermaid's Tear, Evangeline had laid awake almost all night long, thinking, worrying and stressing, listening to the sea shanties below, waves crashing against the dock, and the chaotic racket of a tavern she used to love listening to.

"Rise and shine, *Evelyn*." Nerissa burst through the door, giving Evangeline a fright, using air quotes around her fake name. "If you work for me you need to look the part. We can't have you wearing that filth you came in with, even if it is just for one day. Believe it or not, Greystone has standards."

Evangeline caught the gown Nerissa threw to her, not seeing much difference between Nerissa's filthy clothing and her own. She had seen some of the pirates on the dock; these rotting human beings would not look twice at the dried blood, grime and rips in her clothing. Still, she took the gown without a fuss, appreciating the clean clothes and changed once Nerissa closed the door. Thin, cheap fabric, worn at the seams, threads pulling apart; she was officially a peasant. Running her fingers through her tangled mess of hair, undoing what was left of her braid, her fingers combed out the loose strands, dried blood and forest debris. She braided it sloppily and gathered the strength needed to walk downstairs to the bar.

The tavern in the early hours was bright and cosy; the large fireplace reminding her of home and the layout not too different from The Wolf and Raven. Nerissa was sweeping by the main door, pushing the powdery snow back outside, let in by the male barman, Jack, as he lugged barrels in from outside.

She had not met Jack officially yet, he ignored her presence as if she were a ghost, but Evangeline admired his short sword, she could tell he took good care of the leather sheath; it was the only thing he did take care of, from the state of him.

Evangeline was tasked with pouring drinks, something she was not completely foreign to, having on occasion poured drinks in several inns back home. By the time noon came round, Evangeline was yet to say a single word, and this seemed to suit Nerissa fine.

In a daze, the day passed on without her as if her body were moving on its own accord and her mind watched from afar. Looking back, she would not have been able to replay the day as her mind was elsewhere. Standing at the bar pouring drinks for hours on end became second nature and allowed her mind to drift, which only made things worse. If any of the regulars spoke to her, she was too distracted to answer and only poured them another drink.

"As soon as the sun sets, we're leaving." Arthur called to her as he entered the tavern, grabbed a tankard from the bar and headed toward the fireplace, plopping down on a large, burgundy chair.

It was barely an hour away. This was it. She was going home. Evangeline stepped back from the bar, placing the half-filled tankard she was in the middle of pouring down in front of her disgruntled customer. Placing a hand on her chest hoping to calm her pounding heart, she found herself struggling to breathe. There was too much smoke; from the cigars, pipes, fireplace, her own mind, she needed air.

She darted outside, and not knowing where to go, rushed to the back of the tavern, passing Arthur's cart with Calypso reined and ready to go. She hopped the fence toward the cellar stairs and sheltered between two barrels. Hugging her knees and sliding against the wall to the ground, she hoped she was invisible to all and could just disappear into melting snow beneath her.

She had to go home.

Not wanting to think any more about it, she looked up and

noticed the swinging tavern sign that she had missed on her way there. *The Lost Lady.* The picture on the sign was a young girl, barely a teenager, perhaps Morana and Vesna's age, on her knees, hands clasped together and looking up desperately. The girl's ice white hair equally matched her tattered white gown. It was an old sign, weathered and worn but to Evangeline it looked like a little ghost girl and perhaps a local legend to Greystone.

Evangeline shook her head at the sheer coincidence before her. Of all the places she could have wound up, she landed in a tavern called The Lost Lady. However, that was not the only coincidence. The moment she had lost all energy and about to give up was the moment a cart came into her proximity. A cart that was taking her to a safe place, on its way to The Lost Lady pub, where Ravenhill was on its delivery route.

She thought back to the moment in the forest when she had heard the cart coming. Just before a voice inside told her to keep going and to listen. The voice warned her before she heard it. It was guiding her, just like the voices did in the spirit world. Those voices were inside her, but they were not her own. Were they? If she were being guided in the spirit world how could she be guided now? No. It was just her. Her survival streak urging her on, picking up sounds that she had not processed yet.

Evangeline could not ignore the twisting of her stomach, the twang of her heart; there was something in the back of her mind that she had refused to look at, something that had awakened when she entered the spirit world and had put her on edge ever since. Something she knew Felicity shared. The reason why Sienna and Zorya were so surprised at how they broke the curse and how their visions connected. The spirit world had revealed itself to them, causing the veil to appear.

Crunching footsteps in the snow approached Evangeline, shattering her train of thought. Nerissa came toward her carrying two bottles, without her cigar and wearing a feathered hat and large cloak.

"Here." Nerissa said, presenting one of the bottles. "Take it and drink." She added when Evangeline hesitated.

"Thank you." Evangeline whispered. She took a sip but winced and shivered.

"What? You've never had rum before?" She laughed as

Evangeline shook her head and went back for more. She needed the drink.

"I suppose you're used to wine fit for a king?" When Evangeline did not answer, Nerissa's tone changed. "Look, I came out here to talk to you. I sense a battle going on inside you, one that I have had some experience in. I was not born here, I'm sure you're aware of this due to my accent and colour." She rolled up her sleeve and held her arm out next to Evangeline's hand. "I mean look at us, I'm kissed by the sun and you're paler than the snow we're sitting on. That's not the point, what I am trying to tell you is that I was raised in a small coastal town by my mother. She was a landlady too, and when the news got out that my father was the infamous pirate; Captain John Bellamy, the entire town turned on me. I was shunned by everyone and treated awfully just because I was the spawn of a pirate. My mother kicked me out to raise her own social standing, she had lost almost all of her customers and they outrightly blamed me. My friends, whom I had known my whole life bullied and beat me. On top of all this, my half-brother tried to kill me to keep our mother's blood pure. Eventually I stowed away on a merchant vessel and got as far away from there as possible. I felt guilty of course and wanted to go back but I couldn't understand *why* I wanted to return. My mother was there, and they say family means everything and I could tell she still cared but that wasn't enough for me."

"I have a choice." Evangeline said, thinking over the words.

"Exactly. You need to decide if those ties are strong enough to pull you back home." Nerissa got to her feet, took a long swig of her rum and adjusted her hat. "You can always stay here and rough it with these pirates. I could do with the extra help and I love a good story. You've got a good one, I can tell. It's your choice, so pick a path and follow it."

"What happened to your brother?" Evangeline asked, stopping Nerissa in her tracks before she left. "When he tried to kill you?"

"I drowned him in the well." Nerissa left Evangeline alone again to finish the bottle of rum. She drank a little before hearing Calypso shuffle about at the cart, banging on the wood, so she got to her feet and walked around the pub to Calypso's side.

Stroking Calypso's neck, settling her down, Evangeline began to think. With everyone she ever loved dead, gone or hating her, there was only one strong tie pulling her back. No matter how much she loved him, was it enough to bring her home? Would it change his opinion of her, for better or worse? Was her mental state worth pushing to the side just to cling to more moments with him? Would she be happier by his side in a place she hates or happier in a place she can find herself but without him? Could she abandon her family, her love, her home, her life for a stranger in a strange place, everything completely foreign to her? Perhaps the only way to find out what makes you happy is to cut all strings and set yourself free.

Evangeline looked back at the tavern doors as Nerissa burst her way through, along with Arthur.

"I'm going to need more wine if those shamans come back again."

"Shamans?" Evangeline whispered to herself.

"Oh, she speaks!" Arthur exclaimed, feigning a stumble. He stroked Calypso's mane and hopped on his cart, fiddling with his wares in the back.

"It is time." Nerissa said, by Evangeline's side. "What will you do?"

Evangeline smiled genuinely, for the first time since her journey started. She made up her mind and decided. She chose a path, hoping it was the right one.

The only way out is through.

To be continued...